THE CORPS *is respectfully dedicated to the memory of
Second Lieutenant Drew James Barrett, III, USMC
Company K, 3d Battalion, 26th Marines
Born Denver, Colorado, 3 January 1945
Died Quang Nam Province, Republic of Vietnam,
27 February 1969
and
Major Alfred Lee Butler, III, USMC
Headquarters 22nd Marine Amphibious Unit
Born Washington, D.C., 4 September 1950
Died Beirut, Lebanon, 8 February 1984*

"Semper Fi!"

*And to the memory of Donald L. Schomp
A marine fighter pilot who became a legendary U.S. Army
Master Aviator
RIP 9 April 1989*

D0003654

LINE
OF
FIRE

I

In the early months of 1942, a Major of the U.S. Army Ordnance Corps in Australia was forced to reconsider his long-held belief that he'd passed the point where the Army could surprise him.

The Pacific & Far East Shipping Corporation's freighter *John J. Rogers Jr.* docked at Melbourne after a long and perilous voyage from Bremerton, Washington. In addition to desperately needed war matériel, it off-loaded 800 identical, sturdy wooden crates. Each of these was roughly three feet by three feet by four feet, weighed 320 pounds, and was strapped with steel, waterproofed, and otherwise prepared for a long sea voyage.

These crates were loaded aboard trucks and taken to the U.S. Army Melbourne Area Ordnance Depot, a requisitioned warehouse area on the outskirts of the city. Because they were in waterproof packaging and inside storage space was at a premium (and because the Ordnance Corps Major could not

1

believe the shipping manifest), the crates were placed on pallets—each holding four of the crates—and stored outside under canvas tarpaulins.

It was two weeks before the Ordnance Corps Major could find time to locate the shipment, remove the tarpaulin, cut the metal strapping, pry open the crates, then tear off the heavy tar-paper wrapping.

He found (as the manifest said, and indeed as was neatly stenciled onto the crates in inch-high letters) that each of the crates did indeed contain US SABERS, CAVALRY MODEL OF 1912, W/SCABBARDS, 25 EACH.

The sabers and their scabbards were packed five to a layer, and each crate held five layers. It took him a moment to do the arithmetic:

If he had 800 crates, and there were twenty-five cavalry sabers, with scabbards, in each crate, that meant he had 20,000 cavalry sabers, with scabbards. They all looked new; they had probably never been issued. The Ordnance Major was aware that the last horse-cavalry unit in the U.S. Army, the 26th, had been dismounted in the Philippines; their mounts were converted to rations for the starving troops on Bataan; and the cavalrymen went off to fight their last battle as infantrymen.

On the face of it, cavalry sabers were as useless in modern warfare as teats on a boar hog. A lesser man than the Ordnance Corps Major would have simply pulled the tarpaulin back in place and tried to forget both the US SABERS, CAVALRY MODEL OF 1912, W/SCABBARDS and the goddamned moron who used up that valuable-as-gold shipping space sending them all the way to Australia.

But the Ordnance Major was not such a man.

He gave a good deal of thought to how he could make them useful, yet the best he could come up with was to convert them to some kind of fighting knives, perhaps like the trench knives of World War I. On investigation, however, this proved to be impractical. The blades were too heavy and the hilts too awkward.

He'd just about concluded that the sturdy crates the goddamned sabers were packed in had more potential use to the war effort than the sabers, when he had another idea. This one seemed to make sense.

And so a contract was issued to an Australian firm (before the war it had made automobile and truck bumpers) to convert the sabers into Substitute Standard machetes—at a cost of U.S. $2.75 each. The blades were cut down to sixteen inches and portions of the hilts were ground off. The scabbards, meanwhile, were run through a stamping press. In one operation the press cut the scabbard to size and sealed its end.

And so when First Lieutenant Joseph L. Howard, USMCR, Commanding Officer of Detachment A, USMC Special Detachment 14, decided he needed a dozen machetes for a military operation, he was given MACHETES, SUBSTITUTE STANDARD, W/SHEATHS which had begun their military careers as US SABERS, CAVALRY MODEL OF 1912, W/SCABBARDS.

Actually, he got more than a dozen. Lieutenant Howard had had previous experience with the U.S. Army Ordnance Corps (as a sergeant), and he'd learned then that he was lucky to get half—or a quarter—of what he'd requested.

This request proved an exception to that rule. He requisitioned one hundred machetes, and he got one hundred MACHETES, SUBSTITUTE STANDARD, W/SHEATHS.

The mission Lieutenant Howard drew the machetes for involved a parachute drop of both personnel and equipment. Since there were no specially designed cargo containers, or parachutes, available for the equipment (most importantly, shortwave radios), ordinary personnel parachutes had to be adapted.

Cushioning the radios against the shock of landing was rather simply accomplished by wrapping them securely in mattresses.

But that wasn't the only problem. The standard personnel parachute was designed for a standard soldier carrying normal equipment—that is to say, it could handle a "drop weight" of 200 to 225 pounds. The mattress-wrapped shortwave radios weighed approximately 110 pounds.

Since lightly loaded parachutes fall more slowly than heavier ones, and thus drift more, Howard's radios would not fall to earth anywhere near his personnel.

This was a matter of critical concern, because Lieutenant Howard intended to drop upon a small landing area in the mountains of Buka Island.

Approximately thirty miles long and no more than five miles wide, Buka is the northernmost island in the Solomons chain. That places it just north of the much larger Bougainville and

146 nautical miles from the Japanese base at Rabaul on New Britain.

On Buka, there was a Japanese fighter base and a garrison of Japanese troops variously estimated from several hundred to several thousand.

There was additionally a detachment of the Royal Australian Navy's Coastwatcher Establishment. This consisted of one officer, Sub-Lieutenant Jakob Reeves, RAN Volunteer Reserve, and approximately fifty Other Ranks, all of whom had been recruited from the native population.

Sub-Lieutenant Reeves remained behind when the Japanese occupied Buka; he was provided with a shortwave radio and a small quantity of arms and ammunition; and he was ordered to report on the movement of Japanese ships and aircraft from Rabaul, Bougainville, and of course from Buka.

From the beginning, these reports had been of enormous value for both tactical and planning purposes. But by June 1942, when Lieutenant Howard was preparing his drop, their importance had become even more critical: The United States planned to land on the island of Guadalcanal and to capture and make operational an airfield the Japanese were already building there. The invasion of Guadalcanal was not only the first Allied counterattack in the Pacific War, some considered it to be the campaign that could decide the outcome of the entire war in the Pacific.

Since there were no Allied air bases within fighter range of Guadalcanal, initial aviation support for the invasion of Guadalcanal would fly from aircraft carriers. But launching and recovering aircraft from carriers was a difficult, time-consuming operation, and aviation-fuel supplies were finite. These difficulties could be minimized, however, if the Navy could be informed when Japanese aircraft took off from Rabaul or other nearby bases and headed for the invasion area.. That was the function of the Coastwatcher Station on Buka.

Unfortunately, Sub-Lieutenant Reeves' shortwave radio went off the air during the preparations for the invasion. The Coastwatcher Establishment saw two likely explanations for Reeves' absence: One, the radio itself had broken down (this was the most hopeful scenario). Or two (and much worse), the Japanese had captured Sub-Lieutenant Reeves.

An overflight of his location, conducted at great risk, returned with aerial photographs of a grassy field. The grass had been stamped down to form the letters RA, for radio. Sub-Lieutenant Reeves needed another radio. Good news, considering the alternative.

USMC Special Detachment 14, whose mission in Australia was to support the Coastwatcher Establishment, had a number of brand-new, state-of-the-art Hallicrafters communications radios; and it would be a fairly easy thing to air-drop one to Sub-Lieutenant Reeves. The problem was that Reeves' knowledge of radios was minimal. He almost certainly would not know how to set one up and get it operational. Thus, the planners decided to send someone to Buka who could handle such things.

Additionally, the planners felt it would be useful to have a second aircraft spotter on Buka. Not only could Sub-Lieutenant Reeves use the help, but there was the further question of what to do should he become *hors de combat* from either enemy action or tropical illness—more a certainty than a probability.

It was decided, consequently, to parachute a radio operator-technician into Buka with the radios. Sergeant Steven M. Koffler, USMC, was a parachutist as well as a radio operator-technician. Unfortunately, he couldn't tell the difference between a bomber and a scout plane, and there was no time to teach him. Neither did Sergeant Koffler have the tropical jungle survival skills he was sure to need.

On the other hand, though Lieutenant Howard was not a parachutist, he not only had the necessary survival skills, he had as a sergeant taught classes in identification of Japanese aircraft and warships. And so Howard volunteered to jump in with Sergeant Koffler and the replacement radios.

When faced with the question of ballast for the cargo parachutes (to bring their drop weight up to the norms for personnel parachutes), Lieutenant Howard suggested small arms and ammunition. For these were heavy, fairly indestructible, and valuable to Ferdinand Six—the radio call sign for Sub-Lieutenant Reeves' detachment.

But Lieutenant Commander Eric Feldt, Royal Australian Navy Volunteer Reserve, disagreed. Feldt, who was commanding officer of the Coastwatcher Establishment, pointed out that the mission of the Coastwatchers was not to fight the Japanese but to hide from them. Ferdinand was the bull who preferred to sniff flowers rather than fight, he reminded Lieutenant Howard and Major Edward F. Banning, USMC, the commanding officer of USMC Special Detachment 14.

A small quantity of small arms and ammunition should be dropped to replenish losses, he maintained. But what Howard and Koffler certainly needed were machetes. Machetes were not only useful for hacking through the jungle, they made effective—and *silent*—weapons.

Major Banning deferred to Commander Feldt's expertise. And the mattress-wrapped radios were ballasted primarily with MACHETES, SUBSTITUTE STANDARD. Their scabbards were left behind.

The airdrop on Buka went off more or less successfully. And Sub-Lieutenant Reeves was on the whole pleased to have what Feldt and Banning sent him. He was, as expected, delighted with his new radios. On the other hand, he entertained early doubts about the wisdom of dropping a pair of sodding Yanks in his sodding lap. He was not on Buka to nursemaid sodding children. One of them didn't even know enough about parachutes to keep from breaking his arm on landing.

The Other Ranks of Ferdinand Six, however, had no complaints about the drop, and they were especially overjoyed with the MACHETES, SUBSTITUTE STANDARD. Their own machetes were in short supply and worn out, while the new ones were high-quality steel of a more modern and doubtless better design. There were even enough of them to equip the women and the older boys with one. The men, as a general rule of thumb, went about with two.

[Two]
FERDINAND SIX
BUKA, SOLOMON ISLANDS
28 AUGUST 1942

The commanding officer of the U.S. Marine Garrison on Buka Island and the senior representative of His Britannic Majesty's government there—that is to say, Lieutenant Joe Howard and Sub-Lieutenant Jakob Reeves—elected to locate their command conference at a site where the subjects to be discussed and the decisions made relative thereto would not become immediately known to their respective commands.

They selected for this purpose the tree house, a platform

built a hundred feet off the ground in an ancient enormous tree. Large enough for three or four people to stand or sit comfortably, the tree house was their primary observation post. Since it was normally manned from daybreak to dark, as soon as Sub-Lieutenant Reeves finished climbing up the knotted rope, he ordered the man on duty, Petty Officer Ian Bruce, Royal Australian Navy Native Volunteer Reserve, to go catch a nap.

Petty Officer Bruce was armed with a Lee-Enfield Mark I .303 rifle and two MACHETES, SUBSTITUTE STANDARD, and he was wearing a loincloth and what might be described as a canvas kilt. He was a dark-skinned man with a mass of curly hair; his teeth were stained dark and filed into points; and his chest and face were decorated with scar patterns.

"Yes, Sir!" PO Bruce replied crisply, in Edinburgh-accented English. He and many of his fellows had been educated in a mission school operated by Protestant nuns from Scotland.

He went nimbly down the rope, and then Lieutenant Joe Howard climbed up.

Howard, who wore a three-month-old beard, was dressed in Marine Corps utilities. The trousers had been cut off just over the knees, and the sleeves torn out at the shoulders. He was armed with a Thompson .45 ACP caliber machine gun and what had once been a U.S. Army Cavalry saber.

He found Reeves sitting with his back against the trunk of the tree. He was wearing a battered and torn brimmed uniform cap, an equally soiled khaki uniform tunic, the sleeves of which had been cut off, and khaki shorts and shoes, the uppers of which were spotted with green mold. His hair hung down his neck, and he was wearing a beard even longer than Howard's. A 9mm Sten submachine gun and a large pair of Ernst Leitz Wetzlar binoculars hung from his neck on web straps.

"I passed the distillery on the way here," Reeves said. "It's bubbling merrily."

"Sugar we have, salt we don't," Howard said.

"Yes," Reeves agreed. "And what do you infer from that?"

"That we can either die drunk or go get some salt. And maybe some other things."

Reeves chuckled. Despite his initial doubts, he had come to admire Joe Howard since he dropped from the sky three months before. In fact, he'd grown fond of him.

"The last time the cannibals attacked a Japanese patrol,"

Reeves said evenly, "they had three hundred people up here for a week."

"But they didn't find us."

"They came pretty sodding close."

"We need salt," Howard repeated. "And we really could use a couple of hundred pounds of rice. Maybe even some canned smoked oysters, some canned crab. Koffler said he would really like to have a Japanese radio. I'm not even mentioning quinine or alcohol or other medicine."

"If I were the Japanese commander, and I heard that an outpost of mine had been overrun by cannibals who made off with smoked oysters, medicine, and a radio, I think I'd bloody well question if they were really cannibals."

"I think they know, Jake. By now, they must."

"And if they suspected that the cannibals were led by an Australian, or for that matter by an American Marine—and I think probably by now they've heard us talking to Pearl, which would suggest an American presence—then one thought that would occur to me would be to arrange an ambush for the cannibals the next time they came out of the sodding jungle."

"We need salt," Howard said.

"You keep saying that, mate."

"That's not debatable."

Reeves shrugged, granting the point.

"Which means we have to get some from the Japs. We would get the same reaction from stealing a fifty-pound bag of salt as we would carrying off whatever we find."

"The last time we were lucky."

"Where does it say you can't be lucky twice in a row?"

"In the sodding tables of probability, you jackass!" Reeves said, chuckling.

"I'll take Ian Bruce," Howard said. "And a dozen men. I can make it back in six days."

"No," Reeves said, smiling, but firmly.

"Jake, that sort of thing is my specialty."

"I know Buka. You don't," Reeves said. "For one thing."

"We can't afford to lose you, Jake. If you weren't around, the natives would take off, and Christ knows, I wouldn't blame them."

"Precisely my point," Reeves said. "Except that they wouldn't just take off. There would be a debate whether they should convert you to long pig or sell you to the Japanese."

"You don't mean that," Howard said.

"About the long pig? Or selling you to the Japanese?" Reeves asked. "Yes, I do, mate. Both. My use of the word 'cannibal' was not to be cute. You don't think the good nuns put those scars on Ian's face, do you?"

Their eyes met for a moment and then Reeves went on:

"We'll leave Ian Bruce here with Steve Koffler, one or two other men, and most of the women. That'll keep the station up, and there'll be enough people to carry things off if the Nips should luck upon them while we're gone."

Howard thought that over for a minute and then looked at Reeves again.

"Ian and Koffler have become friends. We'll leave Patience behind too. The two of them might just get Koffler off safe in case the Nips do come. Do you disagree?"

Though Miss Patience Witherspoon was also educated by the nuns in the mission school, she immediately forgot all they taught her about the Christian virtue of chastity the moment she laid eyes upon Sergeant Steven M. Koffler, USMC. Not only were Patience and Koffler both eighteen years old, she found him startlingly attractive.

Her unabashed interest in Sergeant Koffler had not been reciprocated, possibly because Patience's teeth were stained dark and filed to a point, and her not-at-all-unattractive bosom and stomach, which she did not conceal, were decorated with scar tissue.

Lieutenant Howard did not know, and did not want to know, whether time had changed Koffler's views about Patience. And if his views had changed, whether she crawled into his bed at night.

But, he realized, Reeves was right again. If the requisitioning mission went bad, or if the Japanese should luck upon this place while they were gone, Ian and Patience were Koffler's best chance of survival. Perhaps his only chance.

"No, you're right, of course," Howard said.

"And of course, with you along with us, we will have the benefit of your warrior skills."

"Bullshit."

"I wouldn't want this to go to your head, old boy, but the chaps are beginning to admire you. Very possibly it's your beard. Theirs don't grow as long as ours. But in any event, if we both go, and if something unpleasant should happen to me,

I think—I said *think*—that the chaps would probably come back here with you."

Howard met his eyes.

"I was thinking we should leave at first light tomorrow."

"No. I think we should leave now. That way we can move the rest of the day and through the night, and then sleep all day tomorrow."

Reeves stood up.

"I'll have a word with Ian," he said. "And you can have a word with Koffler."

[Three]
HENDERSON FIELD
GUADALCANAL, SOLOMON ISLANDS
28 AUGUST 1942

The twin-engine, twenty-one-passenger Douglas aircraft known commercially as the DC-3 and affectionately as the Gooneybird was given various other designations by the military services that used it: To the U.S. Army, for instance, it was the C-47; to British Empire forces it was the Dakota; and the U.S. Navy—and so The Marines—called it the R4D.

An hour out of Espiritu Santo for Guadalcanal the crew chief of the MAG-25 (*M*arine *A*ir *G*roups consisted of two or usually more Marine aircraft squadrons) R4D came out of the cockpit and made his way past the row of high-priority cargo lashed down the center of the fuselage. At the rear of the cabin, a good-looking, brown-haired, slim, and deeply tanned young man in his middle twenties had made himself a bed on a stack of mailbags.

The other two passengers, a Marine Lieutenant Colonel and an Army Air Corps Captain, both of whom carried with them the equipment, clothing, and weapons specified by regulation for officers assigned to Guadalcanal, were more than a little curious about the young man dozing on the mailbags.

For one thing, he had boarded the aircraft at the very last moment; the pilot had actually shut down one of the engines so the door could be reopened. For another, his only luggage was a bag made out of a pillowcase, the open end tied in a knot. He was wearing khaki trousers and a shirt, the collar points of which were adorned with the silver railroad tracks of a captain, and Marine utility boots, called "boondockers." All items of uniform were brand new. In fact, the young Captain had even failed to remove the little inspection and other stickers with which military clothing comes from stock.

The crew chief, a staff sergeant, started to reach for the Captain's shoulders to wake him, but stopped when the Captain opened his eyes.

"Sir," the crew chief said, "Major Finch wants you to come forward."

"OK," the young Captain said, stretching and then getting to his feet.

He followed the crew chief back up the cabin to the cockpit door. The crew chief opened the door, held it for the Captain, and then motioned him to go first.

The Captain went as far forward as he could go, then squatted down, placing his face level with the Major's in the pilot's seat.

"You wanted to see me, Sir?"

"Oh, I got curious. I sort of expected you would come here on your own to say thank you."

"I am surprised the Major has forgotten what he learned in Gooneybird transition: 'Unauthorized visitors to the cockpit are to be discouraged.' "

The Major laughed.

"Speaking of unauthorized, Charley, how much trouble can I expect to get in for giving you this ride?"

"None, Sir. I'm still assigned to the squadron. I'm just going home."

"Why does that sound too simple?" the Major asked. He looked at the copilot, a young first lieutenant. "Mr. Geller, say hello to Captain Charley Galloway, of fame and legend."

"How do you do, Sir?" Lieutenant Geller said, smiling and offering his hand.

"You may have noticed, Mr. Geller, what a superb R4D pilot I am . . ."

"Yes, Sir, Major Finch, Sir, I have noticed that, Sir," Lieutenant Geller said.

"The reason is that my IP was Charley here."

"At Fort Benning," Galloway said, smiling, remembering.

"We drove the Air Corps nuts," Finch said. "Here I was, a brand-new *major,* and *Sergeant* Galloway was teaching me—

and ten other Marine officers—how to fly one of these. The Army doesn't have any flying sergeants."

Lieutenant Geller dutifully laughed.

"I think maybe I should have busted my check ride," Finch said. "Then maybe I would be flying fighters instead of this."

"But tonight you will be back on Espiritu Santo," Galloway said, "drinking whiskey with nurses and going to bed in a cot with real sheets."

"I understand creature comforts are a little short at Henderson," Finch said.

"You haven't been there?" Galloway asked, surprised.

"This is my first trip."

"Creature comforts *are* a little short at Henderson," Galloway said. "Let me give you a little protocol: *Nice* transient copilots, Mr. Geller, pump their own fuel out of the barrels into the tanks."

"No ground crews?" Finch asked.

"And no fuel trucks. What gas there is comes in on High Speed Transports . . ."

"What's a High Speed Transport?" Geller asked.

"A World War One destroyer with half its boilers removed and converted to troop space," Galloway explained. "High Speed only in the sense that they're faster than troop transports.

"Anyway, gas comes in fifty-five-gallon barrels lashed to the decks. The Navy either loads them into landing barges, or, if time is short, throws them over the side—they float, you know—and then the Marines take over—getting it to shore, off the barges and to the field. The heat and humidity are really nasty. You don't have to move many fifty-five-gallon barrels of Av-Gas very far before your ass is dragging. So please, Mr. Geller, don't stand around with your finger up your ass watching somebody else fuel this thing up."

"No, Sir," Geller said.

"How come there's no Navy shore parties to handle supplies?" Finch asked.

"You've been in The Corps more than three weeks, Jack," Galloway said. "You should know that the Navy doesn't give The Corps one goddamn thing it doesn't have to."

"That sounds a little bitter, Charley," Finch said. There was just a hint of disapproval in his voice.

"Sailors I get along with pretty well," Galloway said. "It's the *Navy* I have problems with."

Finch chuckled, then asked, "Are you going to tell me why you needed this off-the-manifest ride to Henderson?"

"Because some Navy two-striper on Espiritu decided that I should get back to Guadalcanal on one of those High Speed Transports."

"What's wrong with that?"

"I get seasick," Galloway said.

"Bullshit."

"My executive officer is a brand-new first lieutenant with maybe 350 hours' total time. And he's one of my more experienced pilots."

"Now that we're telling the truth, are you all right to fly? Or did you just walk out of the hospital?"

"I'm all right. I didn't get hurt when I went in. I got sunburned and dehydrated, that's all."

"Is that straight, Charley?"

"Yeah, I'm all right."

"What happened, Charley?"

"I really don't know. I never saw the guy who got me. A Zero, I'm sure. But I didn't see him. The engine nacelle started to come off, and then the engine froze. And caught fire. So I remembered what *my* IP had taught me about how to get out of an F4F and got out."

"How long were you in the water?"

"Overnight. A PT boat picked me up at first light the next morning."

"Jesus!"

"God takes care of fools and drunks," Galloway said. "I qualify on both counts."

Geller, Finch noticed, *is looking at Galloway as if he was Lazarus just risen from the dead.*

"Tell me about Henderson," Major Finch asked, sensing that Galloway would welcome a change of subject.

"It's not Pensacola," Galloway replied. "The Japs started it, and had it pretty well along when we took it away from them— which is obviously why we went in half-assed the way we did. If they'd gotten it up and running, Jesus Christ! Using captured construction equipment, our guys made it more or less usable."

"Why captured construction equipment?" Geller asked.

"Because the construction equipment the First Marines took

with them never got to the beach. It, and their heavy artillery, and even a bunch of Marines, sailed off into the sunset the day after they landed because the Navy didn't want to risk their precious ships. Right now, at least half of the ration is captured Jap stuff."

"My God!" Finch said.

"Actually, some of it's not bad," Galloway went on. "I mean it's not just rice. There's orange and tangerine slices, crab and lobster and shrimp, stuff like that."

"What's the field like?" Finch pursued.

"Twenty-six hundred feet," Galloway answered. "They're working to lengthen it. It gets muddy when it rains, and it rains every day. We have a lot of accidents on the ground because of the mud."

"Dirt? Not pierced-steel planking?"

"Dirt. And there's talk—maybe they even started on it—of making another strip for fighters, a couple of hundred yards away."

Galloway suddenly stood up. His legs were getting cramped.

"Would you like to sit in here, Sir?" Geller asked politely.

"No. No, thank you," Galloway said, and then smiled. "Tell me, Mr. Geller, have you ever seen a P-400?"

"What the hell is a P-400?" Finch asked.

"No, Sir," Geller said.

"It used to be the P-39," Galloway said. "The story is they renamed it the P-400 because everybody knew the P-39 was no goddamned good. They were supposed to be sent to Russia—"

"That's the low-wing Bell with the engine behind the pilot, and with a 20mm cannon firing through the propeller nose?" Geller interrupted.

"Right. The cannon was supposed to be used against German tanks. But then somebody told them a 20mm bounced off German tanks, so the Russians said, 'No, thank you.' So then the British were supposed to get them. They flew just enough of them—one, probably—to learn they were no good. So they said, 'No, thank you,' too. So they sent them to Guadalcanal."

"To the Marines?" Geller asked.

"No. There's an Army Air Corps squadron. They have a high-pressure oxygen system, said to be very effective to twenty-five thousand feet, which would be very helpful; the Japanese often come down from Rabaul at high altitude. Except we don't have the gear to charge the oxygen system, so they can't fly above twelve, fourteen thousand feet. And aside from that, it's not a very good airplane in the first place."

"Then why the hell are you so anxious to get back to this paradise?" Finch asked, without thinking, and was immediately sorry.

The Marine Corps finally did something right and made Galloway a captain and gave him a squadron, Finch thought. *He wants to get back because good Marine captains—and Galloway is probably a better captain than he was a tech sergeant—want to be with their squadrons.*

Not surprising Finch at all, Galloway ignored the question.

"We have pretty good Intelligence," Galloway went on. "The Australians left people behind when the Japs started taking all these islands."

"I don't follow you, Charley," Finch said.

"They left behind missionaries, government employees, plantation owners, people like that. They commissioned them into the Australian Navy and gave them shortwave radios. Just as soon as the Japs take off, we know about it. And we get en route reports, too. Which gives us enough time to get the Wildcats into the air and at altitude before they get there. The P-400s and the dive bombers—we had thirty Douglas SBD-3s; there were eighteen left the last time I was there—take off and get the hell out of the Japs' way."

"You mean the P-400s are useless?"

"No. Not at all. They're useful as hell supporting the First Marine Division. But they can't get up high enough to attack the Japanese bombers, and they're no match for the Japs' Zeroes. So they get out of the way when the Japs have planes in the area. I really feel sorry for those Air Corps guys. The P-400 is the Air Corps version of the Buffalo."

Finch knew all about the Buffalo. It was a shitty airplane. VMF-211 flew them in the Battle of Midway (VMF is the designation for Marine Fighter squadrons). For all practical purposes the squadron had been wiped out. The only survivors were the pilots lucky enough to have been assigned Wildcats.

Galloway lost a lot of buddies with VMF-211 at Midway, he thought. *We all did. In the old days, you knew just about every other Marine Aviator.*

"You want to drive this awhile, Charley?" Finch asked as he started to unfasten his seat and shoulder harness. "I need to take a leak and stretch my legs."

He got out of his seat and Galloway slid into it. Finch paused to take down a Thermos bottle of coffee from its rack and pour an inch of it into a cup. He drank that. Then he poured more into the cup and leaned over to hand it to Galloway.

Galloway's hand was on the throttle quadrant. Apparently the synchronization of the engines was not to his satisfaction.

Ordinarily, Finch thought, *my ego would be hurt and I would be pissed. But in this case, in the interest of all-around honesty, I will concede that Captain—formerly Tech Sergeant—Charley Galloway has forgotten more about flying the R4D than I know.*

"Coffee, Charley?" he asked, touching Galloway's shoulder.

Finch brought the R4D in low over the ocean, making a straight-in approach toward Henderson Field, which was more or less at right angles to the beach. He called for wheels down as he crossed the beach, and maintained his shallow angle of descent until he reached the runway itself.

There was no chirp as the wheels touched down, just a sudden rumbling to tell him that he was on the ground.

He chopped the throttles, put the tail on the ground, and applied the brakes, stopping before he reached the control tower, which was to the right of the runway. To his left he saw parts of three hangars, but couldn't tell if they were damaged or simply under construction.

He saw other signs of damage around. There was an aircraft graveyard to the left. People were cannibalizing parts from wrecks, including the P-400s Galloway talked about.

A FOLLOW ME jeep appeared on the runway, and he followed it toward the control tower. A Marine in the jeep jumped out and showed him where he was to park the airplane.

He spotted a familiar face, or more accurately a familiar hairless head, thick neck, and massive chest belonging to Technical Sergeant Big Steve Oblensky. He was glad to see him. Tech Sergeant Oblensky had been very kind to a very young Lieutenant Finch when he reported to his first squadron. Oblensky's uniform consisted of utility trousers, boondockers, and a Thompson submachine gun slung from his bare shoulder.

Oblensky, who had more than enough time in The Corps to retire, had been a Flying Sergeant when Major Finch was in junior high school. Long ago he'd busted his flight physical, but had stayed in The Corps as a maintenance sergeant. He had been Maintenance Sergeant of VMF-211, Finch recalled, until Charley Galloway stole him when he formed his VMF-229.

He was not surprised to see Oblensky. Half the crates lashed down the center of the fuselage were emergency shipments of aircraft parts, and Big Steve was not the sort of man to order emergency shipments only to see them diverted by some other maintenance sergeant. Or for that matter, by the MAW Commanding General.

"Shut it down, Geller," Finch ordered and got out of his seat.

When he reached the rear door of the aircraft, he saw a sight he never expected to see. Technical Sergeant Oblensky ran up to his squadron commander, Captain Charles M. Galloway. But instead of saluting him, he wrapped his arms around him, lifted him off the ground, and complained, "You little bastard, we all thought you was dead!"

"Put me down, for Christ's sake, you hairless ape!"

Major Finch recalled that Galloway and Oblensky had been in VMF-211 for a long time before the war. Galloway had then been a technical sergeant.

Oblensky set Galloway back on his feet. But emotion overwhelmed him again. He swung his massive fist at Galloway's arm in a friendly touch, or so he intended. It almost knocked Galloway off his feet.

"Goddamn—it's good to see you!"

"Christ, watch it, will you?" Galloway complained.

But he was smiling, Finch noticed.

"Hello, Oblensky, how are you?" Finch called as he climbed down the stairs to the ground.

Oblensky looked, and when recognition dawned on his face, he came to attention and threw a very crisp salute.

"Major Finch, Sir. It's good to see you, Sir."

Finch returned the salute.

Oblensky is obviously glad to see me. But not as glad as he is to see Galloway. Whatever the reason, whether because they were sergeants together, or because Charley is just back, literally, from the mouth of death, I'm just a little jealous.

"There's some stuff on board for VMF-229, Oblensky," Finch said as the two shook hands.

"I better get it," Oblensky said, then turning to Galloway, he remembered the appropriate military courtesy before he went on. "Captain, Ward and Schneider are flying out on this thing.

I mean, if you wanted to say hello or so long, or something, Sir."

He pointed to a fly tent erected behind the control tower, between the tower and the tree line. Galloway saw a half dozen jeeps near there, each rigged for stretchers. Several of these had red crosses painted on their hoods.

"How bad are they hurt?" Galloway asked.

"Mr. Schneider's got a busted ankle and took some hits in the legs. Mr. Ward busted his ribs and took some little shit, shrapnel, glass, whatever, in the face. He's not so bad off. I don't know why they're evacuating him."

"And the others?" Galloway asked softly.

"Mr. Jiggs and Mr. Hawthorne didn't make it, Sir," Oblensky said. "Everybody else is all right."

Galloway turned to Finch.

"Thank you for the ride, Sir," he said.

"Anytime, Charley," Finch said, putting out his hand. "Be careful. Get to be one of those old, *cautious* birdmen we hear about."

Galloway freed his hand and saluted, then walked off toward the fly tent.

He found First Lieutenant James G. Ward, USMCR, sitting on a cot, holding his shirt on his lap. He was bare-chested except for the adhesive tape wrapped around his upper torso; his head was wrapped in bandages; the parts of his face that were visible looked like someone had beaten him with a baseball bat; and his neck and shoulders were decorated with a dozen small bandages.

What did that idiot say? "He's not so bad off"? What's bad off, then?

"Hello, Jim," Galloway said. "I'd ask how you are, except that I'm afraid you'd tell me."

Ward, startled, jumped to his feet.

"My God, am I glad to see you!"

"Yeah, me too," Galloway said.

He was fond of Jim Ward for many reasons . . . and not just because Jim Ward was responsible for his initial meeting with Mrs. Carolyn Ward McNamara, who was Jim's aunt. Carolyn's last letter to Galloway was signed, *"all of my love, my darling, always, to the end of time."* And Galloway felt pretty much the same about her.

"These idiots want to evacuate me!" Ward said indignantly,

gesturing toward a group of medical personnel at the far end of the fly tent.

"Really? I wonder why?"

"All I've got is some busted ribs."

"Have you looked in a mirror lately?"

"I took some shards from the windscreen," Ward protested. "And I guess I banged my face against the canopy rails or something. But the bandages and the swelling will be gone in a week." He saw the look on Galloway's face and added indignantly, "Go ask them if you don't believe me."

"Where's Schneider? More importantly, how is Schneider?"

First Lieutenant David F. Schneider, USMC, a graduate of the Naval Academy and the nephew of an admiral, had only one redeeming feature, in Galloway's judgment. The arrogant, self-important little shit had a natural ability to fly airplanes.

"He's in pretty bad shape," Jim Ward said. "He broke his ankle. I mean bad. And he took a bullet and some shrapnel in his leg. They've been keeping him pretty well doped up."

He pointed to a cot at the far end of the fly tent near where the medical personnel were gathered.

"You stay here," Galloway ordered. "I'll ask why you're being evacuated."

"I can fly *now,* for Christ's sake."

"Yeah, sure you can," Galloway said.

He walked to the foot of Schneider's cot. Schneider's face looked wan, and his eyes, though open, seemed to be not quite focused on the canvas overhead. A cast covered his foot and his left leg nearly up to his knee; and his upper right leg was covered with a bandage from his knee to his crotch. Like Ward, he was peppered with small bandages.

"Hey, Dave, you awake?" Galloway called softly.

Schneider's eyes finally focused on Galloway and recognition came. He smiled and started to push himself up on the cot.

"We heard you were alive, Sir. I'm delighted."

"What happened to you?"

"I took some hits in the leg, Sir. And as I was landing, I found that I was unable to operate the right rudder pedal. I went off the runway and hit a truck, Sir."

"How's the truck?" Galloway asked jokingly.

"I understand it was one of the trucks the Japanese rendered inoperable, Sir," Schneider said, seriously. "I regret that I totaled the aircraft, Sir."

"Well, by the time you get back, we'll have a new one for you."

"Yes, Sir."

"Anything I can do you, Dave?"

"No, Sir. But thank you very much."

"I just came from Espiritu Santo, Dave. What they'll probably do is keep you there no more than a day and then fly you to the new Army General Hospital in Melbourne."

"Not to a Navy hospital, Sir?" Schneider asked, disappointed.

Galloway knew the reason for Schneider's disappointment: Ensign Mary Agnes O'Malley, NNC, might not be serving at the hospital where he was assigned. Mary Agnes O'Malley was a sexual engine who ran most of the time over the red line, and in recent times she liked having Schneider's hands on her throttle.

Jesus, as doped up as he is, he's still thinking about Mary Agnes, hoping she'll be there to nurse him in a way not ordinarily provided. Sorry, Dave, even if you go to a Navy hospital, and Mary Agnes was there with her libido in supercharge, it'll be some time before you'll be bouncing around on the sheets again.

"Hey, Dave," Galloway said. "Hospitals are hospitals."

"Yes, Sir."

A small-boned little man in utilities walked up to the cot, swabbed at Schneider's arm with a cotton ball, and then gave him an injection. At first Galloway thought he was a Navy corpsman, but then he saw a gold oak leaf on the little man's collar. He was a lieutenant commander.

He was not wearing a Red Cross brassard, Galloway noticed, and there was a web belt with a Colt .45 automatic pistol in its holster dangling from it.

He looked at Galloway coldly and walked away. When Galloway looked down at Schneider again, his eyes were closed. Galloway walked after the doctor.

"Got a minute, Doctor?"

The little man turned and again looked coldly at Galloway.

"Certainly I have a minute. Obviously there is very little for me to do around here. What's on your mind?"

"Lieutenant Ward, over there," Galloway said, jerking his thumb toward Ward, "doesn't think he really has to be evacuated."

"What are you, his priest or something?"

"I told him I would ask, Commander," Galloway replied.

"OK. He has broken ribs. He can't fly with broken ribs, OK? His nose is broken, OK? And there is a good chance he has some bone damage in that area. We won't know until we can get a good EN&T guy to take a good look at him, OK? In addition to that, he has a number of small penetrating wounds, each of which, in this fucking filthy humid environment, is likely to get infected, OK? So I made a decision, Chaplain: Either I let this guy hang around here, and not only get sicker, OK? And take up bed space I'm going to need soon, OK? And eat rations, which we don't have enough of as it is, OK? Or I could evacuate him, OK? I decided to evacuate him. OK?"

"OK," Galloway said. "Sorry to bother you."

"I don't know how long you've been around here, Chaplain," the doctor said. "But you better understand that these pilots are all crazy. For example, I just got word that a lunatic in the hospital on Espiritu Santo went AWOL to come back here. The son of a bitch was suffering from exposure and dehydration after he got shot down and floated around in the goddamned ocean for eighteen hours."

"You don't say?"

"Anything else on your mind, Chaplain?"

"No, thank you very much, Doctor."

The doctor turned and walked away. Galloway went back to Jim Ward.

"What did he say, Skipper?"

"He said get on the airplane, Mr. Ward. He said unless you do, your wang will turn black and fall off."

"Come on, I can fly."

"Have a good time in Australia, Jim," Galloway said.

"Oh, shit!" Jim Ward said, resigned to his fate.

When Lieutenant Colonel Clyde W. Dawkins, USMC, wearing a sweat-soaked tropical areas flight suit and a .45 automatic in a shoulder holster, raised his eyes from his desk, he saw Captain Charles M. Galloway, USMCR, standing at the entrance to his tent. Though Dawkins looked hot and hassled, his voice was conversational, even cordial, when he spoke:

"Please come in and have a seat, Captain Galloway, I'll be with you in just a moment."

"Thank you, Sir," Galloway said.

Galloway was worried. He had served under Dawkins for a

long time, and he knew Dawkins: When he was really pissed, before he really lowered the boom, he assumed the manner of a friendly uncle.

A full two minutes later, Dawkins looked at him.

"I must confess a certain degree of surprise, Captain Galloway. From the description of your physical condition and mental attitude furnished by the medics on Espiritu Santo, I expected a pathetic physical wreck, eyes blazing with a maniacal conviction that the entire war will be lost unless he is there to fight it himself."

"Sir, I'm all right. All I was doing was sitting around reading three-month-old copies of the *Saturday Evening Post.*"

"In case this has not yet come to your attention, Captain, the Naval Service, in its wisdom, has certain designated specialists, called doctors, who determine if people are fit, or not fit, to return to duty. What makes you think your judgment is superior to theirs?"

Galloway opened his mouth to reply, but Dawkins went on before he could. "How the hell did you get back here, anyway?"

"I caught a ride, Sir."

"And did you really think you could get away with just getting on a plane and coming back here?"

Galloway made no reply.

"They want you court-martialed for breaking into some supply room. What the hell is that all about? What did you steal, anyway?"

Galloway waved his hand, indicating his uniform.

"They wouldn't give me my uniform back, Sir."

Dawkins glowered at him for a full thirty seconds, and then said, "If I wasn't so glad to see you, you sonofabitch, I'd *personally* kick your ass all over this airfield, and *then* send you back there in irons."

"I thought I should be here, Sir," Galloway said.

"Are you really all right, Charley?"

"I looked like a corpse when they fished me out of the water, and I never want to get that thirsty again, but yes Sir, I'm all right."

"What do you mean, you looked like a corpse?"

"My skin was all puckered up."

"You realize how lucky you were?"

"Yes, Sir."

"Jiggs and Hawthorne weren't lucky," Dawkins said.

"Yes, Sir. Oblensky told me."

"And you know about Ward and Schneider?"

"Yes, Sir. I just saw them. Ward's unhappy about being evacuated."

"Well, following the sterling example of his squadron commander, he'll probably go AWOL and come right back."

"I didn't have the chance to ask Big Steve about aircraft," Galloway said, hoping to change the subject.

"You have eight left. Christ only knows when we'll get more. I think the Air Corps is down to about six of their P-400s. Have you seen Dunn?"

"No, Sir. I came right here."

"He is now officially an ace. I put him in for a DSC," a Distinguished Service Cross. "They bumped it down to a DFC," a Distinguished Flying Cross.

"You should have known they would," Galloway said.

Dawkins nodded. "That's why I put him in for the DSC. If I'd have put him in for a DFC, they would have bumped it down to a Good Conduct Medal."

Galloway chuckled.

"You're credited with three and a half," Dawkins said.

"Anything unusual I should know?"

Dawkins shook his head.

"Same drill. We generally get thirty minutes' notice from the Coastwatcher people, via either Pearl Harbor or Townsville. That gives us enough time to get off the ground and to altitude. By then the radar can usually give us a vector. We shoot them down or they shoot us down. That will go on until one side or the other runs out of airplanes. Right now, unless we get some help from the Navy, that looks like us."

"There was a bunch of F4F pilots on Espiritu. Right out of Pensacola."

"That's academic. We don't have airplanes for them to fly."

Their eyes met for a moment, and then Galloway said, "I suppose I better go see Dunn and let him know I'm back."

As the next senior officer present for duty, First Lieutenant William Charles Dunn, USMCR, assumed command of VMF-229 after Galloway was shot down and presumed dead. Bill Dunn was twenty-one years old; he stood five feet six, weighed no more than 135 pounds, and looked to Dawkins like a college cheerleader. He became an ace the day he took over VMF-229.

Dawkins nodded, and then stood up and offered his hand. "I'm glad you came through, Charley. God knows how, but I'll deal with the people you've pissed off."

"Thank you, Sir."

Galloway had gone no farther than two hundred yards from Dawkins' tent when a siren began to wail. He looked at the control tower. A black flag—signifying *air base under attack*—was being hoisted on the flagpole.

He started to trot toward the area where the aircraft of VMF-229 were parked in sandbagged revetments. Then, realizing that he really had no reason to rush to his airplane, he slowed to a walk: The F4F with CAPT C. GALLOWAY USMCR painted below the canopy track was now at the bottom of the sea.

Soon he heard the peculiar sound of Wildcat engines starting, and then the different sound of R4D engines being run up to takeoff power. He looked down the runway in time to see the R4D he'd flown in to Guadalcanal begin its takeoff roll. A moment later it flashed over his head.

No more than sixty seconds later, the first F4F with MARINES painted on its fuselage bounced down the runway and staggered into the air, followed almost immediately by half a dozen others.

From his position, he could not see into their cockpits and identify their pilots.

He kept walking toward the squadron area.

The next time the Japanese come, I will bump one of my eager young lieutenants out of his seat. Will I be doing that because I really think that a squadron commander's place is in the air with his men? Or was that doctor on Espiritu right, that anyone who does such things when he hasn't been ordered to is by definition out of his mind?

II

[One]

U.S. MARINE CORPS RECRUIT DEPOT
PARRIS ISLAND, SOUTH CAROLINA
31 AUGUST 1942

Prior to his enlistment in The Marine Corps, George F. Hart, USMCR, was employed by the Saint Louis, Missouri, Police Department. Specifically, the twenty-four-year-old fifth son and eighth child of Captain (of the Saint Louis police) and Mrs. Karl J. Hart was the youngest (ever) detective on that organization's Vice Squad. Law enforcement was something of a family tradition.

After immigrating to the United States from Silesia, George's paternal grandfather, Anton Hartzberger, joined the force a month after he became an American citizen. He retired as a sergeant.

Two of Anton's sons, George's father and his Uncle Fred (legally Friedrich), went on the cops, as did two of George's brothers and a pair of cousins. Uncle Fred was a harness bull sergeant and happy to be where he was . . . though he thought it would be nice if he made lieutenant later, because of the

25

pension. George's father, Karl, was promoted to Captain shortly after he was placed in charge of the Homicide Bureau; and he had ambitions for higher rank. But he believed his ambitions were damaged all along by the perception that he was one more stupid Kraut—of which, it must be admitted, the Saint Louis police had a more than adequate supply.

When Georg Friedrich Hartzberger was in the eighth grade, Sergeant Karl Hartzberger took his wife and his children to a judge's chambers. They emerged the Hart family, with all their given names Anglicized.

After he graduated from high school, George found employment as a truck driver's helper for a well-known Saint Louis brewery—despite misgivings that he wasn't big or strong enough to handle it.

Legally, he should have been over twenty-one before taking employment in the alcohol industry. But that provision of law was enforced by the police department, none of whose members saw reason to inquire just how old Captain Hart's kid was.

And so for close to three years, he manhandled beer kegs and cases of bottled beer from loading dock to truck, and from truck to saloon or store basements, or to wherever those in the business of slaking the thirst of their fellow citizens chose to keep their supplies of brew.

George Hart was sworn in as a police officer when he was twenty-one. By then the regimen of beer-keg tossing had given him a remarkable musculature. While he wasn't built like a circus strongman—as many of his coworkers were—he was extraordinarily strong. For example, he could (and often did, when sampling his employer's wares) cause an *unopened* beer can to explode by crushing it in his hand.

He had also been inside just about every hotel, motel, restaurant, tavern, bar and grill, saloon, and whorehouse in both Saint Louis and East Saint Louis, its neighbor across the river in Illinois.

The usual period of rookie training—riding around with an experienced officer so as to become familiar with the city and with police procedures—was very short for Officer Hart. He already knew the city, and there wasn't much about the police department that he hadn't already learned before he joined the cops.

Afterward, he was assigned as a plainclothes officer to the Vice Squad. The mission of the Vice Squad was the suppression of gambling, prostitution, narcotics, and crimes against nature. As a practical matter, as long as the girls in the houses behaved themselves (which meant they didn't roll their clientele or sell them narcotics), the whorehouses were left pretty much alone. Nor did the police get very excited about a bunch of guys sitting around playing poker or shooting crap.

For the most part that left the drug dealers, the fairies, and the pimps—especially black pimps who preyed on young women, especially really young, fourteen-, fifteen-year-old white country girls who came to Saint Louis seeking fame and fortune. And also, for obvious reasons, the Squad came down hard on badger operations: A guy takes a girl to a hotel room expecting to get a five-dollar piece of ass; instead he finds some guy waving a badge at him, saying he's a cop, and wanting twenty bucks not to run him in and cause him severe public humiliation. And then there were the fucking unwashed hillbillies who came to Saint Louis to find a job, found that a job meant work, and decided it was easier to rent out their four-teen-year-old daughters to make their moonshine money. These guys really offended Officer George Hart's sense of decency.

Hart had been working plainclothes Vice about six months when he was awarded his first citation. He was in a bar down by the river, just nosing around, when two guys stuck it up. One of them had a .38 Smith & Wesson Military and Police, the other one had a .22 Colt Woodsman. Hart wasn't going to do anything about it except remember what they looked like, but a uniform walked in off the street and tried to be a hero. When the robbers shot him, there was nothing Hart could do but shoot the robbers. He killed one; the other would be paralyzed for the rest of his life.

Four months after that, he was in another bar, just nosing around, when a guy came looking for his wife. He found her where he thought she would be, with some other guy, and shot her. He then saw Hart taking out his pistol and was making up his mind whether to shoot the boyfriend or Hart, when Hart shot him.

He already had a citation, so they bent a few civil service rules and made him a detective and kept him in Vice.

He was a detective three weeks when he tried to arrest an unimpressive-looking guy he caught in the act of selling a bag of marijuana leaves. Confident of both his professional skill and his unusual strength, he attempted to make the felony arrest without calling for assistance from other police officers.

Not only did the marijuana vendor successfully resist arrest, he sent Detective Hart to Sacred Heart Hospital with a broken nose, several broken ribs, and three broken fingers on his right hand. When he was subsequently apprehended, it was learned that he had been taught the fine points of street fighting in Tijuana, Mexico, where he was ultimately deported.

After Hart's broken appendages and ribs were healed, Sergeant Raphael Ramirez gave Detective Hart off-duty instruction in the manly art of self-defense as practiced in the Mexican-American neighborhoods of El Paso, Texas, where Sergeant Ramirez lived before moving to Saint Louis and joining the cops.

Detective Hart proved to be an apt pupil. He was never again injured in the line of duty.

Then the goddamn war came along.

Near the courthouse there was a bar, Mooney's, where most of the patrons were either cops or otherwise connected with the law enforcement community. Civilians (unless they were young, female, and attractive) quickly sensed they were not welcome. The other exception was members of the Armed Forces, possibly because they are by definition not civilians.

The Army, Navy, and Marine Corps recruiting offices were in the courthouse, and the enlisted personnel of these offices felt quite at home in Mooney's. Over a period of time, Detective Hart struck up an acquaintance with Staff Sergeant Howard H. Wertz, USMC, one of the Marine recruiters.

They were of an age, shared a Teutonic background, and even looked very much alike. When they were together, Detective Hart talked to Sergeant Wertz about the cops, and Sergeant Wertz talked to Detective Hart about The Marine Corps.

Now and again the question of Detective Hart's possible military service came up. Though it had been decided early on that police work was an essential service and its practitioners exempt from the draft, in Sergeant Wertz's judgment the draft deferment for police officers would not last long. Soon they too would be summoned by their friends and neighbors to military service.

After a while Sergeant Wertz suggested to Detective Hart that he might not have to worry anyhow, since he might not pass the physical examination. Whether Hart was fit for service or not, Sergeant Wertz suggested, would be a good thing to know. A few days after that, he told Detective Hart he had a buddy at the Armed Forces Induction Center who would run Detective Hart through the examination process "off the books," as a special favor.

The results of the physical were a mixed blessing. Detective Hart was in really splendid physical condition, which was nice to know. At the same time they were a little unnerving, for if Sergeant Wertz was correct and the police deferment was eliminated, Hart would go into the Armed Forces.

Perhaps it might be a good idea, Sergeant Wertz suggested, to start looking around to see what Detective Hart could get from the services in exchange for his immediate enlistment, rather than waiting for his Draft Board to send him the *Your Friends and Neighbors Have Selected You* postcard.

Two days after that, Sergeant Wertz told his friend Detective Hart the good news: The Marine Corps just happened to be looking for a few good men with police backgrounds who would be utilized in law enforcement areas. The only problem was that "The Program" (as Sergeant Wertz called it) was nearly full and about to close. So Hart would have to make up his mind quickly.

When Detective Hart consulted him, his father was enthusiastic: "If you have to go, George, and it looks like you'll have to, that's the way to do it. Otherwise they'll hand you a rifle and turn you into cannon fodder."

Private Hart was in The Marine Corps three days when he learned from a personnel clerk at Parris Island that the Marines not only did not have a law enforcement recruitment program, they'd never had one. In other words, he was like anyone else who had enlisted in The Corps: He'd be assigned where The Corps decided he would be of the greatest value. In his case it was The Marine Corps' intention to hand him a rifle, teach him how to use it, and assign him to a rifle company as a rifleman—a/k/a cannon fodder.

One of the reasons Private Hart looked forward to graduation from Parris Island was that afterward he would be given a short leave. During that time he planned to return to Saint Louis, locate Staff Sergeant Wertz, and break both of the sonofabitch's arms.

But Staff Sergeant Wertz was not the only Marine noncom who, in his view, deserved such treatment.

Private George F. Hart, USMCR, was in the fifth week of his recruit training when he decided to render as-painful-as-possible bodily harm to Corporal Clayton C. Warren, USMC. He did not actually intend to *kill* Corporal Warren, who was one of the assistant drill instructors of his platoon, but the thought of breaking Corporal Warren's arm was, well, satisfying.

Though every man in the platoon had the same wish, Private Hart believed he was the only one with the necessary expertise to (a) do it and (b) get away with it. He wished to do so for two reasons. One was personal, and the other was For the Good of the Service (at least as he saw it).

And today was the day.

The first time Private Hart saw Corporal Clayton C. Warren at Parris Island, he thought the guy was one of the hillbilly pimps he had made in Saint Louis. Warren bore an astonishing physical resemblance—tall, bony, sharp-featured, no chin, and a large, fluid Adam's apple—to a shitkicker from Arkansas or someplace like that who had prostituted his fifteen-year-old *wife* rather than get a goddamn job.

And when Corporal Warren first opened his mouth, thus proving he was indeed a hillbilly shitkicker, the likeness was even more astonishing. Hart had to remind himself that *his* shitkicking hillbilly was doing three-to-five; it couldn't possibly be the same man.

Hart understood the necessity and value of the rigorous recruit training program of The Marine Corps. In his judgment, it had three aims: First was to bring the recruits up to a standard of physical strength and endurance which would permit them to fight the enemy; many of them had never lifted anything much heavier than a schoolbook. Second, it was intended to give them the necessary military skills, from the obvious (how to accurately fire and care for a rifle) to the less obvious (how to live in the field on nothing but what you carried on your back). Many of Hart's fellow recruits had never held a firearm until they came to Parris Island; and they'd never slept anywhere but on a soft bed.

Third, and most important, was to teach a bunch of civilians discipline: that is, to do whatever they were told to do, to the best of their ability, whenever they were told to do it. This was surely the most difficult training task the drill instructors and their assistants faced, and Hart was well aware that not many students were going to like the curriculum.

All of this having been said, it was Hart's judgment that The Marine Corps had made a mistake (despite the Parris Island Holy Writ that this kind of mistake was not possible). They had placed at least part of the responsibility of turning civilians into Marines into the hands of a semiliterate, sadistic, hillbilly shit-kicker who got his rocks off by humiliating and physically abusing anyone he suspected of having more brains than he did. That meant all but one or two of the men in the platoon.

Corporal Clayton C. Warren, USMC, was not only a really vicious prick, but a dangerous one. On three occasions, for instance, Hart saw him actually trip men running up an inclined log on the obstacle course. One of the men broke his arm; it was only luck that the other two suffered only minor sprains and abrasions.

And he took delight in making trainees run around the drill field with their rifles held over their heads until they collapsed from exhaustion. A few times this was punishment for some sort of offense, but often it was because Corporal Clayton C. Warren, USMC, just liked to see people run until they dropped.

There was a long list of similar outrages, all falling under the category of acts against the general Good of the Service.

Hart's personal troubles with Corporal Clayton C. Warren, USMC, were based on Warren's notion that Hart was a fucking college boy. This category of *Homo sapiens* seemed to trigger Warren's most intense feelings of inferiority, and thus his most vicious impulses.

There were a dozen fucking college boys in the platoon—real and perceived: Corporal Clayton C. Warren's definition of a fucking college boy was anyone older than eighteen who could read without moving his lips. And yet—even taking into consideration that Warren was likely making him paranoid—Hart was convinced that Warren had him identified as the most offensive of all the fucking college boys.

Warren's actual offenses against Hart himself began with blows to the face (three times, with his fist); to the solar plexus (three times); to the kidneys (twice). He'd kicked Hart in the shins (three times); in the head, while doing push-ups (twice); and once in the side during a rest break.

He also described Hart's relationship with his mother in words that Hart found insufferable—even considering the source, and his experience as a vice cop.

* * *

According to the mimeographed Training Schedule thumb-tacked to the barracks wall, the second period of post-lunch instruction today was Hand-to-Hand Combat. There was a similar period yesterday. Hand-to-Hand Combat was one of Corporal Warren's favorites. He could hurt people with the blessing of The United States Marine Corps.

Yesterday he dislocated the shoulders of three recruits, skill-fully stopping just short of pulling their joints apart. Still, he'd strained them enough to leave enough pain to last for days.

He also ground into the dirt the faces of each student he honored with Hands-on Instruction—with sufficient force to embed pebbles and twigs in their skin.

Corporal Warren's method of instruction went something like this: The trainees would be seated in a semicircle on the ground; Corporal Warren would select one of them—"You, motherfucker!" He'd then instruct the trainee in the Approved Marine Corps Technique of killing the enemy with a knife.

The trainee would be handed a sheathed trench knife. Similarly armed, Corporal Warren would attack the trainee. In a second or so the trainee would find himself on his back, with Corporal Warren's sheathed knife pressing painfully against his Adam's apple.

"You're dead, cocksucker!"

Next Corporal Warren would tell the trainee to attack him, to demonstrate the proper method of defense against a knife attack.

"Now really try to kill me, shitface!"

The trainee—who was not only in awe of Corporal Warren but traumatized by the situation—would make a clumsy attempt to stab Warren with his sheathed knife. He would immediately find himself on his back, with Warren's knee grinding one side of his face into the ground, or else on his stomach, with Warren twisting his arm to the point of shoulder dislocation.

"You're dead, you stupid motherfucker!"

Private Hart noticed with satisfaction that today's instruction period was going very much like yesterday's. He also noticed that the drill instructor, who sometimes watched Corporal Warren in action, seemed to be occupied with the other half of the platoon.

"You, college boy!" Corporal Warren said, indicating Private Hart.

Private Hart rose to his feet. Corporal Warren threw him a sheathed trench knife.

"Try to kill me, college boy!"

Private Hart successfully resisted the terrible urge to obey the order, and moments afterward found himself on his back with Corporal Warren's sheathed knife pressing painfully against his Adam's apple.

"Fucking fairy motherfucker, you're dead!"

He spat in Private Hart's face and then contemptuously got off him.

Private Hart had dropped his knife.

"Pick it up, college boy, and really try to kill me!"

Hart picked up the knife. He crouched and spread his arms, then advanced on Corporal Warren.

Warren smiled.

Private Hart threw the trench knife from his right hand to his left. When Corporal Warren's eyes followed, for a split second, the passage of the knife, Private Hart kicked Corporal Warren in the groin.

As Warren's eyes, now registering shock, returned to him, Hart took one step toward him, grabbed his right arm, twisted it, flipped Warren over his extended right leg, and followed him to the ground as he fell. He placed his knee between Warren's wrist and elbow and tensed his muscles to break the arm.

He felt a hard blow in the back, between the shoulder blades, and felt himself flying through the air.

What the hell?

His face slid a foot through the dirt and pebbles. The breath was knocked out of him.

He heard the crunch of boots on the dirt and a pair of highly shined service shoes and the cuff of sharply creased khaki pants appeared in his view.

"On your feet!"

He recognized the voice of the drill sergeant before he saw his face.

Shit, he saw what happened. He kicked me.

Private Hart, breathing hard, came to attention.

"Look at me," the drill instructor said evenly.

He was a leathery-faced, leanly built staff sergeant in his early thirties. His eyes were gray and cold.

"Try *me,* tough guy," the drill instructor said, and Hart felt a jabbing at his stomach. He looked down and saw that he was

being offered a trench knife, butt first. The sheath had been
removed.

He looked into the drill instructor's face again.

He looks, Hart thought, *more contemptuous than angry.*

"Go on, tough guy, take it," the drill instructor said, and
jabbed Hart in the stomach again with the butt of the trench
knife.

Hart shook his head and blurted what came into his mind:
"I don't have anything against you."

The drill instructor's eyes examined him with renewed interest.

"Meaning you think you could hurt me?"

Again, Hart blurted what came into his mind:

"I don't know. But I've got no reason to cut you."

There was a moment's silence.

" 'Ten'hut!" the drill instructor barked. "Fow-wud, Harch!
Double-time, Harch!"

Hart's compliance was Pavlovian. He started double-timing
across the parade ground. After a moment, he became aware
that the drill instructor was double-timing a step or two behind
him, just within his peripheral vision.

He came to the end of the parade ground, then crossed a
narrow macadam road and moved between two barracks
buildings.

"Column left, Harch!" the drill instructor ordered when they
reached the far end of the long frame building. "Detail, halt!"

Hart stopped and stood at attention. The drill instructor
stepped in front of him.

What the fuck do I do now? Let him beat me up?

"Who taught you to fight?" the drill instructor demanded,
and then, without waiting for a reply, "What did you do before
you came in The Corps?"

"I was a cop."

"A cop?"

"A detective," Hart said.

"Where?"

"Saint Louis."

"Were you really going to break his arm?"

"He's a vicious, sadistic sonofabitch," Hart heard himself
say. "Yeah, I was going to break his arm. Nobody calls me a
motherfucker."

"He's on his way out of here," the drill instructor said.

"Before the war, there's no way an asshole like Warren would have made corporal, much less been assigned here. But he *is* here, and you just made him—made a DI—look like an asshole in front of the platoon. Maybe I should have let you break his arm—we could have said it was an accident."

Jesus Christ, he's talking to me like a human being.

"I'll fix it with the Captain somehow," the drill sergeant said, obviously thinking out loud. "If I can get you transferred to another platoon, can you keep your mouth shut about what happened?"

He looked intently at Hart, as if finally making up his mind.

Hart nodded.

"Thank you," he said.

"Stick your thanks up your ass. I'm not doing this because I like you. I'm doing it because it's the best thing for The Corps."

[Two]
ROYAL AUSTRALIAN NAVY COASTWATCHER ESTABLISH-
MENT
TOWNSVILLE, QUEENSLAND
30 AUGUST 1942

The letters USMC were stenciled on both sides of the hood of the gray 1941 Studebaker President, and a stenciled Marine Corps globe and anchor insignia were on each rear door.

The driver was a Marine, a tall, muscular man in his early thirties. He wore a green fore-and-aft cap adorned with the Marine insignia and the golden oak leaf of a major. Otherwise, he was substantially out of uniform. Instead of the forest green tunic prescribed for officers during the winter months in Australia, he wore a baggy, off-white, rough woolen thigh-length jacket that was equipped with a hood and was fastened with wooden pegs inserted through rope loops. The letters RAN, for Royal Australian Navy, were stenciled on the chest.

The passenger, a lean, sharp-featured man of about the same age, wore an identical duffel coat and a Royal Australian Navy officer's brimmed cap, the gold (actually brass) braid of which was both frayed and green with tarnish. There was no visible means to determine his rank.

Lieutenant Commander Eric Feldt, RAN, Commanding

Officer of the Royal Australian Navy Coastwatcher Establishment, turned to Major Edward J. Banning, USMC, Commanding Officer of USMC Special Detachment 14, gestured out the window, and inquired, "Is that for you?"

Banning, who had heard the engines, leaned forward to look out the window, and saw what he expected to see. A United States Army Air Corps C-47 had begun its approach to the landing field.

"I don't expect anyone," Banning said.

"But we couldn't expect the Asshole to let us know he was coming, could we?"

Under practically any other circumstances, Major Ed Banning's sense of military propriety would have been deeply offended to hear a brother officer call another officer an anal orifice. And he would have been especially offended when the insult came from a foreigner, and the officer and gentleman so crudely characterized was a full colonel of the U.S. Marine Corps.

But at the moment, Major Banning was not at all offended. For one thing, he had a profound professional admiration and a good deal of personal affection for Commander Feldt. And for another, so far as Banning was concerned, Feldt's vulgar characterization fit to a T Colonel Lewis R. Mitchell, USMC, Special Liaison Officer between the Commander in Chief Pacific Ocean Areas (CINCPAC—Admiral Chester W. Nimitz) and the Supreme Commander, Southwest Pacific (SWPOA—General Douglas MacArthur).

Banning knew far more about Colonel Lewis R. Mitchell than Mitchell would have dreamed possible, including the fact that Mitchell had been given his present assignment in the belief that he could do less damage to the war effort there than he had been causing as one of a half dozen colonels assigned to the Personnel Division at Headquarters, USMC.

"You really think it's Mitchell?"

"Who else would it be? That's a sodding Dakota, not a puddle-jumper. If it were your Nip, he'd be in a puddle-jumper."

The "your Nip" reference was to First Lieutenant Hon Song Do, Signal Corps, U.S. Army.

"I'm telling you for the last fucking time, Eric!" Banning flared furiously. "Don't you *ever* refer to Pluto as a Nip, mine or anyone else's!"

"Sorry," Feldt said, sounding genuinely contrite. It did not satisfy Banning.

"For one thing, he's a serving officer. For another, he's a friend of mine. And finally, for Christ's sake, he's *Korean,* not Japanese."

Pluto Hon had made a good many trips by puddle-jumper from MacArthur's headquarters to Townsville to deliver to Banning classified messages that could not be entrusted to ordinary couriers. It was a long way to fly in a Piper Cub. Pluto Hon was a good man, a good officer, and he was *not* a fucking Nip.

"I'm really sorry, old boy," Feldt said. "That just slipped out."

"That's your fucking trouble!"

Feldt did not respond.

Banning decided he had gone far enough. In fact, he was chagrined that he had lost his temper.

"Well, what do you say?" he asked. "Should we go down to the field and see if that *is* the Asshole?"

"Sod him," Feldt said. "Let him walk."

"We'd just have to send one of the men back for him," Banning replied as he braked and prepared to turn around. "And if one of my guys were out of uniform, say wearing one of these RAN sleeved blankets, the Asshole would have apoplexy."

Feldt and Banning had been en route from the Coastwatcher Establishment antennae farm to their headquarters when Feldt had spotted the airplane. The airfield was in between; it took them only a few minutes to reach it.

By then the C-47 had landed and taxied to the transient ramp. The door opened as Banning stopped the Studebaker at the hurricane fence between the parking lot and the field itself.

As Banning walked to the policeman guarding the gate, Colonel Lewis R. Mitchell climbed down the short ladder, tugged at his trench coat to make sure it was in order, and marched toward the terminal.

He looks like an illustration: "Field Grade Officer, Dress Uniform, Winter," Banning thought.

He intercepted him and saluted crisply.

"Good afternoon, Sir."

Colonel Mitchell returned the salute but said nothing.

What he's doing is mentally composing something memorable to say to me about the duffel coat.

Colonel Mitchell's lips worked as if he was distinctly uncomfortable.

"Major Banning," he said finally, "a communication has arrived which I have been instructed to place before you."

What the hell is he talking about?

"Yes, Sir?"

Mitchell reached into the inside pocket of his blouse, removed an envelope, handed it to Banning, and then adjusted his uniform again.

The envelope was unsealed. It contained a single sheet of paper. From its feel, even before he saw the red TOP SECRET classification stamped on it, Banning knew that it had come from the Cryptographic Room. The paper was treated somehow to aid combustion. When a match was touched to it, it almost exploded.

URGENT

HEADQUARTERS USMC WASH DC 29 AUG 1942 1105

TO: HEADQUARTERS SOUTHWEST PACIFIC AREA
ATTN: (EYES ONLY) COLONEL L.R. MITCHELL USMC

1. Reference your radio 25Aug42 subject, "Request for clarification of role SWPOA-CINCPAC liaison officer vis a vis USMC Special Detachment 14 and RAN Coastwatcher Establishment,'' which has been referred to HQ USMC for reply.

2. You are advised that you have no repeat no role vis a vis USMC Special Detachment 14 or RAN Coastwatcher Establishment. You are further advised that Commanding Officer USMC SPECDET 14 is under sole and direct repeat sole and direct command of the undersigned and therefore not sub-

ject to orders of any USMC officer in CINCPAC or
SWPOA, regardless of position or rank.

3. In order to insure that there is absolutely
no misunderstanding, you are directed to personally make the contents of this message known to
Major Edward Banning, USMC; LTCOM Eric A. Feldt,
RAN; and 1st Lt S.D. Hon, SigC, USA.

4. Lt Hon is directed to inform the undersigned
of date and time he has seen this message. Major
Banning is directed to inform the undersigned of
the date and time he has seen this message, and to
inform the undersigned when its contents were
made known to LTCOM Feldt. A consolidated reply,
classified Top Secret, will be dispatched by urgent radio.

5. You are further advised that your raising of
this question has called into doubt your ability
to perform the duties of your present assignment.

FOR THE COMMANDANT

HORACE W.T. FORREST
MAJOR GEN, USMC
ASSISTANT CHIEF OF STAFF, G2, USMC

Banning raised his eyes to Colonel Mitchell's.

"Yes, Sir," he said.

"I apparently overstepped my authority and responsibility
as I understood it . . ." Mitchell said.

Jesus Christ, I actually feel sorry for him.

". . . and if an apology is in order, Major, please consider one
extended."

"No, Sir. No apology is required, Sir. They should have briefed you."

"Is that Commander Feldt in the car?"

"Yes, Sir."

"If you will give me that message back, I will show it to Commander Feldt and then see about getting back to Melbourne."

"Colonel," Banning said, "unless you have some pressing business in Melbourne, why don't you spend the night with us, and let us show you what we're doing here?"

"In light of that message, that strikes me as—"

"Sir, it was a question of Need to Know. With respect, Sir, you have not been cleared for what we're doing here."

"I have a TOP SECRET clearance," Mitchell said. "I'm the liaison officer between the two senior headquarters in the Pacific, and I'm the senior Marine officer present at SWPOA."

Banning, aware that he was about to lose his temper, spoke very carefully.

"Colonel, you have two choices. You can get back on that airplane or you can spend the night with us, let us show you why this is all so important."

"You had something to do with that message I just got, didn't you, Major? It was not just a reply to my radio, was it?"

"Sir, when you told me what you wanted me to do, and I told you what you asked was impossible, and when I learned you had sent that radio, I sent a back-channel message—"

"Who told you about my radio? That Oriental cryptographer?"

"That Oriental cryptographer"? Fuck you, Asshole!

Banning came to attention.

"Sir, I will bring this message to Commander Feldt's attention and arrange to have the confirmation of its receipt radioed to General Forrest. Good afternoon, Sir."

He saluted, and without waiting for it to be returned, executed a perfect about-face movement and then marched toward the Studebaker.

"Now see here, Banning!" Colonel Mitchell called after him.

Banning reached the Studebaker, got behind the wheel, and drove off.

"The Asshole, I gather, is not coming to tea?" Commander Feldt asked.

"Sod him," Major Banning said.

* * *

The story that ended with the arrival of Colonel Mitchell in Townsville had its start some months earlier with what Banning now recognized to be a hell of a smart idea on the part of Secretary of the Navy Frank Knox. At the beginning of the war, Knox realized that he was going to read very few honest reports on the functioning of Navy in the Pacific so long as those reports were written by Navy captains and admirals.

Knox concluded that if he was going to get anything like what he actually needed, he'd have to find someone who was not a member of the Navy establishment, yet who understood the Pacific and the Navy's responsibilities there. He found him, in spades, in the person of Captain Fleming W. Pickering. In addition to having been an any-tonnage, any-ocean master mariner (hence Captain) since he was twenty-six, Pickering was Chairman of the Board of Pacific & Far East Shipping Corporation.

Pickering, in other words, had all the necessary credentials that Knox required.

It is a sign of Frank Knox's considerable integrity that he actually chose Fleming Pickering for the job; for their initial encounter was not pleasant, Fleming Pickering being a notably outspoken man with very strong views indeed. They met in connection with Pickering's refusal to sell his forty-two-vessel cargo fleet to the Navy (he did sell the Navy his twelve-vessel passenger-liner fleet). During their meeting (it took place not long after the attack on Pearl Harbor), Pickering told Knox that he should have resigned after that fiasco, and they should have shot the admirals in charge.

Peace between the two was arranged by their mutual friend, Senator Richmond F. Fowler (R., Cal.), and Pickering was commissioned into the Navy as a Captain on Knox's personal staff. He left almost immediately for the Pacific, where he filed regular reports on what the Navy and Marine Corps were actually doing—as opposed to what they wanted Frank Knox to know about.

Unfettered by the restraints he would have endured had he been under the command of CINCPAC, and with a wide network of friends and acquaintances in Australia and elsewhere in the Far East, Pickering put his nose in wherever he wanted to.

Very soon after he learned of the Royal Australian Navy

Coastwatcher Establishment, he realized its great intelligence value. And it didn't take Pickering long after that to realize that he and Lieutenant Commander Eric Feldt were both just about equally contemptuous of the brass hats the Navy sent to work with the Coastwatchers.

As a result, a lengthy radio message from Pickering to Navy Secretary Knox resulted in the formation of Marine Corps Special Detachment 14, Major Edward S. Banning, commanding, under the Marine Corps Office of Management Analysis (its name was purposely obfuscatory). Banning's mission was not only to get along with Commander Feldt at any cost, but to provide him with whatever personnel, matériel, and money Feldt felt he could use.

Shortly after he took command of Special Detachment 14, Banning was made aware of one of the great secrets of the war, a secret that Pickering was also privy to.

Navy cryptographers at Pearl Harbor had broken many (but *not* all) of the codes of the Imperial Japanese General Staff. Decoded intercepts of these messages were furnished to a very few senior officers (in SWPOA, for instance, only General MacArthur and his intelligence officer, Brigadier General Charles A. Willoughby, got them). The operation had its own security classification: TOP SECRET—MAGIC. And the only cryptographic officer at SWPOA (South West Pacific Ocean Area) cleared to decrypt MAGIC messages was a Ph.D. in mathematics from MIT, First Lieutenant Hon Song Do, Signal Corps, U.S. Army. Banning joined "Pluto" Hon on the MAGIC list, as a stand-in for Pickering.

Meanwhile, Fleming Pickering and Douglas MacArthur grew friendly—bearing in mind that to call any relationship with the General "friendly" might be stretching the truth. It was MacArthur's view (and Pickering agreed with him) that the Navy was telling him (like Frank Knox) only what it wanted him to know, and only when it wanted to tell him. As a result, a radio message brought the appointment of Marine Lieutenant Colonel George F. Dailey as liaison officer between CINCPAC and SWPOA, with orders to keep MacArthur as fully briefed as possible.

Dailey had a second function . . . though he wasn't aware of it. A former Naval attaché, he had the security and intelligence background that would enable him, if necessary, to replace Banning as both Commanding Officer of USMC Special Detachment 14 and as Pickering's stand-in on the MAGIC list. Since he had no Need to Know, he was told little about the Coastwatcher Establishment and nothing whatever of MAGIC—not even of its existence.

That issue became moot when the intelligence officer of the First Marine Division was killed in the opening days of the Guadalcanal operation. Officers at Headquarters USMC Personnel, unaware of Dailey's standby role as Banning's replacement, saw only a qualified replacement for the dead First Marine G-2. And so they ordered Dailey to Guadalcanal. And—either taking care of one of their own or (in Banning's judgment) getting rid of the sonofabitch—they ordered Colonel Lewis R. Mitchell to Australia to replace Lieutenant Colonel Dailey.

By the time Mitchell arrived, Captain Pickering had gone to Guadalcanal (where he figured he would be more useful than he was in Melbourne). With Pickering's departure Banning lost his own one-man-removed access to Navy Secretary Knox. And he also had to deal with Mitchell. Colonel Mitchell might not have been a problem—except that he turned out to be what Banning considered the most dangerous of men, a stupid officer with ambition.

Soon after his arrival, Mitchell somehow learned of a priority air shipment of radio equipment Banning had ordered for Feldt from the United States. In short order he demanded to know:

(a) what the equipment was to be used for;

(b) why it was necessary to have it shipped with the highest air priority;

(c) why he had not, as Senior Marine Officer present, been consulted;

(d) what was this half-assed Coastwatcher operation all about anyway; and,

(e) since the United States was paying all the bills, why a U.S. officer was not in charge.

Banning, as politely as possible, told him he did not have the Need to Know.

That resulted in a radio message from Mitchell to CINC-PAC "requesting clarification of his role vis-à-vis USMC Special Detachment 14 and the Australian Coastwatcher organization."

When Pluto Hon showed this to Banning and asked what he

should do about it, Banning told him to delay transmission for twenty-four hours while he considered his choices.

Banning saw two options: He could go directly to General MacArthur. Or he could send a back-channel message to the Office of Management Analysis.

On the one hand, going to MacArthur could raise more problems than it solved: MacArthur believed in the chain of command. Since colonels are *de facto* smarter than majors, majors do not question what colonels do.

On the other hand, back-channel messages are not filed and therefore do not have to be phrased in military-acceptable terminology:

```
URGENT
FROM CO USMC SPECDET 14
VIA CINCPAC MAGIC
TO MARINE OFFICE MANAGEMENT ANALYSIS
EYES ONLY COLONEL RICKABEE

MITCHELL REALLY DANGEROUS X HE WILL SEND MES-
SAGE CINCPAC TOMORROW REQUESTING CLARIFICA-
TION OF HIS ROLE VISAVIS EVERYTHING HERE X CAN
YOU GET HIM OFF MY BACK X REGARDS X BANNING END
```

[Three]
THE FOSTER LAFAYETTE HOTEL
WASHINGTON, D.C.
1415 HOURS 31 AUGUST 1942

Senator Richmond F. Fowler (R., Cal.), was a silver-haired, erect sixty-two-year-old. Despite his attire—he wore a sleeveless undershirt and baggy seersucker trousers held up by suspenders—he still managed to look dignified when he opened the door of his apartment himself in response to an imperious knock.

Fowler occupied a six-room suite on the eighth floor of the Foster Lafayette. It was a corner suite, and so half its windows gave him an unimpeded view of the White House on the other side of Pennsylvania Avenue. Though the suite's annual rental was not quite covered by his Senatorial salary, this was not a problem. The Senator had inherited from his father *The San*

Francisco Courier-Herald, nine smaller newspapers, and six radio stations. And it was more or less accurately gossiped that his wife and her brother owned two square blocks of downtown San Francisco and several million acres of timberland in Washington and Oregon.

A tall, distinguished-looking man in his early forties was standing in the corridor. He was wearing a khaki uniform, shirt, trousers, and overseas cap. The U.S. Navy insignia and a silver eagle were pinned to the cap, and silver eagles were on his collar. The right armpit area of the shirt was dark with sweat. The left sleeve had been cut from the shirt at the shoulder to accommodate a heavy plaster cast which covered the arm from the shoulder to the wrist.

The two men looked at each other for a long time before Senator Fowler finally spoke.

"I am so glad to see you, you crazy sonofabitch, that I can't even be angry."

"May I come in, then?" the other man asked with gentle sarcasm.

"Are you all right, Fleming?" Fowler asked, concern coloring his voice.

"When I get out of these fucking clothes, and you get me something cold—and heavily alcoholic—I will be."

"You want to get in bed? Should I call a doctor?"

"I want a very large glass of orange juice, with ice, and a large hooker of gin," Captain Fleming Pickering, USNR, said, as he walked into the sitting room of the suite. "I have been thinking about that for hours."

"Can you have alcohol?"

"Hey, I have a broken arm. That's all."

"A *compound fracture* of the arm," Senator Fowler said. "Plus, I have been told, a number of other unnatural openings in the body."

With his good hand Pickering started to shove an overstuffed chair across the room.

"What are you doing? Let me do that!" Fowler said and walked quickly to him.

"Right in front of the air-conditioning duct, if you please," Pickering said.

"You'll catch cold," Fowler said.

Pickering ignored him. He took off his cap, tossed it onto a couch, then unbuttoned and removed his shirt and dropped it onto the floor. In a moment his khaki trousers followed.

Fowler looked at him with mingled resignation and alarm.

Pickering suddenly marched into one of the bedrooms and came back a moment later with a sheet he had obviously torn from the bed.

He started to drape it over the upholstered chair.

Fowler, seeing what he wanted to do, snatched it from him and arranged it more neatly.

Pickering collapsed into the chair.

"Anything else I can get you, Flem? Are you in pain?"

"How about a footstool and a pillow?" Pickering asked. "And of course the iced orange juice with gin."

Fowler delivered the footstool and the pillow, which Pickering placed on the arm of the chair, and then he lowered his encased arm onto it.

"You look like hell. You're as gray . . . as a battleship."

"I was feeling fine until they opened the door of the airplane and that goddamned humidity swept in like a tidal wave," he said. "I honest to God think the humidity is worse in Washington than it is in Borneo. Or Hanoi."

"You really want a drink?"

"It will make the gray go away, trust me."

Fowler shook his head and then walked into the kitchen, returning with a bowl of ice and a silver pitcher of orange juice. He went to a bar against the wall, put ice and orange juice in a large glass, and picked up a quart bottle of Gilbey's gin.

"I don't feel comfortable giving you this gin."

"Please don't make me walk over there and do it myself."

Fowler shrugged and splashed gin into the glass. He stirred it with a glass stick and then walked to Pickering and handed it to him.

"I knew that sooner or later you would turn me into a criminal," Fowler said.

"Meaning what?" Pickering asked, and then took several deep swallows of the drink.

"Harboring and assisting a deserter is a felony."

"Don't be absurd. All I did was leave the hospital. My orders permit me to go when and where I please."

"I don't think that includes this. The hospital didn't plan to release you for at least another two weeks."

"Yeah, they told me."

"Does Patricia know about it?"

"We stopped for fuel at Saint Louis. I called her from there."

"And what did she say?"

"She was unkind," Pickering said.

"Are you going to tell me what this is all about?"

"Well, I was getting bored in the hospital."

"That's not it, Flem."

"I want out of the Navy. I told Frank that when I saw him in California. When nothing happened, I tried to call him. But I can't get the sonofabitch on the telephone."

Frank Knox was Secretary of the Navy.

"Did he tell you he'd let you do that?"

"He said we would talk about it when I got out of the hospital. I am now out of the hospital."

"I don't think it's going to happen. You were commissioned for the duration plus six months. What makes you think the Navy will let you out?"

"The Navy does what Frank tells it to. That's why they call him 'Mr. Secretary.' "

"What do you plan to do, enlist in The Marines?"

"Come on, Richmond."

"Well, what?"

"Go back to running the company. That way I could make a bona fide contribution to the war."

"Why do I think I'm not getting the truth?"

Pickering started to get out of the chair.

"What are you doing?"

"I need another of these," Pickering said, holding up his glass.

Fowler was surprised, and concerned, to see that he had emptied it.

"I don't think so," Fowler said.

"Richmond, for Christ's sake. I'm a big boy."

"Oh, God. Stay where you are. I'll get it for you."

Making the second drink just about exhausted the orange juice. Fowler was about to call down for a fresh pitcher when Pickering said, "I want to see Pick before he goes over there."

That, Fowler decided, *sounds like the truth.*

He carried the glass to Pickering and handed it to him.

"Well?"

"Thank you."

"That's not what I mean. You wouldn't let Knox send Pick

out to the hospital. For God's sake, he doesn't even know you're home. Or that you've been wounded."

"It would upset him."

"That's what sons are for, to be upset when their fathers are wounded."

"The odds are strongly against Pick coming through this war."

"Every father feels that way, Flem. The truth is that most people survive a war. I don't know what the percentage is, but I would bet that his odds are nine to one, maybe ninety-nine to one, to make it."

"Most fathers haven't been where I have been, and seen what I have seen. And most sons are not Marine fighter pilots. Jesus, do you think I *like* facing this?"

"I just think you're overstating the situation," Fowler said, a little lamely.

"Just before the *Gregory* was hit, her captain told me what a fine airplane the F4F is. It's probably the last thing he ever said; he was dead a minute later. He was trying to do what you're trying to do, make the Daddy feel a little better. It didn't work then and it's not working now. But I appreciate the thought."

"Goddamn it, Flem, I'm calling it like I see it."

"So am I, goddamn it, and I'm calling it how I see it, not how I would like it to be."

"Well, I think you're wrong."

Pickering shrugged and took another swallow of the orange juice and gin.

"Have I still got some uniforms here?"

"No, I gave them to the Salvation Army. Of course you do."

"How about having the house tailor sent up here? I need to have the sleeves cut out of some shirts."

"Sure."

"I mean now, Richmond."

"You're leaving? You just got here."

"I want to go see Frank. To do that, I'll need something more presentable than what I walked in here wearing."

"Seeing Frank can wait until tomorrow. For that matter, I'll call him and ask him to come here."

"Call downstairs for the tailor. Do it my way."

"Yes, Sir, Captain," Fowler said. He walked to a table and

started to pick up the telephone. Instead he picked up a copy of *The Washington Star* and carried it back to Pickering.

"Here's the paper," he said, unfolding it for him and laying it in his lap.

There were two major headlines:

BATTLE RAGES ON GUADALCANAL
WILLKIE HEADS OVERSEAS

A photo of a Consolidated B-24 four-engine bomber converted to a long-range transport was over the caption,

> Republican Party head Wendell Willkie will travel in this Army Air Corps transport on his around-the-world trip as personal representative of President Franklin D. Roosevelt. He will visit England, North Africa, China and the Soviet Union.

"There are not enough bombers to send to the Pacific," Pickering said bitterly. "But there are enough to give one to a goddamn politician to go all over and get in the goddamned way."

Fowler ignored him.

"Are you hungry, Fleming? Have you eaten?"

"No, and no. But I suppose I'd better have something. How about having them send up steak and eggs?"

Fowler nodded and picked up the telephone. He called the concierge and asked him to send up the tailor, and then called room service and ordered steak and eggs for Pickering. After a moment's indecision he added, "And send two pitchers of orange juice, too, please."

He walked back to Pickering, thinking he could turn the pages of the *Star* for him. Pickering had fallen asleep. His head sagged forward onto his chest. His face was still gray.

"Christ, Flem," Fowler said softly. He walked into the bedroom and came back with a light blanket, which he draped over him, and then he went to the air conditioner and directed its flow away from Pickering.

Then he walked to his own bedroom, in a far corner of the apartment, and closed the door. He took a small address book from the bedside table, found the number he was looking for, and picked up the telephone.

"Office of the Secretary of the Navy, Chief Daniels speaking."

"This is Senator Fowler. May I speak to Mr. Knox, please?"

"One moment, please, Senator. I'll see if he's available."

"Richmond?"

"He's here, Frank."

"Let me speak with him."

"He's asleep. More accurately, he passed out in an armchair in my sitting room."

"How is he?"

"He looks like hell."

"Shall I send a doctor over there?"

"I don't think that's quite necessary. And there's one in the hotel if it should be."

"Do you have any idea what this is all about? What's he up to?"

"Two things. Apparently, you told him you would discuss his getting out of the Navy when he got out of the hospital. He says he is now out of the hospital."

"I'd hoped he would forget that."

"He says he wants to go back to running Pacific & Far East Shipping so that he can make a bona fide contribution to the war effort."

"I wonder what he thinks he's been doing so far?" Secretary Knox asked, and then went on, without waiting for a reply. "There are a number of reasons that's not possible. I suppose I should have told him that when I saw him. But he was a sick man . . ."

"He's still a sick man. I told him, for what it's worth, that I didn't think you'd let him out."

"It's now out of my hands, if you take my meaning."

Fowler took his meaning. There was only one man in Washington who could override Frank Knox's decisions as Secretary of the Navy. He was Franklin Delano Roosevelt.

"You told him?"

"He's being Machiavellian again. He has his own plans for Pickering."

Fowler waited for Knox to elaborate. He did not.

"He is also very anxious to see his son," Fowler said. "His idea is to see you, get out of the Navy, and then go to Florida."

"I offered to have the boy flown to San Diego!"

"I think he wants to see him alone. He's managed to convince himself that the boy will not come through the war."

"He's not the only father who feels that way. You heard what our mutual friend's son has been up to?"

That was an unmistakable reference to James Roosevelt, a Marine Corps Captain. Captain Roosevelt had recently participated in the raid on Makin Island.

The Marine Corps had somewhat reluctantly formed the 1st and 2nd Raider Battalions. They were the President's answer to the British Commandos. The 1st was one of the units participating in the Guadalcanal operation. At about the same time, the son of the President of the United States was paddling ashore from a submarine with elements of the 2nd Raiders to attack Japanese forces on Makin Island.

"I also heard the Germans have taken Stalin's son prisoner. Do you think our mutual friend—make that 'acquaintance'—has considered the ramifications of that?"

"I have brought it to his attention," Knox said, then went on: "Technically, I suppose you know, Fleming Pickering is AWOL."

"I don't think you could make the charge stick. And he has a lot of friends in high places."

"And doesn't he know it?" Knox said, and then went on, again without waiting for a response: "I'm on my way to the White House. I'll get back to you, Richmond. Keep him there. I don't care how, keep him there."

"I'll do what I can," Fowler said, and hung up.

III

HEADQUARTERS, 2ND RAIDER BATTALION
CAMP CATLIN, TERRITORY OF HAWAII
31 AUGUST 1942

When Gunnery Sergeant Ernest W. Zimmerman, USMC, Company A, 2nd Raider Battalion, was summoned to battalion headquarters, he suspected it had something to do with Sergeant Thomas Michael McCoy, USMCR.

Zimmerman was stocky, round-faced and muscular. And he'd been in The Corps almost exactly seven years, having enlisted as soon as possible after his seventeenth birthday. He'd celebrated his twenty-fourth birthday a week before aboard the submarine USS *Nautilus* on the way home to Pearl Harbor from the raid on Makin Island. At the time he was nursing a minor, though painful, mortar shrapnel wound in his left buttock.

Sergeant McCoy—four inches taller and forty-two pounds heavier than Gunny Zimmerman—had celebrated his twenty-first birthday the previous January in San Diego, California. He was then in transit, en route to the Portsmouth U.S. Naval

Prison in the status of a general prisoner. There was little question at his court-martial at Pearl Harbor that he had in fact committed the offense of "assault upon the person of a commissioned officer in the execution of his office by striking him with his fists upon the face and other parts of the body."

He had also been fairly charged with doing more or less the same thing to a petty officer of the U.S. Navy in the execution of his office of Shore Patrolman, both offenses having taken place while PFC McCoy was absent without leave from his assignment to the 1st Defense Battalion, Marine Barracks, Pearl Harbor.

The Marine Corps frowns on such activity. Thus PFC McCoy was sentenced to be dishonorably discharged from the Naval Service and to be confined at hard labor for a period of five to ten years.

However, very likely because it was conducted during the immediate post–Pearl Harbor–bombing period when things were quite hectic, the court-martial failed to offer the accused certain procedural aspects of the fair trial required by Rules for the Governance of the Naval Service.

These errors of omission came to light while the Record of Trial was being reviewed by the legal advisers to the Commander in Chief, Pacific Fleet. It was therefore ordered that the findings and the sentences in the case be set aside.

Another trial was impossible, not only because of the possibility of double jeopardy, but also because the witnesses were by then scattered all over the Pacific.

PFC McCoy was released from the San Diego brig and assigned to the 2nd Raider Battalion, then forming at Camp Elliott just outside San Diego.

There PFC McCoy met Gunnery Sergeant Zimmerman. He almost immediately posed a number of disciplinary problems for Gunny Zimmerman. For instance, while he had apparently learned his lesson about striking those superior to him in the military hierarchy, on two occasions he severely beat up fellow PFCs with whom he had differences of opinion.

But what *really* annoyed Gunny Zimmerman about PFC McCoy's behavior was that it was seriously embarrassing to a Marine officer. Normally, this would not have bothered Gunny Zimmerman—indeed, under other circumstances, he might have found it amusing—but this particular officer was Second Lieutenant Kenneth R. McCoy, USMCR, PFC McCoy's three-year-older brother. Lieutenant McCoy and Gunny Zimmerman had been friends before the war, when Zimmerman had been a buck sergeant and McCoy a corporal with the 4th Marines in Shanghai.

There were very few people in The Corps who enjoyed Ernie Zimmerman's absolute trust and admiration, and Lieutenant "Killer" McCoy was at the head of that short list.

Since all other means of instilling in PFC McCoy both proper discipline and the correct attitude had apparently failed, Zimmerman decided that it behooved him to rectify the situation himself.

He accomplished this by going to the Camp Elliott slop chute, where he politely asked PFC McCoy if he could have a word with him. He led PFC McCoy to a remote area where they would not be seen. He then removed his jacket (and, symbolically, the chevrons of his rank) and suggested to PFC McCoy that if he thought he was so tough, why not have a go at him?

When PFC McCoy was released from the dispensary four days later—having suffered numerous cuts, bruises, abrasions and the loss of three teeth: after a bad slip in the shower—he'd undergone a near miraculous change of attitude.

The change was not temporary. Within three weeks, with a clear conscience, Gunny Zimmerman recommended PFC McCoy for squad leader. The job carried with it promotion to corporal.

And Corporal McCoy performed admirably on the Makin raid. Because of his size and strength, Zimmerman had given McCoy one of the Boys antitank rifles. The Boys, which looked like an oversize bolt-action rifle, fired a larger (.55 caliber) and even more powerful round than the Browning Heavy .50 caliber machine gun.

Although he could not prove it—there were other Boys rifles around—Zimmerman was convinced that McCoy was responsible for shooting up a Japanese four-engine Kawanishi seaplane so badly that it crashed while trying to take off from the Butaritari lagoon.

Nothing heroic. Just good Marine marksmanship, accomplished when the target was shooting back.

And when they were in the rubber boats trying to get off the beach back to the submarine—a disaster—McCoy really came through, really acted like a Marine. His had been one of the few boats to make it through the surf, almost certainly because of his enormous strength. Then, when they reached the sub, which was all that was expected of him, McCoy volunteered to go back to the beach for another load—despite his exhaustion.

Again nothing heroic, but good enough to prove that McCoy had the stuff Marine sergeants should be made of. After they were back at Camp Catlin, Colonel Carlson asked him if anyone should get a promotion as a reward for behavior during the raid. The first name Zimmerman gave him was Corporal McCoy's.

Word reached Gunny Zimmerman an hour before his summons to battalion headquarters that Sergeant McCoy had apparently strayed from the path of righteousness. He'd had a telephone call from another old China Marine, now working with the Shore Patrol Detachment in Honolulu. The Shore Patrol sergeant informed him that Sergeant McCoy apparently took offense at a remark made to him by a sergeant of the Army Air Corps. He expressed his displeasure by breaking the sergeant's nose. He then rejected the invitation of the Shore Patrol to accompany them peaceably.

Zimmerman's old China Marine pal told him, not without a certain admiration, that it took six Shore Patrolmen to subdue and transport Sergeant McCoy to the confinement facility. He was now sleeping it off there.

There seemed little doubt that before the day was over Sergeant McCoy would once again be Private McCoy. Unless, of course, Colonel Carlson wanted to make an example of him and bring him before a court-martial.

In Zimmerman's opinion, busting McCoy would be sufficient punishment. He would be humiliated and taught a lesson. And then in a couple of months they could start thinking about promoting him again.

The facts were that he had been a good corporal and would almost certainly have been a good sergeant.

Good sergeants are hard to find, Zimmerman thought. *Sending him to the brig for thirty days will teach him nothing he doesn't already know, and it might make his attitude worse.*

With a little bit of luck, maybe the sergeant major, or maybe even one of the officers, will ask me what I think should be done to McCoy. Or maybe even I can take a chance and just tell the sergeant major what I think.

Zimmerman went into battalion headquarters, walked up to

the sergeant major's desk, and stood waiting while the sergeant
major went very carefully over a paper that had been typed up
for the Colonel's signature. He finally finished and looked up
at Zimmerman.

He smiled.

"How are you, Ernie?" he asked. "How's the ass these
days?"

"I sit on the edge of chairs."

"Your Purple Heart came through," the sergeant major said.
"You are now a certified wounded hero."

*Is that what this is about? Maybe he hasn't heard about
McCoy yet.*

"Did you send for Zimmerman?" a voice called from the
office. On its door a sign hung, EVANS CARLSON, LTCOL, USMC,
COMMANDING.

"He just this second came in, Sir," the sergeant major called
back.

Colonel Carlson appeared at his office door. He was lean and
tanned, and he was wearing sun- and wash-faded utilities.

"Morning, Gunny," he greeted him. "How's the . . . damaged area?"

Zimmerman popped to attention.

"Morning, Sir," he said. "No problem, Sir."

"Get yourself a cup of coffee, if you'd like, and come on in.
Something's come up."

"Aye, aye, Sir," Zimmerman said.

Though he didn't really want it, he took a cup of coffee. The
reason was that he considered the offer—the suggestion—an
order, coming as it did from the Colonel. At the same time, the
friendliness of the Colonel's gesture made him a little uncomfortable.

Colonel Carlson often made him uncomfortable. Zimmerman was on the edge of being an Old Breed Marine. He hadn't
been to Nicaragua or any of the other banana republic wars,
but he *had* been in The Corps seven years, most of that time in
China, and in all that time he had never met another lieutenant
colonel—for that matter, a major or a captain—who treated
enlisted men the way Colonel Carlson did.

It was sort of hard to describe why. It wasn't as if Carlson
treated the enlisted men as equals, but neither did he treat them
the way they were treated elsewhere in The Corps, the way
Zimmerman had been treated for seven years.

Colonel Carlson talked to enlisted Marines—not just the senior staff noncoms, but the privates and the corporals, too—like they were *people,* not *enlisted men.* Like he was *really* interested in what they had to say.

The motto of the Raiders was "Gung Ho!" Most people in the Raiders, even the ones who had been in China and had picked up a little Chinese, thought that meant "Everybody Pull Together." Zimmerman knew better. He spoke pretty good Chinese, three kinds of it. What *Gung Ho* really meant was more like "Strive for Harmony."

When they were training for the Makin Raid back at Camp Elliott, outside 'Diego, Zimmerman talked about that with McCoy—*Lieutenant* McCoy, the Killer, not Sergeant Shit for Brains McCoy, now behind bars in Honolulu.

The Killer spoke even better Chinese than Zimmerman did, plus Japanese and German and Polish and Russian. So he knew what *Gung Ho* really meant, but he told Zimmerman to keep it to himself.

"What I think is really going on, Ernie," the Killer told him, "is that the Colonel is terrifically impressed with the way the Chinese do things. The Chinese communists, I mean."

"You're not telling me he's a communist?"

It would not have surprised Zimmerman at all if the brass had sent Killer McCoy to the 2nd Raider Battalion to see if he thought Colonel Carlson was a communist.

"No. I don't think so. But there are people in The Corps who do."

"Then how come they gave him the Raider Battalion if they think he's a communist?"

"There are also a lot of people who don't think he's a communist, like Captain Roosevelt's father, for example."

Captain Roosevelt was Executive Officer of the 2nd Raider Battalion. His father was Commander in Chief of the Armed Forces of the United States of America. As a Captain, Colonel Carlson had commanded the detachment of Marines assigned to protect the President at White Sulphur Springs, where the President often went to swim with other people crippled by infantile paralysis.

"We're sort of special Marines, Ernie, *Raiders,*" the Killer said. "The Colonel thinks that the kind of discipline the Chinese communists have would work better for us than the regular kind."

"We're *Marines,* not fucking Chinese communists," Zimmerman protested. "Does he really want to do away with ranks and have just leaders and fighters and technicians, and no saluting, and no officers' mess, and the other bullshit that I been hearing?"

"I think he's been talked out of that," McCoy said. "But I know he wants to make sure the enlisted men use their initiative. There's nothing wrong with that, is there?"

"What does that mean, 'use their initiative'?"

"You tell some PFC to fill sandbags and make a wall of them, he does it because you're a sergeant and he's a PFC and PFCs do what sergeants tell them to do. The Colonel figures he'll get a better wall if the sergeant tells the PFC they need a sandbag wall because that will keep people from getting their balls blown off . . . and then the sergeant helps the PFC make it. Understand?"

"Sounds like bullshit to me."

"That's what I thought when I first heard about it," the Killer said. "But now I suppose I've been converted. Anyway, Ernie, it doesn't make any difference what you think."

"It don't?"

"You're a Marine, a gunny. Marine gunnies do what they're told, right?"

"Fuck you, Ken," Zimmerman said, chuckling.

"That's 'fuck you, Lieutenant, Sir,' Sergeant," the Killer replied.

The funny thing, Zimmerman realized, was that over the months he too had become converted to the Colonel's way of doing things. It seemed to work. Everybody in the Raiders did "pull together" or "strive for harmony," depending on how well you spoke Chinese and translated *"Gung Ho!"*

That was very much on his mind on Makin, when things were going badly and he wouldn't have given a wooden nickel for their chances of getting off the fucking beach alive.

He came across Captain Roosevelt then, and the first thing he thought was that only in the United States of America would the son of the head man have his ass in the line of fire. Then he changed that to "only in The Marine Corps" and finally to "only in the Raiders."

Zimmerman realized that he was now a genuine fucking true believer Gung Ho Marine Raider . . . he was also a guy who had spent five and a half of his seven years in The Corps in the

Fourth Marines in Shanghai, where officers were officers, and enlisted men were enlisted men.

He was not at all comfortable when he stood in Colonel Carlson's office door and the Colonel waved him into a chair without even giving him a chance to report to the commanding officer in the prescribed manner.

"I didn't know you'd done any time with Marine Aviation, Zimmerman," the Colonel said.

"I never did," Zimmerman said, so surprised that he added "Sir" only after a perceptible pause.

"Curious," Colonel Carlson said and handed him a teletype message.

```
PRIORITY
CONFIDENTIAL
HQ FLEET MARINE FORCE PACIFIC
1405 30 AUG 1942

To:     COMMANDING OFFICER
        2ND USMC RAIDER BATTALION

Info:   COMMANDING OFFICER
        21ST MARINE AIR GROUP

1. ON RECEIPT THIS MESSAGE FOLLOWING NAMED EN-
LISTED MEN ARE DETACHED COMPANY ''A'' 2ND
RAIDER BN AND ASSIGNED HQ 21ST MARINE AIR
GROUP.

ZIMMERMAN, ERNEST W 286754 GYSGT
MCCOY, THOMAS M 355331 SGT

2. CO 2ND RAIDER BN WILL ARRANGE TRANSPORT BY
MOST EXPEDITIOUS MEANS, INCLUDING AIR, FROM
PRESENT STATION TO RECEIVING UNIT. PRIORITY
AAA IS AUTHORIZED.

BY DIRECTION: C.W.STANWYCK LTCOL USMC
```

"The Twenty-first MAG is on Guadalcanal," Colonel Carlson said.

"Yes, Sir, I know."

"Then this doesn't surprise you, Gunny? You knew about it?"

"No, Sir. I mean, no, Sir, I didn't know anything about this."

"I'm curious, Gunny," Carlson said, conversationally. "If this question in any way is awkward for you to answer, then don't answer it. But would you be surprised to learn that Lieutenant McCoy had a hand in this somewhere?"

The question obviously surprised Zimmerman. He met Carlson's eyes.

"Sir, nothing the Kill— Lieutenant McCoy does surprises me anymore. But I don't think he's behind this. I think I know where it come from."

"You did know, didn't you, Gunny, what Lieutenant McCoy was doing, *really* doing, when he was assigned here?"

Zimmerman's face flushed.

"I had a pretty good idea, Sir," he said uncomfortably.

"Lieutenant McCoy is a fine officer," Carlson said, "defined first as one who carries out whatever orders he is given to the best of his ability, and second as a gentleman who is made uncomfortable by deception. You know what I'm talking about, Gunny?"

"Yes, Sir. I think so, Sir."

"I saw Lieutenant McCoy in the hospital just before they flew him home. He told me then what he'd really been doing with the Raiders. I then told him I had been aware of his situation almost from the day he joined the Raiders."

Zimmerman looked even more uncomfortable.

"I told him I bore him no hard feelings. Quite the contrary. That I admired him for carrying out a difficult order to the best of his ability. If certain senior officers of The Corps felt it necessary to send in an officer to determine whether or not the commanding officer of the 2nd Raider Battalion was a communist, then it was clearly the duty of that officer to comply with his orders."

"The Killer never thought for a minute you was a communist, Sir," Zimmerman blurted.

Carlson smiled.

"So I understand," he said. "And I hope you have come to the same conclusion, Gunny."

"Jesus, Colonel!"

"I also told Lieutenant McCoy that whatever his primary

mission was, he had carried out his duties with the Raiders in a more than exemplary manner, and that I considered it a privilege to have had him under my command."

"Yes, Sir."

"The same applies to you, Gunny. I wanted to tell you that before you ship out."

"Colonel," Zimmerman said, the floodgates open now, "the Killer told me he arranged for me to be assigned to the Raiders in case he needed me for something he was doing. He didn't tell me what he was doing, and the only thing I ever did was take some telephone messages for him. I didn't even know what the fuck they meant."

"Hence my curiosity about your transfer," Colonel Carlson said. "You said, didn't you, a moment ago, that you thought you knew what was behind the transfer?"

"Yes, Sir. I mean, I don't know for sure, but what I think is . . . when they were forming VMF-229 at Ewa, they was having trouble with their aircraft-version Browning .50s. A tech sergeant named Oblensky, an old China Marine, was. He come to me and McCoy—*Sergeant* McCoy—and me went over there and took care of it for him."

"And you think Sergeant—Oblensky, you said?"

"Yes, Sir. Big Steve Oblensky."

"—was behind this transfer?"

"Yes, Sir. He goes way back. He's too old now, but he used to be a Flying Sergeant. He was in Nicaragua, places like that, flying with General McInerney. He knows a lot of people in The Corps, Sir."

Brigadier General D. G. McInerney was not the most senior Marine Aviator, but he was arguably the most influential.

"And you think that based on Sergeant Oblensky's recommendation, General McInerney, or someone at that level, convinced Fleet Marine Force Pacific that MAG-21 needs you and Sergeant McCoy more than the 2nd Raider Battalion does?"

"Yes, Sir. That's the way I see it."

"I think you're probably right, Gunny," Colonel Carlson said, standing up and offering his hand to Zimmerman. "We'll miss the two of you around here, but I'm sure you'll do a good job for MAG-21."

Zimmerman got quickly to his feet and took Carlson's hand.

"I don't suppose I got anything to say about this transfer, do I, Sir?"

"Yes, of course you do. You've been given an order, and when a good gunny gets an order, he says, 'Aye, aye, Sir.'"

"Aye, aye, Sir."

"Good luck, Gunny. And pass that on to Sergeant McCoy, please."

"Aye, aye, Sir."

Zimmerman did an about-face and marched to the office door. As he passed through it, he suddenly remembered that Sergeant McCoy was at the moment behind bars in Honolulu charged with drunkenness, resisting arrest, and Christ only knows what else.

[Two]
ARMED FORCES MILITARY POLICE DETENTION FACILITY
HONOLULU, OAHU, TERRITORY OF HAWAII
31 AUGUST 1942

Sergeant Thomas M. McCoy, USMCR, had not been provided with a pillow or any other bedclothes for his bunk, a sheet of steel welded firmly to the wall of his cell.

He had remedied the situation by making a pillow of his shoes; he'd wrapped them in his trousers. And his uniform jacket was now more or less a blanket.

He was very hung over, and in addition he suffered from a number of bruises and contusions. The combined force of Navy and Marine Corps Shore Patrolmen, augmented by two Army Military Policemen, had been more than a little annoyed with Sergeant McCoy at the time of his arrest.

They had used, with a certain enthusiasm, somewhat more than the absolute minimum force required to restrain an arrestee. Sergeant McCoy's back, hips, buttocks, thighs, and calves would carry for at least two weeks long thin black bruises from nightsticks, and both eyes would suggest they had encountered something hard, such as a fist or elbow.

When the door of his cell, a barred section on wheels, opened with an unpleasant clanking noise, Sergeant McCoy had been awake long enough to reconstruct as much as he could of the previous evening's events and to consider how they were most likely going to affect his immediate future in The Marine Corps.

Even the most optimistic assessment was not pleasant: He

would certainly get busted. Depending on how much damage he'd done to the Shore Patrol—the bloody gashes on the fingers of his right hand suggested he'd punched at least one of the bastards in the teeth—there was a good chance he would find himself standing in front of a court-martial, and would probably catch at least thirty days in the brig, maybe more.

On the premise that the damage was already done and that nothing else could happen to him, he ignored whoever it was who had stepped into his cell. When whoever it was pushed on his shoulder to wake him, he ignored that, too.

"Wake up, McCoy," the familiar voice of Gunnery Sergeant Zimmerman said as his shoulder was shaken a little harder.

He doesn't sound all that pissed, McCoy decided. And then there was another glimmer of hope: *Zimmerman ain't all that bad compared to most gunnies. Maybe I can talk myself out of this.*

He straightened his legs. That hurt.

Those bastards really did a job on me with their fucking nightsticks.

He pushed himself into a sitting position and looked at Zimmerman, a slight smile on his face.

He saw that Zimmerman had a seabag with him and that Zimmerman was in greens, not utilities.

That's probably my bag. He looked and saw his name stenciled on the side.

"You look like shit," Zimmerman said.

"You ought to see the other guy, Gunny."

"Anything broke?"

"Nah," McCoy said.

"I got your gear," Zimmerman said, kicking the seabag. "Shave and get into clean greens. I'll be back in five minutes. It stinks in here."

"How the hell am I supposed to shave? There's no water or nothing in here."

"Big, tough guy like you don't need any water or shaving cream."

Zimmerman turned around and struck one of the vertical cell bars with the heel of his balled fist. It clanked open. The moment Zimmerman was outside the cell, it clanked shut again.

Exactly five minutes later he was back. McCoy had changed into a clean set of greens.

"Where we going, Gunny?"

"I told you to shave."

"And I told you there's no water, no mirror, no nothing, in here. How the fuck . . . ?"

Zimmerman hit him twice, first in the abdomen with his fist, and then when he doubled over, in the back of his neck with the heel of his hand.

McCoy fell on the floor of the cell, banging his shoulder painfully on the steel bunk and nearly losing consciousness. He was conscious enough, though, to hear what Zimmerman said, almost conversationally:

"I thought I already taught you that when I tell you to do something it ain't a suggestion."

McCoy heard the sound of Zimmerman's fist striking the cell bar again, then he saw the cell door sliding open, and then closing again.

After a moment McCoy was able to get into a sitting position, resting his back against the cell wall. He took a couple of deep breaths, each of which hurt, then he pulled his seabag to him, unfastened the snap from the loop, and dug inside for his razor.

[Three]
UNITED STATES NAVAL AIR STATION
LAKEHURST, NEW JERSEY
1705 HOURS 31 AUGUST 1942

Second Lieutenant Malcolm S. Pickering, USMCR, glanced over at his traveling companion, Second Lieutenant Richard J. Stecker, USMC, saw that he was asleep, and jabbed him in the ribs with his elbow.

Pickering, a tall, rangy twenty-two-year-old with an easygoing look, was considered extraordinarily handsome by a number of females even before he had put on the dashing uniform of a Marine officer. Stecker, also twenty-two, was stocky, muscular, and looked—on the whole—more dependable. They were sitting in adjacent seats toward the rear of a U.S. Navy R4D aircraft. To judge from the triangular logotype woven into the upholstery of its seats, the R4D had originally been the property of Delta Air Lines.

"Hey! Wake up! I have good news for you!"

"What the hell?" Stecker replied. He had not been napping. He had been sound asleep.

" 'You too can learn to fly,' " Pickering read solemnly. " 'For your country, for your future.' "

"What the hell are you reading?" Stecker demanded.

" 'Whether you're sixteen or sixty,' " Pickering continued, " 'if you are in normal health and possess normal judgment, you can learn to fly with as little as eight hours of dual instruction.' "

Stecker snatched the *Life* magazine from Pickering's hand.

"Jesus, you woke me up for that?" he said in exasperation, throwing the magazine back in his lap.

"We have begun our descent," Pickering said. "If you had read and heeded this splendid public service advertisement by the Piper people, you would know that."

"Where the hell are we?" Stecker said, looking out the window.

"I devoutly hope we are over New Jersey," Pickering said. He picked up the magazine, found his place, and continued reading aloud: " 'In the future a huge aviation industry will offer great opportunities to pilots of all ages. Visit your Piper Cub Dealer. He will be glad to give you a flight demonstration and tell you how you can become a pilot now.' "

"Will you shut the hell up?"

"It says right here, 'flying saves you time, gas, and tires.' How about that?"

"You're making that up."

"I am not, see for yourself," Pickering said righteously, holding up the magazine.

Stecker did not look. He was staring out the window.

"I see water down there," he announced.

"And clever fellow that you are, I'll bet you've figured out that it's the Atlantic Ocean."

"You're in a disgustingly cheerful mood," Stecker said.

"I have visions of finally getting off this sonofabitch, and that has cheered me beyond measure. My ass has been asleep for the last forty-five minutes."

"And your brain all day," Stecker said triumphantly, and then added, "There it is."

Pickering leaned across him and looked out the window. The enormous dirigible hangar at Lakehurst Naval Air Station rose surrealistically from the sandy pine barren, dwarfing the eight or ten Navy blimps near it, and making the aircraft—including other R4Ds—parked on the concrete ramp seem toylike.

The Naval Aviators here are at war, Stecker thought. *Every day they fly Navy blimps and long-range patrol bombers over the Atlantic in a futile search, most of the time, for German submarines that are doing their best to interrupt shipping between the United States and England.*

"How'd you like to fly one of those?" Stecker asked. "A blimp?"

"Not at all, thank you. I have had my fucking fill of the miracle of flight for one day."

It was about 1300 miles in straight lines from Pensacola, Florida, to Lakehurst, N.J.

Using 200 knots as a reasonable figure for the hourly speed of the Gooneybird, that translated to six and a half hours. It had taken considerably longer than that. There had been intermediate stops at the Jacksonville, Florida, Naval Air Station; at Hurtt Field, on Parris Island, S.C.; at The Marine Corps Air Station, Cherry Point, N.C.; the Norfolk NAS, Va.; and Anacostia NAS, Md.

They had taken off from Pensacola at first light, just after four A.M. It was now nearly four P.M., or actually five, since they had changed time zones.

"I mean, really," Stecker said.

"Not me. I'm a *fighter* pilot," Pickering said grandly.

"Oh shit," Stecker groaned.

The Gooneybird flew down the length of the dirigible hangar, then turned onto his final approach. There was the groan of hydraulics as the Gooneybird pilot lowered the flaps and landing gear.

"You know, it actually rains inside there," Stecker said.

"So you have told me. Which does not necessarily make it so."

"It really does, jackass."

"Another gem from R. Stecker's fund of useless knowledge," Pickering said, mimicking the dulcet voice of a radio announcer, "brought to you by the friendly folks at Piper aircraft, where you too can learn to fly."

With a chirp, the Gooneybird's wheels made contact with the ground.

"The Lord be praised, we have cheated death again," Pickering said.

"Jesus Christ, Pick, shut up, will you?" Stecker said, but he was unable to keep a smile off his lips.

They taxied to the transient ramp at one end of the dirigible hangar. A two-story concrete block there was dwarfed by the building behind it.

The plane stopped. The door to the cockpit opened, and a sailor, the crew chief, went down the aisle and opened the door. He was wearing work denims and a blue, round sailor's cap. A blast of hot air rushed into the cabin.

He unstrapped a small aluminum ladder from the cabin wall and dropped it in place.

Pickering unfastened his seat belt, stood up, and moved into the aisle. When the other passengers started following the crew chief off the airplane, he started down the aisle.

"Put your cover on," Stecker said. "You remember what happened the last time."

"Indeed I do," Pickering said. It wasn't really the last time, but the time before the last time. He had exited the aircraft with his tie pulled down, his collar unbuttoned, and his uniform cap (in Marine parlance, his "cover") jammed in his hip pocket.

He had almost immediately encountered a Marine captain, wearing the wings of a parachutist—Lakehurst also housed The Marine Corps' parachutists' school—who had politely asked if he could have a word with him, led him behind the Operations Building, and then delivered a brief inspirational lecture on the obligation of Marine officers, even fucking flyboys, to look like Marine officers, not like something a respectable cat would be ashamed to drag home.

Dick Stecker, who'd listened at the corner of the building, judged it to be a really first-class chewing-out. He'd also known it was a waste of the Captain's time and effort. It would inspire Pickering to go and sin no more for maybe a day. He had been right.

If I hadn't said something, he would have walked off the airplane again with his cover in his pocket and his tie pulled down.

When Stecker got off the plane, he found Pickering looking up like a tourist at the curved roof of the dirigible hangar. From that angle it seemed to soar into infinity.

He jabbed him in the ribs.

"I'll go check on ground transportation. You get the bags."

Pickering nodded.

"Big sonofabitch, ain't it?"

Stecker nodded.

"It really does rain in there?"

"Yes, it does," Stecker said, and then walked toward the Operations Building.

There were a corporal and a staff sergeant behind the counter with the sign TRANSIENT SERVICE hanging above it.

Wordlessly, Stecker handed him their orders.

"Lieutenant," the corporal said, "you just missed the seventeen-hundred bus. The next one's at nineteen-thirty."

"That won't cut it," Stecker said. "Sorry."

"Excuse me, Sir," the corporal said politely, turned his back, and gestured with his thumb to the sergeant that the Second Lieutenant was posing a problem.

The sergeant walked to the counter.

"Can I help you, Lieutenant?"

"I'm on my way to the Grumman plant at Bethpage, L.I. I need transportation."

"Yes, Sir. The way you do that is catch the bus to Penn Station in New York City. And a train from there. You just missed the seventeen-hundred bus, and the next one is at nineteen-thirty."

"If I wait for the nineteen-thirty bus I won't get out there until midnight."

"Sir, you just missed the bus."

"We're scheduled for an oh-six-hundred takeoff, Sergeant. I am not about to get into an airplane and fly to Florida on five hours' sleep. If you can't get us a ride, please get the officer of the day on the telephone," Stecker said.

The sergeant looked carefully at the Lieutenant's orders and then at the Lieutenant and decided that what he should do was arrange for a station wagon. This was not the kind of second lieutenant, in other words, who could be told to sit down and wait for the next bus.

"I'll call the motor pool, Sir. It'll take a couple of minutes."

"Thank you, Sergeant."

"Yes, Sir."

Dick Stecker was less awed with the sergeant—for that matter, with The Marine Corps—than most second lieutenants were. For one thing he was a regular; the service was his way of life, not an unwelcome interruption before he could get on with being a lawyer, a movie star, or a golf professional.

More important, he was a second-generation Marine. He

had grown up on Marine installations around the country and in China. While he and Pick Pickering both believed that there were indeed three ways to do things—the right way, the wrong way, and The Marine Corps Way—Pickering viewed The Marine Corps Way as just one more fucking infringement on his personal liberty, and Dick Stecker regarded The Marine Corps Way as an opportunity.

Their current situation was a case in point. The Marine Corps seemed for the moment to have misplaced them—as opposed to having actually *lost* them. So far as they knew, immediately on certification as qualified in a particular aircraft, every other Marine Corps Second Lieutenant Naval Aviator had been transferred to an operational squadron for duty.

Most F4F Grumman Wildcat pilots were assigned to the Pacific, either to a specific squadron or to one of the Marine Air Groups. The Marine Corps had lost a lot of pilots in the battles of the Coral Sea and Midway and in connection with the invasion of Guadalcanal.

It followed that Lieutenants Stecker and Pickering, duly certified as qualified to fly Wildcats, should have been on their way to the Pacific some time ago. Or failing that, they should have been assigned to one of the fighter squadrons forming in the United States for later service in that theater.

But that hadn't happened. They were "temporarily" assigned to the Naval Air Station, Pensacola, Florida (where they'd learned how to fly less than a year before), picking up brand-new Wildcats at the Grumman factory and ferrying them all over the country.

This bothered "Pick" Pickering no end. He wanted to be where the fighting was, not cooling his ass in the United States. He also wallowed in fear that they would be permanently assigned to Pensacola as instructor pilots, spending the war in the backseat of a Yellow Peril teaching people how to fly, while the rest of their peers were off covering themselves with glory in the Pacific.

Dick Stecker had a pretty good idea about why they were doing what they were doing. And while Pickering had listened politely to Stecker's explanation, he didn't accept a word of it. Possibly, in Stecker's view, because it was too simple:

Dick Stecker received his commission from the United States Military Academy at West Point. Since very few Marine officers took their commissions from the Army trade school, this screwed up The Marine Corps' Pilot Procurement Program scheduling insofar as Lieutenant Stecker was concerned.

Pickering received his commission from the officer candidate school at Quantico. The idea of becoming a Marine Aviator never entered his mind until he was given a chance to volunteer for pilot training as an alternative to what The Corps had in mind for him: mess officer.

Before coming into The Corps, Pickering had worked in hotels; he knew how to run bars and kitchens. The Corps needed people with experience in those areas, and The Corps was notoriously nonsensitive to the career desires of newly commissioned second lieutenants, even those whose announced intention was to start fighting the Japs as soon as possible.

But Pickering had a friend in high places. Long before he himself had been commissioned and learned how to fly, Brigadier General D. G. McInerney had been a sergeant at Belleau Wood in 1917. One of his corporals then had been Pick Pickering's father, currently a reserve Navy officer on duty somewhere in the Pacific. The elder Pickering and McInerney had maintained their friendship over the years.

While acknowledging that The Corps did need mess officers, General McInerney decided it needed pilots more, and would just have to make a mess officer out of some other lieutenant who did not possess young Pickering's splendid physical attributes, high intelligence, and tested genetic heritage.

Lieutenants Stecker and Pickering both arrived at Pensacola for training at the same time. Lieutenant Stecker did not think this was pure coincidence. Dick Stecker's father, Jack (NMI) Stecker, now an officer with the First Marine Division on Guadalcanal, had also been at Belleau Wood with General McInerney.

After Pickering and Stecker arrived at Pensacola, their basic flight training was not conducted in accord with the rigidly structured and scheduled system that other young pilots were subjected to. For one thing they were not assigned to a large class. And while they completed the exact syllabus of training everyone else was given, they did not do it as part of any particular training squadron. They took some ground school courses with one training squadron, other ground school courses with other training squadrons. And when it came time for them to actually climb into an airplane, *their* instructor pilots were not just instructor pilots but *senior* instructor pilots. Even though the normal duties of senior instructor pilots were supervision of other instructor pilots and giving check rides, they could and did fit two orphans into their available time, for The Good of The Corps. It was a secret only to Lieutenants Stecker and Pickering that General McInerney inquired every week or so into their progress.

When they completed the course, they did not march in dress whites in a graduation parade to the stirring strains of "Anchors Aweigh" and the Marine Hymn played by a Navy band. Their wings of gold were pinned on one Tuesday afternoon in the office of a Navy captain who seemed baffled by what was going on.

After that they were recommended for fighter training . . . probably, in Dick Stecker's judgment, because none of their IPs felt comfortable announcing that one of *his* students didn't have that extra something special required of fighter pilots—especially with General McInerney in the audience.

And when they went down the Florida peninsula for Wildcat training, they again received the prescribed training, but they got it from pilots who were not only qualified IPs, but were also functioning in operational squadrons. So they were taught *the way it really is,* rather than the way the Navy brass thought it should be.

In fact, because of the quality of their instruction, they were just a shade better pilots than other young aviators of equivalent experience. Pickering considered that he was fully qualified to battle the Dirty Jap right now; Stecker was perfectly happy with the opportunity to get more hours in the Wildcat.

Stecker walked back out to the transient parking ramp. Pickering was nowhere in sight. After a moment, though, Stecker saw him standing near the open door to the dirigible hangar, talking to a Naval officer.

He just doesn't want to believe it really does rain inside there. Well, screw you, pal, you are about to learn that it does.

[Four]
BUKA, SOLOMON ISLANDS
31 AUGUST 1942

Sergeant Steven M. Koffler was awakened in his quarters by Miss Patience Witherspoon. She squatted by his bed and squeezed his shoulder. Miss Witherspoon herself had constructed the bed, of woven grass ropes suspended between poles.

He opened his eyes and looked at her.

The fucking trouble with her, he thought, for perhaps the one-hundredth time, *is her fucking eyes. They're clear and gray. It's as if a real girl is looking out at me from behind that scarred face.*

"There are engine noises, Steven," she said in her soft, precise voice.

"Right," he said.

He swung his feet out of bed and jammed them into his boondockers. They were green with mold, and he had no socks. The three pairs he'd had when they jumped in had lasted just over a month.

He picked up his Thompson submachine gun and checked automatically. As usual the chamber was clear, with a cartridge in the magazine ready to be chambered. He slung the strap over his shoulder before he noticed Patience holding something out to him.

It was his other utility jacket, in no better shape than the one he'd been sleeping in, but Patience had obviously washed it for him.

"I'll save it for later," he said. "Thank you."

"Don't be silly," Patience said, modestly averting her eyes.

He took Mr. Reeves' German binoculars from the stub of a limb on one of the poles that held the hut together and hung them around his neck.

Then he walked to the tree house—there was no real reason for haste. Using the knotted rope, he walked up the tree side to the observation platform.

"What have we got, Ian?" he asked.

"Rather a lot, I would say," Ian replied. "They should be in sight any moment now."

Steve could hear the muted rumble of engines and decided Ian was right. There were many of them.

And a moment later, as he scanned the skies, he saw the first of them. He handed the binoculars to Ian Bruce.

"Never let these out of your hands, Koffler," Mr. Reeves had told him just before he and Howard went off into the boondocks. *"Ian is a rather good chap, but a curious one. Give him half a chance and he'll try to take them apart to see what magic they contain to make things bigger."*

When Ian handed them back a moment later, Steve noticed that the last tiny scrap of leather had finally fallen off the side of the binoculars. A thumbnail-sized area that had been glue still held on. But tomorrow that too would disappear and the binoculars would be green all over.

"Twenty to thirty, I would say," Ian said. "And I thought I could make out another formation a bit higher."

Steve put the binoculars to his eyes again. The spots in the sky were now large enough to be counted. Six 5-plane V's. Thirty. Almost certainly Bettys.

The Betty (designated the Mitsubishi G4M1 Type 1 aircraft by the Japanese) was the most common Japanese bomber. Koffler knew a good deal about the Betty: He could recite from memory, for example, that it was a twin-engine, land-based bomber aircraft with a normal complement of seven. It had an empty weight of 9.5 tons and was capable of carrying 2200 pounds of bombs, or two 1700-pound torpedoes, over a nominal range of 2250 miles, at a cruising speed of 195 miles per hour. Its maximum speed was 250 miles per hour at 14,000 feet. It was armed with four 7.7mm machine guns, one in the nose, one on top, and two in beam positions, plus a 20mm cannon in the tail.

He knew this much about the Betty because there was very little to do on Buka. You could not, for example, run down to the corner drugstore for an ice-cream soda, or—more in keeping with his exalted status as a Marine sergeant—down to the slop chute for a thirty-five-cent two-quart pitcher of beer.

So, to pass the time, you exchanged information with your companions.

Thus Steve learned from Mr. Reeves that when Australians went rooting, they weren't jumping up and down cheering their football team. "Rooting" was Australian for fucking. He also learned that the American equivalent to the Australian term "sodding" was somewhere between "fucking" and "up your ass."

Mr. Reeves also explained to Lieutenant Howard and Sergeant Koffler the Australian system of government and its relationship to the British Crown. Steve never knew that Australia was started as a prison colony. He had too much respect for Mr. Reeves to ask him if his ancestors were guards or prisoners.

Lieutenant Howard, in turn, explained the American system of government to Mr. Reeves, who actually seemed interested.

Lieutenant Howard also shared his detailed knowledge of Japanese aircraft with Mr. Reeves and Sergeant Koffler. And Sergeant Koffler tried to explain the theory of radio wave transmission, but with virtually no success.

He gave the binoculars back to Ian, who kept them to his eyes until he was able to announce, with certainty, "Bettys. I make them thirty-five."

"I counted thirty," Steve said, putting the glasses to his eyes again. Ian was right. There were thirty-five.

And the aircraft flying above them were Zeroes.

The Zero was the standard Japanese fighter aircraft, also manufactured by Mitsubishi, and officially designated the A6M. It was powered by a Nakijima 14-cylinder 925-horsepower engine, and was armed with two 20mm Oerlikon machine cannon and two machine guns, firing the British .303 rifle cartridge.

According to Lieutenant Howard it was a better airplane than anything the Americans or the English had. It was more maneuverable, and the 20mm cannons were not only more powerful but had greater range than the .50 caliber Browning machine guns on Navy and Marine aircraft.

"I count forty Zeroes," Steve said. "I'll get started. If anything else shows up, let me know."

"Right!" Ian said crisply.

Steve went down the knotted rope and walked to where the radio was kept, broken down. That way they could run with it if that became necessary.

He spotted Edward James and whistled at him. When he had his attention, he made a cranking motion with his hands.

Edward James popped to attention and saluted crisply.

"Sir!" he barked.

When he popped to attention, one of the two MACHETES, SUBSTITUTE STANDARD, he had hanging from his belt swung violently.

"Another inch and you'd have cut your balls off," Steve said. It took Edward James a moment to make the translation into what he thought of as proper English.

"Quite, Sir," he said.

He then disappeared into the bush. When he returned a moment later he was carefully carrying a device that looked something like a bicycle. It was in fact the generator that powered Steve's radios. They originally jumped in with two. But one of these was now worn out beyond repair—both physically (the bearings were shot) and electrically (the coils were shorted). How long the other would last, nobody knew. Steve would not have been surprised if it failed to work now.

By the time Edward James returned with the generator, Steve had the radio connected to the antennae. Edward James proudly connected the generator leads to the radio and then went to string the antennae between trees.

Steve took out the code book—also on its last legs and just barely legible—and wrote out his message. He then encoded it.

By the time he was finished, Edward James was back. Steve made the cranking motion again.

"Right, Sir!" Edward James said. He got aboard the generator and started slowly and powerfully pushing its pedals. In a moment the dials on the radio lit up. Steve put earphones on his head, adjusted the position of the telegraph key, and threw the switch on the Hallicrafters to TRANSMIT. Then he put his hand on the key.

The dots and dashes went out, repeated three times, spelling simply:

FRD6. FRD6. FRD6.
Detachment A of Special Marine Corps Detachment 14 is attempting to establish contact with any station on this communications network.

This time, for a change, there was an immediate reply.

FRD6. KCY. FRD6. KCY. FRD6. KCY.
Hello, Detachment A, this is the United States Pacific Fleet Radio Station at Pearl Harbor, Territory of Hawaii, responding to your call.
KCY. FRD6. SB CODE.

*CINCPAC Radio Pearl Harbor, stand by to copy
encrypted message.*

When he was at Pearl Harbor, Lieutenant Howard once told
him, he'd pulled guard duty a couple of times—he was sergeant
of the guard—and got a look at CINCPAC Radio. It was in an
air-conditioned building, so the equipment wouldn't get too
hot. It made it nice for the operators too.

*FRD6.KCY.GA.
CINCPAC Radio to Detachment A: Go ahead.*

The information that thirty-five Bettys, escorted by forty
Zeroes, out of Rabaul and on a course that would take them
to Guadalcanal, had just passed overhead at approximately
15,000 feet was encoded on a sheet of damp paper. Sergeant
Koffler put the sheet under his left hand and pointed his index
finger at the first block of five characters.

As his right hand worked the telegrapher's key, his index
finger swept across the coded message. It is more difficult to
transmit code than plain English, for the simple reason that
code doesn't make any sense.

It took him just over a minute, not quite long enough for the
Japanese to locate the transmitter by triangulation, before he
sent, in the clear, END.

*FRD6.KCY.AKN.CLR.
Detachment A, this is Pearl Harbor. Your transmission is acknowledged. Pearl Harbor Clear.*

Steve made a cutting motion across his throat, and Edward
James stopped pumping the generator pedals.

Steve watched as Edward James proudly disconnected the
generator leads from the Hallicrafters and then smiled at him.

As Edward James left the hut, Miss Patience Witherspoon
came in. She carried a plate on which was a piece of cold roast
pork (though it took quite a stretch of his imagination to
identify it as such) and a baked vegetable, something like a
stringy sweet potato, also cold. It tasted like stringy soap.

"Perhaps," Patience said gently, once she saw the look on his
face, "they will be able to get something you will like from the
Japanese."

And perhaps they've already had their heads cut off by the fucking Japs . . . after telling them where to find us, when the Japs sliced their balls off.

Ah, shit, she means well. I don't want to hurt her feelings.

"This is fine, Patience," he said. "And I'm starved."

She lowered her head modestly and crossed her hands over her breasts. The motion served to bring her breasts to Koffler's attention.

If they weren't all scarred up, they wouldn't look so bad; nothing wrong with their shape, or the nipples.

And then he had a thought that really frightened him: *With the officers gone, no one would ever know if I fucked her.*

IV

Fleming Pickering made a grunting noise and opened his eyes. *It could very well be a groan of pain,* Senator Richmond Fowler thought.

"I seem to have dropped off," Pickering said, pushing himself up in the armchair. "How long was I out?"

"Passed out is more like it," Fowler said. "A couple of hours. How do you feel?"

"Will you stop hovering over me like Florence Nightingale? I'm fine."

"I probably shouldn't tell you this, but you look a hell of a lot better than when you walked in here."

"I feel fine," Pickering said. He sniffed under his armpit. "I smell like a cadaver but I feel fine."

"I was wondering about that," Fowler said. "How do you manage bathing?"

"I take a shower with my arm raised as far as I can, and very carefully. Would you like to watch?"

"I'll pass, thank you just the same. I can live with the smell for a while. And besides, you might want something sent up to eat."

"Was the tailor here?"

"Yes. He did three shirts for you."

"Then I think I'd rather eat downstairs in the grill," Pickering said. He pushed himself out of the chair and walked into the bedroom.

In a moment, Fowler heard the sound of running water. Not without difficulty, he resisted the temptation to go in and help. Fleming Pickering was a big boy.

Five minutes later there was indication that not all was well.

"Oh, shit!" Pickering's voice came from the bedroom, filled with disgust.

Fowler went quickly in. Pickering, stark naked, dripping, stood in the door of the bath, examining water-soaked bandages scattered over his chest and upper stomach. Fowler saw streams of watery blood running down his body.

"I don't suppose you have any adhesive tape?" Pickering asked.

Fowler picked up the telephone.

"This is Senator Fowler. Find Dr. Selleres and send him up here immediately."

"That wasn't necessary," Pickering said.

"Trust me. I'm a U.S. Senator," Fowler said.

Pickering looked at him and chuckled. " 'The check's in the mail,' right? 'Your husband will never find out'?"

"Speaking of wives, I just spoke with yours."

"How'd she know I was here?"

"Where else would you be? Aside from St. Elizabeth's?"

St. Elizabeth's was Washington's best-known mental hospital.

"And?" Pickering replied, not amused.

"And she says, when you get a chance, call."

"I will," Pickering said.

He put his hand to his chest and jerked off one of the bandages. Fowler saw that the wound beneath was still sutured.

"You were almost killed, weren't you?"

"That's like being pregnant, you either are or you aren't. No. I wasn't. I don't think I was ever in any danger of dying."

"I saw the Silver Star citation. You passed out from loss of blood."

"I think that was shock from the arm," Pickering said matter-of-factly. "And I didn't pass out. I just got a little light-headed. Where did you see my citation?"

"Knox sent me a copy. He thought I would be interested."

"Christ, *Knox*. I forgot all about him."

"You will see him tomorrow."

"How do you know that?"

"He called me. How did he know you were here? Same answer. Where else would you go?"

"Is he annoyed?"

"I don't think 'annoyed' is a strong enough word."

"When do I see him?"

"Half past five."

"In the afternoon, obviously. Am I being forced to cool my heels all day, until half past five, as a subtle expression of displeasure?"

"At half past five we are having drinks and a small intimate supper with the President."

"Are you kidding?"

"No. I am not. Knox will be there. And Admiral Leahy. No one else, I'm told."

"What's that all about?"

"I have no idea. When the President's secretary calls me and asks if I am free for drinks and supper, I say, 'Thank you very much.' I don't ask what he has in mind."

"I had hoped to be well on my way to Florida by half past five tomorrow."

"You'll have plenty of time to see Pick. One more day won't matter."

"He is liable to be on orders any day. Considering the shortage of pilots over there, they may not give him much of a pre-embarkation leave, possibly only three or four days. I *don't* have plenty of time."

A knock at the door kept Fowler from having to reply. He went to answer it, and Pickering went into the bathroom and wrapped a towel around his middle.

Or tried to. It was a difficult maneuver with one arm in a cast.

"Hello, Fleming," Dr. Selleres, the house physician, said. He spoke with a slight Spanish accent.

"How are you, Emilio? You brought your bag, I hope? I seem to be leaking all over the Senator's floor."

Dr. Selleres walked to him, took a quick look, and shook his head.

"I'm surprised you were discharged from the hospital," the doctor said. "These wounds are still suppurating."

"They can suppurate as well here as they could in a hospital," Pickering argued reasonably.

"Did you get the cast wet, too?" Selleres said, feeling it. "I don't suppose you've heard of this marvelous new medical technique we have called the sponge bath?"

"I needed a real bath," Pickering said.

"Or so you thought," Selleres said. "Lie down on the bed and I'll do what I can to clean up the mess you've made of yourself."

Once he had Pickering down, the doctor checked his heart and blood pressure and peered intently into his eyes. Fowler was surprised that Pickering didn't protest.

Selleres then swabbed the wounds with an antiseptic solution and applied fresh bandages.

"If you don't kill yourself falling down in a shower or doing something else equally stupid, you can have those sutures looked at in four or five days," Dr. Selleres said.

"I love your bedside manner," Pickering said, smiling at him.

"If I wasn't in love with your wife, you could change your own bandages," Selleres said. "Shall I give her any kind of message when I talk to her?"

"You're going to talk to her?"

"Patricia called and made me promise to check on you in the morning. The Senator had told her you were passed out and wouldn't stir before then. Now I can call her tonight and tell her, unfortunately, that you're going to live."

"Do what you can to calm her down, will you, please?"

"Don't I always?" Selleres said. He put out his hand. "Welcome home, Flem. It's good to see you. And I heard about the Silver Star. Congratulations."

"Thank you," Pickering said. Fowler saw that he was embarrassed.

When he had gone, Pickering got off the bed, tried to fasten the towel around his waist, failed, swore, and walked naked out of the bedroom to the bar in the sitting room.

"Not that it seems to bother you," Fowler said, "but would you like some help getting dressed?"

"I can handle everything but a towel," Pickering said. "Towels having neither rubber bands nor buttons."

He made himself a drink and carried it back into the bedroom. Fowler, after making himself a drink, went to the doorway, leaned on the jamb, and watched Pickering dress. He did not offer to help, although it was obvious that Pickering was having a hell of a hard time pulling his cast through the sleeve of a T-shirt and then forcing it over his head.

"Would you please put braces on my trousers?" Pickering asked as he pulled on boxer shorts.

Fowler went to the dresser and picked up a pair of suspenders.

"If you manage that without too much difficulty, I'll let you put the garters on my socks," Pickering said.

"How do you cut your food?" Fowler asked.

"The same way I tie my tie," Pickering said. "I have some kind soul do it for me."

"We don't have to go out to eat, you know. There's room service."

"Tell me about what Leahy's doing," Pickering said, ignoring the offer.

"What do you want to know?"

"I'm just curious. His role seems to fascinate all the admirals."

"You ever meet him?"

Pickering nodded.

"A couple of times. When he was Governor of Puerto Rico. Interesting man."

"A good man," Fowler said. "The first time I met him was when he was Chief of Naval Operations. If it wasn't for him, the way he fought for construction funds, made Congress understand, we would have a very small Navy right now to fight this war."

"So what's he doing now?" Pickering asked, sitting on the bed and pulling black socks over his feet.

Fowler dropped to his knees and strapped garters on Pickering's calves.

"His title is Chief of Staff to the Commander in Chief of the Armed Forces of the United States . . ." Fowler said.

"Which the Navy brass in the Pacific thinks means that he's

the senior uniformed officer of the Armed Forces, Army and Navy. Is that the situation?"

". . . which sounds very impressive," Fowler went on, ignoring the question. "There was an initial perception that he was to rank above both King and Marshall." Admiral Ernest King was the Chief of Naval Operations; General George C. Marshall was the Chief of Staff of the Army. "He had seniority over both officers, having retired from being Chief of Naval Operations in 1939."

"But?" Pickering interrupted again.

"But Roosevelt quickly torpedoed that," Fowler went on, "—note the Naval symbolism—by saying that Leahy is going to be his legman. His legman *only*."

"I am just a simple sailor," Pickering said. "Unversed in the Machiavellian subtleties of politics. I don't know what the hell you're talking about."

"It means that the master of that art, Machiavellianism, our beloved President, has done it again."

"Done what again?"

"Kept his subordinates off balance. He's very good at that. Marshall and King don't know what to think: Just what authority does Leahy have? Is he speaking as Admiral Leahy, who has a lot of rank but no legal authority? Or is Leahy speaking with the authority of the President?"

"So what exactly does he do?"

"Whatever the President tells him to do."

"Now that I have this explanation, I realize that not only doesn't it have anything to do with me, but that I really don't give a damn about White House or Army/Navy politics."

"You're in the Navy, you should be interested."

"I keep telling you that I'm getting out of the Navy," Pickering said.

"And I keep telling you," Fowler said, getting off his knees, "that I don't think Frank Knox is going to let you go. Can you get your pants on by yourself or will you need help with that, too?"

"If you've put the braces on my pants, I can handle putting them on."

[Two]
PENNSYLVANIA STATION
NEW YORK CITY, NEW YORK
31 AUGUST 1942

"Thanks for the ride, Boats," Lieutenant Stecker said to the bosun's mate who had driven them to Manhattan from Lakehurst.

"Yes, Sir," the bosun said. "You go right through that door and you'll see where you turn in your travel vouchers for a ticket—the sign says 'Rail Transportation Office.' "

"Thanks again," Stecker said and closed the station wagon door.

He picked up his small bag and stood there smiling and waving until the station wagon had driven away.

Lieutenant Pickering stepped off the curb, put his fingers to his lips, and whistled. The noise was startling. In a moment a taxi pulled to the curb.

Pickering bowed Stecker into the cab.

"Foster Park Hotel, please," Pickering said to the driver, and then turned to Stecker. "I don't understand why we didn't have the station wagon drop us at the hotel."

"Because that was not some seaman second class," Stecker explained, "who would not give a damn if you told him to drop you in the middle of the Holland Tunnel. That was a boatswain's mate second class. Boatswain's mates second class do not normally chauffeur people around."

"So?" Pickering asked.

"So he probably was driving us because nobody else could be found to drive us. He did not mind doing so, because he thought we really had to catch the train to Long Island. Still with me?"

"To repeat, so?"

"So now he is returning to Lakehurst thinking he has made a small contribution to the war effort by giving up an evening drinking beer and taking two Marine officers to catch a train. On the other hand, if he dropped us at the hotel, bosun's mates being the clever fellows they are, he would have deduced that we were not bound for Long Island. He would have reported this fact to the chief who runs the motor pool. *'Those two fucking jarhead flyboy second johns didn't go anywhere near fucking Penn Station.'* And the next time we asked for wheels at Lakehurst, we would be told, politely, of course, to go fuck ourselves."

Stecker looked at Pickering to judge his reaction to what he thought of as his Lesson 1103 in The Practical Aspects of Military Service. It was immediately apparent that Pickering hadn't heard at least half of what he had said. Pickering was looking out the window.

Then he leaned forward and slid open the panel between the backseat and the front.

"Where are we going?"

"Foster Park Hotel, Sir."

"By way of Greenwich Village? Jesus, do we look that stupid?"

"This is a shortcut I know, Sir."

"Stop at the next cop you see," Pickering said.

The taxi made the next right turn and then turned right again, now headed uptown toward Central Park.

"A guy's got to make a living," the cabdriver said.

"You picked the wrong sucker," Pickering said. "I used to live here."

"You sure don't sound like no New Yorker."

"Oh, shit," Pickering said, laughing, and then slid the window closed and moved back onto his seat. "Did you hear that? That was a New York apology. Our driver is a mite pissed because I don't sound like a New Yorker; I made him waste his time trying to cheat us because I don't sound like a New Yorker."

"Did you hear what I said about why we're in this cab in the first place?"

"What does it matter?"

Stecker shook his head in resignation and leaned back against the cushion.

Like the other forty-one hotels in the Foster chain, the Foster Park Hotel provided its guests quiet elegance and every reasonable amenity. Andrew Foster learned early on in his career that a large number of people were willing to pay handsomely for hotel accommodations so long as the hotel was centrally located and offered first-class cuisine, well-appointed rooms and suites, and round-the-clock staffing. In every Foster hotel, for example, a room service waiter was on duty on every floor around the clock; a concierge was on duty in the lobby day and night; and complimentary limousine service was provided to and from railroad stations and airports.

Foster Hotels were not, in other words, the sort of places sought out by second lieutenants looking for a cheap place to rest their weary heads for a night.

A bellman, wearing a short red jacket, black trousers, and a pillbox cap tilted at the prescribed angle, rushed to open the door of the taxi when it pulled to the curb before the Foster Park Hotel marquee. As soon as he saw the two second lieutenants emerging from the car, his face showed that he was obviously aware that the Foster Park Hotel was doubtless beyond their limited means.

"May I help you, gentlemen?" he asked politely.

"We can manage, thank you," Pickering said.

"Are you checking in with us, Sir?" the bellman asked in a tone suggesting that this was highly unlikely. Even sharing a small double, a night at the Foster Park would cost these guys half their month's pay.

"I devoutly hope so," Pickering said.

At that point the doorman entered the conversation. He wore a black frock coat, striped trousers, and a gray silk hat, and was far too dignified either to open doors or to wrestle with luggage.

"Good evening, Mr. Pickering. How nice to see you, Sir."

"Hello, Charley, how are you?" Pickering said.

The doorman snatched Stecker's small bag from his hand and passed it to the bellman.

"Put the gentlemen's luggage in 24-A," the doorman ordered as he relieved Pickering of his small bag and gave it to the bellman.

Twenty-four-A and 24-B were a pair of terraced four-room suites that overlooked Central Park. The only more prestigious accommodation in the Foster Park was 25, the Theodore Roosevelt Suite, whose nine rooms occupied the entire front of the 25th floor.

The doorman walked quickly to open the door for the two lieutenants.

"Is there anything I can do for you, Mr. Pickering?" he asked as Pickering walked past him.

"Don't get between me and the men's room," Pickering said. "The last time I met nature's call was somewhere over Maryland."

The doorman chuckled.

"I believe you know where to find it, Sir."

"How could I forget?" Pickering said.

The resident manager of the Foster Park Hotel, in a gray tailcoat and striped trousers, was standing a discreet distance from the entrance to the gentlemen's facility when Lieutenants Pickering and Stecker came out.

"Good evening, Mr. Pickering," he said. "A pleasure to have you in the house, Sir."

"And it's always a pleasure to be here."

"There are no messages, Sir, I checked. And I had a small bar set up in 24-A. If there is anything else?"

"Very kind of you. I can't think of a thing. Thank you."

"Have a pleasant evening, Sir."

"We're going to try," Lieutenant Stecker said.

"Starting, I think," Pickering said, "with a snort in the bar."

There were perhaps two dozen people in the dimly lit bar, mostly couples and quartets sitting at tables, but with several pairs of single men at tables and two other single men sitting at the bar.

There were also two strikingly attractive young women sitting together at a table in the corner.

The bartender addressed Pickering by name, adding, "Famous Grouse, an equal amount of water, and a little ice, right?"

"You have the memory of an elephant," Pickering said. "Give my cousin one of the same."

"I'm not related to him," Stecker said, almost a reflex action, and then: "Did you see what's sitting in the corner?"

"Yes, indeed. I think he works for the Morgan Bank."

"I meant the blonde and her friend," Stecker said, even as he realized that Pickering had again successfully pulled his chain.

"Oh," Pickering said. "Her."

The bartender delivered the drinks. Pickering sipped his and then got off the stool.

"You keep the target under surveillance while I check on the car," he said. "Try not to slobber and drool."

He walked out of the bar carrying his drink, then through the lobby to the revolving door to the street. When he caught the doorman's eye, he motioned him over.

"What's up?" the doorman asked, his tone considerably less formal than it had been.

"The two ladies in the bar," Pickering said. "Are they what I think they are?"

The doorman now looked distinctly uncomfortable.

"Jesus, Pick."

"Answer yes or no."

"Yes and no. They are. But they aren't working the bar, Pick. I know better than that."

"Tell me, Charley."

"I don't know if they're free-lancing, working the bars at the Plaza or the St. Regis, or whether they're a couple of Polly Adler's girls. Or somebody else's. They come in every couple of nights, have a couple of drinks, and leave. They never so much as make eyes at any of our guests."

"They know you know?"

"Sure."

"I want to go to bed," Pickering said, and then when he saw the look in Charley's eyes, added, *"Alone.* And early. My buddy, on the other hand, is randy. Since we have to get up at four goddamn A.M., I'm in no mood to prowl the nightclubs. Getting the picture?"

"Sure. Which one?"

"He likes the blonde."

"Who wouldn't? That'd be expensive, Pick."

Pickering reached into his trousers pocket and came up with a wad of bills. He counted out three twenty-dollar bills and handed them to Charley.

"Not that much, Pick. All he's going to do is rent it for a little while."

"I don't want him to know that, right? If there's any left over, leave it in an envelope at reception."

"I understand."

"Get rid of the other one."

"You must be tired."

"I'm in love."

"No shit?"

"No shit."

"Hey, I'm happy for you, Pick."

"I appreciate this, Charley."

"Don't be silly. Anytime. Anything, Pick."

Pickering smiled at him, touched his arm, and walked back toward the bar.

Charley signaled with his finger to the bellman standing on the other side of the lobby to join him.

"There's a blonde in the bar," he said. "Tell her there's a telephone call for her. Bring her here. If I'm not back, tell her to wait."

"OK. What's going on?"

"None of your goddamn business," Charley said. He went to the concierge's desk.

"Mr. Pickering's guest will probably ask a young lady to join him for a nightcap in 24-A."

"I understand," the concierge said. "I'll take care of it."

Charley the doorman and the concierge had been employees of the Foster Hotel Corporation long enough to know that Andrew Foster had one child, a daughter. His daughter had one child, a son. The son's name was Malcolm S. Pickering. Charley the doorman met Pick Pickering when Pick was sixteen and was spending the summer at the Foster Park learning the hotel business: first as a busboy; later, when he proved his stuff, as a baggage handler; and finally, before the summer was over, as a bellman.

[Three]
BETHPAGE STATION
LONG ISLAND RAILROAD
0530 HOURS 1 SEPTEMBER 1942

Second Lieutenant Malcolm S. Pickering, USMCR, reached into the passenger compartment of the Derham-bodied Packard Straight Eight 280 limousine and pushed at the shoulder of Second Lieutenant Richard J. Stecker, USMC. When this failed to raise Stecker from his slumber, he pinched Stecker's nostrils closed, which did.

"Jesus Christ!" Stecker said, sitting up abruptly and knocking Pick's hand away.

"And good morning to you, Casanova," Pick said. "Nap time is over."

Stecker snorted.

"You have a hickey on your neck," Pick said.

"Fuck you."

"That was simply an observation, not an expression of moral

indignation. I'm *glad* you had a good time . . . you *did* have a good time?"

"None of your fucking business."

"You sounded like you were having a good time. It sounded like a first-class Roman orgy in there."

"Do I detect a slight hint of jealousy?" Stecker asked as he climbed out of the limousine. "You had your chance. She told you she had a girlfriend she could call."

"I paid attention to the Technicolor clap movies I was shown. *I* don't go around picking up fast women in saloons, thus endangering *my* prospects for a happy home full of healthy, happy children borne for me by the decent, wholesome girl of my choice after the war."

"Oh, shit!" Stecker said. "And just for the record, she's a legal secretary."

"I gather you intend to see her again?" Pick asked.

"Jesus Christ," Stecker said angrily, suddenly remembering. "I didn't get her phone number!"

"She's probably in the book," Pick said.

"Yeah," Stecker said. "Christ, I hope so."

"Will there be anything else, Mr. Pickering?" the chauffeur of the Foster Park limousine said.

"No, I don't think so. Thank you very much. I'm sorry you had to bring us out here at this ungodly hour."

"No problem, Mr. Pickering, glad to be of service."

"When you see Charley," Pickering said, "tell him I said thank you very much."

"I'll do that, Mr. Pickering. And you take care of yourself."

"Thank you," Pickering said as he shook the chauffeur's hand.

Pickering and Stecker picked up their bags, walked twenty yards to the head of the taxi line, and climbed in the first one.

"Grumman," Pickering told the driver. "Use the airfield entrance."

At least, Stecker thought, *he remembers that much. We did not roll up to the airfield gate in the limousine.*

In Stecker's opinion, the key to success as a second lieutenant was invisibility. Second lieutenants should be neither seen nor heard. With Pickering, that was difficult. Pick was a living example of Scott Fitzgerald's line about the rich being different from you and me.

During their basic flight training at Pensacola, second lieutenants were furnished quarters, two men to a tiny two-room apartment in a newly constructed, bare-frame wooden bachelor officer's quarters building. Such facilities proving unsatisfactory to Second Lieutenant Pickering, he rented a penthouse suite in the San Carlos Hotel in downtown Pensacola and commuted to flight school in his 1941 Cadillac convertible.

The two of them made a deal: Stecker paid for their liquor (acquired tax-free at the Officer's Sales Store). In exchange he got to live in the suite's second bedroom. He did not want to be a mooch, but he couldn't refute Pickering's argument that he was going to have to pay for the suite whether the second bedroom was used or not. So why not?

Not without a little surprise, Stecker quickly learned that Pickering was not a mental lightweight or even someone taking a free ride from his wealthy parents. For instance, the Cadillac had not been a gift. It was purchased from Pick's earnings during his last college summer vacation. He had worked as head bellman in a Foster hotel. Stecker was astonished to learn not only how much head bellmen earned, but how important a head bellman is to a successful hotel operation.

Pick had also worked in hotel kitchens enough to have made him a professional-level chef. Stecker never ceased to be amazed that Pickering could tell the precise doneness of a grilled steak—rare, medium, or medium-rare—by touching it with the tip of his thumb.

For a while grilling steaks for Pensacola maidens on the terrace of their hotel suite was a very profitable enterprise, carnally speaking. But then Pick fell in love.

Not with one of the maidens, but with a widow (a *young* widow, his age) who wanted nothing to do with him. Part of Pick's infatuation with her, Stecker suspected, was that she spurned his attentions. A most unusual occurrence where Pick was concerned; from what Stecker had seen, females ran toward Pickering with invitation in their eyes, not away from him.

The widow, Martha Sayre Culhane, was the daughter of the Number-Two Admiral aboard Pensacola NAS, Rear Admiral R. B. Sayre. Her husband, a Marine First Lieutenant, a Naval Aviator, had been killed on Wake Island.

Pick was of course a formidable suitor, but he got no further with Martha Culhane than some dinner dates and movies. And she flatly refused to marry him.

Stecker was absolutely convinced that she had not let Pickering into her pants.

But he was faithful to her, witness last night, when a smashingly beautiful woman with an uncontrollable lust for Marine Aviators had a friend who felt very much the same way. Pick hadn't even wanted to meet her.

That was either incredibly stupid or admirable.

Because Stecker had grown very fond of Pickering, he gave his buddy the benefit of the doubt. It was admirable. Sir Pick, riding off to the Crusades, vowing to stay chastely faithful to Maid Martha while she remained pure and untouched in Castle Pensacola.

Stecker looked out the window and saw they were riding beside the hurricane fence that surrounded the Grumman plant. Up ahead he could see the floodlighted area around the gate. Since the cab was not permitted inside the fence, they got out of it by the gate.

Stecker saw a white-hat inside the guard shack. That was unusual. Although there was a small Navy detachment assigned to the factory, the security force was civilian. The officers and white-hats were here to get aircraft through the production lines and out to the fleet and air bases, not to guard the plant.

Pickering paid the cabdriver, and Stecker walked to the gate, taking a copy of their orders from his pocket as he did so.

"Excuse me, Sir," the white-hat said, saluting as he came out of the guard shack. "Is your name Pickering?"

"He's Pickering," Stecker replied with a gesture in the general area of the taxi. He was suddenly afraid that something unpleasant was about to happen. The insignia on the white-hat's sleeve identified him as an aviation motor machinist's mate first class. Sailors holding the Navy's second-highest enlisted grade are not ordinarily found in guard shacks at quarter to six in the morning.

"You're Lieutenant Stecker, then, Sir?"

"Right."

"Wait right there please, Lieutenant," the white-hat said, and went back in the guard shack. Stecker saw him pick up a telephone and dial a number.

The white-hat came back out of the guard shack as Pickering walked up. The white-hat saluted him. Stecker found nothing wrong with the return salute Pickering rendered.

He returns *salutes just fine. What gets him in trouble are those vague gestures supposed to be salutes that he gives those senior to him in the military hierarchy.*

"Gentlemen," the AMMM1st said, "the senior naval representative aboard would like a word with you. If you'll come with me I have transport."

The transport turned out to be a Chevrolet pickup truck painted Navy gray. When they had all crowded into the cab, Stecker said, "I wonder why I have this feeling that we're in trouble?"

"May I speak freely, Sir?"

"Please do."

"Where the fuck have you two been? They've been looking for you since yesterday afternoon."

"Who is 'they'?"

"First it was Lieutenant Commander Harris. Then, when you didn't show up last night, Commander Schneebelly. He's the senior naval representative, and he's been shitting a brick."

"Do you have any idea what it's all about?"

"I know there was a message from the Navy Department. I don't know what was in it. Where the hell have you been? Night on the town? I hope she was worth it."

"This officer was carousing and consorting with loose women," Pickering said piously. *"I* myself went to bed early, and of course, *alone.* I should have known that if I associated with *him,* he would sooner or later get me in trouble."

"Why don't I believe that, Lieutenant?" the petty officer asked.

"That he would get me in trouble?"

"That you went to bed early and alone. You could have come out here and done that."

"I have to keep an eye on him. He tends to run amok."

"This may not be as funny as you seem to think it is," Stecker said. "Did you do anything at Pee-cola I don't know about?"

"Can't think of a thing," Pick said truthfully.

The pickup pulled up before the Operations Building, a Quonset hut.

"Here we are," the petty officer said. "Good luck. Commander Schneebelly sometimes gets a little excited."

They stepped out of the truck and walked into the Quonset hut.

A chief petty officer was leaning on a counter. He stood erect when he saw them.

"Good morning, Chief," Stecker said.

"Mr. . . . ?"

"Stecker, and this is Mr. Pickering."

"Commander Schneebelly will see you now, gentlemen," the chief said, pointing to a closed door.

Motioning Pickering to follow him, Stecker walked to the door and knocked.

"Come!"

"Stand at attention when we get in there and keep your mouth shut," Stecker said softly, and then opened the door and marched in.

He came to attention before Commander Schneebelly's desk.

"Sir, Lieutenants Stecker and Pickering reporting as ordered, Sir."

Commander Schneebelly was short and plump; he wore both a pencil-line mustache and aviator's wings.

He pursed his lips.

"Stand at ease, gentlemen," he said softly, and then far less softly, "Where the hell have you two been?"

"Sir, our orders state 'not later than zero six-thirty' this morning," Stecker said. "Sir, with respect, it's zero five fifty-five."

"That's not what I asked, Mister!" Commander Schneebelly snapped. "And I can tell time, thank you. Don't tell me what your orders say. I asked you, *where have you been?*"

"Permission to speak, Sir?" Pickering said, and Stecker winced.

"Speak!"

"Sir, this is all my fault. We spent the night at my grandfather's house. Lieutenant Stecker wanted to come right out here, but I talked him out of it."

Commander Schneebelly considered that for a moment.

"Goddamn it, Mister, don't you have the brains you were born with? Doesn't your grandfather have a telephone? Is there some reason you couldn't have called out here and said that you would report in this morning?"

"No excuse, Sir," Pickering said.

"Goddamn it, son, you're an officer in the Naval Service. You've got to learn to think."

"Yes, Sir."

Commander Schneebelly glowered at both of them for another thirty seconds. But it seemed longer. He then handed Pickering a sheet of teletype paper.

URGENT
NAVY DEPT WASH DC 1530 31AUG42

TO: FLAG OFFICER COMMANDING
      NAS PENSACOLA FLA
      SENIOR NAVAL REPRESENTATIVE
      GRUMMAN AIRCRAFT CORPORATION
      BETHPAGE LI NY

1. THIS MESSAGE CONFIRMS VARIOUS TELEPHONE CONVERSATIONS OF THIS DATE BETWEEN CAPT D.W. GOBLE, AND COMM F.L. TAYLOR, NAS PENSACOLA; COMM J.W. SCHNEEBELLY AND LTCOM B.T. HARRIS, OFFICE OF NAVAL REPRESENTATIVE, GRUMMAN AIRCRAFT CORP BETHPAGE LI NY AND CAPT J.T. HAUGHTON, OFFICE OF SECNAV.

2. THE SECRETARY OF THE NAVY DESIRES THE PRESENCE OF 2ND LT M.S. PICKERING, USMCR AND 2ND LT RICHARD J. STECKER, USMC IN WASHINGTON, D.C. NOT LATER THAN 1600 1 SEPTEMBER 1942.

3. SENIOR NAVREP GRUMMAN WILL AT THE EARLIEST POSSIBLE TIME DIRECT SUBJECT OFFICERS TO SCHEDULE AN INTERMEDIATE STOP AT ANACOSTIA NAS ARRIVING THERE AT NOT LATER THAN 1600 HOURS DURING FERRY FLIGHT BETHPAGE DASH PENSACOLA AND BE PREPARED TO SPEND NOT MORE THAN TWENTY-FOUR HOURS IN WASHINGTON.

4. SENIOR NAVREP GRUMMAN WILL BY THE MOST EXPEDITIOUS MEANS, PREFERABLY TELEPHONE, INFORM OFFICE SECNAV OF (A) TRANSMITTAL TO SUBJECT OFFICERS OF ORDERS IN 2. AND 3. ABOVE; (B) OF DEPARTURE OF SUBJECT OFFICERS FROM BETHPAGE AND ESTIMATED TIME OF ARRIVAL AT ANACOSTIA.

BY DIRECTION:

HAUGHTON, CAPT, USN, ADMINISTRATIVE OFFICER TO SECNAV

Pick read it and then looked at Commander Schneebelly.

"May I show this to Mr. Stecker, Sir?"

Schneebelly made an impatient gesture signifying that he might.

What the hell is this? Stecker wondered.

"What the hell is this all about?" Commander Schneebelly asked. "Do you know?"

"No, Sir," Stecker said.

"No, Sir," Pickering parroted.

"I have been just a little curious," Schneebelly said, "and so, I am sure, have people at Pensacola. What possible interest could the Secretary of the Navy have in two second lieutenants?"

Neither Stecker nor Pickering replied.

"All right. Now let me tell you what's going to happen. I have personally drawn up a flight plan for you. It is approximately 230 air miles between here and Anacostia, passing over Lakehurst NAS. At a cruising speed of 280 knots, that indicates an approximate flight time of forty-eight minutes. We will figure on one hour, just to be safe. We will also schedule your arrival time at Anacostia for 1500 hours, rather than 1600. That means you will take off from here precisely at 1400 hours. Between now and 1400, you will ensure that your uniforms are shipshape, and get yourselves haircuts. You will not leave the plant grounds, and you will keep me, and/or the chief, advised of your location at all times. Clear? Any questions?"

"Sir, what about test-flying the airplanes?" Stecker asked.

"The airplanes will have been test-flown before you sign for them. I'll do it myself, as a matter of fact."

"Sir, with respect, I'd prefer to do that myself."

"No one particularly cares what you would prefer to do, Mister."

"Sir, with respect, that's called for by regulations."

"You really are a wise guy, aren't you, Mister?"

"I don't mean to be, Sir."

"Very well, Mister, you will conduct the pre-ferry test flight."

"Thank you, Sir."

"Chief!" Commander Schneebelly called, raising his voice.

The door opened and the chief stuck his head in.

"Chief, these officers are going to conduct pre-ferry test flights of their aircraft and then they are going to get haircuts and have their uniforms pressed. Would you please go with them and see that they have every possible assistance?"

"Aye, aye, Sir."

"Don't let them out of your sight, Chief."

[Four]
THE FOSTER LAFAYETTE HOTEL
WASHINGTON, D.C.
1710 HOURS 1 SEPTEMBER 1942

There was a knock. And Senator Richmond F. Fowler went to the door of his suite to answer it.

Two young men were standing in the hotel corridor. One wore a suit that bulged under the left armpit. The other was a Lieutenant Commander of the United States Navy in high-collared whites. From his shoulder was suspended the golden cords of an aide to the President of the United States.

The collars of both were wilted by sweat, and there were sweat-soaked patches under the jacket armpits.

"Good evening, Senator," the Secret Service agent said. "I'm Special Agent McNulty of the Presidential detail."

Fowler nodded at him but did not speak.

"We have a White House car, Senator, whenever you and Captain Pickering are ready," Secret Service Agent McNulty said.

"Please thank the President," Senator Fowler said, "and tell him that both the Captain and I are quite able to walk across the street and would prefer to do so."

"There has been a change of plans, Senator," the Naval aide said. "I'm Commander Jellington, Sir, the President's Naval aide."

Fowler looked at him and waited for him to go on. When he did not, Fowler said, "Is the change of plans really a matter of national security, Commander? Or are you going to tell me what the change is?"

"Dinner will be aboard the *Potomac,* Senator," McNulty answered for him.

"Hence, the *Naval* aide, right?" Fowler said. "Come in."

"Thank you, Sir," they said almost in unison.

"Actually, Sir," Commander Jellington said, "the President

sent me to be of whatever assistance I could to Captain Pickering."

"Rendering assistance to Captain Pickering is right up there with trying to pet an alligator—a *constipated* alligator," Fowler added. "You stand a good chance of having the friendly hand bitten off at the shoulder."

He led the two down a corridor to the sitting room, which was on the corner of the building.

"There has been a change of plans, Fleming," Fowler announced to what looked like an empty room. "We are going to dine on the *Potomac.*"

"What does *that* mean?" Pickering's voice came from a high-backed leather chair placed directly in front of the room's air-conditioning duct.

"The *Potomac* is the Presidential yacht, Sir," Commander Jellington said.

Pickering rose from the chair. He was dressed in a T-shirt and boxer shorts. He was shoeless, but wearing calf-high black stockings held in place by garters. Bandages across his chest could be seen through the thin cotton of the T-shirt.

Neither the Naval aide nor the Secret Service agent seemed to notice anything out of the ordinary.

"Good afternoon, Captain Pickering," the Naval aide said. "Sir, I'm Commander Jellington. The President thought I might in some way be helpful to you."

"Whenever you and the Senator are ready, Sir," Agent McNulty said, "we have a White House car."

"The last I heard," Pickering said, glowering at Senator Fowler, "this was going to be cocktails and a simple supper across the street." He gestured with his right arm toward the White House; in his hand he had a bottle of Canadian ale. "And starting at half past six. It's only five something."

"The President has apparently changed his mind," Fowler said. "We are going to dine aboard the *Potomac.* And may I suggest that it behooves you, Captain, as a Naval officer, to manifest a cheerful and willing obedience to the desires of your commander in chief?"

"That sonofabitch," Captain Pickering said. "I should have known he'd pull something like this."

The eyes of Special Agent McNulty widened. He was not used to hearing the President referred to in such terms, much less by someone about to be honored with the great privilege of an intimate dinner with the President aboard the Presidential yacht.

"I think we should all remember that Captain Pickering is a wounded hero," Senator Fowler said, a touch of amusement in his voice, "just recently released from the hospital. And we all know that wounded heroes are a little crazy and have to be humored, don't we?"

"Fuck you, Senator," Captain Pickering said.

McNulty was more than a little uncomfortable. It was one of those situations not neatly covered by regulations and policy.

On one hand he took very seriously (his wife said "religiously") his duty to protect the President of the United States from all threats, real or potential: Here was a man who'd obviously been drinking, who angrily referred to the President as "that sonofabitch," who was just out of the hospital, and was quite possibly at least a little off the tracks, mentally speaking. A rational man did not say "Fuck you!" to a man like Senator Richmond Fowler.

On the other hand Senator Fowler seemed more amused than disturbed by Pickering's behavior, and it could be presumed that the Senator was at least nearly as concerned with the safety of the President as the Secret Service.

McNulty realized that he had two options: He could get on the phone and tell the supervisory agent on duty that he had a potential loony here who'd been at the bottle and should not be allowed anywhere near the President. The trouble was that the loony was not only the President's personal invitee, but a very close personal friend of Senator Fowler. Indeed, he was living in the Senator's hotel suite; and the Senator had *not* gone bananas when this Pickering guy told him to fuck himself.

Option two was to say nothing but keep a close eye on him.

"Commander," Senator Fowler said, "Captain Pickering has a nice fresh uniform in that bedroom. Perhaps you'd be good enough to help him into it?"

"You stay where you are, Commander!" Captain Pickering ordered. He marched across the room, entered the bedroom, and closed the door.

A moment later it opened again.

"Commander," Captain Pickering said, almost humbly, "if you wouldn't mind, I could use some help."

"Yes, Sir," the Naval aide said.

Special Agent McNulty decided that for the time being, option two seemed best.

"I'll give you a hand, Jellington," he said and followed him into Captain Pickering's bedroom.

[*Five*]
THE WASHINGTON NAVY YARD
1750 HOURS 1 SEPTEMBER 1942

Two limousines drove onto the wharf, where they were immediately stopped by neatly dressed men in business suits. The first limousine held a Naval aide to the President of the United States and a member of the Secret Service Presidential Security detail. There was a wave of recognition; then the limousine, a Cadillac, was given a wave of permission to drive farther down the wharf.

Instead, the Secret Service agent got out of the Presidential 1941 Cadillac.

He indicated the second limousine, a 1942 Packard 280.

"Senator Fowler and Captain Pickering are in that one," McNulty said to his Secret Service colleagues. "I'll identify them for you."

One of his colleagues asked the obvious question: "Why aren't they riding in the White House car?"

"Because the Senator's Packard is *air conditioned,* and the White House car *isn't,*" McNulty said.

He opened the front-seat passenger door in time to hear Senator Fowler say, "Now for God's sake, Fleming, when we go on board, watch your mouth. You've been at the sauce all afternoon."

"Just pull up behind the other car," McNulty said to Fowler's chauffeur.

There was a twenty-foot-high wall of corrugated paper boxes on the wharf, leaving just enough room for a car to pass between it and the small white ship tied up at the wharf.

Or a truck, Fleming Pickering decided, once he was out of the Packard. *That stuff is intended for a ship's galleys. This place really is a working Navy yard, not just a place for the President to park his yacht.*

He looked down the hull of the *Potomac.* Perfect paint. Not a speck of rust. A lifeboat, forward, had been swung out on davits. The tide was such that the main deck was within a couple of inches of the wharf; a simple gangplank was in place.

I wonder how they get Roosevelt on here when the Potomac *is much lower or higher than the wharf?*

The answer came immediately: *Hell, a couple of Secret Service guys make a basket of their hands and carry him on. How else? Christ, maybe Fowler's right and I am half in the bag.*

"Right this way, please, gentlemen," Commander Jellington said, and led them to the gangplank.

Two sailors in undress white uniforms stood at either side of the gangplank at parade rest.

Join the Navy and see the Potomac, Pickering thought cynically and then was immediately ashamed of the cynicism.

The sailors came to attention as he started onto the gangplank.

"Good evening," Pickering said and smiled at them.

A full Lieutenant and two more sailors stood on the deck at the end of the gangplank.

At the last moment Pickering remembered his Naval courtesy, and that the *Potomac* was legally a ship of the line.

"Permission to come aboard, Sir," he asked.

"Granted."

Pickering saluted the National Colors and then the officer of the deck.

"The President asks that you join him on the fantail, Sir," the officer of the deck said, and gestured toward the stern of the ship.

Canvas had been hung from the overhead to the rail along the dock side of the *Potomac*, obviously to shield the vessel from the eyes of the curious. But when he reached the fantail, he saw the river side was open. Or at least only covered by mosquito netting.

The President was sitting in an upholstered wicker chair, facing away from the wharf.

What the hell is the protocol? Do I just walk in and say hello?

There was another Naval officer on the fantail, wearing a somewhat wilted white uniform, with four stars on each shoulder board, the insignia of a full admiral.

Admiral William D. Leahy, Chief of Staff to the President, was sitting on a wicker couch and holding a glass of what looked like iced coffee.

He looks, Pickering thought, *a good deal older than the last time I saw him.*

He then remembered hearing somewhere that while Leahy had been Ambassador to Vichy France, his wife had suddenly taken ill and died. It was said that Leahy had taken it badly.

That probably explains why he looks so old, Pickering thought. Then he wondered, *What the hell am I supposed to do? Salute him? Jesus Christ, what am I doing in the Navy?*

Franklin Delano Roosevelt solved Pickering's dilemma. He looked over his shoulder, saw him, and smiled.

"Fleming, my dear fellow!" he said. "How good to see you! Come in and sit down by me."

"Good evening, Mr. President," Pickering said. Something was tugging at his hat. He had without thinking about it tucked it under the cast on his left arm. He looked and saw a white-jacketed Navy steward smiling at him.

"Let me have that, please, Sir."

Pickering raised his arm, and the uniform cap disappeared. He then walked across the deck to Roosevelt.

Roosevelt offered his hand. The grip was surprisingly strong.

"Good evening, Mr. President," Pickering repeated.

Jesus, he does get to me. I already said that.

"I believe you know Bill Leahy, don't you, Fleming?"

"I have had that privilege," Pickering said. "Good evening, Admiral."

"Pickering," Leahy said.

"Sit down and tell me your pleasure," Roosevelt said. "Does your medical condition permit alcohol?"

"It demands it, Sir," Pickering said.

The steward who had snatched his cap was back at his side.

"What may I get you, Sir?"

"Scotch, please. Water. Not much ice."

"And there is my favorite Republican," Roosevelt said, beaming at Senator Fowler. "Richmond, it's good to see you."

"Mr. President," Fowler said formally, making a nod that could have been a bow.

While Pickering was lowering himself into the wicker chair beside Roosevelt, he felt the *Potomac* shudder as the propellers were engaged.

Christ, they were waiting for us to get under way!

"How are you, Admiral?" Fowler asked.

"Very well, thank you, Senator."

"Richmond," the President said, "could I ask you to excuse us a moment? There's a little business I'd like to get out of the way, before we . . ."

"Of course, Mr. President," Fowler said.

One of the stewards held open for Fowler a sliding glass door to an aft cabin and then stepped inside after him. A second steward put a glass in Pickering's hand and then followed the first into the aft cabin.

"I'd like you to do something for me, Fleming," Roosevelt said, laying a hand on Pickering's arm.

"I'm at your command, Sir."

"But there are a few matters I'd like to get straight, if you will," Roosevelt said, "about your previous contributions to the war effort."

"Of course, Mr. President."

"I understand that you met with Bill Donovan right after the war started, isn't that so?"

"Yes, Sir, it is."

William S. Donovan, a New York lawyer, had been asked by Roosevelt to establish an organization to coordinate all United States intelligence activities (except counterintelligence, which was handled in the U.S. and Latin America by J. Edgar Hoover's FBI). The organization evolved first into the Office of Strategic Services (OSS) and ultimately into the Central Intelligence Agency (CIA).

"I understand that your talk with Donovan didn't go well."

"That's correct, Sir."

Where the hell did he hear that? Did Donovan tell him? Or Richmond Fowler?

Roosevelt laughed.

"Forgive me. But you and Bill are the immovable object and the irresistible force. I'm really not at all surprised. I would love to have been a fly on the wall."

"Actually, Sir, it was quite civil. He asked me to become sort of a clerk to a banker whom I knew, and I respectfully declined the honor."

Pickering sensed Leahy's eyes on him, glanced at him, and was surprised to see what could have been a smile on his lips and in his eyes.

"And then, as I understand it," Roosevelt went on, "when you went to The Marines and offered your services, they respectfully declined the honor?"

"They led me to believe, Mr. President," Pickering replied, smiling back at Roosevelt, who was quietly beaming at his play on words, "that as desperate as they were for manpower, there was really no place in The Corps for a forty-six-year-old corporal."

"And then you went to Frank Knox, and he arranged for you to be commissioned into the Navy?"

That wasn't the way it happened. Frank Knox came to me and asked me to accept the commission.

"Yes, Sir," Pickering said.

"Admiral Leahy and I have just about concluded that was a mistake," Roosevelt said.

"So have I, Mr. President. I—"

"I don't think the President means to suggest that you're not qualified to be a Naval captain, Captain," Leahy broke in quickly. "I certainly don't. Your conduct aboard the *Gregory* put to rest any doubts about your competence. And I was one of those who never had any doubts."

"I didn't mean that the way it sounded, Fleming," Roosevelt said.

"I respectfully disagree, Admiral," Pickering said. "I should not be a Naval officer, period."

"Now with *that,*" Roosevelt said, "I agree."

"As soon as I can discuss the matter with Secretary Knox, Mr. President, I intend to ask him to let me out of the Service."

"I know," Roosevelt said. "He told me. I'm afraid that's quite impossible, Fleming. Out of the question."

"I don't quite understand," Pickering said.

"You're familiar, of course, with the Office of Management Analysis in Headquarters, U.S. Marine Corps?"

Pickering thought a moment, came up with nothing, and replied, "No, Sir. I am not."

"Does the name Rickabee mean anything to you, Pickering?" Leahy asked.

"Yes," Pickering replied immediately. "Yes, indeed. Outstanding man."

"He heads the Office of Management Analysis," Roosevelt said a trifle smugly.

"Yes, Sir," Pickering said, feeling quite stupid. He had never actually met Lieutenant Colonel F. L. Rickabee, USMC, but he had seen how efficiently the man could operate. He had, in fact, vowed to find Rickabee in Washington, to shake his hand, and say thank you.

Among the long list of Navy brass actions in the Pacific that were outrageously stupid in Fleming Pickering's view was their handling of the Royal Australian Navy Coastwatcher Establishment.

When the Japanese began their march down the Solomon Islands chain toward New Guinea, Australia, and New Zealand, the Australians hastily recruited plantation managers, schoolteachers, government technicians, shipping officials, and even a couple of missionaries who had lived on the islands. They hastily commissioned these people as junior officers in the Royal Australian Navy Volunteer Reserve and left them behind on the islands, equipped with shortwave radios and small arms.

They were in a position to provide—at great risk to their lives—extremely valuable intelligence regarding Japanese Army and Navy movements, strength, location, and probable intentions. But the Navy arrogantly judged that information coming from natives who were not professional Navy types couldn't possibly be genuinely valuable.

Later, when the value of the Coastwatcher-provided intelligence could no longer be denied, the Navy brass decided that it was now far too important to be left to the administration of the lowly Royal Australian Navy Reserve Lieutenant Commander who was in charge. The U.S. Navy would take over and do it right, in other words.

Pickering heard of the situation from an old friend, Fitzhugh Boyer, who had been Pacific & Far East Shipping's agent in Melbourne and was now a Rear Admiral in the Royal Australian Navy. Fitz Boyer introduced him to Lieutenant Commander Eric Feldt, who was running the Coastwatcher Establishment, and who cheerfully confessed to being a little less than charming to the detachment of U.S. Navy officers who had shown up in Townsville to take over his operation.

Fitz Boyer told Pickering that it was unfortunately true that Feldt did indeed tell the captain who led the detachment that unless he left Townsville that very day, he was going to tear his head off and stick it up his anal cavity.

That same day Pickering fired off an URGENT radio to Frank Knox, recommending that a highly qualified intelligence officer be sent to Australia as soon as possible, with orders to place himself at Feldt's disposal, and with the means to provide Feldt with whatever assistance, especially financial, Feldt needed.

Nine days later, Major Edward J. Banning, USMC, former Intelligence Officer of the Fourth Marines in Shanghai, got off a plane in Melbourne carrying a cashier's check drawn on the Treasury of the United States for a quarter of a million dollars. He was accompanied by a sergeant. Within days the balance of Marine Corps Special Detachment 14, along with crates of the very best shortwave radios and other equipment, began to arrive by priority air shipment.

Banning and Feldt were two of a kind; they hit it off immediately. Not only that, Banning and his detachment proved to be precisely what Pickering had hoped for but thought he had little chance of getting.

Soon after a pair of U.S. Marines was parachuted onto Buka Island to augment the Coastwatcher operation there, Pickering confessed to Banning that he was astonished at the high quality of the people Frank Knox had sent him; and he was equally surprised that they'd arrived so quickly. And Banning replied that the man responsible was Rickabee.

"Mr. Knox is a wise man," Banning said. "He gave this job to Colonel Rickabee, together with the authority, and then let him do it."

That was the first time Pickering heard of Rickabee. But before he was ordered home, he'd had many other dealings with the man; and each contact confirmed his first impression: Rickabee was a man who got things done.

"Colonel Rickabee and you have many things in common, Fleming," Roosevelt said, smiling. "For instance, some people—not *me,* of course, but *some* people—think you both have abrasive personalities."

Roosevelt waited for a reply, got none, and then went on.

"Another way to phrase that is that neither of you can suffer fools. As I'm sure you've learned, fools find that attitude distressing. That doesn't bother you, I know, but it does affect Rickabee."

"I don't think I follow you, Mr. President."

"When Admiral Leahy let the word out that the promotion of Lieutenant Colonel Rickabee to brigadier general was being considered, it was not greeted with enthusiasm. Quite the reverse."

"I think he would make a splendid general officer," Pickering said.

"So do I," Leahy said. "I've known him for a long time. Even before I was Chief of Naval Operations, he did special jobs for me. And he has done special jobs for me since."

"We have reached a certain meeting of the minds vis-à-vis Colonel Rickabee," Roosevelt said. "General Holcomb, the Marine Commandant, has recommended his promotion to colonel. Though I was prepared to send his name to the Senate for confirmation as a brigadier general without the approval of The Marine Corps, Admiral Leahy tells me that would have been counterproductive . . . and not only because it would have caused a lot of talk, which is exactly what Rickabee and the Office of Management Analysis does not want or need."

Jesus Christ, what bullshit! Pickering fumed. *A damned good man can't get promoted because of the prima donnas!*

"Colonel Rickabee's promotion doesn't solve the problem," Admiral Leahy said. "Which is, in rank-inflated Washington, that a general officer is needed to head up the Office of Management Analysis."

"Yes," Pickering thought out loud, "I can understand that."

"Good," Roosevelt said. "That's where you come in, Fleming."

"Sir," Pickering said, surprised, "I wouldn't have any idea whom to recommend for that. Nor would I presume to make such a recommendation."

"That's been done for you," Roosevelt said. "What Leahy and I have concluded is that the man in charge of the Office of Management Analysis should be someone who not only has experience at the upper levels of the Navy Department, say working closely with the Secretary of the Navy . . ."

Christ, he's not talking about me, is he?

". . . but who has also had firsthand experience with the war in the Pacific, and most importantly . . ."

Jesus H. Christ, he is!

". . . is a Marine with extensive combat experience, say someone who won the Distinguished Service Cross in the First World War, and who in this war has been awarded the Silver Star, the Purple Heart, and the Legion of Merit."

What's he talking about, the Legion of Merit?

"Are you beginning to get the picture, Fleming?" Roosevelt asked.

"Mr. President . . ."

Roosevelt reached to the table beside him, opened an oblong box, and took a medal on its ribbon from it.

"Captain Pickering," he said, motioning for Pickering to lean over to him. He pinned the medal to Pickering's uniform. "It is my great privilege, on the recommendation of the Commanding General, First Marine Division, to invest you with the Legion of Merit for your distinguished service as Acting G-2, First Marine Division, during combat operations on Guadalcanal."

"I don't deserve a medal for that," Pickering protested. "I was just filling in—the G-2 was killed—until they could get someone qualified in there."

"I think we can safely leave that judgment to General Vandergrift," Roosevelt said. "He made that recommendation, of course, without being aware that Admiral Leahy and I had something in mind for you."

"Mr. President, you can't really be thinking of—"

"Your name was sent to the Senate this afternoon, Fleming, for their advice and consent to your commission as Brigadier General, USMC Reserve. Now I realize that Richmond Fowler and I agree about very little, but I rather suspect that when I ask him to support your nomination, he'll come along . . . in a bipartisan gesture."

"I will be hated in The Marine Corps," Pickering said.

"Possibly," Admiral Leahy said. "But you're already hated in the Navy, so nothing is lost there. And no Marine is likely to criticize a fellow Marine with a record like yours. General Vandergrift does not hand out decorations like the Legion of Merit lightly."

The President raised his voice slightly.

"Commander Jellington!"

The glass door to the cabin slid open.

"Yes, Mr. President?"

"Commander, would you ask the other gentlemen to join us, please?"

"Yes, Mr. President."

Even though both Brigadier General D. G. McInerney, USMC, and Commander Jellington, USN, had given him an intense briefing on protocol in the presence of the President of the United States, the first of the President's other guests promptly forgot all he'd heard when he walked onto the fantail of the *Potomac* and saw Fleming Pickering with his arm in a cast.

"Jesus *Christ*, Dad!" he demanded. "What *happened* to you?"

V

[One]
FERDINAND SIX
BUKA, SOLOMON ISLANDS
4 SEPTEMBER 1942

As Sergeant Steven M. Koffler, USMC, knelt before the key of his Hallicrafters and waited for the dials to come to life, he was suffering from a severe case of the I-Feel-Sorry-for-Me syndrome.

In his judgment, with the exception of the inevitable failure of the Hallicrafters (which could happen at any time), everything that could go wrong had gone wrong.

When the officers left seven days ago to see what they could steal from the Japanese, they planned to be back in five or six days. They were now overdue. That probably meant they were not going to come back.

And that meant that the Japanese would probably be here sooner rather than later.

Although he was a uniformed member of an armed force engaged in combat against enemy armed forces and thus entitled under the Geneva Convention to treatment as a prisoner of war, Koffler was well aware that the Japanese had different views of such obligations than Americans.

Back in Townsville, to make sure that Sergeant Koffler and Lieutenant Howard really knew what they were letting themselves in for, Commander Feldt had explained the differences in some detail:

If the Japanese captured them, presuming they did not kill them outright, Koffler and Howard should hope for a Japanese officer who believed they were indeed U.S. Marines and thus entitled to treatment as fellow warriors.

That meant he'd have them executed according to the Code of Bushido: First they would dig their own graves. Then a member of the Japanese Armed Forces of equal or superior rank would behead them with a Japanese sword. Following the execution, prayers would be said over their graves, and entries would be made in official Japanese records of the date and place of their execution and burial. Presuming the records were not destroyed, that would be handy, after the war, for the disinterment of their remains and their return to the United States.

It was equally possible, Commander Feldt went on matter-of-factly, that they'd be regarded as spies and not soldiers. In that case, they'd be interrogated—read tortured—then executed in a less ritualistic manner. With a little luck they'd get a pistol bullet in the ear. More likely they'd serve as targets for bayonet practice. Of course, no record would be kept of their execution or place of burial. Thus they'd be listed officially as missing in action and presumed dead.

Later, Lieutenant Howard pointed out why Commander Feldt had gone so thoroughly into the unpleasant details: He wanted to make sure they knew how important it was for them not to get captured.

"So far as Feldt is concerned," Lieutenant Howard said, "we should have absolutely no contact with the Japs. None. But if we are captured, we should not give them any information. When the Cavalry was fighting the Apaches after the Civil War, they always saved one cartridge for themselves. The Apaches were worse than the Japs. They liked to roast their prisoners over slow fires. You understand?"

"Yes, Sir."

The dials came to life. Koffler threw the switch to TRANSMIT

and worked the key. The dots and dashes went out, repeated
three times, spelling out, simply, FRD6. FRD6. FRD6.

Detachment A of Special Marine Corps Detachment 14 is attempting to establish contact with any station on this communications network.

There was no reply. He put his hand on the key again.

FRD6. FRD6. FRD6. FRD6. FRD6. FRD6.

There was a reply:

KCY.???.KCY.???.KCY.???
This is the United States Pacific Fleet Radio Station at Pearl Harbor, Territory of Hawaii. Is there someone trying to contact me?
KCY.FRD6.KCY.FRD6.KCY.FRD6.
FRD6.KCY. FRD6.KCY URSIG 2X1.GA.
Detachment A of Special Marine Corps Detachment 14, this is the United States Pacific Fleet Radio. Your signal is weak and barely readable. Go ahead.

Fucking radio. Fucking atmospherics. Fucking sunspots.
Fuck fuck fuck.

KCY.FRD6.SB CODE.
CINCPAC Radio Pearl Harbor, stand by to copy encrypted message.
FRD6.KCY. RPT URSIG 2X1. GA.
Detachment A of Special Marine Corps Detachment 14, this is the United States Pacific Fleet Radio. Repeat, your signal is weak and barely readable. Go ahead.

After six tries, Detachment A of Special Marine Corps Detachment 14 was able to relay to the United States Pacific Fleet headquarters in Pearl Harbor that an enemy bomber force of twenty Betty bombers, escorted by an estimated thirty Zero fighters, had passed overhead at an approximate altitude of 13,000 feet on a course that would take them to Guadalcanal.

FRD6.KCY. AKN. CLR.
*Detachment A, this is Pearl Harbor. Your trans-
mission is acknowledged. Pearl Harbor Clear.*
KCY. FRD6. FU2 AND GOOD AFTERNOON. FRD6.CLR.

FU was not in the list of authorized abbreviations, but it was
not difficult for the United States Pacific Fleet operator in Pearl
Harbor to make the translation; every radio operator knew
what it meant. He had just been told to attempt a physiologi-
cally impossible act of self-impregnation. Since regulations did
not permit the transmission of personal messages and/or greet-
ings, the Pearl Harbor operator concluded that wherever
FRD6 was, and whoever he was, he had really stuck his neck
out by getting drunk on duty.

[Two]
FOSTER LAFAYETTE HOTEL
WASHINGTON, D.C.
1525 HOURS 4 SEPTEMBER 1942

Because Fleming Pickering ate lunch late that afternoon, when
there was a knock at Senator Fowler's door, he thought it was
the floor waiter come to remove the remnants of the tray of
hors d'oeuvres they had sent him from the Grill Room.

But it wasn't the floor waiter, it was the concierge. He was
helping a mousy-looking little man carry two large stacks of
cardboard boxes. Each box bore the corporate insignia of
Brooks Brothers.

He knew what they were.

"Put them in that bedroom, please," he said, pointing.

When he signed the receipt the mousy-looking man handed
him, he said, "Please tell Mr. Abraham that I'm grateful for the
quick service. And for sending you down here personally."

"Our pleasure, Captain Pickering," the mousy little man
said. "You told Mr. Abraham, 'as soon as possible.' And I had
a nice lunch on the train."

Once they were gone, Pickering looked at the boxes now
neatly stacked on the bed and the chest of drawers, shook his
head, exhaled audibly, and went back into the sitting room.

Yesterday afternoon, after Pick and Jack Stecker's boy left,
Dr. Selleres got him to the office of an orthopedic surgeon.

Selleres' pretext was to make a more comfortable cast for
Pickering's arm. But his actual motive was to have the arm
X-rayed—which was done. Then it was placed in a much less
substantial cast than the Navy had given him at San Diego.

Though Pickering had been reluctant to go, he was now
pleased that he did. For one thing, Selleres got on the phone
afterward and assured Patricia that her husband's arm was well
on the way to recovery . . . and not about to fall off or develop
gangrene. But more important, he could now put his arm
through a shirtsleeve.

Pickering, who was wearing a light seersucker robe, boxer
shorts, and a pair of the Foster Lafayette's throwaway cotton
shower slippers, went back to the leisurely postprandial rest
that the man from Brooks Brothers had interrupted. He
poured himself another cup of black coffee—the last the silver
pitcher held—sat down on the couch, put his feet up on the
coffee table, and picked up *The New York Times*.

There came another knock at the door.

That has *to be the floor waiter.*

"Come in."

He heard the door open and sensed movement in the room,
but no one appeared to roll the room service cart away.

"Get me another pot of coffee, would you, please? I won't
need any sugar or cream."

"General Pickering, I'm Captain Sessions, Sir, from Management Analysis."

Pickering looked over his shoulder. A tall, well-set-up young
man was standing in the open door. His black hair was styled
in a crew cut, and he was wearing a well-fitting, if sweat-
dampened, green elastique summer uniform. He carried a
heavily stuffed leather briefcase and a newspaper.

"I thought you were the floor waiter," Pickering said.
"Come in, please." Then he blurted what he was thinking:
"That's the first time anyone has called me that. 'General.' "

"Then I'm honored, General."

"I'm about to order some coffee. Can I get you anything?"

"Would iced tea be possible?"

"How about a cold beer, Captain? That's what I really
want."

"A general officer's desire is a captain's command, Sir."

Pickering chuckled.

Nice kid. He's not much older than Pick.

Pickering picked up the telephone. "This is Captain—strike that—*General* Pickering. Would you send the floor waiter to clear things away, please? And have him put a half dozen bottles of Feigenspan ale in a wine cooler with some ice." He stopped. "That all right? Feigenspan?"

"Just fine, Sir."

"Thank you," Pickering said to the telephone and hung it up. "What can I do for you, Captain?"

"Colonel Rickabee's compliments, Sir. He asked me to express his regrets for not coming here himself. He's playing golf with the Deputy Commandant."

Playing golf? Jesus Christ!

"War is hell, isn't it, Captain?"

"General, with respect, Colonel Rickabee regularly meets with the Commandant; or if the Commandant is not available, with the Deputy Commandant. The back nine holes at the Army & Navy Country Club is a fine place to hold a confidential conversation."

"My mouth ran away with me," Pickering said. "Sorry."

"I can understand why it sounded a bit odd, General."

"We're back to, 'what can I do for you, Captain?' "

"There's a good deal of paperwork to be signed, General—"

"I'll bet," Pickering interrupted.

Sessions smiled, and then went on, "—but first things first. Has the General seen *The Washington Star*?"

Pickering shook his head and reached for the newspaper Sessions extended to him.

"It's on the lower right-hand corner of the second section, General."

Pickering found what Sessions thought he should see:

SHIPPING MAGNATE ENTERS MARINE CORPS

Washington Sept 3 — The White House this afternoon announced that it had been advised by the Senate of its consent to the appointment of Fleming Pickering as Brigadier General, USMC Reserve.

Presidential Press Secretary Stephen Early said that Pickering, an old and close friend of the President, will head the Marine Corps Office of Management Analysis, which has responsibility for increasing efficiency of Marine Corps' supply acquisition and distribution.

Pickering, who before the war was Chairman of the Board of Pacific & Far East Shipping Corporation, has been serving as a temporary Captain, U.S. Navy Reserve, and only recently returned from the Pacific, where he was a Special Representative of Navy Secretary Frank Knox on logistics matters.

"Both the President and Secretary Knox felt that Pickering would be more effective as a Marine officer," Press Secretary Early reported. "He brings to his new duties not only his extensive shipping experience, but those of his previous service as a Marine."

He said that Pickering was three times wounded and earned the Distinguished Service Cross and the Croix de Guerre as a Marine in France in World War I.

"And like the President," Early added, "he has a son in The Marine Corps." Captain James Roosevelt participated in the recent Marine Corps raid on Makin Island. Second Lieutenant Malcolm S. Pickering recently completed training as a Marine Corps fighter pilot and is believed en route to the Pacific.

Pickering will assume his new duties, according to Early, "just as soon as he can get into uniform."

"Not that I am one to believe much that I read in any newspaper," Pickering said, "but this really strays from the truth, the whole truth, and nothing but, doesn't it?"

"Actually, we were very pleased with it, General."

"We? Who's we?"

"Colonel Rickabee and me, Sir. He saw it first and told me to get a copy before I came over here."

"Just for openers, I am not an old and close friend of Mr. Roosevelt."

"And the Office of Management Analysis does not, as you know, Sir, have anything to do with logistics," Sessions said, smiling. "But it is almost always to our advantage if people have the wrong idea. And, General, with respect, there are people in this town who would kill to have *The Star* report that they are old and close friends of Mr. Roosevelt."

Pickering considered that and chuckled.

"I'm sure you're right, Captain," he said. "You're an interesting young man. What's your background? How'd you get involved . . . in your line of work?"

Before he could reply, there was another knock at the door.

"May I, Sir?" Sessions asked.

He went to the door and opened it. The floor waiter and a busboy came in, wheeled the floor service tray out, and left behind a tray of pilsener glasses and two silver champagne buckets, each holding three bottles of ale buried in ice.

"Help yourself," Pickering said, "there's an opener on the bar."

"This is very nice," Sessions said, indicating the champagne buckets.

"They are very nice to me here, probably because my wife's father owns the place."

"Yes, Sir, I know," Sessions said, opening a bottle of ale and handing it to Pickering. He glanced at Pickering as he spoke and saw coldness in his eyes.

"General, we have to know all there is to know about our people. That applies to everybody."

"I'm sure," Pickering said. "You were telling me how you got into this?"

"I served in China, Sir. With then Captain Ed Banning."

"You know Ed Banning?"

"I'm privileged to be his friend, Sir."

"That speaks highly of you, Captain."

"Sir, this may be a little out of line, but I think I should return the compliment. Ed Banning thinks the world of you."

"Two questions at a tangent, Captain?"

"Yes, Sir?"

"What about our two people on Buka? You know about them?"

"Yes, Sir. They're still there. Banning is trying to figure out a way to relieve them."

Pickering nodded. "I said two questions. I meant three. Number two: When you were in China, did you happen to meet a young man, a corporal, named McCoy?"

Sessions smiled. "Sir, I am happy to report that I am the man, over his bitter objections, who sent the Killer to Officer Candidate School."

"He went to OCS with my son. But I guess you know that."

"Yes, Sir."

"Do you happen to know where McCoy is? The reason I ask—"

"Sir, the Killer's one of us—"

"I suppose I should have guessed that," Pickering said.

"He's on convalescent leave, Sir."

"He was wounded?" Pickering asked, concern in his voice.

"On the Makin raid. But not seriously. The Colonel thought he was entitled to the full thirty days of convalescent leave. He ordered him to take it."

"Question three: Sergeant John Marston Moore?"

"Philadelphia Naval Hospital, Sir. He took some pretty bad shrapnel wounds on Guadalcanal."

"Is he going to be all right?"

"He'll be on limited duty for a while, Sir. But he will be all right."

"What else do you know about Moore?" Pickering asked innocently. But Sessions knew the question behind the question. He decided to answer it fully.

"He's privy to MAGIC, Sir. You authorized that clearance."

"And didn't tell anybody. Which is why he was sent to Guadalcanal, why he's in the hospital."

"Yes, Sir. I'm familiar with the details."

"You're apparently on the MAGIC list?"

"Yes, Sir. Colonel Rickabee and I both, Sir."

"Not McCoy?"

"No, Sir. Lieutenant McCoy does not have the Need to Know, Sir."

"I appreciate your candor in answering these questions, Captain."

"General, you're the boss."

"Two parts to that statement," Pickering said, "both of which I'm having difficulty accepting."

"Well, then, Sir, why don't we make it official?"

"I beg your pardon?"

"One of the things the General has to do to become a general, General, is sign his resignation from the Navy and his acceptance of his commission as a Marine general. Plus no more than four or five hundred other forms, all of which I just happen to have with me, all neatly typed up."

Smiling, he held up the briefcase.

"I even have two spare fountain pens," Sessions went on, "and these." He took from the briefcase two pieces of metal, each the size of a license plate. They were painted red and had a silver star fastened to their centers.

"What's that?" Pickering asked, even as he belatedly recognized the plates for what they were.

"That is what brigadier generals mount on their automobiles, fore and aft. I also drew your General's Flag, and the National Colors from Eighth and Eye before I came over here. But I left those in the car." Headquarters, United States Marine Corps, is at Eighth and I streets, in the District of Columbia.

"What am I supposed to do with a General's Flag?"

"It will be placed in your office, General, which at this very moment is being equipped with the appropriate furniture."

"And who got thrown out of his office so I could have one?"

"A Colonel LaRue, Sir," Sessions replied immediately. "The Colonel is the Marine representative to the Inter-Service Morale and Recreation Council. He was, Sir, very much aware that he was the senior officer in our little building. I don't think Colonel Rickabee was heartbroken when he had to tell him that we required his office space for our General, General."

"Oh, Christ," Pickering said, shaking his head.

"We'll still be pretty much sitting in each other's laps, Sir, but at least there will be nobody in the building but us from now on."

"Well, that's something, I suppose."

"Sir, Colonel Rickabee suggested that we drive down to Quantico this afternoon if you feel up to it."

"Oh? Why?"

"Uniforms, Sir. Colonel Rickabee said to tell you that the

concessionaire there, a fellow named A. M. Bolognese, not only has very good prices, but is an old friend of his. He could probably turn out some uniforms for you in a couple of days."

Pickering gestured toward the bedroom.

"They just arrived. I called Brooks Brothers and they sent a man down on the train with them."

Sessions laughed. "Major Banning said that was the way you were, Sir. By the time he thought of something, you'd done it."

"I wish I'd known about this man with the good prices. I hate to think of the bill I'm going to get from Brooks Brothers."

"What exactly did you order, Sir?"

"I told them to send me whatever I would need."

"General, while you're signing all this stuff, why don't I take a look at it?"

"Somebody who knows what he's doing should," Pickering said. "Thank you."

"You'll find a little red pencil check mark every place you're to sign your name, General," Sessions said, going to a desk and unloading the briefcase. "Everything is in at least four copies, all of which have to be signed."

"What if I had broken my right arm?"

"Then you would make a mark, Sir, and I would sign everything, swearing that was your mark."

Pickering laughed.

"OK, Captain," he said and walked to the table and sat down.

Sessions uncapped a fountain pen and handed it to him. "If you run out of ink, Sir, there's a spare pen."

"You think two is going to be enough?"

"With a little luck, Sir."

By the time he'd taken the documents from one stack, signed his name in the places marked, and put them on a second stack, Pickering had concluded that Sessions was not exaggerating about how many there were. His fingers were stiff from holding the pen.

He got up and walked into the bedroom. The cardboard boxes had been opened, emptied, and piled by the door. An incredible amount of clothing was now spread out on the bed. And still more clothing was hanging from doorknobs and the drawer pulls of the two chests of drawers.

Sessions, who was bent over the bed, pinning insignia to an elastique tunic, looked over his shoulder at Pickering.

"They took you at your word, Sir. There's everything here but mess dress."

"Is mess dress expensive?"

"Yes, Sir. Very expensive."

"Then it was a simple oversight which Brooks Brothers will remedy as soon as humanly possible."

"The only thing we don't know is whether or not it will fit you, Sir."

"It should. I've been buying clothing there since I was in college."

Sessions handed him a shirt.

"There's only one way to know for sure, General."

Three minutes later, Flem Pickering was examining Brigadier General Fleming Pickering, USMCR, in the full-length mirror on the bathroom door.

I feel like one of the dummies in the Brooks Brothers windows. I may be wearing this thing, but I am not, and there is no way I could be, a Marine general.

That Navy captain business was bad enough, but at least I have the right to wear those four gold stripes. I am an any-ocean, any-tonnage master mariner, entitled to wear the four stripes of a captain.

This is different.

"That fits perfectly," Sessions said. "Let's see about the cover."

He handed him a uniform cap. The entwined golden oak leaves decorating its brim—universally called "scrambled eggs"—identified the wearer as a general officer.

Pickering put it on and examined himself again.

The hat makes me look even more like a Brooks Brothers dummy.

"Looks fine, Sir," Sessions said.

"Looks *fraudulent,* Captain," Pickering said.

There was another knock at the door.

"Shall I get that, General?"

"Please," Pickering said. "Thank you."

He turned from the mirror and started gathering up the other uniforms on hangers and putting them into closets. Then he went back to the mirror and looked at himself again.

"Good afternoon, General," a strange voice said. "I'm Colonel Rickabee."

Pickering turned. A tall, thin, sharp-featured man was standing in the door to the bedroom. He was wearing a baggy, sweat-soaked seersucker suit and a battered straw snap-brim hat. In one hand he carried a well-stuffed briefcase identical to Sessions', and in the other he held a long, thin package wrapped in brown waterproof paper.

"I'm very happy to meet you, Colonel," Pickering said. "But I'm afraid I have to begin this conversation with the announcement that I feel like a fraud standing before you in a Marine general's uniform."

Rickabee met his eyes for a moment and then walked into the room. He put the briefcase on the floor and the long, thin package on the bed. He took a penknife from his pocket and slit the package open.

He pushed the paper away from a Springfield Model 1903 .30-06 caliber rifle, picked it up, and handed it to Pickering.

"The General inadvertently left this behind when he checked out of the hospital, Sir. I took the liberty of having it sent here, Sir."

Pickering took the rifle, and then (in Pavlovian fashion) worked the action to make sure it was unloaded. After that he raised his eyes to Rickabee.

"Thank you, Colonel," he said. "It means a good deal to me."

"I thought it would, General," Rickabee said. "That's almost certainly the only Springfield in the United States which has seen service on Guadalcanal."

Pickering met his eyes again and after a moment said, "General Vandergrift told me to take it with me. When they ordered me off the island."

"Yes, Sir. So I understand. May I say something, General?"

Pickering nodded.

"If General Vandergrift and Major Jack Stecker both think of you as a pretty good Marine, Sir, I don't think you should question their judgment."

It was a long time before Pickering spoke. Finally he said, "Funny, Colonel, I have been led to believe—by the President, by the way—that you have an abrasive personality. That wasn't abrasive, that was more than gracious."

Rickabee met his eyes for a moment and then changed the subject.

"I see the General has dealt with the uniform problem."

"Before I knew about the man at Quantico with the good prices."

"Well, at least you're in the correct uniform for me to welcome you back into The Corps."

"Thank you," Pickering said. "I was just wondering what to do with my Navy uniforms. Send them home, I guess. Or find somebody who can use them."

"Thank you, Sir," Rickabee said. "We accept."

"You know someone who can use them?"

"Down the line, I'm sure, they can be put to good use," Rickabee said.

"I see," Pickering said, shaking his head. "OK. They're yours."

"Sessions has told the General, I hope, that we're setting up an office for him?"

Pickering nodded.

"There has been a slight delay. The former occupant squealed like a stuck pig and complained to everybody he could think of," Rickabee said with obvious delight. "He lost his last appeal and has been ordered to clear out by noon tomorrow. If the General has some reason to come into the office tomorrow, we will of course make room for him, but I would respectfully suggest that he wait one more day."

"Are you going to keep talking to me in the third person?"

"Not if the General does not wish me to."

"The General does not," Pickering said with a smile.

"Aye, aye, Sir."

"I thought that tomorrow I would go into Philadelphia to see Sergeant Moore. Is there any reason I can't do that?"

"You can go just about anywhere you want to, General," Rickabee said. He picked the briefcase up from the floor, unlocked it, opened it, and handed Pickering an envelope. "Your orders came in this morning, Sir."

Pickering opened the envelope.

THE WHITE HOUSE
Washington, D.C.

3 September 1942

Brigadier General Fleming W. Pickering, USMCR,
Headquarters, USMC, will proceed by military and/or
civilian rail, road, sea and air transportation (Priority
AAAAA-1) to such points as he deems necessary in
carrying out the mission assigned to him by the
undersigned.

United States Armed Forces commands are directed
to provide him with such support as he may request.
General Pickering is to be considered the personal
representative of the undersigned.

General Pickering has unrestricted TOP SECRET
security clearance. Any questions regarding his mission
will be directed to the undersigned.

W. D. Leahy, Admiral, USN
Chief of Staff to the President

When Pickering finished reading the orders, Rickabee said,
"They're much like your old orders, except that Leahy has
signed these."

"It sounds as if we work for Leahy."

"Sometimes we do," Rickabee said matter-of-factly. "In any
event, this should answer your question about whether or not
you can go to Philadelphia."

"It's a personal thing. That boy worked for me. If I had done
what I was supposed to do, he would never have been on
Guadalcanal."

Pickering saw in Rickabee's eyes a sign that he hadn't liked
that statement.

"OK," he said. "Let's have it."

"Nothing, Sir."

"Rickabee, if we're going to work together, I'm going to
have to know what you're thinking."

Rickabee paused long enough for Pickering to understand
that he was debating answering the challenge.

"Would you mind changing the last part of what you said to read, 'He would never have been on Guadalcanal, where he might have been captured and compromised MAGIC'?" Rickabee asked finally.

Pickering's face tightened. He was not used to having his mistakes pointed out to him. He felt Rickabee's eyes on him; they were wary and intent.

"Yes, I would," Pickering said, "but only because it reminds me of how incredibly stupid I can sometimes be. Still, consider it changed, Rickabee."

"I felt obliged to bring that up, Sir," Rickabee said. "And there is one other thing . . ."

"Let's have it."

"Ed Banning tells me you have a somewhat cavalier attitude toward classified documents."

"He never said anything to me about that!" Pickering protested.

"He and Lieutenant Hon kept a close eye on you, Sir. And just to be doubly sure, he had your quarters kept under surveillance."

Jesus, he's not making this up.

"I didn't know that."

"He didn't want you to," Rickabee said. "But we're not going to be able to do that here."

"I'll be more careful."

"General, you are authorized an aide-de-camp and an orderly. With your permission I would like to charge them with the additional responsibility of making sure that nothing important gets misplaced."

"I feel like a backward child," Pickering said.

"I don't see Japanese lurking in the bushes," Rickabee said. "Or, for that matter, Germans. J. Edgar Hoover is doing a good job with counterintelligence. But other agencies don't particularly like our little shop. They could do us a lot of damage, Sir, if they could show that our security isn't ironclad."

"Other agencies like who, for example?"

"All of them. Any of them. Maybe in particular the FBI, and Donovan's people, whatever they're calling themselves this week, and of course, ONI."—the Office of Naval Intelligence.

"In other words you're telling me the same thing is going on here that's going on in the Pacific? There are two wars? One against the Japanese and the other against ourselves?"

"Yes, Sir, I'm afraid it is."

Good Christ, I'm stupid. Why should I think things would be any different here? And he's right, of course. Bill Donovan would love nothing better than to run to Franklin Roosevelt with proof that I was endangering security, and/or behaving like a blithering idiot.

"If you feel it's necessary, Colonel, you can lock me in a sealed room at night."

"That won't be necessary, Sir. But I would like to be careful, by having your aide—"

"I don't suppose Lieutenant McCoy would be available for that, would he?"

"What I was thinking, Sir, was Sergeant Moore. We can commission him—he was in line for a commission before we sent him to Australia—and he's cleared for MAGIC."

"Yes, of course," Pickering said. "That's a good idea."

"And I'll work on the orderly/driver/clerk, whatever we finally call him. We've been recruiting people with the right backgrounds. There's three or four going through Parris Island right now, as a matter of fact."

"I leave myself in your hands, Rickabee," Pickering said. "My orders to you are to tell me what I can do to make myself both useful and harmless."

Rickabee looked into his eyes for a moment and then smiled.

"As far as useful, Sir—was that Feigenspan ale I saw in the cooler in the other room?"

[Three]
THE 21 CLUB
21 WEST 52ND STREET
NEW YORK CITY, NEW YORK
5 SEPTEMBER 1942

Ernest J. Sage stepped out of a taxi and rather absently handed the driver a five-dollar bill.

"Keep it," he said.

Ernest Sage was forty-eight years old, superbly tailored, slightly built, and very intense. His hair was slicked back with Vitahair because he liked it that way, and not because it was the number-three product in gross sales of American Personal Pharmaceuticals, Inc., of which he was Chairman of the Board and President.

"Good afternoon, Mr. Sage," the 21 Club's doorman said. After somewhat belatedly recognizing Sage, he rushed to the cab.

"Howareya?" Ernest Sage said, managing a two-second smile as he walked quickly across the sidewalk and down the shallow flight of stairs behind the wrought-iron grillwork.

Ernest Sage was late for an appointment. He disliked being late for any appointment.

The man inside the door was quicker to recognize him than the outside man had been. He had the door open and was smiling by the time Sage reached it.

"Good afternoon, Mr. Sage," he said, with what looked like a warm, welcoming smile.

"Howareya?" Ernest Sage replied. "I'm late. Has anyone been asking for me?"

"No, Sir, Mr. Sage."

"I'll be in the bar."

"Yes, Sir, Mr. Sage. I'll take care of it."

He made his way to the bar. At its far end was the man Ernest Sage was meeting. He was sitting on a barstool with his back against the wall . . . on a *very special and particular* barstool. This one was reserved by almost sacred custom for humorist Robert Benchley, or in his absence for another of a small group of 21 Club regulars—newspaper columnists, actors, producers, or a select few businessmen who'd earned the favor of the Kriendler family, the owners of 21.

The individual sitting there now was not famous or even well known. But he had obviously earned the approval of the Kriendler family. As evidence of that, a smiling Al Kriendler was in the process of handing him a drink.

Sage remembered hearing that Bob Kriendler was about to go in The Marine Corps. Perhaps he was already in . . .

Does that explain why Al's personally handing him a drink? Or is he just showing his respect to a nice-looking kid in a Marine uniform?

The young man was wearing the summer uniform prescribed for first lieutenants of The United States Marine Corps—khaki shirt, trousers, and necktie with USMC tie clasp.

"Hello, Ken," Ernest Sage said, touching his back. "Sorry to be late. The goddamned traffic is unbelievable."

"Hello, Mr. Sage," First Lieutenant Kenneth R. McCoy, USMCR, said. "No problem. I just got here."

"Oh, you know each other?" Al Kriendler said.

"For reasons that baffle me," Ernest said, "Ernie thinks the sun rises in the morning because Ken wants it to."

"Well, I would say Ernie has very good taste," Al Kriendler said.

The bartender, who was familiar with Ernest Sage's drinking habits, slid him a Manhattan with an extra shake of Angostura bitters.

Ernie Sage—properly Ernestine Sage—was Ernest Sage's only child, and Ernest Sage loved her very much. At the same time he was aware of the facts of growth and maturity. And so he had pondered the inevitability of her one day transferring her affections to a young man.

Though he'd dwelt at length on every possible Worst Case, he'd never dreamed that the reality would be as bad as it turned out. It was not that he didn't like Ken McCoy. Ken McCoy was beyond question a really fine young man.

Ernest Sage would have been happier, of course, if there had been some family in McCoy's background—some money, frankly—and if he had a little better education than Norristown, Pennsylvania's, high school offered. But such things weren't insurmountable, in his view. In fact, under other circumstances, he could have resigned himself to Ken McCoy. Ernie could have done a hell of a lot worse.

But the circumstances were that the war was not even a year old, that he saw no end to it, that Ken McCoy was already wearing three Purple Hearts and a Bronze Star for valor in combat, and that his nickname in the Marines was "Killer."

Purple Hearts and Bronze Stars and nicknames weren't in themselves hugely significant. But in Ernest Sage's mind, they added up to a significant conclusion: The chances of Ken coming through the war alive and intact ranged from slim to none.

In Worst Possible Case Number Sixty-six, for instance, Ken came home missing a leg, or blind. And Ernie was condemned to a life of caring for a cripple.

If that makes me a heartless prick, so what? I'm worried about the life my daughter will have. What's wrong with that?

The funny thing was that Ken McCoy not only understood

Sage's concerns but agreed with them. And yet Sage almost had a harder time dealing with that than if Ken had run off with her to a justice of the peace the day after he met her.

"I'm not going to marry her, Mr. Sage," Ken had told him. "Not while the war is on. I don't want to leave her a widow."

It was another reason he genuinely liked Ken McCoy.

The real problem, in fact, wasn't McCoy, it was Ernie. She had reduced the situation to basics. She was a woman in love. What women in love do is stick to their man and have babies. She didn't even much give a damn whether she was married to Ken or not—she wanted his baby.

"Look, Daddy," she had told him over lunch in the Executive Dining Room of the American Personal Pharmaceuticals Building. "If Ken does get killed, I would at least have our baby. . . . And it's not as if the baby and I would wind up on charity."

Ernest Sage had clear and definite ideas about moral values and a good moral upbringing. He had, for example, taught Sunday School classes for six goddamned years in order to set a proper example for his daughter. So it wasn't at all easy for him to go to her lover to discuss her intention to become pregnant by him. But Ernest Sage did that. He had to.

And again Ken McCoy surprised him . . . and made him uneasy—not because Ken was going to do his daughter wrong (he wasn't), but because he kept acting just exactly the way Ernest Sage himself would have acted if he had been in the boy's shoes.

"Yeah, I know she wants a kid," Ken said. "But no way. That'd be a rotten thing to do to her."

That was why Ernest Sage couldn't help liking and admiring Ken McCoy. Ken was very much like himself—a decent man with enough intelligence to see things the way they were, not through rose-colored glasses.

Goddamn this war, anyway!

"Miss Sage is here, Mr. Sage," one of the headwaiters said softly in his ear. "Your regular table be all right, Sir?"

Women were not welcome at the bar. Since they weren't actually *prohibited,* however, Ernie felt free to sit there, to hell with what people think. But whenever he could, her father tried to make her sit at a table.

"Yeah, fine," Sage said, looking toward the entrance for his daughter. She was tall and healthy looking, slender but not thin; her black hair was cut in a pageboy. She wore a simple skirt and blouse, with a strand of pearls that had belonged to her maternal grandmother.

He waved. She returned it, but there was a look of annoyance on her face when she saw the headwaiter rushing to show her to a table.

He noticed, too, that male eyes throughout the room followed her.

She stood by the table until they joined her.

"Hi, baby," Ken McCoy said.

"Is that the best you can do?" Ernie Sage asked.

"What?"

She grabbed his neatly tied necktie, pulled him to her, and kissed him on the mouth.

"Jesus Christ," he said, actually blushing when he finally got free.

"Hi, Daddy," Ernie said, smiling at him and sitting down.

When she smiled at him, he could not be angry with her.

"What may I get you, Miss Sage?" a waiter asked.

"What's good enough for The Marine Corps is good enough for me."

"Bring us all one," Ernest Sage said.

"Thank you for asking how my day was," Ernie said. "My day was fine. I was told my copy for Toothhold was 'really sexy.' I wonder what that man does behind his bedroom door if he thinks adhesive for false teeth is sexy?"

"My God, kitten!" Ernest Sage said.

Ken McCoy laughed. "Don't knock it until you try it."

"OK, darling, I'll bring some home. There's a case of it on my filing cabinet."

Ernie McCoy was a senior copywriter at the J. Walter Thompson advertising agency. Ernest Sage took a great deal of pride in knowing that she had the job on her own merits and not because American Personal Pharmaceuticals billed an annual $12.1 million at JWT.

"I learned something interesting today," Ernest Sage said, "which I saved until we could all be together."

"What's that?" Ernie asked.

"There was a story in the *Times* that Fleming Pickering has gone into The Marines. As a general."

"I thought he was a captain in the Navy," Ernie said, looking at McCoy for an explanation.

"I know," McCoy said. "He called me today."

I'll be goddamned, Ernest Sage thought. *He didn't call me. I haven't heard from the sonofabitch since the war started, and we have been friends since before our kids were born. And if he called Ken McCoy, that means he called him at Ernie's apartment, which means he knows they're living together. Well, why the hell should that surprise me? Flem arranged for that boat they were shacked up in at the San Diego Yacht Club. Goddamn him for that, too.*

It had been a longtime, pleasant, and not entirely unreasonable fantasy on the part of Mr. and Mrs. Ernest Sage and Captain and Mrs. Fleming Pickering (the ladies had been roommates at college) that one day Ernestine Sage and Malcolm S. Pickering would find themselves impaled on Cupid's arrow, marry, and make them all happy grandparents.

Instead, Pick Pickering joined the Marines, made a buddy out of Ken McCoy when they were in Officer Candidate School, and took him to New York on a short leave. Pick moved into one of the suites in the Foster Park and passed word around New York that he was in town and having a nonstop party over the weekend. Ernie Sage went to the party and bumped into Ken McCoy. End of longtime, pleasant, and not entirely unreasonable fantasy. Start of unending nightmare. As soon as Ernie saw Ken, she knew he was the man in her life. With that as a given, there was absolutely no reason not to go to bed with him four hours after they met.

"I *waited,* Daddy," Ernie said. "Until I was sure. I'm *sure.*"

If it wasn't for my goddamned father, Ernest Sage often thought, *I could at least threaten to cut her off without a dime.*

When Ernie was four, Grandfather Sage set up a trust fund for the adorable little tyke, funding it with 5 percent of his shares (giving her 2.5 percent of the total) of American Personal Pharmaceuticals, Inc. Control of this trust was to be passed to her on her graduation from college, her marriage, or on attaining her twenty-fifth year, whichever occurred first. Ernie had graduated Summa Cum Laude from college at twenty.

"Oh?" Ernest Sage asked.

"What did he want?"

"Well . . . I'm sorry about this. It's orders. I can't go to Bernardsville with you this weekend."

"Why not?"

"I've got to go to Philadelphia and then to Parris Island."

"You're on leave, hospital *recuperative* leave," Ernie said angrily. "You're supposed to have thirty days!"

"Come on, baby, I was only dinged," McCoy said.

Yeah, Ernest Sage thought, *and if whatever it was that dinged you in the forehead had dinged you an inch deeper, you'd be dead. They don't hand out Purple Hearts for dings.*

"What are you going to do in Philadelphia?" Ernie asked.

She doesn't argue with him. She'll argue with her mother and me till the cows come home. He tells her something and that's it.

"A guy's in the hospital there I have to see," McCoy began, then interrupted himself. "You know him, baby, as a matter of fact. Remember that kid who we put up on the boat? Moore? On his way to Australia?"

"Yes," Ernie said, remembering. "What's he doing in Philadelphia? *In the hospital* in Philadelphia?"

"He got hurt on Guadalcanal," McCoy said.

"Oh, God!" Ernie said. "Was he badly hurt?"

"Bad enough to get sent home."

"I thought he was going to *Australia!*" Ernie said, making it an accusation.

"Until this morning I thought he was in Australia," McCoy said.

"Why are they sending you to see him?"

"They're going to commission him," McCoy said. "Pickering was going there to swear him in, but it turns out he has an infection and they won't let him travel."

"An infection?" Ernest Sage asked.

McCoy nodded. "He says it's not serious, but—"

"Patricia told your mother," Sage said to Ernie, "that Flem just walked out of the hospital in California. Before he was discharged, I mean. He's a damned fool."

"Daddy!"

"Well, he is," Sage insisted, and then thought of something else. "What do you have to do with him, Ken?"

"He's now my boss," Ken said.

"I still don't understand why you have to go to Philadelphia," Ernie said.

"I told you. Moore's getting commissioned. I'm going to swear him in, take care of the paperwork."

"I want to go," Ernie said.

McCoy considered that a moment.

"If he's in the hospital, I want to see him," Ernie went on.

"From Philadelphia, I'm going to Parris Island," McCoy said.

"For how long?"

"Couple of days. I'm driving."

"Any reason I can't go?"

"Yes, there is."

"Well, I can at least go to Philadelphia."

"All I'm going to do is swear him in, handle the paperwork, and then head for Parris Island."

"Today's Friday. Tomorrow's Saturday. We could have all day in Philadelphia, and then you could drive to Parris Island on Sunday," Ernie said reasonably.

He shrugged, giving in.

"Your mother will be disappointed," Ernest Sage said. "And where would you stay in Philadelphia?"

"I don't know. The Warwick, the Bellvue-Stratford . . ."

"You're not married, you can't stay in a hotel together," Ernest Sage blurted.

"Talk to Ken about us not being married," Ernie said. *"I'm* not the one being difficult on that subject."

"Jesus, baby! We've been over that already!"

"What we're going to do, Daddy, is spend the night in Bernardsville and drive to Philadelphia in the morning. Why don't you call Mother and ask her to meet us somewhere for dinner? The Brook, maybe, or Baltusrol?"

There is absolutely nothing I can do but smile and agree, Ernest Sage decided. *If I raise any further objections, she won't go to Bernardsville at all.*

"Baltusrol," he said. "They do a very nice English grill on Friday nights."

He raised his hand, caught the headwaiter's attention, and put his balled fist to his ear, miming his need for a telephone.

As he waited for the telephone, he had a pleasant thought: *What did he say? That Fleming Pickering is now his boss? Jesus, maybe they'll give him a desk job.* But an unpleasant thought immediately replaced it: *Bullshit! Flem Pickering was supposed to be working for the Secretary of the Navy, which any reasonable person would think meant shuffling paper in Washington, and the next thing we hear is that he got all shot up and earned the Silver Star, taking command of some goddamn* destroyer *when the captain was killed.*

He looked at his daughter. She was feeding Ken McCoy a bacon-wrapped oyster. If he'd been an angel, her look couldn't have been more transfixed.

All I want for you, kitten, is your happiness.

"Elaine," he said a minute later to the telephone, "we're in Jack and Charley's, and what Ernie wants us to do is have supper at Baltusrol.

"Yes, I know you've made plans for the weekend, but something has come up.

"Elaine, for Christ's sake, just get in the goddamn car and go to Baltusrol. We'll see you there in an hour."

"You want an oyster, Daddy?"

"Yes, thank you, kitten."

VI

Both Gunnery Sergeant Ernest W. Zimmerman and Sergeant Thomas McCoy were considerably relieved when the R4D made contact again with the earth's surface. It was Gunny Zimmerman's third and Sergeant McCoy's second flight in a heavier-than-air vehicle. Though these previous experiences had a happy outcome (they survived them), that success did not relieve their current anxieties. In fact, if they'd had a say in the matter, both would have traveled by ship from Hawaii to wherever The Corps was sending them.

They were not given a choice. Their orders directed them to proceed by the most expeditious means, including air; and a AAA priority had been authorized.

They flew from Pearl Harbor to Espiritu Santo aboard a Martin PBM-3R Mariner, the unarmed transport version of the amphibious, twin-engine patrol bomber. Flight in the Mariner was bad enough, both of them privately considered during

135

the long flight from Pearl, but if something went wrong with an amphibian like that—should the engines stop, for example—at least it could land on the water and float around until somebody came to help them.

The flight from Espiritu Santo in the R4D was something else. It was a land plane. If they went down in the ocean it would sink, very likely before they could inflate the rubber rafts crated near the rear door.

During the flight they were warm, though not uncomfortably so. But by the time the R4D completed its landing roll and taxied to the parking ramp, they were covered with sweat, and wet patches were under their arms and down the backs of their utility jackets.

The crew chief came down the fuselage past the crates of supplies lashed to the floor and the bags of mail scattered around, and pushed open the door.

By the time Zimmerman and McCoy stood up, a truck was backed up to the door. That meant they had to climb onto the bed of the truck before they could get to the ground. The Marine labor detail on the truck bed unloading the cargo were mostly bare-chested, wearing only utility trousers and boondockers. They were tanned and sweaty.

The sergeant in charge of the detail told Zimmerman where he could find the office of MAG-21. They put their seabags onto their shoulders and started to walk across the field.

The office turned out to be two connected eight-man squad tents, with their sides rolled up. The tents were surrounded by a wall of sandbags.

A corporal sat on a folding chair at a folding desk, pecking away with two fingers on a Royal portable typewriter. When Zimmerman walked into the tent, he saw another kid, bare-chested, asleep on a cot.

"Can I help you, Gunny?" the corporal asked.

"Reporting in," Zimmerman said, and handed over their orders. The corporal read the orders and then looked at Zimmerman.

"Sergeant Oblensky around?" Zimmerman asked.

The corporal ignored him.

"Lieutenant?" the corporal called.

The blond-headed kid on the cot raised himself on his elbows, shook his head, and then looked around the tent, finally focusing his eyes on Zimmerman.

"Do something for you, Gunny?" he asked.

Jesus, he's an officer. He don't look old enough to have hair on his balls.

"Zimmerman, Sir. Gunnery Sergeant Ernest W. Reporting in with one man."

"My name is Dunn," the kid said. "I'm the OD. Welcome aboard. Now, where the hell did you come from?" He looked at the corporal. "Those the orders?"

"Yes, Sir," the corporal said and handed them to him.

He read them and then looked up. "MacNeil," he asked, "where's the skipper?"

"On the flight line, Sir. Him and the exec, both."

"See if you can find him," Dunn ordered. "Or the exec. One or the other."

"Aye, aye, Sir."

"I don't understand your orders," Dunn said to Zimmerman. "A transfer from the 2nd Raider Battalion to an air group seems odd, even in The Marine Corps."

"Yes, Sir," Zimmerman agreed.

Lieutenant Colonel Clyde W. Dawkins, a tall, thin, sharp-featured man in his thirties, appeared a few minutes later, trailed by Captain Charles M. Galloway. Both were wearing sweat-darkened cotton flying suits. Dawkins also wore a fore-and-aft cap and a Smith & Wesson .38 Special revolver in a shoulder holster, while Galloway had on a utility cap that looked three sizes too small for him, and a .45 Colt automatic hung from a web pistol belt.

Zimmerman and McCoy popped to attention. Dawkins looked at them and smiled.

"Stand at ease, Gunny," he said, and then asked Dunn, "Where's MacNeil?"

"I sent him to look for you, Sir. These two just reported in." He handed Dawkins the orders.

Dawkins read them and made very much the same observation Dunn had: "I don't understand this. A transfer from the 2nd Raider Battalion to the 21st MAG?"

He handed the orders to Galloway and looked quizzically at Zimmerman.

"It wasn't my idea, Colonel," Sergeant McCoy volunteered. "I didn't ask to come to no fucking air group!"

"Shut your mouth!" Zimmerman said as Galloway opened his mouth to offer a similar suggestion.

Colonel Dawkins coughed.

"We've met, haven't we, Gunny?" Galloway said to Zimmerman.

"Yes, Sir. I went down to fix your Brownings when you was at Ewa."

"I thought that was you," Galloway said. "Oblensky at work, Colonel."

"Oh?"

"The gunny was good enough, in exchange for a portable generator, to make our Brownings work. I remember Oblensky saying at the time, 'We need him more than the Raiders do.' "

"Oh," Dawkins said. "And was Sergeant Oblensky right, would you say, Captain Galloway?"

"I think Sergeant Oblensky has managed to convince somebody that we need him, both of them, more than the Raiders, Sir."

"Persuasive fellow, Sergeant Oblensky," Dawkins said. "I wondered what happened to that generator. One moment it was there, and the next, it had vanished into thin air."

"On the other hand, Colonel, the gunny here, and his right-hand man, I guess, did make those machine guns work."

"That's a Jesuitical argument, Captain, that the end justifies the means," Dawkins said, trying without much success to keep a smile off his face. He turned to Sergeant McCoy. "Did I hear you say, Sergeant, that if things were left up to you, you would not be here in the fucking air group?"

"No, Sir. I mean, I didn't ask for this, Sir."

"Well, we certainly don't want anyone in our fucking air group who doesn't want to be in our fucking air group, do we, Captain Galloway?"

"No, Sir."

"Since Sergeant Oblensky, Captain Galloway, is your man, I will leave the resolution of this situation in your very capable hands."

"Aye, aye, Sir," Galloway said.

"Might I suggest, however, that since the sergeant doesn't want to be in our fucking air group, he might be happier in the 1st Raider Battalion. Only the other day, Colonel Edson happened to mention in passing that he had certain personnel problems."

"That thought ran through my mind, Sir," Captain Galloway said.

"How about that, Sergeant?" Colonel Dawkins asked solicitously. "How you would like to go to the Raider Battalion here on Guadalcanal? The Fucking First, as they are fondly known."

"I'd like that fine, Sir," Sergeant McCoy said happily. "I'm a fucking Raider."

Colonel Dawkins was suddenly struck with another coughing fit. Motioning for Lieutenant Dunn to follow him, he quickly left the tent; and a moment later they were followed by Captain Galloway, similarly afflicted.

Colonel Dawkins was first to regain control.

" 'I didn't ask to come to no fucking air group,' " he accurately mimicked Sergeant McCoy's indignant tone, " 'I'm a fucking Raider.' "

That triggered additional laughter. Then there was just time for the three officers to hear, inside the tent, Sergeant Zimmerman's angry voice . . . "When I tell you to shut your fucking mouth, asshole, you shut your fucking mouth." . . . when another sound, the growling of a siren, filled the air.

All three of them were still smiling, however, when they ran to the revetments and strapped themselves into their Wildcats.

[Two]
ROYAL AUSTRALIAN NAVY COASTWATCHER ESTABLISHMENT
TOWNSVILLE, QUEENSLAND
6 SEPTEMBER 1942

Staff Sergeant Allan Richardson, USMC, senior staff noncommissioned officer of USMC Special Detachment 14, did not at first recognize the single deplaning passenger of the U.S. Navy R4D as a field grade officer of the USMC.

Although Sergeant Richardson was himself grossly out of the prescribed uniform—he was wearing khaki trousers, an open-necked woolen shirt, a Royal Australian Navy duffel coat, and a battered USMC campaign hat—he had been conditioned by nine years in the prewar Corps to expect Marine officers, especially field-grade Marine officers, to look like officers.

The character who stepped off the airplane was wearing soiled and torn utilities, boondockers, no cover, and he was carrying what looked to Richardson's experienced eye like a U.S. Navy Medical Corps insulated container for fresh human blood. A web belt hung cowboy-style around his waist, and two ammunition pouches and a .45 in a leather holster were suspended from it.

Richardson stared at the insulated containers until he was positive—red crosses in white squares were still visible under a thin coat of green paint—that the containers had almost certainly been stolen. By then the character was almost at Richardson's Studebaker President automobile. When Richardson looked at him, he saw for the first time that not only was USMC stenciled on the breast of the filthy utilities, but that a major's golden oakleaf was pinned to each collar point.

At that point Richardson did what all his time in the prewar Corps had conditioned him to do: He quickly rose from behind the wheel, came to attention, and saluted crisply.

"Good afternoon, Sir!"

"Thank Christ, a Marine," Major Jake Dillon, USMCR, said with a vague gesture in the direction of his forehead that could only kindly be called a return of Sergeant Richardson's salute.

Dillon, a muscular, trim, tanned man in his middle thirties, opened the rear door of the Studebaker, carefully placed the ex–fresh human blood container on the seat, and closed the door.

"How may I help the Major, Sir?" Richardson asked.

"I'm here to see Major Banning," Dillon said as he walked around to the passenger side of the car and got in.

"Who, Sir?"

Richardson had heard Dillon clearly. Indeed, Major Ed Banning himself was the one who sent him to the airport when they heard the R4D overhead. But as a general operating principle, the personnel of USMC Special Detachment 14 denied any knowledge of the detachment or its personnel.

"It's all right, Sergeant. My name is Dillon. I'm a friend of Major Banning's."

When he detected a certain hesitancy on Sergeant Richardson's part, Dillon added: "For Christ's sake, do I look like a Japanese spy?"

"No, Sir," Richardson said, chuckling. "And you don't look like a candy-ass from MacArthur's headquarters, either. The Major really hates it when they show up here."

Dillon smiled.

"I'll bet," he said. "I'll also bet that you would be able to put your hands on a cold beer to save the life of an old China Marine, wouldn't you?"

"I don't have any with me in the car, Major, but I'll drive like hell to where you can get one."

"Bless you, my son," Dillon said, making the sign of the cross.

"That wasn't the regular courier plane, was it?" Richardson asked a minute or so later as he headed for the Coastwatcher Establishment. But it was really a statement rather than a question.

"No, that was a medical evacuation plane from Guadalcanal, headed for Melbourne. I asked them to drop me off."

"No cold beer on Guadalcanal?"

"No cold beer, and not much of anything else, either," Dillon said. "The goddamn Navy sailed off with most of our rations still on the transports. We've been living on what we took away from the Japs."

"Yeah, we heard about that," Richardson said.

When Major Edward F. Banning, USMC, Commanding Officer of USMC Special Detachment 14, glanced into the unit's combined mess hall and club, he saw Major Dillon sprawled in a chair at the table reserved for the unit's half-dozen officers. He was working on his second bottle of beer.

Sergeant Richardson, smiling, holding a bottle of beer, was leaning against the wall.

When Banning walked into the room, Richardson pushed himself off the wall and looked a little uncomfortable.

"I'm afraid to ask what you've got in the blood container, Jake," Banning said.

"There was film in it," Dillon replied. "Richardson put it in your refrigerator for me."

"What kind of film?"

"Still and 16mm. Eyemo."

"That's not what I meant."

"Of heroic Marines battling the evil forces of the Empire of Japan. With a cast of thousands. Produced and directed by yours truly. Being rushed to your neighborhood newsreel theater."

"You may find it hard to believe, looking at him, Sergeant

Richardson," Banning said, "but this scruffy, unwashed, un-
shaven officer was once famous for being the best-turned-out
Marine sergeant in the Fourth Marines."

"Don't give me a hard time, Banning," Dillon said.

"We was just talking about the Fourth, Sir," Richardson
said. "We know people, but we wasn't there at the same time."

"How are you, Jake?" Banning asked, walking to him and
shaking hands. "You look like hell."

"I was hungry, dirty, and thirsty. Now I'm just hungry and
dirty, thanks to Sergeant Richardson."

"Well, I'll feed you, but I won't give you a bath."

"You got something I can wear until I get to Melbourne? My
stuff is there."

"Sure. Utilities? Or something fancier?"

"Utilities would be fine," Dillon said.

"See what you can do, Richardson, will you?" Banning ordered. "Major Dillon will be staying in my quarters."

"Aye, aye, Sir," Richardson said. "You want to give me that
.45, Major, I'll get it cleaned for you."

Dillon hesitated, then stood up and unfastened his pistol
belt.

"Bless you again, my son," he said.

"Anytime, Major," Sergeant Richardson said with a smile
and then left.

Dillon looked at Banning.

"I think I better go have that bath now, while I'm still on my
feet."

"You sick, Jake, or just tired?"

"I hope to Christ I'm just tired. What you can catch on that
fucking island starts with crabs and lice and gets worse.
They've got bugs nobody ever heard of, not to mention malaria."

"If you want a *bath,*" Banning said, as he led Dillon, still
clutching his beer bottle, from the mess hall, "I'll ask Feldt. All
I have is a shower."

"Shower's fine. How *is* Commander Charming?"

"He might even be glad to see you, as a matter of fact,"
Banning said. "You didn't show up here in a dress uniform,
taking notes, and telling him how to run things."

"Speak of the devil," Dillon said as he saw Commander
Feldt coming down the corridor. He raised his voice slightly.
"Well, there's the pride of the Royal Australian Navy."

"Hello, Dillon," Feldt said, offering his hand. There was even the suggestion of a smile on his face. "How are you?"

It was not the reception Dillon expected. He wouldn't have been surprised if Feldt completely ignored him, and even less surprised if Feldt was grossly insulting and colorfully profane.

"Can't complain," Dillon said.

"You *look* like something the sodding cat dragged in."

Commander Feldt then disappeared.

Three minutes later, in Banning's room, he surprised Dillon again. The shower curtain parted and a hand holding a bottle of scotch appeared.

"Have a taste of this, Dillon," Feldt said. "It might not kill the sodding worms, but it'll give them a sodding headache."

"Bless you, my son," Dillon said.

"Sod you, Dillon," Feldt said, but there was unmistakable friendliness and warmth in his voice.

When Dillon came out of the shower, Feldt was sprawled on Banning's bed, holding the bottle of scotch on his stomach. Banning was sitting on his desk.

"So how are things on Guadalcanal?" Feldt asked.

I am probably, Dillon realized, *the first man he—or Banning, for that matter—has talked to who has been on the island.*

"What I really can't figure is why the Japs haven't gotten their act together and thrown us off," Dillon said.

Feldt grunted.

"Are those stories true about the Navy sailing away with the heavy artillery, et cetera, or are you sodding Marines just crying in your sodding beer again?"

"They're true," Dillon said. He walked naked to the bed, took the bottle from Feldt, and drank a swallow from the neck. "If it wasn't for the food the Japs left behind, the First Marine Division would be starving. And if it wasn't for the engineer equipment the Japs left behind, Henderson Field simply wouldn't exist. The fucking Navy sailed off with almost all of our engineer equipment still aboard the transports."

Feldt looked at him a moment and then swung his feet off the bed.

"Cover your sodding ugly nakedness, Dillon," he said. "I asked one of the lads to fix you a steak."

"Thank you," Dillon said.

"Just for the record, you have the ugliest, not to mention the smallest—I will not dignify it by calling it a 'penis'—pisser I have ever seen on a full-grown man."

"Sod you, Eric," Dillon said.

"But for some inexplicable reason, I am glad to see you. What are you doing here, anyway?"

"Flacking," Dillon said as he pulled an undershirt over his head.

"What in the sweet name of Jesus is 'flacking'?"

"I am a flack," Dillon replied. "What flacks do is 'flack,' hence 'flacking.'"

"What is this demented sodding compatriot of yours rambling about, Banning?"

"I'm a press agent, Eric," Dillon said. "My contribution to the war effort will be to (a) encourage red-blooded American youth to rush to the Marine recruiter and (b) shame their families, friends, and neighbors into buying war bonds. That's what flacks do."

"I don't think he's trying to pull my sodding leg, Banning, but I haven't the faintest sodding idea what he's talking about."

"Neither do I," Banning said.

"I'm on my way home with six wounded heroes, two of whom I have yet to cast," Dillon explained as he pulled utility trousers on. "Said wounded heroes will be put on display all over America, with a suitable background of flags and stirring patriotic airs."

"You don't sound very enthusiastic about it, Jake," Banning said.

"I almost got out of it," Dillon said. "I almost had Vandergrift in a corner."

Major General Alexander Archer Vandergrift, USMC, was Commanding General, First Marine Division.

"*You* almost had *Vandergrift* in a corner?" Banning asked incredulously.

"I went and asked him if I could have a company," Dillon replied and then stopped. *The alcohol is getting to me,* he thought. *I'm running off at the mouth.*

"And?" Banning pursued.

"He said, 'Thanks very much, but captains command companies and you're a major.' And I said, 'I would be happy to take a bust to captain, or for that matter back to the ranks.'"

"And?"

"He said he would think about it, and I really think he did. But then we got a fucking radio from Headquarters, USMC. The Assistant Commandant is personally interested in this fucking wounded-hero war bond tour, it seems, and he wanted to know what was holding it up. And that blew me out of the fucking water."

"It's important, Jake," Banning said, more because he felt sorry for Dillon than because he believed in the importance of war bond tours.

"Bullshit," Dillon said. "They have civilians in uniform who could do as well as I can. I'm a Marine. Or I like to think I am."

"Yours not to reason why, old sod," Feldt said, "yours but to ride into the sodding valley of the pracks."

"Flacks," Dillon corrected him automatically.

"Flacks, pracks, flicks, pricks, whatever," Feldt said cheerfully. "You about ready to eat?"

"I'm a prick of a flack, who used to be a flack for the flicks," Dillon heard himself say.

Jesus, I'm drunk!

"Actually, old sod, I would say you're a prickless prack," Feldt said. And then he laughed. It was the first time Dillon could remember hearing him laugh.

The steak was not a New York Strip, charred on the outside and pink in the middle. It was thin, fried to death, and (to put a good face on it) chewy. But it covered the plate.

And it was the first fresh meat Jake had in his mouth for six weeks. He ate all of it with relish.

"Jesus, that was good!"

"Another, old sod?" Feldt asked.

"No, thanks."

"You haven't told us what you're doing here, Jake," Banning said.

"Well, I'm on my way home. I thought maybe you'd want me to call your wife—"

Dillon stopped abruptly.

Too late, Dillon remembered that Mrs. Edward F. Banning did not get out of Shanghai before the Japanese came. She was a White Russian refugee whom Banning had married just before the Fourth Marines were transferred from Shanghai to the Philippines.

You're an asshole, Dillon, and don't blame it on the booze.

"—Shit! Ed, I'm sorry!" he went on, regret in his voice. "That just slipped out."

"Forget it," Banning said evenly.

"Or get you something in the States," Dillon went on somewhat lamely.

"Send us Pickering back," Feldt said. "If you want to do something useful."

"Amen," Banning said, as if anxious to get off the subject of Mrs. Edward F. Banning. "The minute he left, the assholes in MacArthur's headquarters held a party, and then they started working on us."

"That figures," Dillon said. "I'll make a point to see him, talk to him."

"I don't think it will do any good," Banning said.

"I don't know. It sodding well can't do any sodding harm," Feldt said. "That *would* be a service, old sod."

"Consider it done," Dillon said. "He still works for Frank Knox. Hot radios from the Secretary of the Navy often work miracles. Is there anything in particular?"

"Ask him to get that sodding asshole Willoughby off our back," Feldt said.

Newly promoted Brigadier General Charles A. Willoughby, USA, was MacArthur's intelligence officer. He was one of the "Bataan Gang," i.e., the men who escaped by PT Boat with MacArthur from the Philippines.

"Since he is the theater intelligence officer," Banning said, "Willoughby feels that all intelligence activities should come under him. In his shoes I would probably feel the same way. But it really isn't Willoughby who's the problem so much as the people he has working for him."

"Willoughby," Feldt insisted, "is a sodding asshole, and so are the people working for him."

"They want us to route our intelligence through SWPOA," Banning said. (MacArthur's official title was Supreme Commander, *S*outh *W*est *P*acific *O*cean *A*reas.)

"So Willoughby can look important," Feldt said.

"Do you?"

"Yes and no," Banning said. "When possible, the Coastwatchers communicate with CINCPAC Radio directly. We monitor everything, of course. So if our people can't get through to them, we relay to CINCPAC. If that happens, we send a copy to SWPOA." (CINCPAC: Commander in Chief, Pacific, the Navy's headquarters at Pearl Harbor.)

"Willoughby wants our people to communicate with SWPOA, and he'll pass it on to CINCPAC," Feldt said. "We have been ignoring the asshole, of course."

"So far successfully," Banning said. "But, oh how we miss Captain Pickering. He could get Willoughby off our back."

"Speaking of 'our people,'" Dillon said, remembering the two boys on Buka. *It was one thing,* he thought, *to have your ass in the line of fire in a line company on Guadalcanal—having your ass in the line of fire was what being a Marine was really all about—and something entirely different to be one of two Marines on an enemy-held island with no chance of being relieved.*

"Good lads," Feldt said. "Every time I want to say something unpleasant about you sodding Marines, I remind myself there is an exception to the rule."

"So far they're all right, Jake," Banning said. "All right being defined as the Japs haven't caught them yet. Buka, right now, is probably the most important station."

"How are they?" Dillon asked. When neither Feldt nor Banning immediately replied, he went on: "I'm headed for the Fourth General Hospital. Barbara's there. She'll ask me about Joe."

"Lie to her," Feldt said. "That would be kindest."

Lieutenant (J.G.) Barbara T. Cotter, NNCR, was engaged to First Lieutenant Joseph L. Howard, USMCR, who was now on Buka with Sergeant Steven M. Koffler.

"Why are you going to the Fourth General?" Banning asked.

"I have four wounded heroes; I need two more. I'm going to hold an audition at the hospital to fill the cast. Don't change the subject. Tell me about Joe and Koffler. I don't want to lie to Barbara."

"They are on the edge of starvation," Feldt said. "They are almost certainly infested with a wide variety of intestinal parasites. The odds are ten to one they have malaria, and probably two or three other tropical diseases. They have no medicine. For that matter they don't even have salt. They are already two weeks past the last date they could possibly be expected to escape detection by the Japanese."

"Jesus!" Dillon said.

"Tell Barbara that if you like," Feldt said in a level voice.

"What about getting them out?"

"Out of the sodding question, old sod," Feldt said.

"Well, what the hell are you going to do when they are caught?" Dillon asked angrily. "You just said—Banning just said—that Buka is, right now, the most important station."

"When Buka goes down, Jake," Banning said, "we will start parachuting in replacement teams. The moment we're sure it's down, we start dropping people. Giving Willoughby his due, he has promised us a B-17 within two hours when we ask for one."

"A B-17? Why a B-17?"

"Because when we jumped Joe and Koffler in there—Christ, two Jap fighter bases are on Buka—we used an unarmed transport. It was shot down. Fortunately, after Joe and Koffler jumped."

"And nothing can be done?"

"I don't know. We haven't given it much thought," Feldt said, thickly sarcastic. "But perhaps someone of your vast expertise in these areas has a solution we haven't been able to come up with ourselves."

"Eric, I'm sorry you took that the wrong way," Dillon said.

Feldt didn't reply; but a moment later he stood up and leaned over to refresh Dillon's glass of scotch.

"What makes you think you can get a replacement team on the ground?" Dillon asked after a long silence.

"The operative word is 'teams,' plural," Banning replied. "We have six, ready to go. We will jump them in one at a time until one becomes operational. And then we'll have other teams standing by to go in when the operating team goes down."

"Jesus Christ!" Dillon said.

"If we're not able to inform CINCPAC and Guadalcanal when the Japanese bombers take off from Rabaul and the bases near it, our fighters on Henderson Field and on carriers will not be in the air in time to deflect them. That would see a lot of dead Marines," Banning said. "Viewed professionally, the mathematics make sense. It is better to suffer a couple of dozen losses to save a couple of hundred, a couple of thousand, lives. The only trouble is that I—Eric and I—know the kids whose lives we're going to expend for the common good. That makes it a little difficult, personally."

Dillon raised his eyes to Banning's.

"So tell Barbara the truth, Jake. Tell her that we continue to hear from Joe at least once a day, and that so far as we know he's all right."

"Speaking of the truth, old sod," Feldt said, "Banning told me a wild tale. He claims you've dipped that miniature wick of yours into most of the famous honey pots in Hollywood."

The subject of Buka was closed, and Jake knew that he could not reopen it.

"I cannot tell a lie, Commander Feldt," Dillon said. "The story's true."

[Three]
UNITED STATES NAVAL HOSPITAL
PHILADELPHIA, PENNSYLVANIA
0930 HOURS 6 SEPTEMBER 1942

"May I help you, Lieutenant?" Lieutenant (J.G.) Joanne McConnell, NNC, asked.

"We're looking for Sergeant Moore, John M.," McCoy said. "They told us he was on this ward."

"He is, but—this isn't my idea—the rule is no visitors on the ward before noon."

"This is official business," McCoy said.

"Nice try," Lieutenant McConnell said. "But I don't think Commander Jensen would buy it. Maybe you, but not the lady. Commander Jensen runs a tight ship."

"Who's he?"

"She. She's supervisory nurse in this building."

McCoy took a wallet-sized leather folder from his pocket, opened it, and held it out for Lieutenant McConnell to see.

It held a badge that incorporated the seal of the Department of the Navy, an identification card with McCoy's picture on it, and the statement that the bearer was a Special Agent of the Office of Naval Intelligence.

"If the Commander shows up, you can tell her I showed you that and asked you where I can find Sergeant Moore, and that you told me."

"I never saw one of those before," Lieutenant McConnell said. "I hope he's not in some kind of trouble?"

"No. As a matter of fact, I'm about to make him an officer and a gentleman."

"He's a really nice kid," the nurse said.

"What shape is he in?"

"He still has to walk with a cane, but he's going to be all right."

"Why isn't he on recuperative leave?"

"He is. He was gone for a couple of days, but then he came back. He has family in Philadelphia, but—I didn't ask why he came back."

"Where is he?"

"Six-sixteen, second door from the end of the corridor on the left."

"Is he in there alone?"

"The scuttlebutt is that there was a telephone call from some captain in the office of the Secretary of the Navy ordering him a private room. It is one of the reasons he is not one of Commander Jensen's favorite people."

"Real chickenshit bitch, huh?" McCoy said.

"Ken!" Ernie Sage said.

"You said that, Lieutenant," Lieutenant McConnell said, smiling, "I didn't."

Sergeant John Marston Moore, USMCR, wearing a T-shirt and hospital pajama pants, was in bed when McCoy pushed open the door and walked in.

The top of the bed was raised to a nearly vertical position. And spread out before him on the food tray was the balsawood framework of a model airplane wing, to which Moore was attaching tissue paper covering.

He looked up with curiosity, then annoyance, and finally surprised recognition as the Marine officer and the girl walked into the room.

"Jesus!" he said.

"And the Virgin Mary," McCoy said. "I thought I told you to remember to duck, asshole."

"Ken!" Ernie said, and then, "Hello, John, how are you?"

"Surprised," Moore said. He looked at McCoy and went on, "I read in the papers about the Makin Island raid. I thought you would have been in on that."

"He was," Ernie said. "And almost got himself killed."

"No, I didn't," McCoy said.

Ernie walked to the bed and handed Moore a package. He removed the covering. It was a box of Fanny Farmer Chocolates; its cover didn't fit very well.

"Well, thanks," Moore said a little uncomfortably.

"I told you he wouldn't want candy," McCoy said.

"Don't be silly. I love chocolate," Moore lied, and quickly opened the box to prove it.

A pint flask of scotch lay on top of the chocolates. His face lit up.

"I hate people who are always right," Ernie said.

"He's a Marine. Marines always know what's important."

"God!" Ernie replied.

"Speaking of Marines," Moore said. *"General* Pickering. What's that all about?"

"He told me he called you," McCoy said.

"He called, but all he did was ask how I was, and if he could do anything for me. He didn't even tell me he was a general. I saw that in the newspaper. And he didn't tell me you were coming, either."

"Well, he's now a brigadier general; he's our boss; and just as soon as we finish the paperwork, he will have an aide-de-camp named Lieutenant Moore."

Moore didn't seem especially surprised.

"I wondered what they were going to do with me," he said.

"Now you know," McCoy said. "As soon as you get out of here, you go to Washington."

"I can leave here today," Moore said.

"You're entitled to thirty days' recuperative leave," McCoy said. "You want to tell me about that?"

"What do you mean, tell you about it?"

"Why aren't you out chasing skirts, getting drunk?"

"I can't chase too well using a cane. And when I get drunk, I fall down a lot."

"I mean, what the hell are you doing here making model airplanes?" McCoy pursued.

"Ken, that's none of your business!" Ernie snapped.

Moore looked at McCoy for a full thirty seconds, and then shrugged his shoulders.

"Going home was a disaster," he said. "For reasons I'd rather not get into. Before I went over there, I was . . . involved with a woman. Unfortunately she was a married woman. More unfortunately, she went back to her husband. So that leaves what? There's a couple of bars outside the gate here where you can go and have a couple of drinks without being treated like a freak—"

"What do you mean, a freak?" Ernie asked.

"Wounded guys are still a novelty," Moore said. "I am uncomfortable in the role of wounded hero . . . because I know goddamn well I'm no hero."

"You got the Bronze Star," McCoy said evenly.

"Not for doing anything heroic," Moore said, and then closed off further discussion of the subject by going on, "so I drink in local bars at night and make model airplanes during the day. Or is that against Marine Regulations?"

"I have to make him wear his ribbons, too," Ernie said. "I'll tell you what you're going to do today, John. You're going to put on your uniform and spend the day with us. I don't care if either one of you like it or not, I want to be the girl who has two wounded heroes on her arm."

McCoy saw Moore's eyes light up at the suggestion.

"You're going to be here all day?" Moore asked.

"Ken has to go to Parris Island tomorrow," Ernie said.

"I don't suppose I could go with you, could I?" Moore asked.

The door burst open.

Commander Elizabeth H. Jensen, NNC, a short, plump woman in her thirties, marched into the room. She folded her arms across her amply filled stiff white uniform bosom, glowered at McCoy, and announced, "I would like to know exactly what you think you are doing in here!"

"We are about to have a drink to begin the day, Commander," McCoy said, taking his credentials from his pocket and holding them up before Commander Jensen's eyes, "but aside from that, what else we're doing in here is none of your business. If I need you, however, I'll send for you."

[Four]
UNITED STATES ARMY 4TH GENERAL HOSPITAL
MELBOURNE, AUSTRALIA
7 SEPTEMBER 1942

Now shorn, shaved, and dressed in a splendidly tailored officer's green elastique uniform, Major Jake Dillon sat with his hand wrapped around a glass of scotch at a small table in the Officer's Club. Two young and quite attractive members of the Navy Nurse Corps sat on either side of him.

He had flown in this morning from Townsville on a Royal

Australian Air Force airplane that Commander Feldt arranged.

One of the nurses was Lieutenant (J.G.) Joanne Miller, NNCR, a tall, slim nurse-anesthesiologist who wore her fine blond hair in a bun. The other was Lieutenant (J.G.) Barbara T. Cotter, NNCR, a psychiatric nurse. She was also a blonde, but her hair was shorter. She was also not quite as tall as Lieutenant Miller, and a bit heavier—but by no means unpleasantly so. The two were part of a very small group of Navy nurses-with-special-training temporarily assigned to the Army Hospital. They were roommates and had become friends.

The U.S. Army 4th General Hospital was one of the very few facilities in Australia that had never been a major logistical problem. The Royal Melbourne Hospital was originally completed in late 1940. It was an enormous, fully equipped medical establishment that had simply been turned over to the United States Army for the duration of the war. The only thing it lacked was officer's billeting and an officer's club; but it was no problem to convert facilities originally intended for use by the medical school to those purposes. That was where Dillon and the two nurses were now sitting.

"There's a pretty one, Jake," Lieutenant Miller said, nodding toward a tall, good-looking Marine first lieutenant coming into the room, walking with a cane. He wore parachutist's wings pinned on his tunic.

"You stay away from that guy, honey," Dillon said, recognizing the officer.

"Why do you say that, Jake?" Lieutenant (J.G.) Barbara T. Cotter, NNCR, asked, surprised.

After a moment Jake Dillon said, "I don't know. There's something about that guy I don't like."

"You know him?"

Dillon nodded. "I met him once in the States. I just remembered where."

"I thought your criterion was 'handsome hero,'" Joanne Miller said.

"'Handsome, *wounded* hero,'" Jake corrected her and then looked at Barbara Cotter. "Handsome, honey, not pretty."

"Sorry. It's just that I've never been out with a man when *he* was looking for handsome men," Barbara said, and both women laughed.

"Thanks a lot, girls," Jake said. "Buy your own booze."

"I guess the one at the end of the bar won't qualify, huh, Jake?" Barbara asked. Jake looked in the direction of her nod.

An officer, an aviator, was standing at the bar looking down at his drink. He had a large bandage over his nose; the adhesive tape holding it extended to his jawline and temples. Under the bandage, his face was a large bruise from the lip line to above his eyes.

"Jesus, what happened to him?" Dillon asked.

"It's not as bad as it looks," Joanne said. "He slammed his face into a control panel. There were some fractures in the nasal passage area; they went in and straightened things out."

"I know him," Jake said, surprise in his voice. "Excuse me."

He got up and went to the young officer at the bar.

"I'm Jake Dillon, Lieutenant. Don't we know each other?"

The young officer looked at him.

"No, Sir. I don't think so."

"Lakehurst," Dillon insisted. "Charley Galloway? A light colonel—what the hell was his name?—jumped out of your airplane and his chute didn't open?"

Recognition came.

"Yes, Sir," Lieutenant Jim Ward said. "You were the press agent—excuse me, public relations officer, right?"

"I don't think press agent is a dirty word," Dillon said. "I thought it was you."

They shook hands.

"If you're alone," Dillon said, "I'm not. Want to join us?" He nodded toward the table where the girls were sitting.

"That's the best offer I've had in a long time," Ward said.

"The smaller one is taken," Dillon said.

"I admire your taste."

"Not by me, but taken," Dillon said.

As they walked to the table, Dillon saw the parachutist officer glance at them, and then saw recognition in his eyes. He did not respond.

"Ladies, I would love to introduce this wounded, handsome hero to you, but I just realized I've forgotten his name," Dillon said.

"Jim Ward," Ward said.

"He's a pal of a pal of mine," Dillon went on. "Captain Charley Galloway."

The women rather formally shook hands with Ward.

"We've met before too," Joanne said. "I passed the gas when they fixed your face. Are you supposed to be drinking?"

"Well, I hadn't planned on driving anywhere," Ward said.

"Speaking of Charley?" Dillon said.

"He's on the 'Canal," Ward said. "Commanding VMF-229."

"Christ, I wish I'd known that," Dillon said. "I just came out of Henderson."

Ward looked at Dillon with an interest he had not shown before.

"What were you doing on Guadalcanal?" he asked.

"I suppose most people would say I was getting in the way," Dillon replied, and went on: "How's Charley doing?"

"He was shot down. He floated around all night and then a PT boat picked him up. Aside from that, he's fine."

"What happened to you?" Dillon asked.

"I made a bad landing," Ward said. "And bumped my nose on the control panel."

"He lost—temporarily, by the grace of God—the use of his right eye when his windshield was shot away," Joanne said matter-of-factly. "Plexiglas fragments. When he landed, his gear collapsed, and the airplane's nose hit the ground with such force that the seat was ripped loose. The main reason they sent him here was that they couldn't believe he walked away from that crash with nothing more than broken ribs and a broken nose."

"Jesus," Dillon said.

"I really hope your deep research into my background also came up with the fact that I'm single, available, and that dogs and old ladies like me," Jim Ward said.

"So how are you?" Dillon asked.

"Until about five minutes ago I was feeling sorry for myself," Jim Ward said.

"Why?" Joanne asked.

"Just before I came in here tonight, I was told that I couldn't go back to the squadron until my ribs healed, and that for the next three to four weeks I will be an assistant morale and welfare officer of the detachment of patients. Among other things I am to make sure the bingo games are honest."

"Be grateful, for Christ's sake," Dillon said.

Lieutenant Jim Ward looked directly at Lieutenant Joanne Miller.

"Oh, I am now," he said.

She looks uncomfortable, Dillon thought, *but not displeased.*

"Excuse me, Major," the officer wearing parachutist's wings and walking with a cane said, "but aren't you Major Dillon?"

"That's right."

"Correct me if I'm wrong, Sir, but haven't we met?"

"Yeah. At Lakehurst," Dillon said. "We were just talking about that."

"Why don't you pull up a chair, Lieutenant? And sit down?" Joanne Miller said.

Why the hell did I do that? she thought. *Because I wanted him to take the strain off his leg? Or because ol' I-bumped-my-nose-on-the-control-panel here is making a pass at me? Or because I don't like my reaction to the pass? I will not get emotionally involved with him or any of the others. I don't want to go through what Barbara's going through.*

"With the Major's permission?" the parachutist officer asked.

"Yeah. Go ahead. Sit down," Jake said. "The ladies are Lieutenants Miller and Cotter. You remember Jim Ward?"

"No, I can't say that I do," the parachutist said, glancing at Ward and dismissing him. "I'm Dick Macklin," he said to the women. "I'm very pleased to meet you."

Dillon did not like the way Macklin was smiling at Barbara Cotter.

He remembered now why it was he didn't like Lieutenant Macklin. Not specific details, just that when they had been at Lakehurst, Macklin had been chickenshit. He was perfectly willing to throw an enlisted man to the wolves so he would look good—a PFC or a corporal, Jake now remembered, although he couldn't come up with a face or a name.

All good Marine officers have contempt for such officers. But in Jake Dillon's case, the contempt was magnified by his own experience with chickenshit officers. He had far more time in The Corps as a sergeant than he did as a field-grade officer and gentleman.

If you make a pass at Barbara, I'll break your other fucking leg. Why did I tell this sonofabitch it was all right to sit down? As a matter of fact, if you make a pass at either one, I'll break your other fucking leg.

"May I ask, Sir," Macklin said, "if you're a fellow patient?"

"Just passing through," Dillon said.

"On your way to Guadalcanal?"

"No," Dillon said.

"We had press people with us," Macklin said. He raised his stiff leg. "That's where I caught this. I went in with the first wave of parachutists when we hit the beach at Gavutu."

"Then we went in at about the same time," Dillon said, wearing a patently insincere smile. "I went in to Tulagi with Jack Stecker's 2nd Battalion of the Fifth."

"Really?" Barbara Cotter asked. It was the first time Jake had said anything about what he had done at Guadalcanal. Without thinking about it, she'd decided that as a press agent, Jake had gone in after the beach had been secured.

"Jack Stecker and I were sergeants in the Fourth," Dillon said. "He let me tag along."

That's not surprising, Barbara thought.

Jake was like Joe Howard. Both were Marine Mustangs (officers commissioned from the ranks); she knew the type. They felt somehow cheated if they weren't where the fighting was. This was admirable, unless of course you were in love with one of them, in which case they were damned fools.

Barbara hadn't believed a word Dillon told her about Joe Howard being all right. What she didn't already know, or guess, about the Coastwatchers and Joe's chances of survival, she had learned from Yeoman Daphne Farnsworth, Royal Australian Navy Women's Volunteer Reserve. Daphne not only worked with the Coastwatchers, she had become involved with Sergeant Steve Koffler before the two Marines parachuted onto Buka.

"What happened to you, Ward?" Macklin asked, obviously not wanting to swap war stories with Dillon.

"I thought the guy said 'stand up,' " Jim Ward said. "What he said was 'shut up.' "

"He got hurt flying out of Henderson with VMF-229. With Charley Galloway," Dillon said. "You remember Charley, don't you, Macklin?"

"No, Sir," Macklin said, searching his memory.

Jim Ward not only remembered Lieutenant Macklin from Lakehurst; he'd picked up on Dillon's contempt; and was just as annoyed as Dillon with Macklin's raised-leg, look-at-me-the-hero attitude.

"Sure, you do," Ward said. "He was our instructor pilot on the Gooneybird. *Tech Sergeant* Galloway?"

"Oh, yes, of course."

"Captain Galloway, now," Jim Ward added. "My squadron commander."

"Really?" Macklin asked.

From the look on Macklin's face, Ward saw that he had struck home. Nothing else he could have said would so annoy a Regular Marine officer with a commission from Annapolis than to be told that a technical sergeant he had tried to push around now outranked him as an officer and a gentleman.

Meanwhile, Lieutenant Richard B. Macklin might not have been a prince among men, or even a very decent human being, but he was no fool. He saw that his high hopes to get to know one of the nurses, perhaps even carnally, were not going to come to fruition.

Although Dillon had claimed that the blonde with the big boobs was taken, she kept looking at Dillon with something like affection. And the other one kept stealing looks at the aviator.

He had been done in, he realized, by the natural tendency of female officers to be attracted to field-grade officers and/or aviators. He didn't understand this—as far as he was concerned, it took far more courage to jump out of an airplane than it did to fly one—but that was unfortunately the way things were.

"How long are you going to look like that?" Dillon asked Ward.

"I beg your pardon?"

Joanne Miller understood the question.

"He ought to look more or less human in a week or ten days; at least the black-and-blue will have gone away," she said. "The ribs will take six weeks or so to heal."

"I can fly now," Ward said. "I didn't want to come here and they shouldn't have sent me."

That's not bullshit intended to impress the girls and me, Jake decided. *This kid is a Marine.*

"Where are you from, Ward?"

"Philadelphia. Or just outside. Jenkintown."

"Right. Where Charley's girlfriend is from, right?"

"She's my aunt," Jim Ward said.

"What about you, Macklin? Where are you from?"

"California, Sir. Near San Diego."

"Where'd you go to school?"

"The Naval Academy, Sir."

Jake Dillon Productions, Jake thought, *has just completed final casting of his epic motion picture, or at least newsreel feature epic,* Wounded Marine Heroes of 1942.

But I won't tell either of them just yet. Ward will be genuinely pissed when he hears what I'm going to do to him. And I suspect that Macklin will be so pleased I'm taking him out of harm's way that he'll piss his pants.

He remembered a story going around the aid stations on Gavutu and Tulagi about the 2nd Parachute Battalion officer who'd taken a minor flesh wound to his calf and had to be pried, screaming and hysterical, from a piling on the seaplane wharf where he had been hit.

There was absolutely no question in Jake's mind that that officer was now sitting at his table.

VII

Sergeant Steven M. Koffler, USMC, woke suddenly and sat up, frightened. His guts were knotted and he had a clammy sweat.

It was from a nightmare, he concluded after a moment, although he couldn't remember any of it.

The feeling of foreboding did not go away. Something was wrong. There was enough light in the hut for him to see that Patience was gone. That was not unusual. Since she had moved in with him, she habitually rose before he did and was out of the hut before he woke.

But then, slowly, it came to him, what was wrong. He heard no noise. There was always noise, the squealing of pigs, the crying of children, the crackling of a fire, even hymn singing.

That image sent his mind wandering: *They don't sing hymns here, like in church. It has nothing to do with God. It's just that "Rock of Ages" and "Faith of Our Fathers" and "God Save the King" and "Onward Christian Soldiers" and the other ones are*

160

the only music these people have ever heard. He corrected himself: *Plus the Marine Hymn, which of course me and Lieutenant Howard taught them.*

Why can't I hear anything?

He felt another wave of fear and reached for the Thompson. He checked the action and then stuck his feet in his boondockers and stood up.

He went to the door of the hut and looked out. No one was in sight.

Where the fuck is everybody?

With his finger on the Thompson's trigger, he left the hut, took one quick look to confirm that no one was visible, then ran into the jungle behind the hut. He moved ten feet inside it, enough for concealment, and then he moved laterally until he found a position where he could observe the other huts.

There was no one there. The fires had gone out.

Even the fucking pigs are gone!

The sonsofbitches ran off on me!

Well, what the hell do you expect? he asked himself. *If I wasn't here, they're just a bunch of fucking cannibals; the Japs don't give a shit about cannibals unless they're causing trouble. The worst thing the Japs would do would be to put them to work.*

With me here, they're the fucking enemy. The Japs would kill them, slowly, to show they're pissed off. And they'll do it so it hurts, to teach the other cannibals it's not smart to help the White Man. Like cutting off their arms and legs, not just their heads, and leaving the parts laying around.

A chill replaced the clammy sweat.

What the fuck am I going to do now?

He was suddenly, without warning, sick to his stomach. When that passed, he had an equally irresistible urge to move his bowels.

He moved another fifteen yards through the jungle and watched the camp for another five minutes. Finally he walked out of the jungle and started looking in the huts.

The radio was still there.

Why not? What the hell would they do with the radio?

And he found some baked sweet potatoes, or whatever the hell they were, and some of the smoked pig.

A farewell present? Merry Christmas, Sergeant Koffler? How the fuck long are those sweet potatoes and five, ten pounds of smoked pig going to last me?

Oh, shit!

There came the sound of aircraft engines, a dull roar far off.

Fuck 'em! What the fuck do I care if the whole Japanese Air Corps is headed for Guadalcanal?

He walked to the tree house. They'd left him the knotted rope, he found to his surprise. He used it to walk up the trunk.

"Good morning, Steven," Patience Witherspoon said. She was sitting on the floor of the platform, wearing an expression that said she expected to be kicked.

Ian Bruce was leaning against the trunk.

"You heard the engines, Sergeant Koffler?"

"Fuck the engines, where the hell is everybody?"

"The men went to seek Lieutenant Reeves," Ian said. "The women have gone away from here."

"Gone where?"

"You would not know where they have gone," Ian said with irrefutable logic. *"Away."*

"Why?"

"If it has not gone well with Lieutenant Reeves, the Japanese will come looking for us. If they find this place, with the radio, they may believe there were no other white men. You will come with us to where the women are making a camp. We may be able to hide you."

"You think something fucked up, went wrong, don't you?"

"I think something has fucked up. Otherwise Lieutenant Reeves would have returned when he said he would return."

"Why wasn't I told?"

"Because I knew you would forbid it," Ian Bruce said. "Lieutenant Reeves left you in charge; he told me I was to take your orders as if they had come from him."

"What are you doing up here, then?" Steve asked.

"Watching for the Japanese aircraft," Ian said. "We will need the binoculars."

"They're in my hut," Steve replied automatically.

"I will get them," Patience said, and quickly got to her feet and started down the knotted rope.

"If we're going to hide in the goddamned jungle," Steve asked, "why are we bothering with this shit, anyway?"

"Because," Ian Bruce said, again with irrefutable logic, "we do not know that Lieutenant Reeves is dead. We only believe he is. Until we know for sure, or until the Japanese come, we will do what he wishes us to do."

"Semper Fi, right?"

"I do not understand."

"Yeah, you do," Steve said.

"Is that English?"

"It's Marine," Steve said. "It means . . . you do what you're expected to do, I guess. Or try, anyway."

"I see," Ian Bruce said solemnly.

[Two]
USMC REPLACEMENT DEPOT
PARRIS ISLAND, SOUTH CAROLINA
2250 HOURS 7 SEPTEMBER 1942

Because he was on a routine check of the guard posts, the officer of the day happened to be at the main gate when the 1939 LaSalle convertible pulled up to the guard and stopped. It had been a long and dull evening and showed little prospect of getting more interesting.

"Hold it a minute," the OD said to his jeep driver.

"Aye, aye, Sir," the driver said and stopped the jeep.

The OD got out and walked toward the LaSalle. The driver was apparently showing his orders to the guard, for the beam of the guard's flashlight illuminated the interior. The OD saw that the car held two lieutenants, neither of whom was wearing his cover.

But what the hell, it's almost eleven o'clock.

"Welcome to sand flea heaven," the OD said. "Reporting in?"

"Just visiting," McCoy replied.

He was a first lieutenant, the OD saw, not any older than he himself was. But he was wearing a double row of ribbons, including the Bronze Star and what looked like the Purple Heart with two clusters on it. The other one was a second lieutenant, and he too was wearing ribbons signifying that he had been wounded and decorated for valor.

Am I being a suspicious prick, or just doing my job? the OD wondered as he reached to take the orders from the guard.

The orders were obviously genuine. They were issued by Headquarters, USMC, and ordered First Lieutenant K. R. McCoy to proceed by military or civilian road, rail, or air transportation, or at his election, by privately owned vehicle, to

Philadelphia, Penna., Parris Island, S.C., and such other destinations as he deemed necessary in the carrying out of his mission for the USMC Office of Management Analysis.

What the hell is the Office of Management Analysis?

"Well, as I said," the OD said, smiling, "welcome to sand flea heaven."

"I know all about the sand fleas," McCoy said, smiling. "But how do I find the BOQ?"

"How do you know about the sand fleas and not the BOQ?" the OD asked, and immediately felt like a fool as the answer came to him: This guy was a Mustang. He had gone through Parris Island as an enlisted man before getting a commission. He knew about sand fleas. But Marine boots do not know where bachelor officers rest their weary heads.

"Follow the signs to the Officer's Club," the OD said. "Drive past it. Look to your right. Two-story frame building on your right."

"Thank you," McCoy said.

The guard saluted. McCoy returned it. McCoy drove past the barrier.

"Interesting," the OD said to the guard. "Did you see the ribbons on those officers?"

"Yes, Sir. And one of them had a cane, too."

"I wonder what the hell the Office of Management Analysis is?" the OD asked, not expecting an answer.

"I'll tell you something else interesting, Sir," the guard said. "The sergeant major is looking for them. At least for Lieutenant McCoy. He passed the word through the sergeant of the guard we was to call him, no matter when he came aboard."

"Him? Not the OD? Or the General's aide?"

"Him, Sir."

"Well, in that case, Corporal, I would suggest you get on the horn to the sergeant major. Hell hath no fury, as you might have heard."

"Aye, aye, Sir."

"Does this place fill you with fond memories?" McCoy asked as they drove through the Main Post, an area of brick buildings looking not unlike the campus of a small college.

"I would rather go back to Guadalcanal than go through here again," Moore said.

"How's your legs?"

"I won't mind lying down."

"Well, you wanted to come."

"And I'm grateful that you brought me. I was going stir crazy in the hospital."

"I think what you need, pal, is a piece of ass. I also think you're out of luck here."

"Says he, the Croesus of Carnal Wealth," Moore replied.

"What?"

"Says he, who doesn't have that problem."

"What Ernie and I have is something special," McCoy said coldly.

"Hell, I realized that the first time I saw you two looking at each other in San Diego," Moore said. "My reaction then, and now, is profound admiration, coupled with enormous jealousy."

"Your lady really did a job on you, huh?"

"When I got her letter, in Melbourne, I was fantasizing about getting to be an officer and marching into the Bellvue-Stratford in my officer's uniform with her on my arm. . . . 'Dear John,' the letter said."

"Hell, your name *is* John," McCoy said. "And you have your officer's uniform, three sets of khakis, anyway. . . ."

"And thank you for that, too. I wouldn't have known where to go to buy them."

"Horstmann Uniform has been selling uniforms to The Corps since Christ was a corporal," McCoy said. "And as I was saying, your Dear John letter lady is not the only female in the world."

"So I keep telling myself," Moore said.

"Well, there's the club, and it looks like it's still open. Would you like a drink?"

"I'll pass, thank you," Moore said. "But go ahead if you want to."

"I've got a couple of pints in my bag," McCoy said. "I didn't really want to go in there anyway." A moment later he said, "That must be it."

Moore looked up and saw a two-story frame building. McCoy drove around behind it and parked the car. Since he'd packed Moore's two spare khaki uniforms in his own bag, there was only one to carry.

A corporal was on duty in the lobby of the Bachelor Officer's Quarters.

McCoy told him they were transients and needed rooms; and the corporal gave them a register to sign, then handed each of them a key.

"End of the corridor to the right, Sir. Number twelve."

"Thank you," McCoy said and walked up the stairs.

Halfway down the corridor he swore bitterly: "Shit! Sonofa-*bitch!*"

Moore saw the source of his anger. A neatly lettered sign was thumbtacked to one of the doors. It read, RESERVED FOR KILLER MCCOY.

He walked quickly to the sign and ripped it down. He started to put his key to the lock in the door, but it opened before he could reach it.

"Well, if it isn't Lieutenant McCoy," a man wearing the three stripes up, three lozenges down insignia of a sergeant major said, standing at rigid attention. "May the sergeant major say, Sir, the Lieutenant looks just fine?"

"That fucking sign isn't funny, goddamn you!" McCoy flared. "What the hell is the matter with you, anyway?"

The sergeant major was not as taken aback as Moore expected him to be. He seemed more hurt and disappointed than alarmed by McCoy's intense and genuine anger.

"Aw, come on, Ken," he said.

McCoy glowered at him for a moment and finally said, "I don't know why the hell I'm surprised. You never did have the brains to pour piss out of a boot. How the hell are you, you old bastard?"

"No complaints, Ken," the sergeant major said with obvious affection in his voice, taking McCoy's hand.

And then he saw Moore, and a moment after that, there was recognition in his eyes.

"I believe I know this gentleman, too, don't I?"

"I don't think so," McCoy said. "Moore, this is Sergeant Major Teddy Osgood. We were in the Fourth Marines together."

"Yeah, sure," Moore said. "I remember you now, Sergeant Major. When I left here—"

"Oh?" McCoy asked, curious.

"Captain Sessions came down here and pulled me out of boot camp," Moore explained. "The sergeant major . . . how do I say it?"

"Handled the administrative details," the sergeant major furnished.

"I remember you telling Captain Sessions that you had known the Killer—Ooops!—*Lieutenant* McCoy in China."

"If you think that was funny, you asshole, it wasn't," McCoy said.

But he was not, Moore saw, furious anymore.

"I see neither one of you paid attention when you went through here. Is that *three* Purple Hearts, Ken?"

"Two of them are bullshit," McCoy said. "Moore took some mortar shrapnel on Guadalcanal. He needs to lie down."

"This is a field-grade officer's suite, all kinds of places to lay down," Osgood said. "Would you like a drink, Lieutenant?"

"Yes, thank you, I would," Moore said.

"Get in bed, I'll make the drinks," McCoy said.

"That Captain said you was with the 2nd Raider Battalion," Osgood said to McCoy.

"I was."

"You were on the Makin Island raid?"

McCoy nodded.

"And now?"

"I'm doing more or less what Captain Sessions does," McCoy said.

"Yeah, I figured that. When the TWX came in saying you was coming, the G-2 shit a brick. What the hell do you people do, anyway?"

McCoy didn't immediately reply. He dug in his bag, fished out a pint of scotch, poured some in a glass, and handed it to Moore, who by then had crawled onto one of the beds.

"The name is the Office of Management Analysis," he said finally. "We're sort of in the supply business."

"Yeah, sure you are. That's why every time we get some boot who speaks Japanese, who has civilian experience as a radio operator, or who's lived over there, we notify you, right? So they can pass out rations, right?"

"Right," McCoy said.

"Well, I got a dozen, thirteen people, lined up for you to talk to tomorrow, three who speak Japanese . . . what do you call them?"

"Linguists," McCoy said.

". . . half a dozen amateur radio operators, and a couple of guys who are going to cryptography school."

"Great," McCoy said. "Everything laid on for me, us, to talk to them?"

"You tell me when and where and I'll have them there."

"You got someplace?"

"Yeah. I'll take care of it," Osgood said. "I'll send a car for you in the morning. You have to make your manners with the G-2, I guess?"

"I suppose we'll have to," McCoy said.

"There's another guy, Ken. He don't speak Jap, and he's no radio operator, but he's interesting."

"Why interesting?"

"Well, for one thing, he used to be a cop. Actually a vice squad detective. Saint Louis."

"A vice squad detective?" Moore asked, laughing.

"Maybe *he* could do something to solve your problem, Lieutenant," McCoy said, and then added, "I don't understand, Teddy."

"He went after one of his DIs, was going to break his arm."

"Sounds like my kind of guy," Moore said.

Osgood looked at him and smiled. "The word is that the DI, an assistant DI, is a real asshole."

"And this guy broke his arm?" McCoy asked.

"No. The platoon DI saw what he was up to and stopped him. He said the guy really knows how to use a knife. If he had wanted to cut the DI, kill him, he would be dead, the DI said. But all he wanted to do was break his arm. I guess he figured he could get away with that."

"They court-martial him?"

"No. For what? The DI said, 'Try to kill me.' The guy was just obeying orders. The platoon DI came to me and explained the situation, and I transferred the guy to another platoon."

"Is this guy a sleaze, Teddy?" McCoy asked.

"What do you mean?"

"I mean, what does he look like, what does he act like?"

"I don't know. I never actually seen him. His platoon DI's a friend of mine, and he must have sort of liked this guy or he wouldn't have come to me about him."

"Or, like you said, the assistant DI is an asshole and he figured he deserved a broken arm. I want to see him, Teddy. Can you arrange that?"

"No problem," Osgood said. "I'll have him there with the others."

"You want another one of these?" McCoy asked, extending the pint of scotch to Moore. He suspected, correctly, that Moore was both exhausted by their trip and in pain.

"Please," Moore said, taking the bottle.

"What about now?" McCoy said. "Let's see how he reacts to getting up in the middle of the night."

"You're serious, aren't you?" Osgood asked.

"Yeah, I'm serious," McCoy said. He looked at Moore. "After I talked to your new boss, I talked to Captain Sessions. He said I should also ask about getting your new boss an orderly, or a driver, but really somebody to pick up the papers he leaves lying around when he's not supposed to."

"Oh," Moore said.

"He also used the word 'bodyguard,' but said we shouldn't say it around your boss."

"Yeah," Moore said, understanding.

"Why not?" Sergeant Major Osgood said. "Everybody knows people in the supply business need bodyguards. Who is your boss, anyway?"

"None of your fucking business," McCoy said. "Since you asked."

The sergeant major chuckled. He went to the bedside table, pulled open a drawer, took out a mimeographed telephone directory, found the number he was looking for, and dialed it.

"This is the sergeant major," he said. "Roll Private Hart, George F., out of the sack. Have him standing by in full field gear in five minutes. I'll send a vehicle for him."

Private Hart was not surprised when the lights in the squad bay came on in the middle of the night. That happened all the time. Nor was he particularly surprised when the drill instructor marched down the aisle between the rows of double bunks, his heels crashing against the wooden, washed-nearly-white flooring, and stopped at his bunk.

At least I'm out of the sack and at attention, he thought, taking some small solace from the situation.

It was not the first time since he had been transferred to his new platoon that he'd been singled out for what was euphemistically called "extra training." This most often consisted of an order to get dressed and take a couple of double-time laps around the barracks area with his rifle held over his head. But a couple of times they woke him at two in the morning to practice "basic elements of field fortification." That meant digging a man-sized hole with his entrenching tool and filling it up again. Then they let him shower and get back in the sack.

He understood now why they'd done those things. His new DI and his assistants wanted to make sure he was not a wiseass who had to be broken to fit the Marine mold. Although what he had almost done to Corporal Clayton C. Warren, USMC, had not officially happened and was supposed to be kept as quiet as possible to protect the dignity of the DI Corps, they knew about it, obviously, and so they wanted to make sure about him.

For his part, he'd obeyed their orders without complaint and to the best of his ability. And the DI here and his assistants, while they were a stiff-necked bunch of bastards, were at least a reasonably fair trio of stiff-necked bastards—a marvelous improvement over Corporal Clayton C. Warren, USMC.

It was against Holy Writ to meet the eyes of a DI; one was required to stare off into space. So it was a moment before Private Hart became aware that the DI whose face was an inch and a half from his was *the* DI, Staff Sergeant Homer Hungleberry, USMC, and that Staff Sergeant Hungleberry was attired in his boondockers and skivvies only.

"Caught you with your cock in your hand, did I, Hart?"

"Sir, no, Sir."

"What have you done that I don't know about, Hart?"

What the fuck is he talking about?

"Sir, I don't know."

"When I find out, and I *will* find out, I will have your ass twice. Once for doing something I don't know about and once for lying to me about it."

"Sir, yes, Sir."

"So there is something?"

"Sir, no, Sir."

"Utilities, full field gear, helmet, piece, in five minutes!"

"Sir, aye, aye, Sir."

Staff Sergeant Hungleberry withdrew his face from Private Hart's, did a left-face, and marched back down the aisle between the rows of double bunks. When he reached the light switch, he turned off the lights.

Private Hart, in the dark, located a set of utilities, his socks, boondockers, field equipment, and helmet and carried them down the aisle toward the head, where one 40-watt bulb (the others were ritually unscrewed from their sockets) was allowed to burn all night.

The firewatch, a boot required to stay awake all night, was in the head.

"What the fuck did you do now?" he inquired.

"Does it fucking matter?" Hart replied as he hastily pulled on his utilities, the field equipment, his socks, and shoved his feet into his boondockers and tied them.

"You did something," the firewatch said helpfully. "And he *knows.*"

"Fuck you," Private Hart said as he put his helmet on his head.

How the hell am I going to get my piece? My fucking piece is in the fucking arms rack, and the fucking arms rack is locked.

The answer came: *When he comes out of his room, he will find me standing at fucking attention by the arms rack waiting for him to unlock the sonofabitch.*

Staff Sergeant Hungleberry, now fully dressed, appeared. He examined Private Hart, who was standing at rigid attention.

"You have hearing problems, Hart?"

"Sir, no, Sir."

"Do I speak indistinctly? Or was I maybe talking in Chinese?"

"Sir, no, Sir."

"Then you did understand me to say, 'Utilities, full field gear, helmet, and piece in five minutes'?"

"Sir, yes, Sir."

"Then where is your fucking piece?"

"Sir, in the arms rack, Sir, and the arms rack, Sir, is locked, Sir."

"Do you really think I would ask you to take your piece from a locked arms rack?"

"Sir, no, Sir."

"Then get your fucking piece from the arms rack!"

The sonofabitch unlocked the fucking rack before he came storming down the aisle!

"Sir, aye, aye, Sir!"

He retrieved his piece, U.S. Rifle, Springfield, Model of 1903, Serial Number 2456577, from its assigned place, third from the right on the squad bay side, worked the action to ensure that it was empty, and came to attention again.

"You are still telling me that you have no idea why the sergeant major wants to see you?"

The sergeant major? What the fuck does the sergeant major want with me at midnight?

"Sir, yes, Sir. I don't know why the sergeant major wants to see me, Sir."

" 'Ten-HUT! Right SHOULDER, Harms! Right Face! Foh-wud, Harch! Open the door when you get to it!"

Private Hart marched off, opened the door when he came to it, marched through it, down the shallow stairs and toward the next barracks.

"Detail, HALT!"

After approximately two minutes, which seemed like much longer, the headlights of a Chevrolet pickup truck illuminated the area, and then the truck stopped about eight inches from Private Hart.

He could faintly but clearly hear the conversation between his DI and the corporal driving the truck.

"What the fuck is going on here?"

"Beats the shit out of me. All I know is I was told to come here and get some boot named Hart and take him to the BOQ."

"The BOQ? I thought the sergeant major sent for him."

"To the sergeant major at the BOQ," the corporal clarified.

"Shit!"

"That's all I know, Sergeant," the corporal said righteously. "You coming, or just him? That *is* him?"

"Hart, get in the fucking truck!"

"Sir, aye, aye, Sir."

The opening and then slamming of the passenger door told Private Hart that his DI had decided his duty required him to accompany him to the sergeant major at the BOQ.

The sergeant major at the BOQ? What the hell is going on?

Ten minutes later the pickup stopped in front of a two-story frame building in a part of Parris Island Private Hart had never been to.

He saw a man he had never seen before. But to judge by the stripes on his sleeves and his assured manner as he approached the truck, he was certainly the sergeant major.

"Who are you?"

"Hungleberry, Sergeant Major."

"That Hart?"

"Yes, Sergeant Major."

"What took you so long?"

"We was ready when the truck got there," Staff Sergeant Hungleberry said righteously.

"Get him out of the truck and march him to room twelve. Left corridor, last door on the right. Report to the officers."

"Right," Sergeant Hungleberry replied. Then he raised his voice: "Out of the truck, Hart!"

Hart got out of the truck.

"'Ten-HUT! PORT, Harms! Lu-eft, FACE! Foh-wud, HARCH! Up the stairs and into the building."

When Private Hart passed the sergeant major, the sergeant major leaned forward to get a good look at Private Hart. Private Hart could smell his breath; he had been in enough bars to recognize the smell of whiskey there. Indeed, his experience as a vice squad detective had given him the expertise to make a professional judgment: The sergeant major had been drinking scotch, and in quantities sufficient to place in grave doubt his ability to walk a straight line or to close his eyes and touch his nose with his finger.

Jesus Christ, now what? What the fuck is this all about? I've heard they take people out behind barracks and beat the shit out of them. Is that why nothing happened to me for trying to break that asshole's arm? They were saving me for this? Are the sergeant major, drunk—and maybe a couple of drunken officers— really going to teach me that they just won't tolerate trying to break a DI's arm?

Staff Sergeant Hungleberry marched Private Hart to the door to room 12, then barked, "De-tail, HALT!" and knocked at the door.

"Come!"

Staff Sergeant Hungleberry marched Private Hart into the room, again ordered, "De-tail, HALT!" and then barked, "Sir, Staff Sergeant Hungleberry reporting to the Lieutenant with a detail of one, Sir!"

"Put your detail at ease, Sergeant," the officer ordered conversationally.

"Aww-duh, HARMS! Puh-rade, REST!"

"I said, 'at ease,' Sergeant," the officer said.

"At EASE!"

After Private Hart complied, he dared to look around the room. There were two officers, both young. One was a second lieutenant, sprawled on a bed, a whiskey glass resting on his chest. He was wearing khakis. His field scarf was pulled down and the top three buttons of his shirt were open.

Hart recognized the Purple Heart among the ribbons pinned to the shirt.

The other officer was a first lieutenant, and he too had ribbons pinned to his shirt, including the Purple Heart. In the fleeting instant when their eyes met, Private Hart's professional experience told him, *this guy can be one mean sonofabitch.*

"You're his DI?" the mean-looking officer asked.

"Yes, Sir. Staff Sergeant Hungleberry, Sir."

"OK, Sergeant. Tell me, is this guy going to be a Marine or not?"

The question surprised Hungleberry. It was a moment before he replied: "I guess he'll be all right, Sir."

That's the nicest thing anybody has said about me since I came to this fucking hellhole.

"I didn't ask for a guess, Sergeant. I asked whether this guy will make a Marine or not?"

The hesitation this time was longer.

"Yes, Sir, in my opinion, he'll be all right."

"Thank you," the officer said. He turned to the dresser behind him and picked up a pint of scotch. "Sorry to keep you out of the sack at this time of night, but we want to talk to him."

He tossed the pint to the sergeant major, who had come into the room.

"Take the sergeant someplace and give him a little taste, Teddy, would you, please?" the officer said.

"Aye, aye, Sir," the sergeant major said. In a moment Hart heard the door close.

"My name is McCoy," the officer said. "That's Lieutenant Moore."

"Yes, Sir."

"I understand you're a tough guy," McCoy said.

Hart could not think of a proper reply to that. He did not answer.

"I understand you tried to break your DI's arm. Yes or no?"

"Yes, Sir."

"I also understand you know how to use a knife?"

"Yes, Sir."

"Why didn't you kill the DI? Everybody seems agreed that he's an asshole."

"I didn't want to go to Portsmouth, Sir."

"Good reason," McCoy said. "I asked you a question before. Are you a tough guy or not?"

"I used to be a cop, Lieutenant," Hart said. "I suppose I'm as tough as most cops."

"Tougher than some?"

"Yes, Sir."

"You look like you could use a drink," McCoy said. "Lean your piece against the wall."

The offer completely surprised Hart. McCoy saw his hesitation and laughed.

"Go ahead," he said. "You're not the first guy to go through here, including me, who wanted to kill his DI. You're the first sane one I've met who actually tried to."

He walked to Hart, took his rifle from him, and motioned him into a chair. He leaned the rifle against a wall, and then he poured whiskey into a glass and handed it to him.

"You want some water?"

"No, thank you, Sir."

"Why did you want to be a cop?"

"My whole family is cops."

"When you were a cop, did you ever use your weapon? Kill somebody? Or try to?"

"Yes, Sir."

Hart took a sip of the whiskey. For the first time he saw Moore's cane.

"Which? Tried to? Or did?"

"I had to kill a couple of people, Sir, when I was a cop."

"Is that why you joined the crotch?" Moore asked somewhat thickly. "To kill people?"

What did he say? The crotch?

Hart saw McCoy flash Moore an angry look, but then he turned to Hart: "Answer the question."

"A goddamn recruiter lied to me," Hart blurted.

"No shit?" McCoy replied sarcastically. "I thought a cop would be smarter than that."

"This was a clever sonofabitch," Hart said, and a split second later remembered to append, "Sir."

"What did he tell you?" McCoy asked.

"That The Corps wanted guys who had been cops to be sort of cops for The Corps, Sir."

"And you believed him?"

"I believed the sonofabitch who told me I'd get a commission when I got through here," Moore said.

He's drunk, Hart realized.

"You have a commission." McCoy chuckled.

"Yeah, now."

"You're plastered," McCoy added, still chuckling, as if the realization pleased him. "You've been an officer forty-eight hours and already you're guilty of conduct unbecoming an officer and a gentleman. Try not to fall out of bed."

"Fuck you, McCoy."

McCoy shook his head and turned to Hart.

"You know what a full background investigation is?"

"Yes, Sir."

"I want straight answers now. Don't try to be clever. If we ran one on you, what would it turn up?"

Hart considered the question. Before he had formed a reply, McCoy went on.

"You're German, right? You or anybody in your family ever been involved with the German-American Bund? Anything like that?"

"No, Sir."

"How about the Communist Party? You, or anybody close, family, friends, ever been involved with that? Maybe the Abraham Lincoln Brigade?"

"No, Sir."

"Now don't get hot under the collar, but you're not a secret faggot, are you?"

"Jesus Christ, McCoy!" Moore complained.

"Are you?"

"No, Sir."

"How do you feel about rich people?"

"Excuse me?"

"How do you feel about rich people. I mean, really rich people?"

"I never met any," Hart replied, hesitated, and added, "Sir."

"The Lieutenant is asking," Moore explained, carefully pronouncing each syllable, "if you would be comfortable working with someone who is enormously wealthy, or whether you would disgrace the crotch by pissing in the potted palms."

What the fuck is this all about?

McCoy laughed.

"He doesn't usually get this pissed on a couple of drinks. I'm beginning to be sorry I brought you down here with me."

"I'm not pissed," Moore said. "How could I possibly be pissed? I've only had two or three little nips."

"You answer the question," McCoy said. "How do you think . . . could he work with the General?"

"I think the General would like him," Moore said. "But then, I have been wrong before."

"Hart, what we're looking for is someone to be a bodyguard for a general. The General is not going to like the idea of having a bodyguard. Could you handle something like that?"

"I didn't know generals had bodyguards," Hart blurted.

"Most of them don't. This one needs one."

"I really don't know."

"Your other option is taking your piece on a ship and going to a line company in someplace like Guadalcanal," Moore said. "They shoot people on Guadalcanal. It smarts when they shoot you."

"You've gone too far," McCoy flared. "Shut your fucking mouth!"

"Aye, aye, Sir," Moore said and threw McCoy an insulting mockery of a salute.

"The other qualification is the ability to keep your mouth shut," McCoy said to Hart.

"I think I could do that," Hart said.

"Yeah, so do I," McCoy said. "OK. Decision made. If you don't get along with . . . the officer we're talking about, we'll find something else for you to do. But one last time, if a CBI turns up something you're concealing from me, I will personally guarantee that you'll spend the rest of the war in an infantry line company."

"No, Sir. I know there's nothing in my background that would keep me from getting a security clearance. That's what you're talking about, isn't it? A Secret Clearance?"

"No," McCoy said. "Not Secret. We start with Secret and go up from there. Go find the sergeant major, would you, and ask him to come in here?"

"Aye, aye, Sir."

It took Hart several minutes to find Sergeant Major Osgood and Staff Sergeant Hungleberry. When they went back to the room, Lieutenant Moore was throwing up into a wastebasket.

"Jesus!" Sergeant Major Osgood said.

"I took him out of the Naval Hospital in Philadelphia, Teddy," McCoy explained. "That was dumb. He's not nearly as healthy as he thinks he is. He took some nasty mortar hits on the 'Canal."

"He going to be all right?"

"Hung over," McCoy said. "Teddy, we'll be taking Hart with us. Same deal as before, with Moore. I want him to disappear from his company and I don't want anybody talking about it."

"You got it, Ken."

"I don't know what's going on," Staff Sergeant Hungleberry said.

"That's right, you don't," Sergeant Major Osgood said. "What you're going to do now is take Hart to collect his stuff and then bring him back here. If anybody asks any questions tonight, refer them to me. I'll fix things with the brass in the morning."

"OK," Hungleberry said, doubtfully.

"What about the other guys, Ken?"

"I'll make my manners with the G-2 first thing in the morning, and I want to see them as soon as possible after that."

"Aye, aye, Sir. You going to need any help with him?"

"I was thinking of giving him a cold shower," McCoy said.

"Fuck your cold shower," Lieutenant John Marston Moore said. And then he was nauseated again.

[Three]
TASIMBOKO, GUADALCANAL
0530 HOURS 8 SEPTEMBER 1942

In early September, intelligence from Native Scouts attached to the First Marine Division reported several thousand Japanese in the vicinity of the village of Tasimboko, twenty miles down the coast from Henderson. Previous intelligence had placed the Japanese strength at no more than three hundred.

The inclination was to disbelieve this report, since it had not come from an established source and there were no confirming data from other sources. But arguing for it was the reputation of the Native Scouts. They had originally been part of the Royal Australian Navy Coastwatcher Establishment. Not only were they men of incredible courage, they had never been wrong before.

On 6 September 1942, an operations order was issued by Headquarters, First Marine Division, ordering the formation of a provisional battalion. After formation it would proceed by sea from Lunga Point to a beach near Taivu Point, from where it would stage a raid on the village of Tasimboko. The primary purpose of the raid was to confirm or deny the presence of several thousand Japanese and to destroy whatever Japanese matériel came into their hands.

The provisional battalion consisted of elements of the 1st Raider Battalion and the 1st Parachute Battalion. These "elements" were all that was left of them after the invasion. The parachute battalion had taken severe losses.

Lieutenant Colonel "Red Mike" Edson was senior to the 1st Parachute Battalion commander, and thus he was placed in command.

Transport from the port of departure (the beach near First Marine Division headquarters) to the raid site was to be by high-speed transport. This was something of a misnomer. High-speed transports were World War I destroyers with half their boilers removed; the space was converted to troop berthing. Removal of the boilers had lowered the vessels' speed to approximately that of an ordinary transport, but the ex-destroyers had retained most of their armament.

When the high-speed transports appeared offshore, it was immediately evident that there were not enough of them to carry the entire provisional battalion. And so hasty amendments were made to the operations order. These called for the 1st Raider Battalion to board the transports, invest and secure the beach near Tasimboko, and then hold in place until the transports could return to Lunga Point, board the 1st Parachute Battalion, and transport them to the raid area.

The Raiders began to land east of Tasimboko at dawn.

Largely because Gunnery Sergeant Joseph J. Johnston took one glance at him and decided that the large, muscular, mean-looking sonofabitch was just what he needed, Sergeant Thomas McCoy's reception at Company A, 1st Raider Battalion, was considerably warmer than it had been at Headquarters, 21st Marine Air Group.

For one thing, Able Company was considerably understrength. It took losses during the initial invasion a month before when the 1st Raider Battalion, under Lieutenant Colonel "Red Mike" Edson, landed near Lunga Point on Tulagi, a small island twenty-odd miles across SeaLark Channel from Guadalcanal.

And they'd gotten no replacements. Like every other Marine on Guadalcanal, Sergeant Johnston was very much aware that the goddamn Navy sailed away from the beaches with a hell of a lot of Marines, equipment, ammunition, and heavy artillery still in the holds of the transports. And even if some available bodies were ashore, it was unlikely that Colonel Edson would have asked for them: They would have been bodies, not Raiders. Raiders were special to begin with, and they'd been molded into something really special by their training and their first combat.

There had been additional losses since the invasion, most of them due to what The Corps called "noncombat causes." That translated to mean there were a great many very sick Raiders, brought down by tropical disease, mostly malaria, but including some diseases the surgeons and corpsmen had never heard of, much less seen before.

In Sergeant Johnston's opinion, the "rest" they gave the 1st Raiders before they were brought across SeaLark Channel to Guadalcanal had not restored them to what they were before. What it did was keep a great many more people from getting sick.

So Company A—for that matter, the entire 1st Raider Battalion—was understrength. And the available Marines were on the edge of sickness or near exhaustion (or both) from the lousy chow, the high heat and humidity, and all the necessary manual labor they had to perform.

But there was one particular personnel shortage Sergeant Johnston was especially aware of. He was a great admirer of one particular weapon in The Marine Corps arsenal, the Browning Automatic Rifle—a combination rifle and a machine gun that fired the same .30-06 cartridge.

The weapon, known as the BAR, was considerably lighter than the standard .30 caliber Browning machine gun; but like a machine gun, it was capable of full automatic fire: As long as you held the trigger back and there were cartridges in the magazine, the weapon would continue to fire.

Cartridges were held in a 20-round magazine that was

quickly replaceable when emptied. In fact, it was easier and quicker to change a BAR's 20-round magazine than it was to recharge with a stripper clip the nonreplaceable five-shot magazine of a Springfield rifle.

The BAR was commonly equipped with a bipod, two metal legs fixed to the barrel near the muzzle. They permitted accurate fire at great distance. And it had a well-earned reputation for reliability. The trouble was that at about sixteen pounds, it was twice as heavy as the Springfield rifle. The heavy weight, coupled with the recoil, meant that few men indeed could fire the BAR from the shoulder. Sergeant Johnston was one of them; and when he saw Sergeant Thomas McCoy, one of his first thoughts was that he was looking at somebody else who just might be able to do it.

"Your jacket says you made the Makin Island raid."

"I made the fucker, Sergeant."

"What'd you do?"

"I had a Boys."

The Boys Rifle was developed by the Royal Army after World War I as an antitank weapon. It was a .55 caliber bolt-action rifle, which in size—it weighed thirty-six pounds—was to the BAR what the BAR was to the Springfield. It was a weapon Sergeant Johnston admired as other men might admire a Rolls-Royce or a Renoir.

"You had a Boys? We're talking about the same weapon? A British .55 caliber Boys?"

"I had a fucking Boys," Sergeant McCoy said with quiet pride.

Sergeant Johnston had heard that Lieutenant Colonel Evans Carlson, who commanded the 2nd Raider Battalion, had authorized his men to arm themselves with any weapon they wished. This was the first proof he'd had of that.

"You do any good with it?"

"I shot up a fucking Jap airplane," McCoy replied. "Put a dozen rounds in the sonofabitch. It tried to take off, got fifty feet in the air, and fucking blew up."

That would explain the Bronze Star for valor that Sergeant McCoy's records recorded, Sergeant Johnston realized. *There was no mention of any specific act, but there wouldn't be if he had shot down an airplane with a Boys.*

"I guess you can use a BAR all right, huh?"

"Yeah, sure."

"Off hand?"

Very few men could fire the BAR off hand—in other words, standing up and holding the BAR like a Springfield.

"Yeah, sure."

"Tell you what, McCoy," Sergeant Johnston said. "I got what you might call a provisional heavy weapons squad I think might be just the place for you."

"What's a provisional heavy weapons squad?"

"Twelve guys instead of eight. Two BARs. Two guys with Springfields. The rest carry Thompsons and ammo bandoliers for the BARs."

"Yeah, maybe. I think I'd like that," McCoy replied.

Sergeant Johnston did not, however, take Sergeant McCoy at his word. He checked his knowledge of the BAR, which proved to be adequate, and then he tested his marksmanship with it. Sergeant McCoy turned out to be a fucking artist firing the BAR.

When Sergeant Johnston saw Sergeant McCoy walking across the beach at Tasimboko, his BAR suspended at waist height from his shoulder, trailed by two Marines loaded down with BAR magazines, firing the sonofabitch in two- and three-shot bursts with all the finesse of a fucking violin player, he began to suspect that giving the provisional heavy weapons squad to Sergeant McCoy had been a correct command decision.

Twenty minutes later, when one of the ammo bearers returned in the dual role of ammunition replenishment and runner, there was proof positive:

"Sergeant McCoy took out a Jap outpost," the guy said, "and then we took a Jap artillery battery. He wants to know what you want him to do now."

"Get your ass back up there and tell him to dig in. We're about to get some air support."

Five minutes later the air support arrived. It consisted of those funny-looking Army Air Corps P-400 fighters, accompanied by Marine SBD bombers.

By the time the bombing and strafing ended, the transports had returned and landed the elements of the 1st Parachute Battalion. And so a general advance on the village was ordered.

It was necessary to ask for additional air support to drive the defenders from the village, but by quarter to ten it was secure.

The intelligence report of the ex–Coastwatcher Establishment Native Scouts proved to be accurate.

The Marines of the provisional battalion spent almost two hours destroying Japanese matériel, almost certainly recently landed. It included several landing craft, one 37mm cannon (McCoy had captured it early on), four 75mm cannon, radios, and large stocks of ammunition and medical supplies.

At 1230 hours, the Marines were ordered to return to the beach to reboard the transports. They took with them two of their own dead and six wounded. They left behind twenty-seven dead Japanese and an uncounted number of Japanese wounded.

Lieutenant Colonel "Red Mike" Edson stood at the sandbagged entrance to the command post of the Commanding General, First Marine Division, until General Alexander Archer Vandergrift sensed his presence. When Vandergrift looked at him, Edson saluted, and then went into the CP.

"How did it go, Mike?"

"Two KIA, six WIA, two seriously."

"I'm sorry."

"The Native Scouts were right, Sir."

"They usually are."

"We destroyed a large amount of matériel. Here's a list, Sir."

He handed the list to Vandergrift, who read it and then looked at him.

"Large quantities of medical supplies would seem to indicate a large force, wouldn't you say?"

"Yes, Sir. And that much ammo translates to a lot of weapons, too, Sir. I took what documentation I could find to G-2 to get it translated, but there's no question in my mind that what we captured was not what the Japanese here took with them into the boondocks when we landed."

Vandergrift nodded but did not reply.

"There's several thousand Japs in that area, General. What I don't understand is why they didn't attack us."

"Conservation of force for future action is often a wise choice," Vandergrift said. "I would guess that after he saw how you landed your force in two segments, the Japanese commander decided that you didn't intend to stay. Therefore there was no point in expending assets to throw you back in the sea."

"Yes, Sir."

"He can better use those assets here," Vandergrift said,

pointing to the map. "Either trying to knock Henderson Field out of operation, or even taking it. I don't like those 75mm cannon. If you captured four, I think we better count on a lot more."

"Yes, Sir. I thought about that."

"Take a look at this, Mike," Vandergrift said, and handed him a sheet of paper with TOP SECRET stamped on it top and bottom.

" 'The operation to surround and recapture Guadalcanal will truly decide the fate of the control of the entire Pacific,' " Edson read aloud.

"From Lieutenant General Harukichi Hyakutake to the 17th Army," Vandergrift said. "Odd how the minds of brilliant men run in the same paths, isn't it, Mike?"

"May I ask where you got this, Sir?"

"No, you may not."

"General, there's a rumor going around that we've broken the Japanese codes."

"Mike, you've got a major flaw," Vandergrift said coldly. "You don't know how to take no for an answer."

"Yes, Sir. Sorry, Sir."

"You can consider this an order, Colonel. You will tell no one, repeat, no one, that I showed you that document."

"Aye, aye, Sir."

Vandergrift met Edson's eyes long enough to convince him that he had made his point, paused long enough to curse himself for showing him the MAGIC intercept in the first place, and then allowed his facial muscles to relax.

"So how were the men?"

"They're tired, General, and I think undernourished."

Vandergrift nodded.

"Are you putting anyone in for a decoration?"

"No, Sir," Edson said. "There were no 'conspicuous acts of gallantry' that I know about. Maybe later. But I *am* going to make one buck sergeant a staff sergeant."

"What did he do?"

"Well, I was up pretty close to the line when we got our air support—which was right on the money, General—"

"I'm glad to hear that."

"—and when the strafing and bombing lifted, I looked around, and marching down this little path in the boondocks was this great big guy with a BAR. He had it suspended from his neck and was firing it from the hip. He had two Marines with spare magazines running to keep up with him. And he was smiling from ear to ear. It looked like a World War One movie with Douglas Fairbanks."

"Really?"

"I figure any man who can smile when he's hauling a BAR around deserves to be a staff sergeant."

"I concur, Colonel," Vandergrift said with a smile.

[Four]
THE FOSTER LAFAYETTE HOTEL
WASHINGTON, D.C.
0755 HOURS 9 SEPTEMBER 1942

Captain Edward L. Sessions, USMC, was standing inside the lobby of the hotel when the LaSalle convertible pulled up at the curb.

He quickly put his brimmed cap on and walked to the curb, reaching it just as the doorman pulled the car door open.

"Good morning," he said. "Let me get in the back."

There were three people in the front seat, two of whom he knew, Lieutenants McCoy and Moore. The man he had come to see, Private George Hart, was at the wheel.

McCoy slid forward on the seat, permitting Sessions to squeeze into the back.

All three of them looked as if they had driven through the night, which was of course the case.

"Let's go somewhere and get a cup of coffee," Sessions said, sitting on the forward edge of the rear seat, trying to get a better look at Hart.

"Turn right on Pennsylvania Avenue," McCoy ordered. "There's a place we can go a couple of blocks away."

"Aye, aye, Sir," Hart replied.

He was very much aware that in the normal course of events he should have been on the drill field at Parris Island at this hour, not at the wheel of a LaSalle convertible, driving past the White House.

"Long ride?" Sessions asked.

"You said it," McCoy said, "and we ran into a patriotic Virginia highway cop who took this new 35-mph speed limit

very seriously. He said he was really surprised that Marines—
of all people, they should know better—would be speeding."

"Get a ticket?"

"No." McCoy chuckled. "Hart still had his badge. Professional courtesy. He let us go."

"You were a detective, I understand, Hart?"

"Yes, Sir."

"How are you, Moore?"

"Fine, Sir."

"He is not," McCoy said. "I should not have let him talk me
into taking him out of the hospital."

"I'm all right, Sir," Moore said.

"Congratulations on the gold bar," Sessions said.

"Thank you," Moore said. "We got you a linguist, Captain.
Just one."

"I thought there were supposed to be three?"

"Two didn't speak a word of Japanese," McCoy said.

"Anybody else?"

"Couple of radio operators. The trip was really a waste of
time."

"Are you including Private Hart in that?"

"Isn't that why you wanted to meet us? To make that decision?" McCoy asked.

"I thought it would be a good idea to talk to Hart before we
take him to see General Pickering," Sessions said. "I wasn't
questioning your judgment, Ken, I just thought it would be a
good idea for me—"

"I know, to talk to him," McCoy said.

"Are you going to tell me why I am annoying you, or am I
supposed to just sit here and suffer in silence?" Sessions said
sharply.

"I'm pissed at me, Captain," McCoy said. "When Moore
got out of bed this morning—correction: yesterday morning—
he passed out."

"I told you, I slipped," Moore interrupted.

"He passed out and fell down . . . hit his leg on a dresser
drawer and opened his goddamned wound. And when they
took a look at him at the dispensary, they wanted to keep him.
I had a hell of a time getting him out."

"I'm all right," Moore insisted.

"Do you think we should take him to Bethesda?" Sessions
asked.

"Sir, I would prefer to go back to Philadelphia," Moore said.

"I should never have taken you out of Philadelphia," McCoy said.

"OK," Sessions said. "Lieutenant Moore, you will return to the Naval Hospital at Philadelphia and you will stay there until properly discharged by competent medical authority. Understand?"

Moore nodded.

"Lieutenant, when an officer receives an order from a superior officer, the expected response is, 'Aye, aye, Sir.' "

"Aye, aye, Sir."

"What the hell's the matter with you, John? You were seriously wounded," Sessions said, far more gently.

"Sir, I'm all right. I'm a little weak, that's all."

"You up to driving to Philadelphia? Or should I make other arrangements?"

"I can ride in a car, Sir."

"There it is," McCoy said. "Make the next right, Hart."

"You guys have your breakfast?" Sessions asked.

"We stopped in Richmond," McCoy said. "But I could have something. Coffee and a doughnut anyway."

"I called General Pickering after you called me yesterday," Sessions said. "He said we could bring Hart by at eight this morning. But when I called from the lobby, there was no answer. I guess he's still asleep. If it makes you feel any better, Lieutenant Moore, neither one of you should be out of the hospital."

"Yes, Sir."

"So there will be time for me to talk a little to Private Hart, and then we'll go see the General. Give him another hour in bed."

An hour later, when Captain Sessions called on the house phone in the lobby of the Foster Lafayette Hotel, there was no answer from Senator Richmond F. Fowler's suite.

"Wait here," Sessions ordered, and then modified that. "You go sit down, Moore, over there. I'm going to check with the desk and see if he left a message."

There was no message at the desk.

"I don't like this," Sessions said to McCoy. "I think we'd better see if we can get somebody to let us into the suite."

"Sir," Private Hart said, "I've got a sort of master key for hotel rooms, if you'd like me to try."

"I told you," McCoy said, smiling, "that Hart would be useful."

"Let's see if your key works, Hart," Sessions said.

There was a Do Not Disturb card hanging from the doorknob of the Fowler suite.

"Fowler's in Chicago," Sessions said. "Pickering told me when I called him."

Hart pushed the Do Not Disturb card out of the way and applied his "key"—the blade of a pocketknife ground square and flat—to the crack in the door. He then pushed the door open and stood back to let Sessions enter.

In the sitting room were the remnants of Fleming Pickering's room service dinner, including the wheeled cart and an empty quart of scotch.

Sessions, with McCoy on his heels, went quickly to Pickering's bedroom.

When they opened the door, the foul smell of human waste met them.

Fleming Pickering, wearing only a sleeveless undershirt, made a failed attempt to pull a sheet over him.

"My God!" Sessions said.

"I seem to be a little under the weather," Fleming Pickering said weakly.

McCoy went to the bed and made an instant diagnosis: "Malaria," he said.

"You think that's what it is, Ken?" Pickering asked.

"Sweating, freezing? You can't control your bowels?" McCoy asked.

"Yes. Made a hell of a mess, haven't I?"

"We've got to get him out of that bed," Hart said matter-of-factly. "In addition to the mess he's made, it's soaking wet."

"There's at least one more bedroom," Sessions said.

"You two get him on his feet," Hart ordered, "and I'll clean him up. Then we'll move him."

"Moore," Sessions ordered, "get on the horn and get the house physician up here. And then call the dispensary at Eighth and Eye and have them send an ambulance over here. An ambulance and a doctor."

"The dispensary where?" Moore asked.

"At Marine Barracks. The number will be in the phone book," Sessions said.

"No," Pickering said, as McCoy and Sessions bent over the bed to pick him up. "Moore, don't call the dispensary. Just the house doctor. His name is Selleres. He can take care of me."

"Call the dispensary, Moore," Sessions ordered.

"Goddamn it, Captain," Pickering said furiously. "I said no."

"Do what the General says, Moore," Sessions said after a moment's hesitation.

Hart came out of the bathroom with wet towels and wiped the waste from Pickering's groin area and from his legs.

"God, that's disgusting, something like this," Pickering said.

"Don't be silly, General," Hart said. "Women do it to their babies three, four times a day."

"Christ!" Pickering said.

"Where's the other bedroom?" Hart asked.

"Down the corridor somewhere, I suppose," Sessions said. Then, with Pickering suspended between them, he and McCoy carried Pickering out of the room.

Hart went ahead of them into the other bedroom and had the covers ripped off one of its twin beds before they dragged Pickering in.

"We've got to get some fluid in him," McCoy said. "He's dehydrated."

"Do you know what you're doing, McCoy?" Sessions asked.

"This isn't the first malaria I've seen."

They lowered Pickering into the bed. Hart covered him with a blanket.

"A minute ago I was sweating," Pickering said. "Now, goddamn it, I'm freezing!"

His body shook with shivering under the blanket. Hart ripped the bedspread and a blanket from the other twin bed and laid it over him.

"Doctor Sellers is on his way," Moore announced from the door.

"Seller*es*," Pickering corrected him. His teeth chattered.

"Yes, Sir," Moore said.

"What the hell are you doing out of the hospital?" Pickering demanded.

"About the same thing you are, General," McCoy said. "Making things a hell of a lot worse."

Dr. Selleres appeared a minute or two later, and immediately confirmed McCoy's diagnosis and immediate treatment.

"Somebody get General Pickering a glass of water," he ordered.

"The water here is undrinkable," Pickering said. "There should be some ginger ale."

"OK, ginger ale. Have you been nauseous?"

"No, but I have had a first-class display of diarrhea."

"The ginger ale may make you nauseous."

"I'll take my chances, thank you," Pickering said. "And aside from ginger ale, what can you do for me?"

"Well, the first thing we do is get you into an ambulance and into a hospital."

"No."

"You have to go to the hospital, General. Period. No argument."

"Jesus Christ! Why can't you do what you have to do here?"

"Well, for one thing, Fleming, we don't have facilities to conduct an autopsy here, and unless you start behaving, that's the next medical procedure you'll need."

"Bullshit."

"No. No bullshit. The facts. How long have you been experiencing symptoms like these?"

"The diarrhea's new. And the goddamned weakness. But the hot and cold spells, a couple of days. Three maybe. Maybe four."

"And you've been treating yourself with aspirin and scotch, right?"

"I thought the scotch had given me the runs," Pickering said.

Hart appeared with a bottle of ginger ale and two glasses, one empty and one with ice.

"Here you are, Sir."

"That's liable to make you sick, Fleming," Dr. Selleres said.

"So you said," Pickering snapped, and then, "I don't have the goddamn strength to sit up."

Hart went to him and held him in a sitting position. McCoy held the glass to his lips.

Sessions went into the sitting room and dialed a number from memory. When Colonel Rickabee came on the line, he told him what was going on. Then he went back into the bedroom.

"An ambulance is on the way," he said, "with a doctor and

corpsmen. The General will be taken to Walter Reed Army Hospital, which has the best malaria treatment facilities in the area."

"You really think I need hospitalization, Emilio?" Pickering asked.

"Only if you want to live, Fleming," Dr. Selleres said.

"Hell!" Pickering said, and then shrugged. He looked at the people standing around his bed. "If I'm going back in the hospital, John, so are you. Can you arrange that, Sessions?"

"It's already been arranged, Sir. He's going in your ambulance."

"McCoy, will you telephone Mrs. Pickering and make sure she doesn't get hysterical when she hears about this?"

"Yes, Sir, if you want me to."

"I'll call her, Fleming," Dr. Selleres said. "If I don't, she'll call me."

Pickering ignored him. He looked at Private George Hart.

"You've just had one hell of an introduction to a prospective boss, son. I would certainly understand why you wouldn't want to work for me."

"Do I have a choice, Sir?"

"Yes, of course, you do."

"I think I'd like very much to work for you, Sir."

Pickering didn't reply for a moment. Then he said, "Sessions, Moore told me that when you snatched him out of Parris Island you made him an overnight sergeant. And he didn't even have to wipe an officer's ass. Can you do as much for this young man?"

"Yes, Sir. If that is the General's desire, Private Hart will be a sergeant before noon."

"That is the General's desire," Pickering said. Then he looked at Dr. Emilio Selleres. "I hate to admit this, but you're right, you sonofabitch. I'm about to throw up."

"Roll over on your side, Fleming," Selleres said.

Outside, there was the wail of a siren.

"Do you suppose that's for me?" Pickering asked. "Or is that Roosevelt out for a morning drive?"

And then he was shaken with chills and nausea.

VIII

"We could have eaten downstairs, you know," Andrew Foster said as he transferred two kippers from a crystal platter to his grandson's plate with all the skill and élan of any of his first-class waiters. Foster was in his sixties, tall and distinguished-looking, with elegantly cut silver hair.

"The service isn't nearly as nice downstairs," Second Lieutenant Malcolm S. Pickering replied, adding, "thank you."

"But on the other hand, I'm not nearly as pretty as any of the half-dozen young women I'm sure you would have found down there."

They were sitting at a glass-topped cast-iron table on the tiled terrace of the penthouse. A striped awning had been lowered enough to shade them from the morning sun, and mottled glass panels in steel frames had been rolled into place to shield them from the wind.

"But they couldn't possibly smell as good as you do," Pick said. "What is that you're wearing?"

"Something your mother gave me. I thought she might come with you, so I bit the bullet and sprayed some on."

"Very nice."

"Perhaps for a French gigolo," Foster said.

"Maybe a little strong." Pick chuckled.

"The last time I had some on, a gentleman of exquisite grace, inhaling rapturously, followed me across the lobby," the old man said, "thinking he'd found the love of his life."

Pick laughed. "It's not that bad."

"I'd be happy to give you what's left of the bottle."

"Thank you, but no thank you," Pick said.

A waiter came to the table and picked up a silver-collar orange juice pitcher.

"More juice, Mr. Pickering?"

"No, thank you," Pick said.

"Have some more," the old man said. "I rather doubt where you're going that freshly squeezed orange juice will be on the menu."

"Point well taken, Sir," Pick said. "Yes, please, Fred."

"Speaking of where you're going, you haven't said where or when?"

"I report to Mare Island on the thirteenth. I'm headed for VMF-229. I'm not supposed to know, but I do. It's on Guadalcanal."

"What is . . . what you said?"

"VMF-229. It's a fighter squadron."

"Do you feel qualified to go, Pick?"

"I think I'm a pretty good pilot."

"I'm sure you are."

"On the other hand, I sometimes think my ego is running away with me," Pick confessed. "I guess I'll just have to wait and see."

"I had an interesting chat, a while back, with a Marine pilot."

"There must be fifteen or twenty in the bar every night," Pick said.

"This was an interesting chap. I had him and his lady to dinner up here. With your mother."

"His 'lady'?"

"Well, she *was* a lady. I liked her and so did your mother, but it came out that their relationship had not yet culminated in holy matrimony.''

"Illicit cohabitation? In the Andrew Foster? Shocking! And the innkeeper had them to dinner? With my mother?"

"Yes, and the innkeeper was very glad that he did. He told me all about your training. I understood at least twenty percent of what he told me. And I think he managed to alleviate some of your mother's concerns—"

"Which is why you had him to dinner, right?"

"Certainly. He was a very impressive man. On his way to the Pacific. Galloway was his name. He said he was to be a squadron commander."

"I don't know the name," Pick said.

"He didn't know yours, either," the old man said. "I asked." The telephone rang.

"Take that, Fred, will you, please?" the old man said. "And remind the operator that I said I didn't want any calls."

The waiter went inside, and Pick could hear him speaking softly on the phone. Then, to his surprise, he reappeared on the terrace, telephone in hand. He plugged it in and handed it to Andrew Foster.

"The inn better be on fire, Fred," the old man said as he took the telephone.

"I thought you had better take it, Mr. Foster."

"This is Andrew Foster.

"No, Mrs. Pickering is not here.

"I'm afraid I have no idea where she is."

"She said she would be at the office from about eleven," Pick said. "What is that?"

The old man handed him the phone.

"Who is this, please?" Pick asked.

"My name is McCoy, Sir. I'm a Marine officer."

"From what I hear, you're a flaming disgrace to the god-damn Marine Corps," Pick said cheerfully.

There was a moment's hesitation, then the caller asked, "Is that you, Pick?"

"How the hell are you, you ugly bastard?"

"Pick, I'm calling from Walter Reed. Your dad's in here."

"Jesus, now what?"

"He's going to be all right. I waited until they gave him a . . . Colonel Rickabee just got the word from the doctors."

"Who's he?"

"He works for your father."

"So what's going on?"

"Your father has malaria. I went to his room in the hotel this morning and found him too weak to even sit up. He's been treating himself with scotch and aspirin. But he's going to be all right. He made me promise to call your mother and see what I could do to calm her down. I called all over, and finally somebody at your house—Talbot, something like that—gave me this number."

"Mother's butler," Pick said. "It's my grandfather's number. That was him on the phone before."

"OK. So what I know is this: He has malaria. There's two kinds, intestinal, and—I forget what they call it, in the brain. That's really bad news. He has intestinal. That's not as bad. What it does is give you chills and fever, and you lose control of your bowels, and you throw up a lot."

"That's not bad, huh?"

"It dehydrates you. He was in pretty bad shape when we found him. But we got him in the hospital, and they're giving him stuff to kill the malaria, and they're putting fluid in him. He's going to be all right."

"Define 'all right,' " Pick said.

"He's sick. He's weak, and embarrassed."

"What do you mean, embarrassed? What the hell's he got to be embarrassed about?"

"He . . . shit his bed. We had to wash him like a baby."

"God!"

"He said I was to tell your mother there was no need for her to do anything foolish, like come to Washington."

"Which means she will be on the next plane. *We* will be on the first plane."

"You better think about that," McCoy said. "You're supposed to be at Mare Island on the thirteenth."

"How do you know that?"

"I checked. Actually, you're supposed to be in Pensacola. What was that all about?"

"I had originally . . ." Pick said, and stopped. "What the hell does it matter?"

"I called all over Pensacola for you. I finally got some Admiral's wife on the phone, and she told me you were on your way to San Francisco."

The Admiral's wife was Mrs. Richard B. Sayre, mother to

Mrs. Martha Sayre Culhane. Upon learning that Lieutenant Pickering was headed for the Pacific, Martha had been even more determined than ever not to marry him. Martha had said it so often he had no choice but to believe her: She could not go through again what she'd already gone through. She couldn't wait around for the inevitable telegram from the Secretary of the Navy expressing his deep regret that her husband had been lost in aerial combat against the forces of the Empire of Japan.

"There's no way you could come here and get back out there by the thirteenth," McCoy said.

"I could get an emergency leave," Pick said.

"Yeah, *you* probably could," McCoy said. There was a hint of disgust in his voice.

"Meaning what?"

"Meaning you're a Marine officer, and you have your orders. There's nothing you could do for your father here except embarrass him by showing up."

"Fuck you, Ken!" Pick flared, but then immediately: "Shit. I'm sorry. You're right, of course."

"Look, he's sick, but in a couple of weeks, a month, he's going to be all right, OK?"

"That's the straight poop?"

"That's straight."

"You going to see him?"

"Yeah, sure."

"Tell him . . . You know what to tell him."

"Yeah. Sure. You'll tell your mother?"

"I'll tell her and she'll come."

"He won't like that."

"Yes, he will, and besides, there's nothing he can do about it."

"OK."

"Thanks for . . . everything, I guess, Ken."

"Take care of yourself, pal."

"You, too."

The line went dead.

Pick held the phone in his hand for a long moment before dropping it into the cradle. Then he raised his eyes and found his grandfather's eyes on him.

"That was Ken McCoy. We went to OCS at Quantico together."

The old man nodded.

"You understood what that was all about?"

"Some of it."

"Dad's in Walter Reed Hospital with malaria. He's apparently pretty sick, but in no danger."

"I gather we should see about getting your mother on an airplane?"

"Just Mother. It was just pointed out to me that I do not have time to go to see him."

"I will take your mother to see him and tell him why you couldn't be there. Is there anything else I can do, Pick?"

Pick raised both hands helplessly.

"What?" he asked.

[Two]
TEMPORARY BUILDING T-2032
THE MALL
WASHINGTON, D.C.
1630 HOURS 9 SEPTEMBER 1942

When First Lieutenant Kenneth R. McCoy pushed open the outer door of the two-story frame building, he noticed a new sign, USMC OFFICE OF MANAGEMENT ANALYSIS, nailed to the side of the building. Previously, there had been no sign at all. Since that made Building T-2032 even more anonymous among the other identical "temporary" frame buildings—they had been there since the First World War—he wondered why Colonel Rickabee had decided to hang a sign.

As he took the stairs to the second floor two at a time, he decided that some brass hat with nothing better to do had probably issued an edict that all buildings would be properly labeled.

It had probably occupied the better part of his time for a month, McCoy mused, *first coming up with the idea, and then deciding in precise detail the size of the sign, and of its lettering, and its color.*

As he reached the second floor, he remembered that a bird colonel and his entourage had been sharing the building.

He was charged with coordinating enlisted morale projects with the Army and Navy, or some such bullshit. I wonder why he doesn't have a sign?

At the top of the stairwell was a small foyer. Access to the rest of the building was barred by a counter; wire mesh went from the countertop to the ceiling.

McCoy recognized one of the two staff noncoms behind the barrier.

"Open up, Rutterman," he said.

Technical Sergeant Harry Rutterman, who had first come to know Lieutenant McCoy as a just-graduated-from-Quantico second lieutenant, threw up his hands in horror.

"Sir, these are classified premises," he said. "Will you please state the nature of your business and show me your identification?"

"You're kidding."

"Not at all, Sir. Less than an hour ago, our beloved commanding officer passed through these portals without challenge, and then ate my ass out for letting *him* in."

"Really?"

"I think you are next on his menu, Lieutenant, if you don't mind my saying so," Rutterman said. "He left word that he wants to see you as soon as you came in."

McCoy extended his identification, a leather folder holding a badge and a photo identification card.

"Pass, friend," Rutterman said, as he pushed a button which operated a solenoid that unlocked a wire mesh door. "And good luck!"

"If I wasn't an officer and a gentleman, Harry, I'd tell you to take a flying fuck at a rolling doughnut," McCoy said as he walked past him.

Colonel F. L. Rickabee's office was at the corner of the far end of the building. Its door was closed. McCoy knocked and said, "McCoy, Sir."

"Come!"

McCoy opened the door, marched in, and stood to attention before Rickabee's desk, even though Rickabee was in civilian clothing.

"Moore?" Rickabee asked.

"He's all right, Sir. It was exhaustion more than anything else."

"Taking him out of the hospital was stupid, McCoy."

"Yes, Sir. No excuse, Sir."

"Sessions told me that General Pickering ordered you to get

in touch with his wife." It was a question more than a statement.

"Yes, Sir. I was unable to reach Mrs. Pickering, but I spoke with his son, Sir."

"That's right, you know him, don't you?"

"We were in OCS together, Sir."

"Where's this man Hart?"

"At the hotel, Sir. I didn't know what to do with him. I was going to ask if you wanted to see him."

"I'll have to go on what Sessions and you feel," Rickabee said. "I'll want to see him when he comes back."

"Sir?"

Rickabee handed him a large manila envelope. McCoy opened it. It contained airline tickets and a sheaf of mimeographed orders.

HEADQUARTERS
UNITED STATES MARINE CORPS
WASHINGTON, D.C.

9 September 1942

LETTER ORDERS:

To: SGT Hart, George F 386751, USMCR
      Company "A"
      Marine Barracks
      Washington, DC

    1. You will proceed this date to San Francisco, Cal., St. Louis, Mo., and such other destinations as may be necessary in carrying out the mission assigned to you by the Office of Management Analysis, Hq USMC.

    2. Travel by government and civilian rail, motor and air transportation is authorized. Priority AAA.

    3. A five (5) day delay en route leave is authorized in connection with these orders.

BY DIRECTION OF BRIG GEN F. PICKERING:

F. L. Rickabee, Col, USMC
Executive Officer, Office of Management Analysis

I'll be damned. He's sending Hart out there to tell Pick his father'll be all right, McCoy thought.

He blurted what popped into his mind: "That was very nice of you, Sir."

" 'Nice' is not one of my character traits, McCoy," Colonel Rickabee said. "One: I think it important that your man Hart understand just who he will be working for. His initial introduction to the General was something less than inspiring. Seeing what he did in civilian life, who he was, will be instructional. Two: I think it is important that General Pickering knows that we think of him as one of our own. Three: Sergeant Hart is entitled to an end of boot-camp leave; and he won't be needed around here anyway for ten days, possibly more."

Bullshit—that was nice of you!

"Yes, Sir. Sorry, Sir. I know that, Sir."

"I would hate to think you were being sarcastic, McCoy."

"Not me, Sir."

"Sessions tells me you told him Mrs. Pickering will be coming to Washington."

"Yes, Sir. I think she will."

"Keep me advised of her schedule. I'd like to meet her plane, or train, whatever."

"Yes, Sir."

"General Pickering, McCoy, can be very valuable to us around here. It thus behooves us to do whatever we can for him."

Bullshit again, Colonel. You like Pickering. You're two of a kind.

"Yes, Sir."

"Get out of here, McCoy."

"Yes, Sir."

[Three]
MUNICIPAL AIRPORT
SAN FRANCISCO, CALIFORNIA
1530 HOURS 11 SEPTEMBER 1942

When Hart entered the terminal after leaving the Transcontinental and Western (TWA) DC-3 that brought him from Chicago, with a stop at Salt Lake City, two shore patrolmen were standing in the middle of the airport aisle. One was a sailor armed with a billy club, and the other was a Marine sergeant, wearing a .45 suspended from a white web belt.

Neither of them looks like much of a cop, former Detective George Hart decided, and then dismissed them from his mind as he headed for a row of telephone booths.

Lieutenant McCoy had given him four telephone numbers for Lieutenant Pickering: the Pickering home, in Marin County; the offices of Pacific & Far East Shipping, in San Francisco; the San Francisco apartment of Mrs. Fleming Pickering; and the Andrew Foster Hotel. If he called the last number, he was instructed to ask for Mr. Andrew Foster, stating he was a friend of Lieutenant Pickering.

His orders were to tell Lieutenant Pickering, without any bullshit, General Pickering's condition when they went into the bedroom of the Foster Lafayette Hotel, and then to tell him that the prognosis was good and that his coming to Washington would have only embarrassed his father.

"Tell Lieutenant Pickering he's doing the right thing by not coming," Lieutenant McCoy said. "And, if you have to, that I wouldn't lie to him. And tell him to call me just before he gets on his plane, and I'll give him the latest poop."

Hart had just taken the list of telephone numbers from his pocket and was about to drop a nickel in the pay phone slot, when there was a sharp rap on the telephone booth window.

It was the sailor shore patrolman. He made a sign with his index finger for Hart to come out of the booth.

"What can I do for you?" Hart asked.

"For one thing, you can show us your orders," the Marine sergeant said.

Hart produced a copy of the orders from the breast pocket of his tunic and handed them over.

The MP read them and showed them to the sailor.

"Anybody with a mimeograph machine could have made these up," he said. "There's no stamp or seal or nothing."

"That thought occurred to me on the way out here," Hart said.

"Where did you get that haircut, *Sergeant*?" the Marine asked.

"Parris Island."

"Boots' hair usually grows back in before they make sergeant," the Marine said. "I think, *Sergeant,* that you better come with us until we can check out these orders."

I was wrong. This guy's not as dumb as he looks. He picked up on the Parris Island haircut.

"How about this, Sergeant?" Hart said, and handed him the leather folder holding the badge identifying him as a Special Agent of the Office of Naval Intelligence and the accompanying photo identification card.

"I'll be damned," the sergeant said. "Sorry."

"No problem. It was the haircut, right?"

"Yeah, and there's two inspection stickers hanging out on the back of your jacket," the Marine said. "So I checked."

"I understand."

"Could I ask you a question?"

"Sure."

"How do you get a billet like that? It would sure be better than standing around an airport all day looking for AWOLs and drunks."

"I really don't know," Hart replied. "That's where they sent me when I got out of Parris Island. I used to be a cop. But I didn't apply for it or anything like that."

"It would sure beat standing around this fucking airport," the Marine repeated, and then smiled and walked off.

Hart went back into the telephone booth and struck out with the first three numbers. After three intermediate people came on the line, the fourth call was finally answered:

"Andrew Foster."

Jesus, I'm actually talking to the guy who owns all those hotels!

"Mr. Foster, my name is Sergeant Hart. I'm trying to locate Lieutenant Malcolm S. Pickering."

"Perhaps I could help you."

"Sir, I really would like to speak to Lieutenant Pickering. It's about his father."

"Is this bad news, Sergeant?"

"No, Sir. The opposite. I was with General Pickering when . . . just before we took him to the hospital. I've been asked to tell Lieutenant Pickering about that. And how the General is doing now."

"I'd be very much interested in hearing what you have to say, Sergeant," Andrew Foster said, "if that's possible. General Pickering is my son-in-law."

After a moment's hesitation, Hart delivered a slightly laundered report of the events in the hotel room, and then the prognosis the doctors at Walter Reed had offered—complete recovery after three to six weeks of rest in the hospital.

"I'm sure my grandson will be delighted to hear this, Sergeant. He's been climbing the walls around here the last couple of days. The problem would seem to be getting you together. Where are you?"

"At the airport, Sir."

"At the passenger terminal?"

"Yes, Sir."

"Across the field from the passenger terminal is Hangar 103," Andrew Foster said. "It says 'Lewis Flying Services' on it. My grandson should be there. He should be somewhere around my airplane. If he is not, call me back here. I'll either know where he is by then, or we can launch a manhunt together."

"Yes, Sir. Thank you very much."

"Sergeant, am I permitted to ask your connection with General Pickering?"

After a brief hesitation, Hart decided to answer this question, too.

"Sir, I've been assigned to look after General Pickering."

"Somehow I don't think that means you're his valet, or orderly, or whatever they call it."

"No, Sir."

"If my grandson's not there, call me, Sergeant."

"Yes, Sir."

There was little activity inside Hangar 103, and no one in Marine uniform. But a young man with a bored look was leaning against the hangar wall next to a battery charger. He was wearing oil-stained khaki trousers and an oil-stained T-shirt under a cotton zipper jacket. His tan and his haircut suggested he was no stranger to military service.

Me and Sherlock Holmes in the airport.

"Excuse me, Sir," Hart said. "I'm looking for Lieutenant Pickering."

"You found him," Pick said.

Hart saluted. "Sergeant Hart, Sir. I work for Lieutenant McCoy, Sir."

Pick did not return the salute.

"OK," he said, his voice even but tense. "No beating around the bush. Let's have it."

"Your father will be all right. They will keep him in the hospital for three to six weeks of rest and treatment. From what I have seen of your father, I'd bet on three weeks."

"Jesus Christ, that's a relief! When you said McCoy had sent you, I was really worried."

"My orders, Sir, are to tell you exactly what happened."

"Go ahead."

When he had finished, Pick said, "Thank you, Sergeant."

There was a moment's silence, and then Pick asked, "They sent you all the way out here to tell me this?"

"Yes, Sir."

"What's your connection with my father?"

"I work for him, Sir."

"Doing what?"

"Whatever he tells me to do, Sir."

"In other words you're not going to tell me. But since you *have* told me you work for McCoy, it wouldn't be unreasonable for me to assume, would it, that you're also involved—suitably draped in a cape—in all those mysterious things McCoy does but won't talk about?"

Hart didn't reply. When it was evident to Pick that he wasn't going to reply, he went on, "I'll rephrase, Sergeant. Would it be unreasonable of me to assume that you are not my father's orderly?"

"I'm not your father's orderly, Sir."

"OK, we'll leave it at that. So what are you going to do now?"

"I have a plane reservation for tomorrow afternoon, Sir."

"Nothing to do right now? How about a hotel reservation?"

"No, Sir."

"Well, we can take care of that, the hotel, I mean."

"That's not necessary, Sir."

"I'll make you a deal, Sergeant. You do two things for me, and I will take care of the hotel and throw in dinner and all the booze you can handle."

"My orders are to do whatever you ask me to do, Sir."

"Great. The first thing is, stop calling me 'Sir.' The second thing is, help me get this heavy fucking battery back in the airplane. I almost ruptured myself taking it out."

Hart knew very little about airplanes, but when he had

walked across the hangar floor to meet Lieutenant Pickering, he noticed a single-engine biplane he recognized as a Stagger Wing Beechcraft. A compartment hatch in the fuselage was open.

Obviously, the battery Pickering was now disconnecting from the battery charger had come out of it.

"Why did you take the battery out?"

Pickering looked at him with amusement in his eyes.

"It was dead, Sergeant," he said. "One recharges dead batteries. It *resurrects* them, so to speak."

"I meant, why recharge it, Sir."

"You've agreed not to call me Sir," Pick said. "Which brings us to what do I call you?"

"My name is George."

"Well, George, the reason I am recharging the battery is that this is my grandpa's airplane. Most light civilian aircraft like this one have been taken over by the armed forces, for reasons I can't imagine. This one, however, Grandpa got to keep because it was essential to his business. Or at least he got our Senator to tell the Air Corps it was essential to his business. He and our Senator, by happy coincidence, are old pals. By the time they had gone through all this, the pilots had gone into the Army Air Corps. You following all this?"

"More or less," Hart said, smiling.

"More or less, *Pick*," Pick corrected him. "You will call me Pick. That is an order."

"Yes, Pick."

"Which left the airplane here unattended, so to speak. Airplanes which are left uncared for tend to deteriorate. The batteries, for example, go dead, and the tires go flat, et cetera. Still with me, George?"

"Yes, Pick," Hart said.

"Better. So Grandpa, who is a master, by the way, of getting people to do things for him, remembered that the U.S. Navy, at enormous expense, had turned his grandchild into a Naval Aviator. Naval Aviators, Grandpa reasoned, know something about airplanes."

"And he said, 'Go check on my airplane,' right?"

"Right. And so I pumped up the tires and took the water that had condensed in the fuel tanks out of the fuel tanks, and pulled the engine around to remove the oil that had accumulated in the cylinders. It was my intention to run up the engine, you see. Running up the engine is something one does when one's airplane has been sitting around."

"And the battery was dead," Hart said.

"And the battery was dead. George, you are a clever fellow, indeed."

"Yes, Pick."

Pick laughed.

"Give me a hand with this, will you?"

The battery wasn't all that heavy, but putting it in its battery compartment was awkward. Hart wondered how Pickering had managed to take it out. Finally it was in place, and connected.

"Now we will open the hangar doors and push the airplane outside," Pick announced.

The huge doors of the hangar moved with an ease that surprised Hart. Pushing the Stagger Wing Beechcraft was easier than he would have thought, too, but obviously one man couldn't do it.

"What were you going to do if I hadn't turned up? You couldn't push it by yourself."

"Run it up in the hangar, of course," Pick said.

"Wouldn't the—wind from the propeller—"

"We Naval Aviators call that 'prop blast,'" Pick furnished helpfully.

"—*prop blast* have blown things around the hangar?"

"I don't know," Pick said. "I never ran an engine up in a hangar."

This guy is a cheerful idiot, Hart decided. And then modified that: *a nice cheerful idiot.*

When the airplane was outside and turned at right angles to the hangar, Pickering opened another compartment in the fuselage and took out a fire extinguisher.

"You know how to work one of these?" he asked. Hart nodded. "Maybe we will be lucky," Pick went on, "but if there is a cloud of smoke and flames, you will extinguish them using this clever device. Think you can remember that?"

"Right, Pick."

"Do not stand where the propeller turns," Pick ordered solemnly. "Getting whacked with a propeller stings."

"Right, Pick."

Pickering pulled the engine through several times and then

climbed into the cockpit. Hart saw him moving around inside, but he had no idea what he was doing.

The window beside Pickering opened.

"Clear!" he shouted, and now he sounded very professional.

Hart picked up the fire extinguisher, wondering if he would have to use it.

There was a whining sound, and then the propeller began to turn, very slowly. The engine coughed and stopped. A small cloud of dark smoke came out of the exhaust ports.

The whining of the starter began again, and then the propeller moved through several rotations as the engine coughed, burped smoke and died again.

It is not going to start, Hart decided, as he watched Pickering's head disappear as he moved around the cockpit.

The whining started again, the propeller turned, the engine coughed, coughed again, discharged an enormous cloud of smoke, and then caught with a mighty roar and began to run.

Hart could see a delighted smile on Pickering's face.

After a few moments the roughness disappeared.

I wonder how long it takes to—what did he say?—run up an engine?

He set the fire extinguisher on the ground and looked up at the cockpit.

Pickering was shaking his head and making gestures. After a moment Hart understood them: he was not to put the fire extinguisher down, but to get into the airplane with it.

Hart made a wide sweep around the wing and went to the fuselage door. It was closed.

The wind—the prop blast—*blew it closed.*

With some effort, he forced it open against the prop blast, laid the fire extinguisher on the floor, and then climbed aboard. The prop blast slammed the door closed. He looked at the door, saw a handle that locked the door, and turned it.

Then he walked to the cockpit. He was surprised at how much room the airplane had—there were four passenger seats—and how plush it was. The seats were upholstered in light-brown leather, and the walls and ceiling were covered with it.

Pickering motioned for him to sit in the second seat in the cockpit. It was George Hart's first visit to a cockpit and he found the array of dials and levers and controls both fascinating and intimidating.

Pickering showed him how to fasten the lap and shoulder harness, and then handed him a set of earphones.

"The intercom button, I just found out," Pickering's metallic voice came over the earphones, "is that little button on the side of the microphone. Can you hear me?"

Hart looked at Pickering and saw he had a microphone in his hand. And then Pickering pointed to a second microphone beside Hart. Hart had finally found something recognizable. The microphone was essentially identical to the ones in Saint Louis police cars.

"What do you mean, you just found out?"

"I never sat up here before," Pickering said.

Bullshit!

There was a popping sound, and then Pickering's voice.

"Frisco Ground Control, Beech Two Oh Oh on the Lewis ramp."

"Beech Two Oh Oh, go ahead."

"Request taxi instructions to box my compass."

What the hell does that mean?

"Beech Two Oh Oh is cleared via taxiway one three right to the threshold area of runway one three."

"Roger, thank you," Pickering's voice came over the earphones. "Understand threshold area of one three. One three moving and clear."

Hart watched with fascination as Pickering released the brakes, advanced the throttle, and the airplane began to move.

He pressed his mike button.

"Where are we going?"

There was another pop in the earphones.

"Aircraft calling Ground Control, say again."

"George," Pickering said, "don't talk into the intercom until I tell you you can. You are worrying Ground Control."

Hart nodded. He had just revealed his enormous ignorance, and it humiliated him.

They taxied a long way to the end of the field. As they neared it, a United Airlines DC-3 came in for a landing. Hart found that fascinating.

He also found Pickering's next act fascinating. He moved the airplane to the center of a large concrete area and carefully jockeyed it into position. He then fiddled somehow with the compass. Then he moved the airplane again, and fiddled with the compass again, and then repeated the process.

"As you can see, I have now boxed the compass," he said.

Hart didn't reply.

"You may express your admiration, we're on intercom," Pickering said.

"I'm impressed. Now what?"

"I am debating whether or not I can fly this thing," Pickering said. "How would you like a little ride, George?"

"What do you mean, whether or not you can fly this thing?"

"I told you. This is my first time sitting up here."

Bullshit. He's pulling my leg.

"I have faith in a fellow Marine," Hart replied.

"How can I resist a challenge like that? Now shut up, George. We are going to talk to the tower." There was another pop in the earphones.

"Frisco tower, Beech Two Oh Oh on the threshold of one three for takeoff."

Jesus, he is going to take me for a ride!

"Beech Two Oh Oh, what is your destination?"

"Couple of times around the pattern. Test flight."

"Beech Two Oh Oh, you are advised you are required to have a departure authorization."

"It's supposed to be there. You don't have it?"

There was a long break.

"Beech Two Oh Oh. You are cleared as number one to take off on one three. The altimeter is two niner niner niner. Winds are negligible."

"Roger, Two Oh Oh rolling," Pickering said and moved the throttle forward.

He lined the airplane up with the center of the runway and pushed the throttle all the way forward.

The Beech quickly picked up speed, and a moment later the rumbling of the landing gear disappeared.

"Beech Two Oh Oh. We don't have your departure clearance."

"Frisco, say again, you are garbled."

"Beech Two Oh Oh, we do not, I say again, we do not have a departure clearance. You are directed to land immediately. You are cleared as number one to land on runway one three."

"Frisco, say again, you are garbled."

There was another pop in the earphones.

"George, you may now express your admiration for that splendid virginal takeoff."

"What the hell was the tower saying to you?"

"Essentially, it means I don't think we ought to go back there," Pickering said. "I think they take their departure clearances, whatever the hell that means, very seriously."

"Meaning you don't have one?"

"What are they going to do to me?" Pickering said. "Send me to Guadalcanal?"

"Jesus Christ, you're crazy!"

"I always wanted to fly this thing," Pickering said. "The temptation was too much. I have a very weak character."

"We're at war, for Christ's sake. They're going to shoot you down. *Us* down."

"I thought about that," Pickering replied. "By the time they get their act together and decide to report this to the military, at least fifteen minutes will have passed. By the time the Army or the Navy gets its act in gear and decides which one will get the honor of shooting down an unarmed civilian airplane, another twenty minutes or so will have passed. And then it will take them five minutes to get in the air and another ten minutes to find us. We've got damned near an hour."

"You are really out of your gourd!"

"And then it would take a real prick of a pilot to shoot down something as pretty as this airplane. I certainly wouldn't do it."

"Holy Christ!"

"That long thin thing down there over the mouth of the bay is the Golden Gate Bridge," Pickering said, pointing. Hart looked where he was pointing. "What I think we will do is fly very low over thataway, then fly under the bridge—something I have always wanted to do—and then we will find home, sweet home."

"You have to be kidding."

"I am a Marine officer and a Naval Aviator. We never kid about important things."

"When you land this thing, they are going to put you in jail."

"First they have to catch me."

"I'm dead goddamn serious."

"So'm I," Pick said with a smile. "Relax and enjoy the ride."

In addition of course to flying under the Golden Gate Bridge in the first place, what surprised Sergeant Hart about their flight was that he wasn't nearly as terrified as he expected to be.

There was plenty of room under the bridge. And Pick didn't seem nervous.

In fact, looking up out of the cockpit at the massive structure as it flashed overhead was both interesting and stimulating.

He was far more afraid five minutes later when it became apparent that Pickering was about to land the airplane on what was obviously not an airfield. It was a field, or an enormous lawn, but it was definitely not an airfield.

But there, goddammit, is one of those dunce caps on a pole. What do they call them? Wind socks. Airports have wind socks. This must be an airport.

A moment later the Beech touched down.

"Where the hell are we?"

"Home sweet home, my son," Pickering said solemnly. "As you may have noticed, we have cheated death again."

"Where the hell are we?"

"This is my parents' place."

"You have your own goddamned airport?"

"Plus a barn that can be used as a hangar," Pick said. "And into which, I devoutly hope, we can get this thing before the military spots us from the air."

"You better hope we can."

"I am always a pessimist," Pickering said. "But I think we got away with it this time, George."

"They're going to catch you eventually," Hart said.

"By then I'll be on Guadalcanal," Pickering said softly. "And even if they do catch me, I will swear that I was alone. So relax, George."

Three minutes later they were closing the doors of a large barn.

[Four]
THE MEN'S BAR
THE ANDREW FOSTER HOTEL
SAN FRANCISCO, CALIFORNIA
1930 HOURS 11 SEPTEMBER 1942

Wearing a superbly tailored double-breasted blue pinstripe suit with a rosebud pinned to his lapel, Andrew Foster walked into the bar and found what he was looking for, two young men in tweed sports coats, gray flannel slacks, white button-down-collar shirts, and loafers. He walked to them.

"Good evening, gentlemen," he said. "I wondered if you had an opportunity to see the newspaper."

He laid *The San Francisco Chronicle* on the bar.

"Good evening, Grandfather," Malcolm S. Pickering said. "I know you've talked to George on the telephone, but I don't think you've actually met, have you? George, this is my grandfather."

"How do you do, Sir?" George Hart said with a weak smile. He'd just seen the headline—MYSTERY AIRPLANE FLIES UNDER GG BRIDGE. It was accompanied by a somewhat-out-of-focus photograph of a Stagger Wing Beech flying up the Golden Gate no more than a hundred feet off the water.

"How do you do, Sergeant?" Andrew Foster said—causing the heads of half a dozen Navy and Marine officers, three of them wearing Naval Aviator's wings, to turn in curiosity. The men's bar of the Andrew Foster was not often frequented by enlisted men.

The bartender quickly appeared.

"What can I get you, Mr. Foster?"

The name intensified the curiosity of the officers. They had heard that the old man sometimes showed up in the men's bar and bought the next round for anyone in uniform.

And here he was.

"A little Famous Grouse, Tony, please," the old man said, and then changed his mind. "Bring the bottle."

"Yes, Sir."

"I've been wondering what happened to you," Andrew Foster said. "I understand you have had a very interesting afternoon."

"Fascinating," Pick agreed. "Well, we went out to the house, Grandfather."

"You had no trouble getting there?"

"Not a bit, Sir."

"Nothing's broken, or anything like that?"

"No, Sir."

"I just had a talk with Richmond Fowler," Andrew Foster said. "He said to tell you that he would do what he could, because of your father; but he could make no promises."

"I see."

The waiter delivered a quart bottle of Famous Grouse, held

it over a glass, and poured. It was nearly full before Andrew Foster said, "Thank you."

He took a large swallow, then turned to his grandson.

"Pick, damn it, I've covered for you before, but this! My God, even for you, this is spectacular!"

"Yes," Pick said, wholly unrepentant. "I rather thought it was myself."

"Why?"

"It seemed like a marvelous idea at the time, didn't it, George?"

"No, it didn't," George said.

"Did it pass through your mind what your father's reaction to this is going to be when he finds out about it?"

"No. But on the other hand, Dad's in no position to say anything to me about it."

"Meaning what?" the old man snapped.

"Meaning that Dad *swam* the Golden Gate. That was considerably more dangerous than flying *up* it and *under* the bridge."

"Christ, will you shut up!" Hart said, aware that their conversation was now the subject of a good deal of attention.

Almost immediately, he was sure that there was reason for his concern. A lieutenant, in greens and wearing wings, walked up to them.

"Lieutenant Pickering, I believe?" he said.

"Well, if it isn't Lieutenant Stecker, the pride of Marine Aviation. I didn't expect you until tomorrow."

"I came out a day early," Lieutenant Stecker said. "I'll tell you about it later."

Hart sensed the question had made Stecker uncomfortable. The proof came when Stecker pulled the newspaper to him, visibly glad for a chance to change the subject.

"I saw this in the airport," he said. "What kind of an idiot would do something like that?"

"As George Washington said to his daddy," Pick said happily, "I cannot tell a lie."

"Will you shut the hell up!" Hart snapped.

"Holy Christ! Really?" Stecker said.

"He's kidding, of course," Hart said.

"He kiddeth not. Oh, excuse me. Lieutenant Stecker, may I present my grandfather, Mr. Foster? And Sergeant Hart?"

"How do you do, Lieutenant?" Andrew Foster said.

"I think we ought to get out of here," Hart said.

"I think the sergeant is right," Andrew Foster said.

"I'm having a fine time right where I am," Pick said.

"Listen to me, you jackass," Stecker flared. "You will either leave here under your own power or I will coldcock you and carry you out."

Pick looked at him a moment.

"For some strange reason, I think you're serious."

"I'm serious."

"Thank you, Lieutenant," Hart said.

"Let's go," Stecker said.

Pick met his eyes for a moment and then shrugged. "I'm outnumbered."

They walked out of the bar.

Halfway across the lobby, Andrew Foster said, "I think you had better either get out of the hotel or go to Sergeant Hart's room. In case someone is looking for you."

"They won't know where to even start looking for me until sometime tomorrow."

"Where's your room, Sergeant?" Stecker asked.

Hart pulled the key from his pocket.

"Eleven-fifteen," he said.

"Let's go," Stecker said, and took Pick's arm and propelled him toward the bank of elevators.

"I don't know why you're pissed," Pick said to Stecker in Hart's room—a three-bedroom-plus-sitting-room suite. "You weren't there. Even if they catch me and stand me before a firing squad, you're not involved."

"You had no goddamned right to involve the sergeant in this," Stecker said. "Jesus Christ, it's a court-martial offense to be wearing civilian clothing! Not to mention the insanity of your flight under the goddamned bridge!"

"George, we have just heard from the Long Grey Line," Pick said.

"The what?"

"Lieutenant Stecker is not only a professional officer and gentleman, but a *West Pointer*. They believe, as a matter of faith, that enlisted men have no brains and have to be cared for like children."

"Oh, fuck you, Pick!" Stecker flared. "I was raised as the dependent of an enlisted man."

"George is not going to get into any trouble," Pick said.

"Says you," Stecker said. "Sergeant, where did you meet this . . . child in an officer's uniform?"

"Lieutenant," Hart said. When he had his attention, he handed him his credentials. "Even if anybody asks, there's no problem about the civilian clothing. This says I can wear it."

Stecker looked carefully at the credentials.

"Are you on duty now?" he asked.

"More or less."

"What does that mean?"

"It means he works for my father, and he came out here to reassure me."

"Reassure you about what?"

"Dad's in the Army Hospital in Washington, with malaria, exhaustion, and Christ only knows what else."

"Why didn't you let me know?"

"I didn't want to worry you."

"How is he?"

"He'll be all right," Hart answered.

"And that's what caused this insanity? Relief that your father's going to be all right?"

"What insanity?" Pickering asked innocently. "I was under the impression that any red-blooded Marine Aviator would jump at the chance to fly under that bridge. What are you, Stecker, some kind of a pansy?"

Stecker looked at him. Finally he shook his head.

"Hand me the bottle," he said. "I think I will get stinko."

"Not until you tell me why you're out here a day early," Pickering said. "Is there some angry Pennsylvania Dutch farmer looking for you with a knocked-up daughter in tow?"

"Give me the goddamned bottle," Stecker said.

Pickering gave it to him.

"My mother was driving me nuts," he said, finally, after he'd taken a pull from the neck. "It wasn't her fault, of course. . . . Fuck it. It doesn't matter."

"What?" Pickering asked softly.

"She's already lost one son in this fucking war. My father's on goddamned Guadalcanal, and now I'm going there. I couldn't stand the way she looked at me. So I came out early. I suppose that makes me the candidate for prick of the year."

"I'm sorry," Pickering said.

"I'll tell you what," Stecker said. "I did not come out here to—"

"To what?"

"You really flew under the bridge?"

"I really flew under the bridge."

"You had enough time in that airplane to feel that confident?"

"Yeah, sure I did. How long were we up there, would you say, George, before we went under the bridge?"

"About twenty-five minutes."

"How much *total* time is what I'm asking."

"Twenty-five minutes. I just told you."

Hart could tell from the look on Pickering's face that he was telling the truth.

"Lieutenant," he said, "can I have that bottle, please?"

"If he gives you the bottle, George, the next thing you know you'll want to go out chasing fast women."

"I know you disapprove, that you will be faithful until death to Saint Martha, the virtuous widow, but what's wrong with that for Hart and me?" Stecker said.

"Now that I think about it," Pickering said, "nothing. Not for any of us."

"Really?" Stecker asked. "What about the sainted widow?"

"Live today, for tomorrow we die, right?"

"Oh, Jesus!" Stecker said.

"Or go to jail," Hart said. "Whichever comes first."

"You guys want me to call some women or not?"

Stecker handed him the telephone.

"Do you want fast women, or *fast* fast women?" Pickering asked.

"Just as long as they don't talk too much before they take off their clothes," Stecker said.

"I know just the girls," Pickering said, and told the operator to give him an outside line.

[Five]
HEADQUARTERS
FIRST MARINE DIVISION
GUADALCANAL
12 SEPTEMBER 1942

When Lieutenant Colonel "Red Mike" Edson returned from the Tasimboko raid on 8 September, his professional assessment then was that several thousand Japanese were in the area, probably newly arrived and well equipped. This was confirmed on the afternoon of 12 September.

Lieutenant Colonel Sam Griffith picked up a Springfield rifle and led two volunteer riflemen on a patrol into the rain forest and up the ridge inland from Henderson Field. Griffith's first combat experience in the war had been with the British Commandos, to whom he had been attached as an "observer."

Griffith returned to report that a large force of Japanese was approaching, almost certainly several thousand of them. It was unsettling news. But worse, the force was both well led and in excellent physical condition: This was almost certainly the group that had elected not to attack Edson's battalion at Tasimboko. And now they were nearby. Only a well-led force in excellent physical condition could have moved through the rain forest and across the steep ridges from Tasimboko in less than four days.

Edson recalled General Vandergrift's words to him after the Tasimboko raid: "Conservation of force for future action is often a wise choice."

That translated to mean they were facing a fellow professional, rather than what they had been facing before, an officer whose rank let him assume command of a motley force of hungry, demoralized, and poorly equipped troops.

Edson also remembered the message General Vandergrift had shown him from Lieutenant General Harukichi Hyakutake to the 17th Army.

"The operation to surround and recapture Guadalcanal will truly decide the fate of the control of the entire Pacific."

The Japanese, Edson and Griffith concluded, were about to go into action on Guadalcanal.

It was later learned that the forces that landed in the vicinity of Tasimboko (an advance element of 750 officers and men during the night of 31 August was followed the next night by

1200 officers and men) were elements of the 124th Infantry Regiment. Following the Imperial Japanese Army custom of naming an elite force after its commander, the unit was designated the *Kawaguchi Butai.* Its commander was Major General Kiotake Kawaguchi. Guadalcanal was not to be General Kawaguchi's first encounter with Americans. He and *Kawaguchi Butai* had spent April mopping up the last remnants of American resistance on the island of Mindanao in the Philippines.

General Kawaguchi's orders from General Hyakutake were to retake the airstrip (Henderson Field) as a first priority. Once that was accomplished, the Americans could no longer send aircraft aloft to intercept Japanese aviation and Naval forces. Then throwing them back into the sea would be a relatively easy matter.

On 12 September, of course, Edson had no way of knowing about any of this. His only information was what he'd suspected—which Griffith now confirmed—that he was about to get involved in a battle with several thousand fresh and probably well-led Japanese troops.

He did what experience had taught him. He ordered several strong patrols to set out at first light to gather more information about the enemy; and he summoned an officer's call to explain the situation to his command.

Edson's situation map showed the disposition of his forces along a T-shaped ridge about a mile south of the Henderson Field runway. The cross of the T was clear, broken ground with four spurs, two on each side of the ridge that formed the 1000-yard-long base.

Baker and Charley companies of the Raiders were on the line. Able and Dog companies were in reserve, close to the line. Raider headquarters and elements of Easy Company (Heavy Weapons) were several hundred yards back from the front, on the base of the T.

Remnants of the badly hurt Parachute Battalion were mixed in with the Raiders. Baker Company, Parachutists, down to seventy men, was next to Baker Company, Raiders. The parachutists of Able and Charley companies were in the wooded area near the bottom of the base of the T. And what was left of the Parachute Battalion command post was near Edson's CP.

It was generally agreed that the Japanese would probably

attack toward Henderson Field from their positions south of the ridge down the long axis of the base of the T.

Marine fields of fire were discussed. It was finally concluded that given the limited resources, all that could be done had been done. They would just have to wait until morning and see what happened.

At about 2100, just as Colonel Edson was about to dismiss his officers, the Japanese attacked. Japanese artillery located east of Alligator Creek opened fire. A moment later a parachute flare burst in light over the south end of Henderson Field. Moments after that, Japanese Naval gunfire began to land on the ridge.

By morning, what had been somewhat impersonally identified as "the ridge" would be forever known as "Bloody Ridge."

IX

[One]
HEADQUARTERS, 1ST RAIDER BATTALION
GUADALCANAL, SOLOMON ISLANDS
0445 HOURS 13 SEPTEMBER 1942

Lieutenant Colonel Merritt "Red Mike" Edson was staring closely at a map of Guadalcanal that covered the small, folding wooden table where he'd spread it. The Japanese had attacked hard last night, and he was trying to make some sense of their movements.

When Colonel Edson glanced up from the map, another Marine was standing beside the table looking down at the map with great interest. He had not been there three minutes before, and he was not a member of the 1st USMC Raider Battalion.

I'm annoyed for some reason, Edson thought. *I wonder why?*

"Good morning, Jack," Edson said. "I didn't see you come in."

"Good morning, Sir," the Marine said crisply, almost coming to attention.

He would have come to attention, Edson thought, *if he wasn't*

*cradling that Mickey Mouse rifle of his in his arms like a deer
hunter.*

Major Jack (NMI) Stecker, USMCR, Commanding Officer,
2nd Battalion, Fifth Marines, was one of the very few people
on Guadalcanal armed with the U.S. Rifle, Caliber .30-06, M1,
known after its inventor as the Garand.

Most of The Marine Corps (including Lieutenant Colonel
Edson) believed that compared to the U.S. Rifle, Springfield,
Caliber .30-06, Model 1903, the Garand was a piece of shit.

Major Jack (NMI) Stecker was sure these people were
wrong. Not only could the eight-shot, semiautomatic Garand
be fired far more rapidly than the five-shot, bolt-operated
Springfield, but it was also his professional judgment that the
Garand was every bit as reliable as the Springfield (minor
Marine Corps heresy) and more accurate (major Marine Corps
heresy).

Before the war, when he was Master Gunnery Sergeant
Stecker, he represented The Corps at the testing of the new rifle
at Fort Benning, Georgia. After that, he regularly and frequently augmented his income by putting his money where his
mouth was when other senior staff noncommissioned officers
questioned the accuracy of the Garand.

On 7 December 1941, Stecker was the senior noncommissioned officer at Quantico. Shortly afterward he was called to
active duty as a captain, and a short time after that, he was
promoted to major.

Though it was rarely put into words, professional Marine
officers often felt a certain ambivalence about Mustang officers.
On the one hand, obviously, The Corps needed more officers
than were available; and just as obviously it made more sense
to put officers' insignia on veteran senior noncommissioned
officers than to commission men directly from civilian life.

On the other hand, there was no substitute for experience. In
the case of Major Jack (NMI) Stecker, for instance, his first
command was his present command, 2nd Battalion, Fifth Marines. Previous to that assignment he had never commanded a
platoon or served as a company executive officer, company
commander, battalion staff officer, or battalion executive officer.

In the minds of many officers, including many who honestly
regarded him as one of the best master gunnery sergeants in
The Corps, Jack (NMI) Stecker had not actually earned either

his promotion to major or his command of 2nd Battalion, Fifth Marines. As they saw it, he got his promotion and his command (over a dozen or so regular officers) largely because he was a lifelong friend of Brigadier General Lewis T. "Lucky Lew" Harris, now assistant First Marine Division commander.

Harris first met Stecker in World War I. Second Lieutenant Lewis T. Harris had been Corporal Jack (NMI) Stecker's platoon leader during an engagement that caused Corporal Stecker to stand out from other Marines, officer or enlisted. In recognition of the conspicuous part he played in that engagement, he was awarded his nation's highest award for valor and gallantry. He was rarely seen wearing it, but he was entitled to top his rows of medals and campaign ribbons with a blue ribbon dotted with white stars which signified that the President of the United States, on behalf of the U.S. Congress, had awarded him the Medal of Honor.

Second Lieutenant Harris was one of the two dozen Marines "whose lives," in the words of the award citation, "had been saved by Corporal Stecker's utter disregard of his own personal safety and painful wounds while manifesting extraordinary courage above and beyond the call of duty in the face of apparently overwhelming enemy force, such actions reflecting great credit upon himself, the U.S. Marine Corps, and the Naval Service of the United States."

"I don't suppose you're here, Jack," Edson said to Stecker, "to tell me we're being relieved by Second of the Fifth?"

It was a remark made in jest. But Stecker did not take it that way.

"No, Sir. But I wouldn't be surprised if we were sent up here to reinforce. I thought I should make the time to come up and look around."

Yes, Edson thought, *of course you did. You may be Lew Harris' lifelong friend, and you do have The Medal, but that's not why they gave you the 2nd of the Fifth. They gave it to you because you are one hell of a good Marine officer, which you proved beyond any question on Tulagi, and again just now, by anticipating the orders you'll probably receive, and by preparing yourself and your battalion for them.*

"Would you like me to . . . ?" Edson asked, gesturing at the map.

"I'd be grateful, Sir, if you could spare the time."

"We had listening posts, here, here, and here," Edson said,

pointing to the map. "They went under in the first couple of minutes." He looked up at Stecker, saw him nod understanding, and then went on: "The main thrust of the attack hit here, where my Baker and Charley companies met. I'm sure it was by accident, but they hit one platoon from Baker and one from Charley."

Stecker nodded again. He knew what that meant. It had caused a command and communication problem that would not have existed had the Japanese attack struck two platoons of one company.

"They used firecrackers. Very lifelike sounds. That caused some confusion," Edson went on. "And then—this was smart—here, here, and here, they cut fire lanes and fired down them. They took us by surprise, Jack. Hell, I didn't expect them to attack at all last night. I was going to send out patrols this morning, right about now, to see what they were up to."

Stecker grunted and nodded, but didn't say anything.

"Then they breached the line between Baker and Charley companies," Edson went on, pointing. "Mass attack. Hundreds of them. Screaming. Unnerving. Charley Company had to withdraw to here," he pointed again, "which made Baker's positions untenable, so they had to pull back—actually, they had to fight their way back—to here."

"Why didn't they pursue the attack," Stecker asked, "since Baker was pulling back?"

"Because the people who couldn't make it back were—are—still fighting. In small groups, as individuals."

Stecker grunted again.

"I have the feeling, Jack," Edson said softly, "that the Japanese didn't quite expect the resistance they got."

Stecker looked at him with a question in his eyes.

"There was no second attack," Edson explained. "There've been skirmishes all night . . . in other words, they have not only the means—though God knows we have killed a lot of them—but the will. But no planned, coordinated, second attack. And they stopped their naval artillery, I thought, before I would have stopped it."

"That means they thought they were going to go right through your lines. The artillery was lifted because they believed *they* would be holding the positions by then."

"That's how I read it."

"They'll be back, Colonel," Stecker said.

"And so I hope, Jack, will you. I've got about four hundred—maybe four hundred and twenty—effectives, and an 1800-yard line to hold."

"What about the Parachute Battalion?"

"They're even more understrength than we are."

"We're all understrength," Stecker said.

"What shape are you in, Jack?"

"I've lost more men to sickness than to the enemy," Stecker said. "But, Jesus Christ, for some reason their morale is higher than I have any reason to think it should be. They'll do all right."

That obviously has something to do with the quality of the officers leading them, Edson thought.

He said: "They're Marines, Jack."

"Yes, Sir. Thank you for your time, Sir. I better go back and try to make myself useful."

[Two]
VMF-229
HENDERSON FIELD
GUADALCANAL, SOLOMON ISLANDS
0605 HOURS 13 SEPTEMBER 1942

Compared with the pilots of VMF-229, the half-dozen Naval Aviators gathered in the sandbag wall tent that served as the squadron office of VMF-229 looked neat and clean enough to march in a parade at Pensacola. This was so despite their recent takeoff from a carrier at sea, a flight of approximately two hundred miles in a tightly packed cockpit, and the faint coating of oil mist that often settled on F4F Wildcat pilots.

They were freshly shaven. Their hair was neatly trimmed. Their khaki flight suits, although sweat-stained under the arms and down the back, had recently passed through a washing machine. The undershirts that showed through the lowered zippers of their flight suits were as blinding white as any dress uniform. The shoulder holsters which held their Smith & Wesson .38 Special revolvers looked as if they had been issued that morning. Even their shoes were shined.

The Commanding Officer of VMF-229, by contrast, needed a haircut. He had obviously not shaved in twenty-four hours. The skin of his nose was sunburned raw. There were deep rings under his eyes. And his hands were dirty. His flight suit (no underwear of any kind was beneath it) was soiled with grease and sweat, and his feet were in battered boondockers. The leather holster that carried his .45 Colt automatic was green with mold.

Two of the office's three chairs were occupied by Captain Charles Galloway and his squadron clerk. The third held a stainless steel pot containing a green-colored liquid that tasted as foul as it looked. Captain Galloway had developed a theory that mixing lime-flavored powder with their water would kill the taste of the chlorine. His theory had proved to be wishful thinking.

The Navy pilots were from the carrier USS *Hornet;* they'd come to transfer to VMF-229 six F4F Wildcats. As Captain Galloway carefully examined the documentation accompanying the aircraft, they stood around uneasily; for he had a number of pointed questions about reported malfunctions that had been ostensibly repaired.

But he was a happy man. As of that morning, VMF-229 was down to three operational aircraft. And six nearly brand-new aircraft, splendidly set up by skilled mechanics in the well-equipped shops aboard *Hornet,* had just arrived.

"You checked the guns?" he asked finally, looking at the full Lieutenant, the most senior of the Navy pilots.

"Our SOP is to check weapons just before entering a threatening, or combat, situation."

"In other words, you haven't checked the guns?"

"No."

"I nevertheless thank you from the bottom of my heart," said Galloway. "We were just about out of airplanes."

"You're welcome," the Lieutenant said somewhat awkwardly.

A small, thin, blond-haired First Lieutenant of Marines, attired in a flight suit quite as filthy as Captain Galloway's, staggered into the tent. He was loaded down with three Springfield rifles, three steel helmets, and three sets of web equipment, each consisting of a cartridge belt, a canteen, a first-aid pouch, and a bayonet in a scabbard. He was trailed by his crew chief, similarly loaded down.

"Sir!" he said.

"Gentlemen, my executive officer, Lieutenant Dunn," Captain Galloway said.

"Sir, the skipper said there's some question of the R4D being able to make it in to take these gentlemen out," Bill Dunn said.

"Really?" Galloway said.

"Yes, Sir," Dunn said seriously. "And in view of the ground situation, he thought these gentlemen should be equipped so they can fight as infantry, if that should be required. I personally don't think that will be necessary."

"But apparently the skipper does?"

"Yes, Sir, but maybe he's just being careful."

Dunn began to pass out the rifles to the Navy pilots. There was little question in Galloway's mind that the last time any of them had touched a rifle was before they'd gone to flight school.

"And are they supposed to wait here until we know whether they'll be needed or not?"

"No, Sir. The skipper seems concerned that Japanese infiltrators may sneak through the lines and attempt to damage our aircraft in their revetments. Unless the situation gets worse, he wants these officers to be placed in the revetments."

"Lieutenant," the Navy pilot said, "what exactly was the word about the R4D?"

"Essentially, Sir, that they don't wish to risk the loss of the aircraft if the Japanese break through our lines, and/or damage the runway with artillery. The aircraft will not be sent until they see how the ground situation develops."

"I see," the Navy Lieutenant said solemnly.

There have been just about enough rounds landing around here to make that credible, Galloway decided. *And there's enough noise from the small arms and mortars a mile away to be scary as hell unless you know what it is.*

"Dunn, is there enough time to have these gentlemen fed before they go to the revetments?"

"There's time, Sir, but Japanese Naval artillery has taken out the mess, Sir. I will get them some C rations, Sir."

"Sorry about that, gentlemen," Galloway said. "And thank you once again, in case I don't see you again, for the aircraft."

"Our pleasure, Captain," the Navy Lieutenant said with a weak smile as he adjusted the interior straps of his helmet.

"Bill, that was a rotten fucking thing to do to those sailors," Galloway said, when Lieutenant Dunn, wearing a very-pleased-with-myself grin, walked back in the tent ten minutes later.

"Yeah, wasn't it?" Dunn replied. "But it will give them something to talk about when they get back to their air-conditioned wardroom. How they personally repelled mass attacks of sword-wielding Japanese."

"After they have a nice shower and a nice shave and have put on nice clean clothes," Galloway said.

The telephone rang.

"Greengiant," Galloway answered it.

"Yes, Sir. They're being serviced. They're brand new, Colonel. Somebody in the Navy must have screwed up.

"I'll pass the word, Sir. Thank you."

He put the field telephone back into its leather case.

"That was the skipper. The ETA on the R4D to take those guys out of here is fourteen hundred."

"They'll be glad to hear that," Dunn said.

"They would be even gladder if you told them at say, thirteen fifty-five."

"Has anyone ever told you, Skipper, that you can be just as much a prick as any of us?"

The telephone rang again.

"Greengiant.

"Yes, Sir.

"I'll send the three remaining aircraft, Sir, and with your permission, Dunn and I will take two of the new aircraft. That'll let us kill two birds with one stone. I don't want to turn them over to somebody else without a test flight.

"Aye, aye, Sir."

He put the phone back in its leather case.

"Coastwatchers report a flight of three twin-engine bombers from Rabaul. Destination unknown, but where else than here?"

"I heard," Dunn said. "It will be a pleasure flying an airplane fresh from the showroom floor."

"Just don't break it," Galloway said as he got up from his chair. "I don't think there's any more where these came from."

When they reached their plane revetments, they found Navy pilots guarding them. Each wore a helmet and firmly clutched a Springfield, as he peered warily over the sandbags toward the general direction of the sound of the small arms and mortar fire.

Three minutes after that, Dunn and Galloway were airborne, climbing slowly, so as to conserve fuel, to a final altitude of 25,000 feet.

No Japanese aircraft appeared.

When their fuel was gone and they were making their descent to Henderson, they encountered a large flight of mixed Navy and Marine F4Fs climbing upward.

"Cactus Fighter leader, Galloway."

"Go ahead, Galloway."

"What's up?"

"There's supposed to be three recon aircraft and twenty Zeroes up here someplace."

"Haven't seen a thing."

"Lucky you."

Galloway pushed the nose of the Wildcat over and down. If there were twenty Zeroes in the air—and if the Coastwatchers said there were, you could bank on it—the worst situation to be in was nearly out of gas and trying to get on the ground.

He allowed the airspeed indicator to come close to the red line before retarding the throttle. When he glanced out the window he could see Bill Dunn.

Dunn—apparently holding the stick with his knees—had both hands free to mimic some guy holding a Springfield rifle to his shoulder and wincing in pain and surprise at the recoil.

Galloway, smiling, shook his head.

[Three]
HEADQUARTERS, FIRST MARINE DIVISION
GUADALCANAL, SOLOMON ISLANDS
1605 HOURS 13 SEPTEMBER 1942

Looking something like a schoolteacher, Major General Archer Vandergrift, commanding the First Marine Division, stood with an eighteen-inch ruler in his hand in front of the situation map in the G-3 Section. A technical sergeant was nearby, armed with a piece of cloth and a red and black grease pencil, prepared to make corrections to the map as necessary.

The "students" were the general staff: the G-1 (Personnel), the G-2 (Intelligence), the G-3 (Plans & Operations), the G-4 (Supply), plus Lieutenant Colonel William Whaling, executive officer of the Fifth Marines; Lieutenant Colonel Hayden Price, commanding 5th Battalion, Eleventh Marines (the artillery); and Lieutenant Colonel Merritt Edson, commanding 1st Raider Battalion.

"I realize you all would rather be with your units, so I'll make this as quick as I can," General Vandergrift said. "I just want to make absolutely sure the left hand knows what the right hand is doing."

He turned to the map.

"Red Mike sent his people out at sunrise to recover what he had lost during the night," he said, using the pointer. "There was not much resistance, and they were able to regain their fighting positions. When the Raiders withdrew last night, they had to leave the food they took from the Japanese at Tasimboko. The Japanese now have it back."

He moved the pointer. "The Parachute Battalion's Able Company, which was here, had no contact with the Japanese last night. We moved it down here, to the level area, so they could support the Raiders when they went out to take back their positions. They got this far when they were taken under fire from concealed positions. The company commander . . . who was that, Mike?"

"McKennan, General. Captain William."

"Right. Good man. He made the correct decision not to get into a major scrap on what was a very narrow front. So he moved around here, got some artillery support, and this time only ran into some sniper opposition. He was where he was supposed to be by about 1500.

"Charley Company of the Raiders was pretty badly hurt last night, here on the right. They were withdrawn and replaced by Able Company, plus what was left of Dog Company, which we have disbanded.

"Edson has pulled his line back about one hundred yards, to here," Vandergrift said. "That shortened it, and it will force the Japanese to attack the open ground here. We have moved the machine guns around to take advantage of that field of fire, and the rifle positions have been built up all along that area.

"I called Mike about three o'clock and told him that I was going to send in the 2nd of the Fifth to back him up, and that as soon as I could find Jack Stecker, I was going to send him up there to look around. He told me that Jack was up there first thing this morning. Why wasn't I surprised?"

There was dutiful laughter.

"The problem of getting 2nd of the Fifth into position is that they have to cross the Henderson runway to get there," Vandergrift continued. "And the runway, obviously, has been about as busy as it can get. Whaling, have you got an estimate from Jack Stecker about when he'll be in position?"

Colonel Whaling stood up. He did not appear happy.

"Sir, I talked to him a few minutes ago. He says it will be long after dark."

"Can't be helped," Vandergrift said. "Jack will do the best he can." He turned to the map and used the ruler as a pointer again.

"Price has moved his 105s out of the woods here and into firing positions here south of the Henderson runway. Are your guns laid in, Price?" Since the Division's 155mm cannon had not been off-loaded during the invasion, the 105mm howitzer was the largest artillery piece available.

Colonel Price stood up.

"If they're not, Sir, they will be within minutes."

"OK. As soon as that happens, everybody but the gunners will move back to about here," Vandergrift said, pointing, "where they will form a secondary line in case the Japanese get through the Raiders and the Parachutists. If that happens, gentlemen, the artillery will be lost, and there won't be very much to keep the Japanese from taking Henderson."

There was no response.

"Are there any additions, corrections, or observations that anyone wishes to make?" Vandergrift asked politely.

There were none.

"That will be all, gentlemen, thank you," General Vandergrift said.

The Japanese attacked at 1830. They directed their major effort to the right of the Raider defense line at almost exactly the point where they'd attacked the previous night.

[Four]
POLICE HEADQUARTERS
SAINT LOUIS, MISSOURI
1405 HOURS 15 SEPTEMBER 1942

When the knock on the frosted glass panel of his office door destroyed his concentration, Captain Karl Hart, commanding officer of the Homicide Bureau, was trying to make sense of a police officer's report of a death the previous evening by gas asphyxiation.

He had just concluded that the reporting officer was not only a functional illiterate, but a genuine goddamn moron to boot.

He ignored the knock and tried to make sense of a sentence that read, so far as he could make out, "body dispozd by coronary's office."

Coronary's *obviously was supposed to mean* Coroner's, *but what the hell was* dispozd?

There was another knock on the frosted glass panel of his door, this time an impatient knock.

"Wait a goddamned minute!"

He reached for his telephone and placed it on his shoulder. Holding it in place with his chin, he started to dial a number.

The doorknob turned, followed by the faint rattling noise it always made when it was being opened. In fury, he turned to face it.

Goddamn it, I said to wait a goddamned minute!

"Is this where I go to have somebody homicided?" Sergeant George Hart asked innocently.

"George," Captain Hart said.

"Hi, Pop."

"George," Captain Hart repeated, and then got up and walked around the desk and put out his hand.

His son shook it.

"Damn," Captain Hart said. "You could have let us know you were coming."

No, I couldn't. That would have required explanations.

"You been out to the house? Seen your mother?"

"I went there from the airport."

"What did she say?"

"She asked was I here, and had I seen you," George reported truthfully.

"Jesus H. Christ!" Captain Hart said. And then, though it

had been a long, long time since he'd done it: *What the hell, why not?* he asked himself as he put his arms around his son and hugged him. "Damn, it's good to see you!"

It's the first time in God knows how long, George realized, *since I was a kid, that Pop's hugged me.*

He felt his eyes water, and that surprised him.

"How much leave they give you?"

"Five days."

"That's all?"

"That's all they give you."

"Jesus, you can hardly get from down there and back in five days," his father said. Then he saw the chevrons on George's tunic.

"You're a sergeant? Jesus, that was quick."

"The Marines recognize good men when they see one," George said.

"Look," his father said, "I got a report on a citizen stuck his head in the oven that's so bad I don't even believe it."

"Since when do you handle suicides?"

"When the guy's brother's a Monsignor and the Commissioner told me he don't want to hear the word suicide. You know the Catholics, they won't bury a suicide in holy ground—"

"Consecrated," George corrected him automatically.

"Consecrated, holy, whatever. I got to talk to the cop—I can't believe this guy, he's so dumb—and then talk to the coroner, and then report to the Commissioner."

"Just out of idle curiosity, what are you going to find out really happened?"

"He slipped on a wet kitchen floor as he was about to light the oven," Captain Hart said, "bumped his head and knocked himself out. And then the gas got him."

"Brilliant." George laughed.

"It was all I could think of," Captain Hart admitted. "Anyway, you don't want to hang around here. I'll meet you in Mooney's in thirty minutes."

"OK."

"Maybe you better call your mother and ask her does she want to eat out someplace?"

"She said she was going to make a pot roast, and I was to bring you home no later than half past six."

"OK. So we'll have a couple of snorts and go home."

"OK, Pop."

"You got some money?"

"Yeah, sure."

"You said you went home from the airport. So what did an airplane ticket cost you? Where'd you get the money?" Captain Hart said, as he took a wad of bills from his pocket and peeled off two five-dollar bills. "Don't argue with me, I'm your father."

"OK, Pop. Thank you."

"Thirty minutes, George," Captain Hart said, and then there was another unexpected gesture of affection. He rubbed his hand over his son's head, but masked the affection by saying, "Jesus, I love your haircut."

Mooney's was crowded. Cops who had come off the four-in-the-afternoon shift change mingled with courthouse people who seldom waited until the clock said five before closing up.

George smiled at familiar faces and even shook a couple of hands, but there was no one in the bar he knew well enough to sit down with.

He found a stool toward the back of the room, near the Wurlitzer jukebox. Before he sat down, he reached behind the Wurlitzer and turned the volume control way down.

"Welcome home, George," Jerry the bartender said, offering his hand. He was a plump young man wearing a black vest and an immaculate white shirt with the cuffs turned up. "Your Uncle George was in a while ago, and Ramirez just left."

"I'll be around a while. My father's coming in."

"Seagram's & Seven? Or a beer?"

"Jerry, you got any Famous Grouse?"

"What the hell is that?"

"Scotch."

The bartender shook his head, no. "I got some Dewar's and there's some . . ." He turned, searched the array of bottles against the mirror and put a bottle of Haig & Haig Pinch Bottle on the bar. ". . . of this."

"That. Straight. Water on the side."

"When'd you start drinking that?" Jerry the bartender asked as he poured a very generous shot in a small, round glass.

"As soon as I found out about it," George said. He took out his wallet and laid a ten-dollar bill on the bar.

"Put that away," Jerry said. "Your money's no good in here."

"Thanks, Jerry," George said, and started to put the twenty back in his wallet. Then he remembered the two fives his father had given him, and took them from his pocket.

The truth of the matter, Jerry, is that I was having a couple of drinks with my pal Pick Pickering—you know, the guy whose grandfather owns Saint Louis' snootiest hotel, the Foster Pierre Marquette, and forty other hotels—right after we flew under the Golden Gate Bridge in his grandfather's airplane; and Ol' Pick said, "George, if we're going to drink as much as I think we are, you better get off that Seagram's & Seven and onto The Bird." So I got onto The Bird, which is what my pal Pick calls Famous Grouse; and I got to like it, right from the first.

Would I bullshit you, Jerry?

He took a swallow of the water on the side and then poured scotch into it.

"My God," Pick said, *"you were a vice cop and I have to teach you about booze? Upon my word as an officer and a gentleman, Sergeant Hart, the way one drinks whiskey—and by whiskey, I mean scotch whiskey—is to mix it in equal portions with just a little bit of ice."*

I wonder why I used to think scotch tasted like medicine? George thought after he'd taken a sip of his drink. *Well, what the hell, when I was a little kid and Pop ate oysters, I used to want to throw up. And now I love them. They're what they call an acquired taste.*

He turned on his stool and caught the arm of a waitress.

"Hey, George," she said, "I thought that was you. You look real nice in your uniform."

"Hazel, could you get me a dozen oysters?"

"You bet your life I could, honey."

When he turned back to the bar, Jerry handed him a newspaper.

"Seen the paper?"

"No, I haven't. Thank you."

He unfolded the paper and spread it on the bar. There was a four-column picture of an aircraft carrier, and below it the headline: AIRCRAFT CARRIER 'WASP' SUNK IN PACIFIC.

He read the story:

> Washington, DC Sept 15 (AP) — In a
> terse announcement this afternoon, the

Navy announced that the aircraft carrier USS 'Wasp' was lost at sea yesterday (Sept 14), with heavy loss of life, while operating in the Solomon Islands area.

The Navy said that initial reports indicate the 'Wasp' was struck by at least three Japanese torpedoes from a submarine in an action which also saw a destroyer sunk, and serious, but not fatal, damage caused to the battleship USS 'North Carolina.'

There was other war news, some of it accompanied by photographs:

In North Africa, German airfields at Benghazi have been attacked by units of the British Long Range Desert Group, and severe damage is reported.

American bombers have attacked Japanese bases in the Aleutian Islands.

The Russian forces defending Stalingrad are in desperate shape. The defense perimeter has been reduced to a thirty-mile area. The German High Command has predicted the fall of the city within a matter of days.

Word has reached London that the Cunard liner 'Laconia,' carrying British military dependent families and Italian prisoners of war, has been sunk off the Cape of Good Hope by the German submarine U-156.

On Guadalcanal, in the Solomon Islands, the Marines have succeeded in turning back a Japanese attack on 'Bloody Ridge' near the American air base, Henderson Field. Severe Japanese losses were reported.

Jesus Christ, Pick and Dick Stecker are on their way to Guadalcanal! It doesn't seem so fucking impersonal if you know people.

An elbow jabbed Hart in the ribs. He turned and saw that he'd been joined by a fellow noncommissioned officer of The United States Marine Corps, Staff Sergeant Howard H. Wertz, USMC, the miserable, lying cocksucker who conned him into joining the crotch by telling him he could be sort of a Marine detective.

Sliding his beer glass around in a little puddle on the bar, Wertz gave him a smirking smile.

"You look good, kid," he said. "Parris Island must have been good for you."

"Yeah, all that fresh air," Hart said. "Still scrounging up all the warm bodies you can for the crotch, are you, Sergeant?"

"You know how it is, kid. You're in The Corps, you do what they tell you."

I don't really want to stick his head in the spittoon or knock his teeth down his throat. How come? Christ knows, I thought about doing just that by the goddamned hour.

"I guess so," Hart said.

"You know what I wondered when I saw you, Hart?"

"Haven't the faintest fucking idea, Sergeant."

"I wondered where you got those chevrons on your sleeve."

"Oh, you wondered about that, huh?"

"Yeah, I mean, what the hell. I'm not normally a suspicious person, but what is it now, eight weeks since you went off to Parris Island?"

Hart did the arithmetic in his head.

"Closer to ten, actually."

"OK, ten, then. You don't get to be a Sergeant in The Corps in ten fucking weeks."

"Some people do."

"You know what I think, Hart? And I'm really disappointed. I think you sewed those stripes on to impress broads."

"Well, I admit it works. Some girls think Marine sergeants are really hot shit."

"Yeah, well, assholes like you wearing stripes they haven't

earned really piss me off. You better have some orders to go with them stripes."

He held out his hand.

"No orders, Sergeant," Hart said. "Sorry."

He reached into the breast pocket of his tunic and took out his leather identification folder. He handed it to Wertz.

Wertz examined with great care the credentials of Special Agent George F. Hart of the Office of Naval Investigation.

"Go fuck yourself, Wertz," Hart said, taking them back.

"I'm not sure I believe that," Wertz said.

"Call me on it, you sonofabitch! Call the MPs and tell them you don't believe it. If I report that I showed you those credentials and told you to get out of my way, and you didn't, you'll be out of Saint Louis on your way to a rifle company so quick your asshole won't catch up with you for a month."

Staff Sergeant Wertz made a decision.

"OK. So I'm sorry."

"Get the fuck out of my sight," Hart said. "I don't want to see you in here again as long as I'm in Saint Louis."

Staff Sergeant Wertz slid off his stool and walked out of Mooney's bar.

"What the hell was that all about?" Jerry the bartender asked.

"Nothing," Hart said. "Forget it."

"You want another one of these?" Jerry asked, holding up the Haig & Haig.

"Yeah, Jerry, please."

I don't feel good about Wertz. Why not?

"Why do I have this feeling that you liked it as well as I did?" Elizabeth "Beth" Lathrop asked, in his bedroom in the suite in the Andrew Foster. When she spoke, neither Beth Lathrop nor George Hart was wearing clothes. And they were both sprawled in more or less close proximity across his bed.

"Cut the bullshit," he said, and swung his legs out of bed and went to the bottle of scotch on the dresser.

When Elizabeth "Beth" Lathrop came into the suite, she was wearing a blue cotton dress he would remember the rest of his life. As he would remember the rest of her, the long blond hair parted in the middle and held in place with a bow in back. And the smell of her perfume. And her blue eyes (matching her dress) and her long delicate fingers.

And now her perfect, pink-tipped breasts and the delicate tuft of blond hair at her crotch and the incredible warm softness within.

"Meaning what?"

"Meaning you did what you were paid to do. Leave it at that, for Christ's sake. Skip the bullshit."

He watched her face in the mirror over the dresser. It tightened, and then she shrugged.

Don't tell me I hurt your feelings, honey. You didn't really expect me to believe that "it was good for me, too" bullshit, did you?

He poured scotch into a glass and glanced over at the bed. She pulled the sheet over her. He lifted the glass toward her and caught her eye.

"Yes, thank you, I will," she said.

He walked to the bed.

"How did a nice girl like you get into this?" he asked. What a damn fool silly question for a vice cop to ask, *he thought as he asked it.*

"You know the rules," she said. "That's one of the questions you're not supposed to ask."

She pushed herself up against the headboard, pulled the sheet over her chest, and then reached for the glass.

"Thank you," she said, politely.

"Professional curiosity," *he said over his shoulder as he went to make himself a drink.* "What was it? Your husband threw you out? There's a kid somewhere, and this is the only way you can feed it? I think you're too smart to get under a pimp."

"No husband. No kid. No pimp. What did you mean, 'professional curiosity'?"

"I've heard a lot of stories . . ."

"I'll bet you have. I bet you ask all the girls, right?"

"I'm a cop. Or was. A vice squad detective."

"Oddly enough, I believe that," she said. "You said 'was'?"

"Now I'm in The Marine Corps."

"I wondered about that," she said. "Pick said you were an old pal from Saint Louis."

"I'm from Saint Louis."

"But you're not old pals?"

He shook his head, no.

"I work for his father."

"Oh, that's right, his father is a captain in the Navy."

"A general in The Marine Corps," he corrected her, laughing. "In Washington."

"Close," she said, and smiled.

He shook his head.

"So that wasn't a threat to make trouble for me?" she asked.

"No. Of course not."

"I've never had any trouble . . . been arrested."

"That's simply a question of time. Maybe it would be good for you. Twenty-four hours in the slam with a dozen girls off the street might make you understand what the hell you're doing to yourself."

"What have we got here, a Marine who used to be a vice detective? With morals?"

"You're so goddamned beautiful! You don't have to fuck every man who comes along!"

"Thank you," she said, "but I don't fuck every man who comes along. The only reason I fucked you was that I couldn't find a third girl for the job."

"You're running a string?" he asked, genuinely surprised. The madams of his acquaintance, and he knew half a dozen, were not at all like this girl. Most were fat and middle-aged, and all were hard as nails, with cold eyes.

"I'm a photographer," she said.

"That's a new one."

"You asked."

"Go on."

"An advertising photographer, nothing special, mostly for catalogs and brochures. The way you get commissions is to be nice to art directors. Then they started asking me if I had friends who might like to earn a little pocket money. Somebody once said that the way to get rich is to identify a need and then fill it. So I provide a service. I have associates. Do we have to keep this up?"

"Pickering's paying for this?"

"Do you have any idea how much housekeeping supplies this hotel uses? Not to mention how many Foster hotels there are? Keeping the heir apparent happy is just good business. They take it off their income tax as 'client relations.'"

"But he knows?" he asked, but it was more of a statement.

"Of course he knows. Pick's a very good-looking fellow, but he's not that good-looking. I shouldn't have to tell you this, but there's no such thing as a free lunch."

He shook his head.

"Did you ever hear that you shouldn't look a gift horse in the mouth?" Beth asked.

"You're so goddamned beautiful! You shouldn't be doing this! You don't have to do this!"

"There's another rule," Beth said. *"Clients are not supposed to worry about the girls."*

"Fuck you!"

"That's all you're supposed to do," Beth said. *"Let's leave it at that. And this time I won't tell you how much I liked it."*

He met her eyes, and then looked quickly away. Beth made him very uncomfortable.

"Have you got a girl back in Saint Louis? Is that it? You're consumed with guilt?"

"No girl back in Saint Louis. No girl anywhere."

"I'm surprised," she said.

"Why should you be surprised?"

"Because you strike me as a nice guy," Beth said.

"You know what's really strange?" George said. *"I really did like doing it with you. I never liked it so much before."*

"I'm pleased."

"So laugh."

"Sorry."

"Goddamn you!"

"I really am pleased," she said. *"I probably shouldn't tell you this, but every once in a while . . . it's not just business."*

"Am I supposed to believe that?"

"Believe whatever you goddamn please!"

Their eyes met.

After a moment she said, *"Why not? It's already paid for."*

"Just for the hell of it, how much?"

"For the three of us, three hundred dollars."

"You could hire every whore in Saint Louis for three hundred dollars."

"Come on," Beth said, making a gesture at his midsection. *"Obviously, you want to."*

He'd never wanted to sink himself in any woman half as desperately as he wanted to be in this one again.

It's all the fucking booze, *he thought, as he walked to the bed and pulled the sheet off her.* The booze, and that insane goddamn airplane ride under the bridge. All of it. I'm a little crazy, that's all. I'm too smart to fall for a whore, even one as beautiful, and nice, as this one.

"What the hell is that you're drinking?" Captain Karl Hart asked his son.

"Scotch. They make it in Scotland."

"Jerry, give me some real whiskey, and give him another of those. When did you start drinking scotch?"

"I don't know. How's the suicide?"

"Accident victim, accident victim," Captain Hart said. "I just checked. The undertaker got the lipstick and rouge off him, and the women's underwear, and I talked to the cop on the scene, and there's no further problem."

Hart had one final thought about Beth Lathrop: *There's one thing you have to say about her, she's not the kind of girl you could bring home to meet the folks.*

[Five]
FERDINAND SIX
BUKA, SOLOMON ISLANDS
15 SEPTEMBER 1942

They decided to move out. They were out of choices.

For one thing they had to eat.

They'd started with more smoked pig than the ten pounds or so Sergeant Steve Koffler found on the morning he thought everybody had taken off and left him: At Ian's orders, Patience had taken twice that much more and hidden it in the rocks by the stream, in a small cave that could be sealed with rocks and protected from wildlife and insects.

And then Ian stalked another wild pig and impaled it on his MACHETE, SUBSTITUTE STANDARD, and for two days the three of them feasted on roast pig. Ian didn't want to risk smoking it, because of the smoke, and Steve figured there was no point in arguing with him. So they roasted it over the last of their dry wood, which was smokeless. The pig was pretty good, even without salt.

But now just about everything was gone. And the men had

not returned from looking for Lieutenant Reeves and Lieutenant Howard. In fact, they hadn't even sent a messenger back—suggesting the unpleasant possibility that they had run into the Japs and would not be returning.

So they took their small arms and ammunition (the British Lee-Enfield rifles and their .303 ammunition) into the jungle and buried them. The rifles in one place, their bolts in another, and the ammunition in still another.

Steve thought that was mostly bullshit. The Japanese were not going to wander around in the jungle looking for rifles and ammo. Nor was he, Ian, or anyone else going to come back and dig them up. They could just as easily have left them in the hut with the radio for the Japs to find.

As he was spreading a layer of dirt on his rifle, he wondered what he should do about reporting in. Should he get on the air and tell Townsville or Pearl Harbor that FRD6 was leaving the net for an indefinite period?

He decided against that. It just might happen that he could come back; but if he had signed off the net, those by-the-book assholes would give him all sorts of static about coming back on.

Though he recognized it as whistling in the dark, the hope that he might get back on the air later almost made him feel comfortable about leaving the Hallicrafters intact. The rotten thing about that was the Japs would probably find it. If he was absolutely certain that the Japs would actually get it, he would have smashed the sonofabitch. But he wasn't certain of that. So in the end he compromised. He took all but one of the crystals that controlled the frequencies, wrapped them in the last remnant of his skivvy shirt, and put them in the pocket of his utility jacket.

He made one last report, this time to Townsville, for the atmospherics were such that he couldn't reach Pearl Harbor. And then he signaled Patience to stop pedaling the generator.

Feeling a strange mixture of sadness and blind rage, he left the hut for what he thought would be the last time.

When he got outside, Edward James and Lieutenant Reeves were in the clearing.

Reeves looked like a walking corpse, and the clothes he had on him were rags.

"What about Lieutenant Howard?" Steve blurted.

"I'm delighted to see you too, old chap," Reeves said. "I appreciate the warmth of your reception."

"We thought you were all dead," Steve blurted.

"We sodding well should be," Reeves said. "Mother did not raise me to be a sodding pack mule."

"What?"

"We struck gold," Reeves reported. "A sodding Nip truck all alone on a ration run."

"No shit?"

"Which we have carried up and down every sodding hill on this sodding island."

"Anybody get hurt?"

"Your lieutenant sprained his ankle. The chaps are carrying him in."

"That's all?"

Reeves nodded.

Sergeant Steve Koffler felt like crying.

[Six]
THE FOSTER LAFAYETTE HOTEL
WASHINGTON, D.C.
1630 HOURS 19 SEPTEMBER 1942

Just after he knocked on the door to Senator Richmond Fowler's suite, Sergeant George Hart noticed a doorbell button nearly hidden in the framework of the door. He had just put his finger out to it when the door opened.

A tall, trim, silver-haired woman in a cotton skirt and fluffy blouse smiled at him.

She really must have been a looker when she was young.

"Sergeant Hart, right?" she asked. "Colonel Rickabee said you were coming over."

"Yes, Ma'am."

She gave him her hand. A wedding ring was her only jewelry, but pinned to her blouse was a cheap metal pin, two blue stars on a white shield background. It signified that she had two members of her immediate family serving in the Armed Forces. George's mother had been wearing one, with one star, when he'd gone to the house from the airport.

"I'm Patricia Pickering," she said, "but I suppose that a detective like you will have already deduced that, right?"

"Yes, Ma'am."

"I'd like to apologize for what my idiot son did to you, Sergeant," she said. "To put that behind us."

"Lieutenant Pickering was very nice to me, Ma'am."

"Was that before or after he flew you under the Golden Gate Bridge?" she responded, gently sarcastic. "That was inexcusable! Stupid enough on his part, and *inexcusable* to take you with him."

He had been following her into the sitting room.

"Dick, this is Sergeant Hart," she said. "Sergeant, this is Senator Fowler."

Jesus Christ, a United States Senator is actually getting out of his chair to shake my hand!

"How do you do, Sergeant?" Fowler said. "I've been hearing a good deal about you lately, all of it good. I'm quite an admirer of your commanding officer."

"Yes, Sir."

"Correction," Senator Fowler said, "I'm quite an admirer of *Colonel Rickabee*. I'm very fond of your commanding officer, but as Mrs. Pickering and I were just saying, he does need a keeper; and according to Rickabee, you're just the man for the job."

"You're putting the sergeant on a spot, Dick," Patricia Pickering said.

"I certainly didn't mean to," Fowler said. "I meant to make the sergeant welcome."

"Thank you, Sir."

"Where are your things, Sergeant?" Patricia Pickering asked.

"Ma'am?"

"Your uniforms. Your clothing."

"Oh. Captain Sessions arranged for me to share an apartment. It's a couple of blocks away. I went there first."

"We were just talking about that, too," Fowler said. "We think it would be better for you and Lieutenant Moore to be in here with the General. Would that pose a problem for you?"

"Sir, I go where I'm told to go. But I don't know what Colonel Rickabee would say. Or General Pickering. Or, for that matter, Lieutenant Moore."

"I don't think Colonel Rickabee will have any objection," Fowler said. "I'll have a word with him. And that should take care of any objections Lieutenant Moore might have. You know him, I gather?"

"Yes, Sir."

"And *General* Pickering's vote doesn't count," Patricia Pickering said firmly. "There's a small suite next door," she went on, gesturing toward the wall behind Hart. "I've asked them to put a door in. It should be there by the time Lieutenant Moore gets out of the hospital. With a little luck, that will be before my husband does."

"For the time being you can stay in the spare bedroom," Fowler said. "Is that all right with you?"

"Sir, I do what I'm told."

Well, I guess if your father owns the hotel, and you want a door put in, they put a door in.

"There's one more thing, Sergeant," Patricia Pickering said. "One of our stewards, a fine old fellow named Matthew Howe, is retired here in Washington—"

What the hell is she talking about?

"—and he is willing—actually, he seemed delighted when I asked him—to look after my husband. He'll be coming in every day to take care of him."

"What Mrs. Pickering is saying, Sergeant," Senator Fowler explained, "is that Howe will take care of General Pickering's linen and pass the canapés, leaving you and Lieutenant Moore free to take care of him in other ways."

"Yes, Sir."

"Our first priority, *your* first priority, is to see that General Pickering does nothing that might hinder his recovery," Senator Fowler said. "Obviously, Mrs. Pickering and I have a personal interest in that. But I would also strongly suggest to you, Sergeant, that he's not going to be much use to The Marine Corps, for that matter to the country, if he winds up back in the hospital. Do I make my point?"

"Yes, Sir."

"And finally," Fowler said, with a vague gesture toward Pick's mother, "Mrs. Pickering is a little concerned that both you and Lieutenant Moore are armed. I have told her that J. Edgar Hoover and the FBI have done their job, and that there is absolutely no danger to General Pickering from the enemy here in Washington."

"Then why do they need guns?" Patricia Fleming asked

quickly, rising to the moment. "My God, Dick, Fleming has his old Marine Corps .45 in there in his dresser!"

She pointed toward the bedroom.

"Mrs. Pickering," Hart said, "every cop carries a gun. Ninety-five percent of cops never take them out of their holsters from the time they join the force until they retire."

Fowler looked at him with approval; Patricia Fleming looked at him dubiously.

"Have you ever had to take yours from its holster?" she asked.

I can't lie to this woman.

"Yes, Ma'am, I've had to do that twice."

"That's why Rickabee assigned him to Fleming, Patricia," Fowler said. "You should find that reassuring."

"I find Sergeant Hart very reassuring," she said. "Everybody carrying a gun disturbs me."

"Speaking of the FBI, Sergeant," Senator Fowler said, "I had a chat with Mr. Hoover this morning. He tells me that since they've come up with very little information about the lunatic who flew his airplane under the Golden Gate Bridge, and since no damage was done, and since the FBI has more important cases to work on, the FBI in San Francisco has been instructed to put that investigation on the back burner."

Hart saw a faint smile in Fowler's eyes and on his lips.

Jesus Christ, Hart thought, remembering the suicide in women's underwear his father had been dealing with back home, *I guess the fix is in everywhere.*

"I would be very surprised if that lunatic was ever hauled before the bar of justice," Fowler added. "You know how these things are."

"Yes, Sir."

"And thank you, Sergeant," Patricia Pickering said, "before I forget it, for getting the lunatic off to war before he got in any more trouble."

She met his eyes and smiled.

"I'm on an Eastern Airlines flight out of here at 9:30 tomorrow morning. My husband pointed out to me this afternoon that I really should get back to San Francisco. After all, you're here to take care of him, and I have a shipping company to run."

"Yes, Ma'am."

"Over his objections, I am going to the hospital to say good-bye before I leave. I'd be grateful if you would go with me."

"Yes, Ma'am."

"It is my intention, Sergeant, to tell my husband that the Secretary of the Navy personally ordered you to report to him the very first time my husband does something stupid."

"Yes, Ma'am."

"I told Frank Knox," Senator Fowler said, "that I would relay that order to you."

"Yes, Sir."

"I was about to ask you," Patricia Fleming said, "to meet me here about half past seven in the morning. But I just had a better idea: Why don't you take the car and go get your things and bring them back? Move in now, in other words? That way we'd both be here in the morning."

"Yes, Ma'am. What car?"

"It's a Buick my husband bought when he first came here. It's parked out in front. The doorman should have the keys."

You didn't really think this woman would have her car parked anywhere else, did you?

"Yes, Ma'am."

"And then we'll all have dinner. Considering what you've already done for me, and what my husband is certain to do to you, that's the very least I can do."

X

[One]
THE WILLARD HOTEL
WASHINGTON, D.C.
0945 HOURS 20 SEPTEMBER 1942

When Major Jake Dillon, USMCR, debarked from the aircraft at Anacostia Naval Air Station at 2100 the previous evening, a message for him stated that a room at the Anacostia Bachelor Officer Quarters had been reserved for him, and that Brigadier General J. J. Stewart, Director, Public Affairs Division, Headquarters, USMC, would see him in his office at 0745 the next morning.

Although Major Dillon was fully aware of the penalties provided for a Marine who failed to appear at the proper time and the proper place in the properly appointed uniform—which was the definition for Absence With Out Leave—it took him no longer than five seconds to put himself at risk of those penalties. *Fuck him,* he thought, *I'm entitled to a good night's sleep and a good breakfast.*

Instead of cheerfully and willingly complying with his lawful orders, Major Dillon caught a cab to the Willard Hotel and obtained the key to the suite Metro-Magnum Studios maintained in the Washington landmark.

He took a long hot shower, sent his uniform to the valet service for an emergency cleaning and pressing, and consumed about half a bottle of Haig & Haig Pinch Bottle scotch, while enjoying his room service dinner of filet mignon with *pommes frites,* topped off with a strawberry shortcake dessert.

In the morning, he rose at eight, had another long hot shower, and then ate a room service breakfast of freshly squeezed orange juice, milk, breakfast steak, two eggs sunny side up, rye toast, and a pot of coffee. He then read *The Washington Star* from cover to cover, excepting only the classified advertisements.

Even in the fresh light of day, his conscience did not bother him vis-à-vis his AWOL status, nor was he concerned about the consequences of his act. *What can they do to me? Send me back to Guadalcanal?* This was not the first time he had been AWOL, and more than likely it would not be the last. And this time he had some justification:

He had just gone through a rough two weeks.

What he—privately, of course—thought of as the road company of *Dillon's Heroes* had made it from Melbourne to Pearl Harbor without any problems. Unfortunately, they arrived in Pearl a day after a hospital ship had come in. For a number of valid reasons, both Army and Naval medical authorities in Hawaii were anxious to send those requiring long-term care home to the States. It obviously made more sense to give the badly wounded priority over Dillon's war bond tour heroes.

And so they had been bumped from available airspace to the States.

At first Jake thought this was probably a stroke of good luck. Compared to the healthy, well-nourished people at Pearl, Dillon's undernourished, wan, and battered heroes looked like death warmed over.

And so he decided to arrange rooms for them in the Royal Hawaiian. Three or four days' rest on the beach and some good food would do them wonders. (He would even look into getting them better-fitting uniforms.)

While they were basking on the beach, he'd go out to Fort Shafter. A former Metro-Magnum Studios lab guy, now commissioned into the Army Signal Corps, was running a photo-

graphic laboratory there. For auld lang syne—if not the war
effort—he would soup the undeveloped film Jake had carried
from Henderson Field in the "borrowed" whole-blood container. The sooner it was souped, the better. Christ only knew
what damage the heat and humidity had already done.

He had no sooner explained the change in plans to the cast
of *Dillon's Heroes*—there was no objection, save from Lieutenant R. B. Macklin, who clearly saw himself as the star of the
troupe and could not wait to get onstage—than they encountered Pearl Harbor Standard Operating Procedure.

In order to keep those returning from exotic areas from
infecting the natives with exotic diseases, returnees were required to submit to a medical examination. Once they had
successfully passed medical muster, they would be permitted to
leave the base and enter the real world.

The Navy doctors took one look at *Dillon's Heroes* and
decided that entry into the real world was out of the question:
All of them—Major Jake Dillon included—would be admitted
to the hospital for more complete physical examinations and
treatment.

It took six days before pressure from Washington forced the
Navy Hospital, reluctantly, to discharge them from the hospital—only on condition that they fly immediately to San Diego
for admittance to the U.S. Navy Hospital there.

Because of all this, Jake was unable to get the Guadalcanal
combat footage souped. And worse, the doctors took away the
whole-blood container, promising to inform his superiors of
his blatant misappropriation of Navy Medical Corps property.

After Jake Dillon's failure to bring them anywhere near the
Royal Hawaiian Hotel or the world-famous beach at
Waikiki—not to mention his ineptitude in dealing with the
medical bureaucracy—*Dillon's Heroes* concluded they were in
the care of a world-class incompetent.

And to judge by his URGENT radio messages to Dillon, Brigadier General J. J. Stewart, Director, Public Affairs Division,
Headquarters, USMC, held a like opinion. He was absolutely
unable to understand how a major could fuck up so simple a
task as bringing eight people from Melbourne—especially since
Brigadier General J. J. Stewart himself had arranged for their
travel.

San Diego turned out to be slightly less a pain in the ass—
only because Jake was able to get the film souped. But that was

just good luck: Jake ran into Tyrone Power in the hospital coffee shop. The actor was taking a precommissioning physical, and then he was driving back to L.A. The two men chatted awhile, and one thing led to another. And so, even though it was now packaged in an ice-filled garbage can, Power carried Jake's film back to Los Angeles in his Packard 220 roadster and dropped it off at the Metro-Magnum Film Laboratory.

The Navy, meanwhile, amazed that any hospital could have discharged *Dillon's Heroes,* wanted to keep them until they were fully recovered. It took four days and several telephone calls from General Stewart to get them released. And it took yet another day to talk the local Marine bureaucrats into issuing them leave orders.

During each of his many icy telephone conversations with Major Dillon, General Stewart not only pointed out that the whole operation was ten days behind schedule, but that he failed to see why the Heroes could not have waited until the end of the war bond tour before taking their leaves.

In short, Jake Dillon was in no great rush to make his 0745 appointment with Brigadier General J. J. Stewart, Director, Public Affairs Division, Headquarters, USMC.

When Major Dillon examined himself in the full-length mirror in his bathroom, his tailor-made uniform now seemed sewn for a bigger brother, and he himself looked like hell. His face was drained of color, his eyes were sunken, and there were bags under them.

It wasn't that bottle of Pinch last night, either, or even the bullshit of the last two weeks. That goddamned Guadalcanal did this to me.

He had a quick image of Guadalcanal—of men standing around in sweat-soaked utilities, weak with malaria or some other goddamned tropical disease, their skin spotted with festering sores.

He forced the image from his mind, adjusted his cover at an angle appropriate to a field-grade Marine feather merchant, and left the Metro-Magnum suite.

"The General will see you now," Brigadier General J. J. Stewart's staff sergeant clerk said.

Dillon tucked his cover under his left arm and marched into the General's office.

"Major Dillon reporting, Sir."

When Stewart raised his eyes, Dillon saw disapproval in them. He was familiar with the look.

I am now going to have my ass chewed. Fuck him.

"My God, Dillon, you look awful!" General Stewart said. "Are you all right?"

"I'm a little tired, Sir."

"You were ill, too, weren't you, Dillon?" General Stewart accused. "You just didn't think you should say so, am I right?"

"Everyone on the island is a little sick, General. I'll be all right."

"Damn it, Major! You've got to take care of yourself. What the hell would I do without you?"

"Probably very well, Sir."

"Under other circumstances, Major, I would *order* you to the dispensary. But we have our mission, don't we? And the mission comes first."

"Yes, Sir."

"Where's your film?"

"I think . . . I hope . . . it will be here today, Sir."

"You didn't bring it with you?"

"No, Sir. I arranged to have it souped on the West Coast."

"At San Diego?"

"No, Sir. At Metro-Magnum."

"I'm not entirely sure that was wise. As a matter of fact, I think it was unwise. Certainly, now that I think of it, there must be footage that we wouldn't want to get into the wrong hands. What were you thinking about?"

"Sir, I was very concerned about possible damage to the raw film from heat and humidity. I know the capabilities of the Metro-Magnum lab. I decided the film was so important that it should get the best possible lab work. That meant Metro-Magnum."

General Stewart grunted.

"You don't think it might get into the wrong hands?"

"No, Sir. I'm sure it won't."

Jesus, I didn't think about that. Morty Cohen probably made a duplicate to show his friends. Are those the wrong hands? Morty will be careful who he shows it to. And what the fuck does "wrong hands" mean anyway? There should be a film record somewhere of those kids crumpled up dead, even if it's lousy public relations.

"And it's being sent here? How?"

"It'll probably come in by air, Sir, to the Metro-Magnum suite at the Willard. I thought that would be safest."

"Well, you're the expert, Dillon. But as soon as possible, I'd like to screen that footage."

"As soon as it gets here, I'll set up a screening for you."

"Good. I'm looking forward to it. And in the meantime have a look at this." He handed Dillon a manila folder. Then he suddenly seemed to remember that Jake was standing with his cover under his arm and his right hand in the small of his back—the position officially described as "at ease." "My God, Dillon, sit down," he added.

"Thank you, Sir."

He opened the folder. The pages inside were fastened with a metal clip. The first of these was a newspaper clipping neatly glued to a sheet of paper.

"Machine Gun" McCoy Hero of Bloody Ridge

By Robert McCandless
INS War Correspondent

With The First Marine Division Sept 14 (Delayed) — "What we expected to find was his body, but what we found was Japanese bodies stacked like cordwood in front of his position, and McCoy, despite his wounds, ready to take on the rest of the Japanese Army," said Marine First Lieutenant Jonathan S. Swain, of Butte, Montana, and the 1st Raider Battalion, describing what he found when he led a counterattack to retake positions lost in the early stages of the battle for Bloody Ridge.

Staff Sergeant Thomas M. McCoy, 21, of Norristown, Pa., and a veteran of the Marine Raider attack on Makin Island, had been placed in charge of three listening posts in front of the Marine Raider line on Bloody Ridge. Two of the listening posts were wiped out in the first thirty minutes of the Japanese attack, and the two Marines with

McCoy in his position were seriously wounded.

This left McCoy in the center of the Japanese attack with a .30 caliber machine gun, plus his personal weapon, a Browning Automatic Rifle.

His orders were to try to fight his way back to the main Marine Raider Line, if it became apparent that he could not hold his position in the face of overwhelming enemy force.

"I couldn't do that," McCoy, a stocky, barrel-chested young man who was a steelworker before becoming a Marine, told this reporter. "Marines don't leave their wounded and run."

So he stayed, using brief interludes in the fierce fighting to render what first aid he could to the men with him, and to recharge the magazines of his Browning Automatic Rifle.

"I had plenty of ammo," McCoy reported, "so all I had to worry about was the machine gun getting so hot it would either jam, or cook off rounds."

(When a great many rounds are fired through the air-cooled Browning Machine Gun, the weapon becomes hot enough to cause cartridges to fire as soon as they enter the action.)

When that happened, McCoy would pick up his Browning Automatic Rifle and fire that until his machine gun cooled enough to fire reliably again.

"There were at least forty Japanese within yards of his position," Lieutenant Swain reported. "There's no telling how many others he killed in the jungle on the other side of the clearing."

McCoy was painfully wounded during his ordeal, once when a Japanese rifle bullet grazed his upper right leg, and several times more when he was struck on the face and chest by Japanese mortar and hand grenade fragments. His hands were blistered from the heat of the machine gun, and bloody from his frantic recharging of automatic rifle magazines.

"I had to order him out of his position," Lieutenant Swain said. "He didn't want to leave until he was sure the wounded men with him had made it to safety."

When he finished the story, Jake raised his eyes to General Stewart.

"One hell of a Marine, wouldn't you agree?" the General said.

"Yes, Sir."

"Take a look at the radio, it's under the news story."

Jake turned the page in the manila folder and found the radio.

URGENT
HQ USMC WASHINGTON DC 1135 20SEP42

COMMANDING GENERAL
FIRST MARINE DIVISION
VIA CINCPAC

1. REFERENCE IS MADE TO THE NEWS STORY BY MR. ROBERT MCCANDLESS, INTERNATIONAL NEWS SERVICE, OF 14SEPT42 DEALING WITH THE EXPLOITS OF SSGT THOMAS M. MCCOY WHICH HAS RECEIVED WIDE DISTRIBUTION THROUGHOUT THE UNITED STATES.

2. IF THE FACTS PRESENTED BY MR. MCCANDLESS ARE TRUE, IT WOULD SEEM THAT SSGT MCCOY SHOULD BE CITED FOR VALOR IN ACTION ABOVE AND BEYOND THE CALL OF DUTY. IF THIS IS THE INTENTION OF YOUR COMMAND, PLEASE ADVISE BY URGENT RADIO THE DECORATION, INCLUDING THE PROPOSED CITATION THEREOF, TO BE RECOMMENDED.

3. SSGT MCCOY, AS SOON AS HIS PHYSICAL CONDITION PERMITS, IS TO BE DETACHED FROM 1ST RAIDER BN AND PLACED ON TEMPORARY DUTY WITH PUBLIC AF-

FAIRS DIVISION, HQ USMC, WASH DC IN CONNECTION
WITH WAR BOND TOUR BEING CONDUCTED BY THIS OF-
FICE. AN AIR PRIORITY OF AAAA IS ASSIGNED. PAD
HQ USMC, ATTN: SPECIAL PROJECTS WILL BE ADVISED
BY URGENT RADIO OF DATE AND TIME OF SSGT MCCOY'S
DEPARTURE FROM 1ST MARDIV, AND HIS ROUTING, TO
INCLUDE ETA PEARL HARBOR HAWAII AND SAN DIEGO
CAL.

4. IN CONNECTION WITH THE ABOVE, IT IS SUG-
GESTED THAT SSGT MCCOY NOT REPEAT NOT BE
AWARDED ANY DECORATION FOR VALOR, INCLUDING
THE PURPLE HEART MEDAL(S) FOR WOUNDS SUFFERED
UNTIL HE IS RETURNED TO THE UNITED STATES. IT IS
CONTEMPLATED THAT A SENIOR USMC OFFICER OR A
HIGH RANKING GOVERNMENT OFFICIAL WILL MAKE
SUCH AWARD(S).

BY DIRECTION OF THE COMMANDANT:

J. J. STEWART, BRIG GEN, USMC
DIRECTOR, PUBLIC AFFAIRS DIVISION
HQ USMC

"If that story is true, and I have no reason to believe it is not,
that sergeant is going to get the Distinguished Service Cross.
Possibly even the Medal of Honor."

"Yes, Sir."

"I am going to recommend to the Commandant the Medal
of Honor," General Stewart said. "But in any event, obviously,
the sergeant belongs on your war bond tour."

"Yes, Sir."

"Do you think it likely that he will encounter on his way
home the same kind of difficulty you did?"

"Yes, Sir. I think he probably will."

"OK. I'll take steps to see that doesn't happen," General
Stewart said firmly. "As soon as I have word on when he's due
here, I'll let you know."

"Yes, Sir."

"I had his records checked. He has a sister in Norristown
and a brother in The Corps. An officer. A first lieutenant.
Here."

"Sir?"

"I thought it would make a very nice human interest photograph. A Marine officer welcoming his brother, a sergeant and a hero, home."

"Yes, Sir."

"His brother is assigned here to headquarters. The Office of Management Analysis, whatever the hell that is. It's in Building T-2032 on the Mall. You know where that is?"

"Yes, Sir."

"Good, because I want you to go over there and see him. I had one of my people call over there and they got the runaround. They said they never heard of Lieutenant K. R. McCoy. I want you to go over there, Jake, and lay your hands on him, tell him—more importantly tell his superiors—that we need him."

"Aye, aye, Sir. Sir?"

"Yes?"

"Sir, would that wait until tomorrow? I really feel a little bushed. I'd sort of like to take it easy today."

"Absolutely," General Stewart said after a moment's hesitation. "First thing tomorrow morning would be fine. Perhaps by then your film will be in from the West Coast, right?"

"Yes, Sir. It should be."

"You take the day off, Jake," General Stewart said magnanimously. "You've earned it."

"Yes, Sir. Thank you, General."

[Two]
TEMPORARY BUILDING T-2032
THE MALL
WASHINGTON, D.C.
0845 HOURS 21 SEPTEMBER 1942

Major Jake Dillon had little trouble finding Building T-2032 among its many twins on the Mall; but because he was more than a little hung over and in a foul mood, he grew rapidly annoyed when there was no answer to his repeated knocking on what seemed to be the building's main door.

"What the fuck are these feather merchants up to?" he inquired aloud.

Then he spotted a less imposing door to the left. And when he tried it, it opened. Inside he discovered a set of interior stairs, which he then climbed. At the top of the stairs, he found himself facing a counter. Above the counter, wire mesh rose to the ceiling. A staff sergeant and a civilian examined him curiously from behind the counter.

"Is this the Office of Management whatever?"

"The Office of Management Analysis, yes, Sir," the staff sergeant said.

"I'm looking for First Lieutenant K. R. McCoy," Dillon said, taking a note from his pocket.

"I'm sorry, Sir," the staff sergeant said immediately. "We have no officer by that name, Sir."

"Then you better tell Eighth and Eye," Dillon said, just the near side of nasty. "They say you do."

"I'm sorry, Sir," the sergeant said. "We have no officer by that name."

Dillon became aware of movement behind him. He glanced and saw a second lieutenant, then turned back to the sergeant.

"I want to see the officer in charge of this outfit, please," Dillon said. "Who would that be?"

"That would be General Pickering, Sir."

There was the buzzing sound of a solenoid; a gate in the wire mesh opened and the Second Lieutenant went through it.

"Would you get word to him that Major Dillon of the Public Affairs Office, USMC, would like to see him?"

"General Pickering will not be in today, Sir. Sorry," the staff sergeant said.

"Well, then, goddamn it, Sergeant, tell whoever is in charge here that I want to talk to him."

"Major Dillon!" the Second Lieutenant said.

Dillon looked at him. There was no recognition.

"Do I know you, Lieutenant? More to the point, do you work here?"

"Yes, Sir," the Lieutenant said. "My name is Moore, Sir. We met in Australia."

"In Australia?" Dillon asked, searching his memory.

"You know this officer, Lieutenant? He's been asking for Lieutenant McCoy."

Recognition came to Dillon.

"You were Fleming Pickering's orderly," Dillon accused. And then associations came. The Lieutenant was wearing the woven gold rope worn by aides-de-camp to General Officers. *"General Pickering will not be in today, Sir."*

The kid's name is Moore. He was a buck sergeant at Picker-ing's house when I went there from New Zealand with Whatsis-name, the First MarDiv G-2 who got himself killed right after we landed on the 'Canal.

"Yes, Sir," Second Lieutenant John Marston Moore, USMCR, replied. "More or less."

"What the hell is going on here, Moore?" Dillon demanded. *General Pickering? What the fuck is that all about?*

"Is the Colonel back there?" Moore asked.

"Yes, Sir," the civilian behind the counter replied.

"Open the gate, Sergeant, please," Moore said. "Major Dil-lon, will you come with me, please?"

The solenoid buzzed. Moore put his hand to the gate and pulled it inward.

"This way, please, Major."

"Lieutenant, what about the log?" the staff sergeant asked.

"Log him in on my authority," Moore said.

Dillon followed him through a door, and then down a corri-dor. He noticed that Moore was walking awkwardly, limping.

"What did you do to your leg?" he asked.

Moore did not reply.

They came to an office at the end of the corridor. Through a partially opened door Dillon saw a skinny civilian sitting at a desk. He had taken off his suit coat. His trousers were held up by a pair of well-worn suspenders.

He glanced up from his desk and saw Moore.

"You want to see me, Moore?"

"Yes, Sir. I think it's important."

The civilian gestured for Moore to enter. Moore motioned for Dillon to precede him.

"This is Major Dillon, Sir," Moore said.

"Who is Major Dillon?" the civilian asked.

"The question in my mind is who the hell are you to ask who I am?" Dillon flared.

The civilian looked at him.

"I think we need some ground rules in here," he said. "Major, I am a colonel in the USMC. If you insist, I will show you an identification card. For the time being, however, I suggest you stand there, at attention and with your mouth shut, until I find out what's going on here."

There was an unmistakable tone of *I-Will-Be-Obeyed* au-thority in the civilian's voice.

Jake Dillon came to attention, wondering, *If he's a colonel, how come the civilian clothes?*

"OK, John, who is this officer?" Colonel F. L. Rickabee asked.

"He's Major Dillon, Sir. He has something to do with Public Relations."

"Fascinating! And what's he doing here?"

"He's looking for Lieutenant McCoy, Sir. I overheard that as I came through the gate."

Rickabee looked at Dillon.

"If you find this officer—Lieutenant McCoy, you said?—what will you do with him, Major?"

"Colonel, Lieutenant McCoy's brother behaved very heroically on Guadalcanal; he is being returned from Guadalcanal to receive a high decoration."

"And you wanted to tell him about that?"

"No, Sir. General Stewart—"

"Who the hell is General Stewart?"

"Public Affairs, Sir. At Eighth and Eye?"

Rickabee nodded. "Go on."

"General Stewart thinks Lieutenant McCoy would be helpful in connection with getting The Corps some good publicity."

"That's out of the question," Rickabee said. "Forget it. Can you relay that to General Stewart or will I have to do it?"

"I think it would be helpful if you spoke with the General, Sir," Dillon said.

"Sir, there's more," Moore said.

"What would that be?"

"Major Dillon and General Pickering are friends."

"Is that so, Major?"

"If we're talking about Fleming Pickering, yes, Sir. We're old friends."

"Sir, Major Dillon is a friend of Major Banning's too. I don't know if—"

"Do you know what Major Banning's doing for a living these days, Major?" Rickabee interrupted him.

"Yes, Sir, I do."

"Damn!" Rickabee said. "But, now that I think of it, maybe you don't. You tell me what you think Banning's doing."

"Colonel, I don't know who you are," Dillon said. "I'm sure what Banning is doing is classified, and I'm not sure you have the Need to Know."

"Show him your badge, Moore," Rickabee ordered. Moore took his credentials from his pocket and showed them to Dillon.

Jesus Christ, what the hell is this? The last time I see this kid, he's a sergeant passing canapés for Pickering, and now he's a Special Agent of the Office of Naval Intelligence!

"That's his Need to Know. And I'm his boss," Rickabee said. "Good enough?"

"Yes, Sir," Dillon said. "Sir—"

"Close the door, John," Rickabee interrupted him. "And you can pull up a chair, Major. If you're a friend of General Pickering, you're obviously not the asshole of a public relations feather merchant I first thought you were."

Colonel Rickabee was just about finished explaining to Major Dillon the change in Fleming Pickering's military status when there was a knock at his door.

"Come!"

"Colonel," Captain Ed Sessions said, putting his head in the door. "There's an Army officer out here asking for General Pickering."

"Tell him the General will not be in today and ask him what he wants."

"I did, Sir. He said he's a liaison officer for General MacArthur. I think maybe you had better see him."

"Douglas MacArthur?"

"Yes, Sir."

"Jesus Christ! Well, go fetch him."

The door closed and then a minute later, reopened.

"Colonel Rickabee," Captain Sessions announced formally, "Colonel DePress."

A lieutenant colonel marched into Rickabee's office. He was in Army Pink and Green uniform, the lapels decorated with the insignia of the General Staff Corps, his brimmed cap tucked under his arm; and he was carrying a leather briefcase chained to his wrist. He saluted crisply before he seemed to notice the man behind the desk was not in uniform.

Rickabee made a vague gesture in the direction of his forehead; the gesture could be loosely defined as a salute.

"I'm afraid General Pickering is not available right now, Colonel," he said. "I'm his deputy. Maybe I could help you somehow?"

"Sir, I have a Personal from General MacArthur to General Pickering."

"I'll see that he gets it," Rickabee said, holding his hand out.

"Sir, my orders from General MacArthur are to personally deliver the Personal."

Rickabee considered that a moment. While they were talking, Rickabee gave the Army Lieutenant Colonel a quick once-over. *He may be a Doggie Feather Merchant,* he decided, *but he wasn't always one.*

On his right sleeve, Lieutenant Colonel DePress was wearing the insignia of the 26th Cavalry, Philippine Scouts, signifying that he had served in combat with that unit. And topping the I-Was-There fruit salad on his breast were ribbons representing the Silver Star and the Third Award of the Purple Heart.

"Colonel," Rickabee said, "not for dissemination, General Pickering is in the hospital."

"I'm sorry to hear that, Sir."

"I'm about to visit him. Would you have the time to come along?"

"Yes, Sir. I would appreciate that, Sir."

"Sessions, is there a car available?" Rickabee asked.

"I'll check, Sir."

"Colonel," Lieutenant Moore said, "I've got General Pickering's car. If you wanted to use that, Sergeant Hart could bring you back."

"OK, done," Rickabee said. "You have the material Sessions packed up for the General, Moore?"

"No, Sir."

"It's on my desk, Sir," Sessions said.

[Three]
WALTER REED ARMY GENERAL HOSPITAL
WASHINGTON, D.C.
1015 HOURS 21 SEPTEMBER 1942

Brigadier General Fleming Pickering, USMCR, had been assigned a three-room VIP suite in the Army Hospital. His rank would have entitled him to a private room in any case, but the hospital authorities had decided that since a VIP suite was available, who was better qualified to occupy it than a man who was not only a brigadier general, but "an old and close friend of the President," according to *The Washington Star?*

The suite was on the third floor. It consisted of a fully equipped hospital room and a sitting room, furnished with a sofa, a pair of upholstered chairs, and a four-place dining table set. These rooms were connected by a smaller room that held a refrigerator and a desk.

When Colonel Rickabee and party entered the suite, they found General Pickering in the small connecting room playing gin rummy on the desk top with Sergeant Hart. Pickering was wearing a silk bathrobe, and Sergeant Hart was in civilian clothing; his shoulder holster and pistol were on top of the refrigerator.

Hart stood up.

"Good morning, General," Rickabee said, and then, "as you were, Sergeant."

"Where he was was about to take me for twenty dollars," Pickering said. "I didn't expect to see you here this morning, Rickabee. And who is that ugly Marine tagging along behind you?"

"How the hell are you, Fleming?" Dillon inquired, walking to Pickering and shaking his hand.

"General," Rickabee said, "this officer has a Personal for you from General MacArthur."

Lieutenant Colonel DePress saluted.

"Good morning, General," he said.

"Good morning," Pickering said.

"May I inquire as to the General's health?"

"You may," Pickering said. "The General's health is a hell of a lot better than I can convince anybody around here that it is."

"I'm glad to hear that, Sir," Colonel DePress said.

"What, Colonel? That my health is better? Or that I can't convince the doctors that it is?"

Colonel DePress, looking uncomfortable, finally managed, "I'm glad to hear the General is feeling better, Sir," and then, somewhat awkwardly—because it was chained to his wrist— opened his briefcase and handed Pickering a large manila envelope.

A signature had been scrawled across the flap and then covered with transparent tape. The signature was General Douglas MacArthur's.

Pickering tore open the manila envelope and took from it a smaller, squarish envelope. A red blob was on its flap.

I'll be damned, Rickabee thought. *Didn't sealing wax go out with the nineteenth century?*

Pickering opened the second envelope and read the letter it contained.

"Will there be a reply, General?" Colonel DePress asked.

"Will you be seeing General MacArthur anytime soon?"

"Yes, Sir. I'll be returning in two or three days, Sir."

"Please tell General MacArthur"—Pickering began and then interrupted himself—"could I send a letter back with you?"

"Of course, General."

"I'll try to do that. If something goes wrong, please tell General MacArthur that I am very grateful for his gracious courtesy, and ask him to offer my best wishes to Mrs. MacArthur."

"I'll be happy to do that, General. And I will check with you before I leave to see if the General has a Personal for the General."

"I'd appreciate that," Pickering said. "Thank you very much, Colonel."

"My pleasure, Sir. With your permission, Sir?"

To judge by the look on his face, General Pickering was baffled by the question. Rickabee knew why: The Army officer was asking ritual permission to leave the Marine general's presence, and Pickering was unfamiliar with the ritual.

"Colonel," Rickabee said, doing his best to finesse the situation, "Sergeant Hart will take you wherever you need to go. And with General Pickering's permission, he'll stay with you as long as you need him."

"Very kind of you, Sir. Just to General Marshall's office would be a great help."

"On your way, Sergeant Hart," Pickering said.

"Aye, aye, Sir," Hart said.

Colonel DePress saluted again. This time Pickering returned it.

When the door had closed on them, Jake Dillon asked, "What the hell was that all about?"

"Goddamn it, Jake," Pickering said. "You're just a lousy major. How about a little respect for a goddamned general?"

"Yes, Sir, Goddamned General. What the hell was that all about?"

Pickering chuckled and tossed him the small envelope from General MacArthur.

So they really are close friends, Rickabee decided. *Dillon isn't just another one of Pickering's suck-up acquaintances.*

"I'll be damned," Dillon said, when he had read the letter.

"Show it to Rickabee and Moore," Pickering said.

Dillon handed it to Rickabee.

OFFICE OF THE SUPREME COMMANDER
GENERAL HEADQUARTERS
SOUTHWEST PACIFIC OCEAN AREAS

13th September 1942
Brigadier General Fleming Pickering, USMC
By Hand of Officer Courier

My Dear Fleming,

I shall probably be among the last to offer my congratulations upon your appointment to flag rank. But you of all people, with your deep understanding of the communications problems in this theater of war, will understand why the news reached here so belatedly; and as a cherished friend and comrade in arms you will believe me when I say that had I known sooner, I would sooner have written to say with what great joy Mrs. MacArthur and I received the news.

Please believe me further that had it been within my power, that is to say if you had been under my command during your distinguished and sorely missed service here, you would long ago have been given rank commensurate with your proven ability and valor in combat.

Mrs. MacArthur joins me in extending every wish for your continued success in the future, and our warmest personal good wishes,

Yours,

Douglas

Pickering waited until Rickabee finished reading, then said, "That's what's known as the old el softo soapo, of which the General is a master, Rickabee."

"I don't think so," Dillon said.

"Neither do I," Rickabee said, thinking aloud. "Those references to his wife made it personal. I think he really likes you."

"The staff over there hated your ass, Flem," Dillon said, "which is the proof of that pudding."

"So what brings you here, Jake, to change the subject?"

"You mean to the States, or here, here and now?"

"Both."

"Well, I am about to win the war by running a war bond tour. I brought eight heroes here from the 'Canal—really seven, plus one asshole who managed to get himself shot and looks like a hero."

"Straight from Guadalcanal or via Australia?"

"I saw Feldt and Ed Banning, if that's what you're asking. And I saw the girls in Melbourne, Howard's and that kid sergeant's."

"That's what I was asking. And Howard and Koffler are still on Buka?"

"That's an unpleasant story, Fleming. They're really up shit creek."

"Damn," Pickering said. "Banning was trying to come up with some way to relieve them."

"I don't think that's going to happen," Dillon said. "Not that Banning wouldn't swap his left nut to get them out of there."

"You understand what we're talking about, Rickabee?"

"Yes, Sir," Rickabee said. "We had a back-channel from Banning this morning—you'll find a carbon of it in that material I had Sessions put together for you—and Ferdinand Six was still operational as of—what?—thirty hours ago."

"When they do go down," Dillon said softly, "Feldt and Banning are going to drop in one team after another until one makes it. So far they have four teams ready to go—two Aussies and two Marines."

"Banning should not have told you that," Rickabee said.

"Banning took his lead from me," Pickering said a little sharply. "I don't think Major Dillon is a Japanese spy or has a loose mouth."

"With respect, Sir," Rickabee said, "there is an absolute

correlation between the number of people privy to a secret and the time it takes for that secret to be compromised."

"That may well be, Colonel," Pickering said icily, reminding Jake Dillon that Fleming Pickering was not accustomed to being corrected, and didn't like it at all. "But in this circumstance, I believe I have the authority to decide who gets told what."

"Yes, Sir. That is correct, Sir." Rickabee said. In Dillon's judgment—looking at Rickabee's tight lips and white face—Rickabee's temper was at the breaking point. Career Marine Colonels are not fond of reservists, period, but they go into a cold, consuming rage when reservists who outrank them bring them up sharp.

"And I brought some film from the 'Canal," Jake said, hoping to change the subject. "From Hawaii to the West Coast in an ice-filled garbage can."

"What did you say?" Pickering asked after a moment, after he had stared Rickabee down. "An ice-filled garbage can?"

"I got one of those insulated whole-blood containers from the medics on the 'Canal," Jake explained. "They took it away from me at Pearl Harbor. So I got a garbage can and put the film in, packed in ice."

"What kind of film?" Pickering asked.

"Combat footage, from the 'Canal. I'm going to make up a newsreel feature. Maybe, if the film is any good, and if there's enough usable footage, a short."

"I'd like to see that," Pickering said. "Where is it?"

"So would I," Rickabee said.

"I had it souped at Metro-Magnum," Jake replied, adding, "Hell, now that I think about it, it may be at the Willard now."

"Find out," Pickering ordered.

"Yes, Sir, General," Dillon said.

"Don't push your luck, Jake," Pickering said.

Jake had no idea if Pickering was kidding or not. He picked up the telephone and called the Willard. He was told that an air freight package had arrived for him thirty minutes before.

"It's there," he said. "I'll get in a cab and go get it."

"If I sent someone to get it, would they give it to him?"

"Probably not. It's probably in a Metro-Magnum can and they guard those like Fort Knox."

"What kind, what size, film is it?"

"Sixteen millimeter."

Rickabee picked up the telephone and asked for the office of the hospital commander.

"Good morning, Sir. Colonel Rickabee, General Pickering's Deputy. The General needs a staff car to transport Major Dillon into Washington and return. And the General will require that a 16mm projector and screen be set up in his sitting room right away.

"No, Sir. The General will not require a projectionist. Just the camera and screen. Plus, of course, the car.

"Thank you, Sir."

He hung up and turned to Dillon.

"There will be a staff car waiting at the main entrance, Major."

"Thank you, Sir."

"I trust you are suitably awed by my power as a general, Jake," Pickering said.

"Yes, Sir, Goddamn General, I am truly awed."

Rickabee and Pickering laughed.

Well, at least I got them laughing. For a moment there, it looked like it was going to get goddamned unpleasant.

[Four]

"Interesting man," Rickabee said after Dillon left . . . and after sending Moore to get a pot of coffee he didn't really want. "I think there's more there than meets the eye."

"He was—I suppose still is—Vice President for Publicity for Metro-Magnum Studios. I don't think they'd pay him the kind of money they did unless he was worth it. Clark Gable told me once that Jake's real value came when movies were in production. He could tell whether the public would like them or not, just from looking at rushes. And he knew how to fix them."

"I wasn't aware you . . . I guess the phrase is 'traveled in those circles'?"

"Oh, no. I never did. I was a skeet shooter. There were some movie people, Gable, Bob Stack, people like that, and Jake, who shot skeet. That's how I met him. Marines can smell each other. Jake was a China Marine, a sergeant, before he went Hollywood. He was a better shot with a sixty-nine-dollar Winchester Model 12 from Sears, Roebuck than Gable was with his thousand-dollar English shotguns."

"What did you shoot, General?" Rickabee asked.

"When my wife was watching, one of the pair of Purdys she gave me for my thirtieth birthday," Pickering said. "When she wasn't, a Model 12. I don't think a better shotgun was ever made."

Rickabee was not surprised.

"I still don't know how you and Jake managed to show up here together," Pickering said.

"He came to the office looking for Lieutenant McCoy."

"What did he want with the Killer?"

"He doesn't like to be called that," Rickabee said.

"To hell with him, I'm a general, I'll call him whatever I want to," Pickering said. "Besides, I am literally old enough to be his father."

"McCoy's brother apparently was quite a hero on Bloody Ridge. An INS reporter has dubbed him 'Machine Gun McCoy.' Dillon's boss, a Brigadier General named Stewart, in Public Relations at Eighth and Eye, found out about our McCoy and wants to make public relations about him. When they started asking us questions, we gave them the runaround, and General Stewart sent Dillon to straighten us out. Moore recognized Dillon—"

"Jake met him at my house in Australia," Pickering interrupted.

"—and brought him into my office."

"So what do we do about McCoy? You want me to call this General—Stewart, you said?—and get him off our back?"

"I thought perhaps you would be willing to call General Forrest. That would keep us out of it entirely. And it would give you a chance to talk to him."

Major General Horace W. T. Forrest was Assistant Chief of Staff, Intelligence, Headquarters, USMC.

"Why do I suspect an ulterior motive, Rickabee? Why didn't *you* just call Forrest?"

"I thought it might be of value, General, to remind General Forrest that you are not just a nightmare of his."

"You really think it's that bad?"

"My job is to see things as they are, General. Let me put it this way: I suspect that General Forrest secretly hopes that your recovery will take some time, maybe until the war is over. He has not come to see you, you may have noticed, or even had his aide call your aide to ask about your condition."

"In that case, get the sonofabitch on the phone," Pickering said. "After you tell me what to say to him."

"The General has been made aware of the problem, Sir. Another general officer, who has no need to know why, has to be discouraged from asking about one of your officers. I'm sure the General will know how to deal with the situation."

"I haven't the foggiest idea . . ." Pickering said, and stopped. Rickabee was already picking up the telephone.

"General Pickering for General Forrest," Rickabee said, and then handed Pickering the telephone.

"Forrest."

"Pickering, General."

"Well, what a pleasant surprise, General. I understand you've been a little under the weather."

"I'm feeling much better, General."

"Ready for duty, General?"

"I've placed myself on limited duty, General, until I can get the doctors to agree with my prognosis."

"Well, General, you really don't want to rush things. You'd better listen to the doctors."

"I have a little problem, General. I thought I could ask your help with it."

"Anything within my power, General."

"It has to do with General Stewart—"

"Public relations type, that Stewart?"

"That's right, General."

"Well, you and I, General, are really not in the public relations business, are we?"

"That's precisely the problem, General. General Stewart apparently has an interest in putting one of my officers into the public eye."

"Who would that be, General?"

"Lieutenant McCoy, General."

"Oh, yes. I know McCoy. What the hell does Stewart want with him?"

"It seems that McCoy's brother did something spectacular on Guadalcanal, General. General Stewart is having him returned for publicity purposes. He found out that Sergeant McCoy's brother is my McCoy and wants to involve him."

"Give him the runaround, General."

"General Stewart is a determined man, General. He sent a major to see Colonel Rickabee."

"Give the major the runaround. I was under the impression that Rickabee was pretty good at that sort of thing."

"Colonel Rickabee is, General. But the Major is about as determined as General Stewart. Which is why I'm asking for your help, General."

"I'll deal with General Stewart, General. Put it out of your mind."

"Thank you very much, General."

"As soon as you feel up to it, General, have your aide call mine and we'll set something up. You and I really have to sit down and have a long talk."

"That's very kind of you, General. I'll do that."

"Good to finally have the chance to talk to you, Pickering," General Forrest said, and the line went dead.

Pickering put the telephone back in its cradle and looked at Rickabee.

"How'd I do?"

"General officers are expected to do very well, General. You didn't let the side down."

"If I were Forrest, I wouldn't like me either," Pickering said. "I wouldn't like it a goddamn bit if somebody I never heard of, who got his commission in a damned strange way, showed up as one of my senior subordinates."

"General, President Roosevelt is the Commander in Chief. There should be no questioning of his orders by a Marine."

"I don't think Forrest is questioning the legality of the order, but I suspect he has some question about its wisdom."

"Who was it, General—Churchill?—who said, 'War is too important a matter to leave to the generals'?"

"I think it was Churchill," Pickering said. "But that leaves me sort of in limbo, doesn't it? As a general who really shouldn't be a general?"

"That question, General, is moot. And who was it that said, 'Yours not to reason why, et cetera, et cetera'?"

"I have no idea, but I take your point."

There was a knock at the door. And then three Army enlisted men in hospital garb appeared. Two of them were pushing a table with a Bell & Howell motion picture projector on it and the third was carrying a screen.

"I believe the General wishes that set up in the sitting room," Rickabee said. "Is that correct, General?"

"That is correct, Colonel," General Pickering said.

[Five]

When Sergeant George S. Hart entered The Corps, he brought one thing with him that few of his fellows had when they joined—a familiarity with violent death.

As a cop, he'd seen—and grown accustomed to—all sorts of sights that turned civilians' stomachs, civilians being defined by cops as anyone not a cop. He'd seen bridge jumpers after they'd been pulled from the Mississippi; people whose dismembered bodies had to be pried from the twisted wreckage of their automobiles; every kind of suicide; people whose time on earth had been ended by axes, by lead pipes, by rifle shots, pistol shots, shotguns.

Even before he joined the force, he'd been present in the Medical Examiner's office while the coroner removed hearts, lungs, and other vital organs from open-eyed cadavers and dropped them like so much hamburger into the stainless-steel scale hanging over the dissection table. All the while, the coroner would exchange jokes with Hart's father.

But none of this had prepared him for the motion picture film Major Jake Dillon brought with him from Guadalcanal.

There were five large reels of film.

"You understand, Fleming," Dillon said to The General (for that was how Hart had begun to look at Fleming Pickering—The General, not the General), "that this is a really rough cut. All my lab guys did was soup it and splice the short takes together. This is the first time anyone has had a look at it."

After Major Dillon told him to kill the lights in The General's sitting room and started to run the film, it was sort of like being in a newsreel theater with the sound off.

The film began with a picture of a small slate blackboard on which the cameraman had written the date, the time, the location, the subject matter, and his name.

For example:

5 August 1942 1540
Aboard USS Calhoun
En route to Guadalcanal
1st Para Bn Prepares for invasion
Cpl H.A. Simpson, USMCR

Then there were Marines; most of them were smiling. They were standing or sitting around, cleaning their weapons, sharpening knives, working ammunition-linking machines for machine gun belts, or writing letters home, stuff like that.

George was getting just a little bored with this when the content changed. They were at the invasion beach.

> **7 August 1942 0415**
> **Tulagi**
> **First Wave, 1st Raider Bn**
> **Cpl H.A. Simpson, USMCR**

The cameraman was in an invasion barge. You could see Marines with all their gear, hunched down, waiting for the boat to touch shore. They were no longer smiling.

Then you could see the beach, a landing pier, burning Japanese seaplanes, and shellfire, and lots of smoke.

And then guys were climbing over the sides of the barge. Then the camera was out of the barge and on top of the pier; parts of the pier had been destroyed.

And then you started to see bodies. The first body was just lying there, with arterial blood pumping out his back. The camera was on that for maybe ten seconds; it seemed a lot longer.

And then you saw two Marines running along the pier. Both of them, at the same time, just fell down. Not like in the movies, where people clutch their chests or their throats and spin around before they fall. These Marines just stopped in mid-stride, fell down, and were dead.

There was a lot that was out of focus, and a lot of gray space, with no images; and then there were more bodies. Some of them now were Japanese.

"I'd like a drink, please," The General said.

"General," Lieutenant Moore said, "you said to remind you when you'd already had the day's ration."

"Lieutenant, ask Sergeant Hart to get me an inch and a half of scotch, please."

"Aye, aye, Sir. Hart?"

"Aye, aye, Sir."

"Help yourself, George, if you like," The General said. "You, too, John."

There was a shot of some Japanese, in pieces, around a small hole in the ground. After a moment Hart decided it had been caused by the impact of a Naval artillery shell.

There was a shot of a Marine lying on his back with his face blown off.

Bodies. Bodies. Bodies.

There was a shot of some Marine with more balls than brains standing up in the open and firing his rifle off hand, like he was on the goddamned rifle range at Parris Island, sling in the proper place and everything.

And then a shot of a couple of Japanese with the tops of their heads blown off, and then a shot of the Marine with the rifle, closer up now, so close that Hart could see that he was an older guy, an officer, a major. He was gesturing angrily at the cameraman and Hart could tell that he was really pissed that the cameraman was taking his picture.

It went on and on and on, Marines running and shooting their weapons, Marines down, with corpsmen bending over them; even a shot of a guy with blood on his face clinging for dear life to one of the supports of the pier, looking like he was hysterical. There was time enough for The General to ask for three more drinks. Hart made them, and two more for himself. The last two he made for The General were an inch and a half, straight up.

Finally it was over; and Major Dillon told Hart to turn the lights on.

"Your people did a fine job, Jake," The General said.

"Yeah," Dillon said. "But there's not much I can put in newsreel theaters, is there?"

"I'd like a copy of that," Colonel Rickabee said.

"Colonel, that would be hard—" Major Dillon said.

"Why, Rickabee?" The General interrupted.

"I want to show it to my people—our people."

"Get him a copy, Jake," The General ordered.

"General Stewart wants to look at this right away."

"Fuck General Stewart," The General said. "He'll have to wait until you get a copy of that for Rickabee."

"OK, Flem. Whatever you say."

"The Navy has a pretty good photo lab at Anacostia, Dillon," Rickabee said. "But I don't know if they can copy motion picture film."

"I've got a pal, used to work in the Metro-Magnum lab," Dillon replied, "who's running the Army lab at the Astoria Studios on Long Island. I know he won't fuck it up, and he could do a quick edit and get rid of the garbage."

"Call him," Fleming Pickering ordered. "See if he can—will—do it. If he will, we can send George to New York."

Hart could see that Colonel Rickabee didn't like that. But he was not surprised that he didn't raise an objection. He had already learned that arguing with The General was usually a waste of breath.

XI

Sergeant George Hart let himself as quietly as possible into the small suite he shared with Lieutenant John Marston Moore. But as he walked on his toes into the bedroom, the lights came on. And when he opened the door, Moore was awake, holding himself up on his elbows.

"I tried not to wake you, Lieutenant."

Moore shook his head, signifying it didn't matter.

"Everything go OK?"

Moore held up a large film can.

"I just dropped off the original with Major Dillon at the Willard," he said. "This is two copies."

"Two?"

"They asked me how many copies I wanted, so I said two."

"Good man," Moore said. "I think The General wants one."

Despite the differences in their ranks and backgrounds, Hart had come to think of Moore as a friend. And his story was too good to just keep, particularly since Moore was one of the very few people in the world who would believe it.

"Veronica Wood has nipples the size of silver dollars," he announced.

Veronica Wood was a motion picture actress. A photograph, showing her in a translucent negligee, her long blond hair hanging down to her waist, was pinned up on barracks walls around the world.

"I'm sure you're going to tell me how you know that," Moore said.

"She was in bed with Major Dillon," Hart said. "I knocked at the door, and he said come in, and I did, and there she was. She said 'Hi!' and smiled at me. She didn't even try to cover herself. They were both stinko."

"I would say that Major Dillon is entitled, wouldn't you?"

"Yeah. Jesus, those movies!"

"They were pretty awful, weren't they?" Moore said, and then added: "But you understand, George, that all they shot was . . . what you saw. It really wasn't all that bad."

"Yeah, and that's why you walk around with a cane, right?"

"Speaking of dollar-sized nipples, Sergeant," Moore said, "you had a telephone call from a lady."

"I did?"

"You did. At midnight. I answered the phone, and she said, in a very nice voice, 'George?' and I said, 'Sorry, he's not here right now, can I take a message?' and she said, no, she'd call back."

"You're probably talking about my mother," George said.

"I really don't think so. This lady didn't sound like a mother. And wouldn't your mother have said, 'Tell him his mother called'?"

"I have no idea—"

"Maybe it was Captain Sessions' secretary," Moore said innocently. "I've noticed the way she looks at you."

"Thanks a lot, Lieutenant."

Captain Sessions' secretary was at least thirty-five, weighed more than a hundred fifty pounds, and had a mustache.

"Consumed with unrequited passion in the wee hours of the morning," Moore went on. "Yearning for the feel of your strong arms around her—"

"My arms wouldn't fit around her," George said. "Beats the

hell out of me. The only person I gave this number to is my mother."

"Jesus, George. If it was your mother, I'm sorry—"

"I don't think it was my mother," George said. "She would have asked where I was at midnight."

"Speaking of midnight, the wee hours," Moore said, "The General called about ten. I am instructed to inform you that he doesn't want to see you before thirteen hundred tomorrow."

"What?"

"You have the morning off. The General also said to remind you that you are not to waste your money eating at the Waffle House or Crystal Burger."

"What does that mean?"

"We are to take full advantage of hotel services. Booze, chow, laundry, whatever. He said I was to consider that an order."

"That's nice," George said.

"I think it's more than nice," Moore said. "I think it's important to him. You took care of his idiot son and now he wants to repay the favor."

"You ever meet him?"

Moore shook his head, no.

"He's a really nice guy," Hart said. "A little wild, but a nice guy."

"Somehow, when I heard he'd flown under the Golden Gate, I suspected he was not a shrinking violet," Moore said. "Where's the car?"

"Out in front. Just about out of gas. I couldn't find an open station."

"Well, then, I'll take a cab to the hospital in the morning, and you get it gassed up before you come."

He let himself fall back on the bed, and rolled on his side.

"Turn out the light when you're finished," he said.

[Two]
HENDERSON FIELD
GUADALCANAL, SOLOMON ISLANDS
1515 HOURS 23 SEPTEMBER 1942

Lieutenant Colonel Clyde W. Dawkins had informed Captain
Charles M. Galloway that part of a squadron of dive bombers
was on its way—half a dozen of them, of VMSB-141s. These
were under Lieutenant Colonel Cooley, an officer Galloway
admired; he'd flown with Cooley years before.

So Galloway was not surprised when he heard odd noises
overhead. He was familiar with the peculiar sound made by
half a dozen thousand-horsepower Wright R-1820-52 engined
Douglas Dauntlesses. What did surprise him, when he stepped
out of VMF-229's sandbag tent squadron office, was the sight
of two Grumman Wildcats about to touch down ahead of the
SBDs.

He could tell that they, too, were replacement aircraft. Their
fuselages glistened, unmarked by the mud carried by every
airplane that landed at Henderson.

Seeing them there—so new and fresh—should have pleased
him. In fact, he wasn't at all pleased, he was hugely annoyed—
on two counts: First, nobody had told him two new Wildcats
were coming—thus denying him the chance to plead for them
for VMF-229. Second, they came in with the SBDs. And that
meant the Navy had fucked up again. . . .

The SBDs were brought in toward Guadalcanal aboard one
of the escort carriers. In order to protect the carrier from
Japanese aviation and to permit it to return to other duties as
quickly as possible, the SBDs took off for Guadalcanal at the
farthest point possible from Henderson—after due consideration of the weather and reserve fuel requirements.

Since the Dauntlesses had a much greater range than the
Wildcats, and since the Dauntlesses and the Wildcats had obviously been launched from the same carrier, one of two things
had happened: Either the Dauntlesses had been launched
within Wildcat range of Henderson, thus endangering the escort carrier that much longer. Or—more likely—the Wildcats
had been launched at Dauntless range and were landing with
near empty tanks.

Wildcats that ran out of fuel and ditched in the ocean were
no different from Wildcats lost in action.

Captain Galloway was again reminded that a lot of really stupid people were running around with a lot of rank on their collar points. There was nothing he could do about that, of course, but there was a chance he could talk Dawkins into giving VMF-229 the two new Wildcats.

He took off at a trot for the sandbagged headquarters of MAG-21.

When he walked into the MAG-21 office, Charley learned that Lieutenant Colonel Dawkins was in the air, taking his turn on patrol. Since the Coastwatchers couldn't always give them warning that Japanese planes were coming, one- and two-plane patrols were always overhead.

The two pilots of the new Wildcats came into the MAG-21 tent a few minutes after Charley Galloway got there. In Charley's judgment, they looked as if they'd graduated from Pensacola last week.

One was wearing a ring knocker ring, Charley noticed without any special glee. The other looked like a troublemaker: Charley saw the spark of intelligence in his eyes . . . but also the far side of mischievousness.

"I'm Captain Galloway," Charley said, putting out his hand. "I've got VMF-229. That was you two coming in in the Wildcats just now?"

The ring knocker came to attention and saluted. This did not surprise Charley.

"Yes, Sir. Lieutenant Stecker, Sir. Reporting aboard, Sir. With Lieutenant Pickering."

"To MAG-21, you mean, Mister?" Charley asked as he returned the salute.

"No, Sir. We're on orders to VMF-229."

He opened his canvas flight bag and handed Galloway a set of their orders. Galloway read them; they were indeed assigned to VMF-229. He managed to conceal his delight fairly successfully.

Since they flew those airplanes in, and they're assigned to me, if I just take these guys—and the airplanes—to the squadron, I stand a much better chance of keeping the airplanes, too. Possession is nine-tenths of the law.

"Welcome aboard, gentlemen," Charley said. "Will you come with me, please?"

Lady Luck smiled on him. Fifty yards from MAG-21, he encountered Technical Sergeant Oblensky.

"Sergeant Oblensky, these officers just delivered two F4F aircraft. As your first priority, will you see that those aircraft are moved to our squadron area? I'd like to have that accomplished before Colonel Dawkins returns from patrol."

"Aye, aye, Sir," Big Steve said. "I'll do that immediately, Sir."

Lieutenant Bill Dunn was in the squadron office when Galloway walked in. He looked with interest at the neat and shiny newcomers.

"Lieutenant Dunn," Captain Galloway said, "these two officers just arrived for duty with us. In new Wildcats. Sergeant Oblensky is moving one of them to our area. Would you please go move the other one, right now?"

"Your wish is my command, Skipper," Dunn said, and quickly left the tent.

Galloway waited until Dunn left the tent, then said, "Lieutenant Dunn is working on being a double ace. He's my executive officer."

He saw increased interest in the eyes of both of his new officers.

"Stecker, you said?"

"Yes, Sir."

"You're an Annapolis man, I see, Mister Stecker?"

"No, Sir. West Point."

West Point? You don't see many of those in The Corps.

"And you, Mr.—"

"Pickering, Sir."

"—Pickering. Where did you get your commission?"

"Quantico, Sir. Officer Candidate School."

"And your flight training?"

"P'Cola, Sir. Both of us."

"And how many hours do you have? You first, Mr. Pickering."

"Four hundred sixty-eight, Sir."

That was a good deal more than Charley expected to hear. The last half-dozen replacements to VMF-229 had averaged about 250 hours total time, very little of that in Wildcats.

"How much in Wildcats?"

"Two twenty-eight, Sir."

"This is not, then, your first squadron assignment?"

"Yes, Sir, it is."

"How did you get so much time in Wildcats, then?"

"They had us ferrying them, Sir, from Bethpage all over the country."

"Both of you, you mean?"

"Yes, Sir."

"You answer this, Mr. Stecker. I want a straight answer: What was your last thought when you took off from the escort carrier?"

"Sir," Stecker hesitated a moment, and then blurted, "that I had better run the engine as lean as possible, Sir, or prepare to take a swim."

"How much fuel remaining when you touched down?"

"About fifteen minutes, Sir."

"You, Pickering?"

"My fuel warning light was lit, Sir."

"And what was your reaction to that?"

"I was scared shitless," Pick said, remembering a moment later to add, "Sir."

"In other words, you're telling me that you knowingly took off with inadequate fuel?"

"It didn't turn out to be inadequate, Sir."

"You're not being flip, are you, Pickering?"

"Sir," Stecker said, "Mr. Pickering raised the question of fuel just before we were to launch and was told to man his aircraft."

"Sir, I think it was a question of getting the carrier turned around as quickly as possible."

In other words, I was right, there was an asshole on that escort carrier, probably wearing commander's boards.

"Where are you from, Pickering? Are you married?"

"San Francisco, Sir. No, Sir, I'm not married."

Galloway looked at Stecker.

"No, Sir. I'm not married. I'm from eastern Pennsylvania, Sir."

"Philadelphia?"

"About seventy miles north of Philadelphia, Sir."

"My girl's from Philadelphia," Galloway said.

Why the hell did I offer that information?

"Yes, Sir," Stecker said.

"And just before I came over here, I was in San Francisco," Galloway said. A quick, entirely pleasant memory of Caroline came into his mind. They'd spent a fair amount of time together in their marble-walled, multiple-showerhead bath. "Had a hell of a time in the Andrew Foster Hotel. You know it?"

"Yes, Sir," Pick said. "We've been there."

Galloway picked up on a look the two of them exchanged. *The Andrew Foster Hotel touched a nerve,* he decided. *They probably got really shitfaced there. In due course a report of conduct unbecoming officers and gentlemen will be forwarded through channels for my attention. I hope they had a good time.*

"What we do here is try to protect the field and the area around it from the Japanese," Galloway explained. "Most of the time—nine times out of ten—we have advance knowledge that they're coming. When we do get it, we get in the air as fast as we can and try to intercept them as far from here as we can."

"May I ask how we get the advance knowledge, Sir?" Stecker asked.

"Primarily from the Coastwatchers. They're Australians who stayed behind when the Japs occupied the islands to the north of us. Guys with real big balls. They radio Pearl Harbor and it's relayed to us here. Other times we get word from our own patrolling aircraft or from carrier-launched patrols. But mostly it's the Coastwatchers who alert us."

"What are those funny-looking airplanes I saw when I sat down?" Pick asked. "The ones with alligator teeth painted on them?"

He didn't say "Sir"; he should know what a Bell fighter is; and those are shark teeth, not alligator teeth. But there's something about this kid I like.

"Those are *shark* teeth, Mr. Pickering," Galloway said. "The aircraft are Army P-400 fighters, and the pilots who man them are as good as any I've ever known. Any further questions?"

"Yes, Sir. When will we go up for the first time?"

"Anxious to get into combat, are you?"

"No, Sir. I was just curious, that's all."

Hell, I'd ask the same question.

"Well, we'll get you a place to sleep and show you the mess. In the morning either Lieutenant Dunn or myself will take you for a little ride and see how well you can fly. If that goes well, you'll go up for real very soon after that. If it doesn't go well, we'll wait until we're sure you won't kill yourself or somebody else."

"Yes, Sir. Thank you, Sir."

Lieutenant Bill Dunn came into the tent.

"Sir, I took the liberty of asking Big Steve to put our squadron numbers on those airplanes."

"Good boy, Bill," Galloway said, and then introduced the newcomers to Dunn.

"Find them a place to sleep and get them settled for this afternoon," Galloway said. "I told them we'll give them an area check ride in the morning."

"Aye, aye, Sir."

"Unless you have a question, Stecker?"

"Sir, more on the order of a request."

"Shoot."

"If we're to have a couple of hours free, would there be time for me to go to 2nd of the Fifth?"

"Second Battalion, Fifth Marines?" Galloway asked. "Why do you want to go there? A buddy's with 2nd of the Fifth?"

"My father, Sir."

There was silence for a moment.

"You don't happen to be Jack (NMI) Stecker's boy, do you, Mr. Stecker?"

"Yes, Sir."

Well, that explains West Point. If they hang the Medal of Honor around your neck, your kids get to go to the Service Academy of their choice.

He then remembered hearing that Major Jack (NMI) Stecker's son, an Annapolis graduate, a Navy ensign, had been killed aboard the battleship *Arizona* at Pearl Harbor on December 7th.

Major Jack (NMI) Stecker is going to be something less than overjoyed to find his other son on this fucking goddamned island as a fighter pilot.

"Find somebody to drive him up there in my jeep, please, Bill," Galloway said.

"Aye, aye, Sir."

[Three]
THE FOSTER LAFAYETTE HOTEL
WASHINGTON, D.C.
0915 HOURS 22 SEPTEMBER 1942

A discreet knock at the door came shortly after a room service waiter rolled in a tray carrying ham and eggs, toast, coffee, a pitcher of freshly squeezed orange juice, a copy of *The Washington Star,* and a rose in a tiny vase.

"Come in," Sergeant George Hart called cheerfully.

The door opened and a man in a paint-stained smock stuck his head in.

"Sorry to disturb you, Sir," he said. "If you'll tell me when it's convenient, I'll come back and finish painting the door."

He pointed at the wall that separated the suite Hart shared with Moore from the one Senator Richmond F. Fowler shared with Brigadier General Fleming Pickering. A tarpaulin concealed the newly installed door.

"Come ahead," George said. "Watching other people work has never bothered me."

The witticism was lost on the painter.

"I'll come back when you've left, Sir."

"I don't plan to leave. Come on in and paint the door."

"Yes, Sir."

George turned his attention to *The Washington Star.*

According to Reuters News Service, there was heavy fighting between the Germans and the Russians on Mamayec Kurgan Hill, outside Stalingrad. Casualties on both sides were described as severe.

British troops had landed at Tamatave on the east coast of Madagascar, with the apparent intention of taking the capital, Tananarive. This was held by reportedly "very strong" Vichy French forces. There was a map, with arrows. George knew who the Vichy French were, they were the ones who'd made peace with the Germans. But he had no idea where Madagascar was. The map was no help.

In the Pacific, the Commander in Chief, Pacific, had announced that six transports, under heavy escort, had made it safely to Guadalcanal, where they successfully delivered the Seventh Marines (to reinforce the First Marine Division), and a "substantial amount" of supplies. There was a map here, too; and George studied this one with interest.

Until he'd seen Major Dillon's movies yesterday, he really hadn't been all that interested in Guadalcanal.

He was reading the comic strips when the telephone rang. Not the one in his suite, one of the telephones in The General's.

He carefully squeezed past the painter working on the door and picked it up. It was The General's phone, not the Senator's. He knew the drill:

"General Pickering's quarters, Sergeant Hart speaking, Sir."

He would then tell them The General was not available at the moment and could he take a message?

"George?"

His heart jumped.

"Jesus Christ!"

"I called last night when I got here," Elizabeth Lathrop said. "Some officer answered and said you would be late."

He could feel her fingernails on his back, smell the soap in her hair, taste the skin of her neck.

"How the hell did you get this number?"

"Where else would Pick's father stay in Washington?"

"What do you want?"

He could tell from her tone that the question hurt.

Jesus Christ, I didn't want to hurt her feelings!

"Well, I happened to be in the neighborhood," she said, more coldly, "and I thought I would just call up and say hi."

"You're in Washington?"

"Yes," she said. "And I thought maybe you'd want to see me."

He thought: *I would kill to be inside you again, with your breasts soft and warm against my chest.*

Detective George Hart of the Saint Louis Vice Squad answered for him without thinking: "Honey, I can't afford you."

The telephone made a clicking noise, then hummed, and then after a moment, there came the dial tone.

"Shit!" Hart said, loudly and bitterly. He slammed the handset into the cradle and said "shit!" again.

The man painting the door looked at him with open curiosity. George glowered at him and the painter looked away.

How the hell can I find her? Call the local cops and ask them as a professional service to a brother vice detective if they have an address or known associates of a high-class whore named Lathrop, Elizabeth, white female, approximately five three, approximately twenty-two or twenty-three, approximately one hun-

dred five pounds, blue eyes, blond hair, no distinguishing scars or bodily blemishes?

That's probably not even her fucking name. That's her professional name. Her real name is probably Agnes Kutcharsky or some shit.

He had just squeezed past the painter when the telephone rang again.

"General Pickering's quarters, Sergeant Hart speaking, Sir."

"Don't you think I know you don't have any goddamned money?"

"Baby!"

"You sonofabitch!"

"I'm sorry. That just . . . I don't know why I said that."

There was a long silence.

"I said I was sorry."

"OK."

"Where are you?"

"The Hotel Washington."

I've seen that marquee. It's around here someplace. Hell, yes, right down the street, a block down from Pennsylvania Avenue, around the corner from the movie theater.

"That's right around the corner."

"Yeah, I know. Do they give you any time off?"

"I'm off now."

"Would you like to come here? And have a drink or something?"

A drink, at half past nine in the morning? Or something?

"Or something," George said.

"I'm in 805," Elizabeth Lathrop said. The phone clicked again before he could open his mouth to say, "I'll be there in a couple of minutes."

It was beautiful outside. The sun was shining and the temperature was just right. *Indian summer,* he thought, as he walked—almost trotted—past the White House. *It's sort of like a dream,* he thought, *walking past the White House, on my way to be with Elizabeth.*

The Washington Theater was showing *Eagle Squadron;* Tyrone Power was playing an American who went to fly for the English. Hart remembered hearing someplace that Tyrone Power was joining The Corps. *From Major Dillon, that's it,* he remembered; he'd heard him tell The General. He wondered if they would send him to Parris Island. It was strange to think of Tyrone Power with all his hair cut off getting screamed at by some asshole like Corporal Clayton C. Warren.

The Hotel Washington was just where his memory placed it. He pushed his way through the revolving door, walked across the lobby to the bank of elevators, and rode up to the eighth floor; 805 was the third door to the left.

When Beth opened the door, she was wearing a white blouse, an unbuttoned sweater, and a tweed skirt. And she wouldn't look at him.

"Hi! Come on in."

"I'm sorry about what I said on the telephone."

She nodded but didn't reply.

"It's only a couple of blocks from the Foster Lafayette to here."

She nodded again.

"So what brings you to Washington?"

Now she looked at him, and there was pain in her eyes again.

"Oh, Jesus!" Hart said, almost moaning.

"Stupid of me, right?" Elizabeth said. "But I decided, what the hell . . ."

He reached out and touched her face; and her hand came up and touched his. Then all of a sudden he was holding her in his arms as tight as he had ever held anybody. He didn't kiss her, he just clung to her, his face buried in her hair. And she was hanging on to him, too, and she was weeping a little, and he realized he felt a little like crying too.

And then he became aware of the warmth of her legs against his, and the softness of her breasts against him, and he grew erect. He pulled his middle away from her.

She pulled her head back and looked at him, and he was right, she had been crying; tears were making a path down her cheeks through her makeup.

"It's all right," she said, sort of laughing. "I would have been disappointed . . ."

She put her hand on his cheek.

There was an imperious rapping at the door.

"Who's there?"

"Assistant manager, Miss Lathrop. Please open the door."

She freed herself from George's arms. Rubbing at her eyes with her knuckles, she went to the door and opened it.

A middle-aged man in a business suit entered without being invited.

Assistant manager, my ass. That's a house detective. I've seen enough of them to know one when I see one.

"You're not allowed up here, Sergeant. The Washington is not that kind of hotel. And, Miss Lathrop, we would appreciate it if you would check out as soon as possible."

As he walked quickly to the ruddy-faced house detective, George took his credentials from his tunic pocket.

"What's going on in here is none of your business," he said.

The house detective took a long look at the credentials and then looked at Hart.

"Take a walk," Hart said. "And don't come back. And the lady will not be checking out. Got it?"

Without a word, the house detective turned and pulled the door open and went through it.

What was that all about? Did he just add up a Marine sergeant going to a hotel room as a guy about to pay for a piece of ass? Or did he take one look at Elizabeth and decide she was a whore? Jesus, she doesn't look like a whore or act like one.

He turned and looked at her.

"Well," she said.

Hart shrugged.

"What was that you showed him?"

"I've got sort of a Marine Corps badge."

"I thought maybe you showed him your vice detective badge," Beth said.

There were tears in her eyes again.

"He's gone. He won't be back."

"Would you just put your arms around me again?" Beth asked softly, looking into his eyes. "And just hold me?"

He held his arms open and she took the few steps to him. When he put his arms around her, she started to cry again. He ran his hands over her back and against her hair and made soothing noises.

And then the warmth of her legs and the softness of her breasts got to him again; and the erection returned. When he tried to pull away from her, she followed him. And then she tilted her head back again and looked into his eyes for a moment. And then her mouth was on his, hungrily, and she dragged him backward onto the bed.

[Four]
WALTER REED ARMY GENERAL HOSPITAL
WASHINGTON, D.C.
1145 HOURS 22 SEPTEMBER 1942

At quarter past ten, Technical Sergeant Harry N. Rutterman put his head in Colonel F. L. Rickabee's office and told him that General Pickering was on the line.

The conversation was a short one:

"There's something we have to talk about, Rickabee," General Pickering said. "Is there some reason you can't come over here, say at quarter to twelve?"

"No, Sir," he said, though he was not telling the precise truth when he said it. His work schedule was a god-awful mess. Adding a meeting with The General would only make it worse. On the other hand, a general's wish was a colonel's command. . . .

"Thank you," Pickering said, and hung up.

When Colonel F. L. Rickabee, at precisely the appointed hour, walked into the sitting room of Brigadier General Fleming Pickering's VIP suite, he found a table set for two. And The General was dressed in uniform—or part of one—and not in a bathrobe and pajamas. Though he wasn't wearing his blouse or a field scarf, there was a silver star on the collar points of his khaki shirt. Rickabee decided that Pickering had a purpose when he pinned on the insignia of his rank.

Otherwise why bother? He's not going anyplace. On the other hand, maybe someone's coming to see him—maybe General Forrest—and he's putting his uniform on for that. And wants some advice from me before he meets him?

"Good morning, General."

"Sorry to drag you away from your office, but I suspect I would have made waves if I had come to you."

"My time is your time, General," Rickabee said. "And I thought you would be interested in this, Sir. It was delivered by messenger yesterday afternoon."

He took a sheet of paper from his inside pocket and handed it to Pickering.

INTEROFFICE MEMORANDUM

DATE: 21 September 1942

FROM: Assistant Chief of Staff,
            Personnel

TO: Director
            Public Affairs Office
            Hq, USMC

HAND CARRY

SUBJECT: Office of Management Analysis
            Hq, USMC

1. Effective immediately, no, repeat no,
public relations activity of any kind will
involve the Office of Management Analysis, or
any personnel assigned thereto.
2. The Public Affairs Office is forbidden to
contact the Office of Management Analysis for
any purpose without the specific permission
of the undersigned.
3. Discussion of this policy, or requests
for waivers thereto, is not desired.

BY DIRECTION OF THE COMMANDANT:

Alfred J. Kennedy
Major General, USMC
Assistant Chief of Staff, G-1

Pickering read it and snorted, then handed it back.

"I suppose that will keep them off our backs. Being a general officer does seem to carry with it the means to get things done, doesn't it?"

"Yes, Sir, it does seem to, General."

"I thought we could save time by having lunch," Pickering said. "I asked them to serve at twelve."

"Very kind of you, Sir."

"You better hold the thanks until you see what they give us. Now that I think of it, I should have ordered some emergency rations."

"Sir?"

"I sometimes have the hotel send over a platter of hors d'oeuvres against the likelihood that lunch or dinner will be inedible."

"I see."

"I am medically restricted to four drinks a day," Pickering said. "I am about to have my second. Would you care to join me?"

You are medically restricted to no more than two drinks a day, General, not four. And somehow I suspect that the drink you are about to have is going to be Number Three or Number Four, not Number Two.

"Yes, Sir. I would. Thank you."

"Scotch all right?"

"Scotch is fine, Sir."

Pickering went into the small room between the sitting room and the bedroom. He returned in a moment with a nearly empty bottle of Famous Grouse.

"My supply of this is running a little low," he said.

"No problem, Sir, I don't have to have scotch."

"Oh, no. There's a couple of bottles left here, and if Hart and Moore haven't been at them, several more in the hotel. But the stock is running low. I have a hell of a stock, however, a hundred cases or more, in San Francisco. Most of it came off my *Pacific Princess* when I chartered her to the Navy."

"Well, they have a rule, no liquor aboard Navy vessels."

What the hell is this all about?

"We have people running back and forth between the West Coast and here all the time, don't we, Rickabee?"

"Yes, Sir."

"Do you suppose it would be possible for one of them to bring a couple of cases of this back here for me?"

"Certainly, Sir. No problem at all, Sir. Captain Lee is at Mare Island right now, Sir. I'll just call him and that'll take care of it. He's leaving tonight, that should get him in here the day after tomorrow."

"One of the little privileges that goes with being a general, right? Being able to get a Marine officer to haul a couple of cases of booze cross country for you?"

Jesus, I don't like this. What the hell is he leading up to?

"If you will call your people in San Francisco, General, and tell them Captain Lee will be coming by?"

The question was directed to Pickering's back. He had turned and walked out of the room again, and he didn't reply.

He returned in a moment with two glasses dark with whiskey. He handed one to Rickabee.

"Here you are, Rickabee."

"Thank you, Sir."

"Who shall we drink to?"

"How about The Corps, Sir?"

"How about those two Marines on Buka?" Pickering said.

"The Marines on Buka," Rickabee said, raising his glass.

"They have names," Pickering said. "Lieutenant Joe Howard and Sergeant Steve Koffler."

He's really pissed about something. Or is he drunk?

"Lieutenant Howard and Sergeant Koffler," Rickabee said.

"Joe and Steve," Pickering said, and took a healthy swallow from his drink. "Did you know, Rickabee, that I made Koffler a buck sergeant?"

"No, Sir, I did not."

"He's only a kid. A long way from being old enough to vote. But I figured that any Marine who volunteers to do what he is doing should be at least a buck sergeant. So I told Banning to arrange it."

"I didn't know that, General."

"Joe Howard's a Mustang," Pickering said. "An old pal of mine, a Marine I served with in France—he was a sergeant and I was a corporal, fellow named Jack (NMI) Stecker—thought that Sergeant Howard would make a pretty good officer and got him a direct commission."

"Yes, Sir. I know Major Stecker, Sir. I knew him when he was a master gunny at Quantico."

"One hell of a Marine, Jack (NMI) Stecker," Rickabee said.

"Yes, Sir, he is."

He is drunk. Otherwise why this trip down Marine Corps Memory Lane?

Further evidence of that came when General Pickering went back into the small room, returned with the bottle of Famous Grouse, and killed it freshening their glasses.

"No problem, I just checked. There's two more bottles where that came from. And then, of course, as a courtesy to a Marine

General, Captain Lee is going to bring me some more, isn't he?"

"Yes, Sir."

"Sergeant Hart had two copies of Dillon's movies made," Pickering said. "Did you know that, Rickabee?"

"Yes, Sir. Lieutenant Moore told me."

"Clever fellow, that Hart."

"Yes, Sir."

"There's more to Moore than you might judge the first time you met him," Pickering said.

"Yes, Sir."

"Dillon's movies were very interesting, weren't they, Rickabee?"

"Yes, Sir. They were."

"Perhaps 'disturbing' would be a more accurate word."

"Disturbing *and* interesting, General."

"I lay awake a long time thinking about those movies," Pickering said. "And this morning, when Moore brought me the second copy Hart had made, I had the hospital send the projector back and watched them again. The projectionist got sick to his stomach."

"Really?"

"Well, what the hell do you expect, Rickabee? He was only a soldier, and we're *Marines,* right?"

Jesus Christ, he is about to get out of hand!

"That's when I called you," Pickering went on, "and asked you to come over here . . . when the soldier was being sick."

"Yes, Sir."

"Those movies triggered a lot of thoughts in my mind, Rickabee. When I saw the shots of Henderson Field, it occurred to me that my son and Jack (NMI) Stecker's son are soon to be among the pilots there . . . if they're not there already."

"Yes, Sir."

"And then I went back a long time, to when Jack and I were going through Parris Island. You go through Parris Island, Rickabee?"

"No, Sir. I came into The Corps as an officer."

"You know, a lot of people think that everybody in The Corps should go through Parris Island. I mean officers, too."

"It would probably be a good idea, General."

"Banning didn't go through Parris Island, either, did he?"

"No, Sir. I believe Major Banning came into The Corps as an officer, Sir."

"Good man, Banning," Pickering said.

"Yes, Sir."

"You know what they teach you as a boot at Parris Island, Rickabee? What they taught me, and Jack Stecker?"

"I don't take The General's point, Sir."

"They taught Jack and me that one of the things that makes Marines special, makes them different, better, than soldiers is that Marines don't leave their wounded, or their dead, on the battlefield."

"Yes, Sir."

"Do you think they still teach that, Rickabee? Or was that something just from the olden days of World War One?"

"No, Sir. I don't think it is."

"You think they taught that to Lieutenant Moore and Sergeant Hart, for example, when they went through Parris Island?"

"Yes, Sir. I'm sure they did."

"And they went back for Moore, didn't they, on Guadalcanal, when he was hit? A couple of Marines with balls went out there and got Moore and the Marines with him because they knew they were either dead or wounded, and Marines don't leave their dead or wounded, right?"

Where the hell is this conversation going?

"Yes, Sir. That's probably just what happened."

There was a knock at the door and two Army medics pushed a rolling cart into the room.

I hope the food sobers him up.

Lunch was vegetable soup, fried chicken, macaroni and noodles, a slice of bread, a banana custard, and a pot of tea.

"Please bring me some coffee," General Pickering said, and then changed his mind. "No. Belay that. I don't want any coffee. Thank you very much."

He took instead another swallow of Famous Grouse. Then he carefully cut a piece of chicken from the breast on his plate and put it in his mouth.

I hope that tastes terrible and he will divert the anger that's inside him to eating out the mess officer.

"Well, the mess sergeant must be drunk," General Pickering said. "That's really good."

"I'm pleased, Sir."

"I wonder what Joe Howard and Steve Koffler are eating on Buka?"

"I'm afraid they're not eating this well, General."

"More to the point, Rickabee," General Pickering asked conversationally, "when did we kick them out of The Corps?"

What the hell does that mean?

"Sir?"

"Well, I would call their physical condition pretty much the same as being wounded, and that's presuming they're still alive. If they were Marines, we'd go get them, wouldn't we? Marines don't get left on their battlefield when they're wounded. Or dead. So that means they're not Marines, right?"

"General, if Major Banning could relieve them, he would."

"Wrong. Major Banning has written them off. You were here when Dillon told me that. As far as Banning is concerned, as far as anybody is concerned, they're dead."

"I'm afraid that's true, Sir. There's absolutely nothing that can be done, given the circumstances."

"I'm going to tell you something, Colonel Rickabee," General Pickering said, just this side of nastily. "This Marine is going to try."

"I'm not sure I take The General's meaning, Sir."

"You can knock off that 'The General this' and 'The General that' crap, Rickabee. And you know damned well what I mean. You just don't want to hear it."

"May I speak bluntly, Sir?"

"You better. Bullshit time is over."

"There's nothing you can do, Sir."

"Maybe not. But I am damned sure going to try. If I have the power to have some captain deliver overnight two cases of booze to me from the West Coast, I ought to be able to divert a little of it to getting those two kids off of Buka."

"Trying to reinforce them would endanger their safety."

"What safety, for Christ's sake? Feldt and Banning are sitting around in Townsville with their thumbs up their ass waiting to hear they're dead."

"I'm sorry to hear that you have lost your confidence in Major Banning."

"I was sorry to lose it. What's happened is that he's forgotten he's a Marine and fallen under Feldt's goddamned British philosophy that no sacrifice is too great for King and Country."

"I can't believe that Ed Banning is capable of forgetting he's a Marine," Rickabee said, aware that he was on the edge of losing his temper.

"Then why is he sitting around waiting for those two kids to get killed?"

I'll be a sonofabitch. Touché, General.

"General, I wouldn't know where to start. I'm exceedingly reluctant to sit here in Washington and second-guess what Banning is doing, the decisions he is forced to make."

"I'm not," Pickering said simply. "And, for a place to start, I want to see McCoy."

"McCoy?"

"Is there some reason that's impossible?"

"Sir, there is an operation in the planning stages—"

"What kind of an operation?"

"We're going to set up a weather observation station in Mongolia, General. The mission was laid on The Corps by the Joint Chiefs. The station will be required later in the war for long-range bombing raids. McCoy is singularly well qualified to take a major role."

"Mongolia?" Pickering asked dubiously, and then: "When does this operation get under way?"

"In about four months, Sir. They're trying to decide the best way to get the people into Mongolia."

"I'm planning to get Howard and Koffler off Buka in the next month, Rickabee. Send for McCoy. I have the feeling there's a very good reason they call him 'Killer.' And in any event, he's a simple ex–enlisted man like me who believes that Marines don't leave their dead and wounded on the battle-field."

"There are a number of professional officers, General, including this one, who don't think so either."

"I've angered you, Rickabee, haven't I?"

What you've done is make me a little ashamed of myself.

"No, Sir. Not at all, Sir. I'll have McCoy here in the morning, and I'll give this some thought."

[Five]
THE FOSTER LAFAYETTE HOTEL
WASHINGTON, D.C.
1910 HOURS 22 SEPTEMBER 1942

"May I help you, Miss?" the desk clerk said to the striking young woman with jet-black, pageboy-cut hair.

"May I have the key to 614, please?" she asked.

Although every effort had been made to prepare him for every possible contingency, the request posed certain problems for the desk clerk.

For one thing, he had no idea who this woman was. For another, 614 was a three-room suite maintained year-round by American Personal Pharmaceuticals, Inc., for the convenience of corporate executives who had business in Washington. For another, the desk clerk was aware that the Chairman of the Board of American Personal Pharmaceuticals, Inc., and his wife had a personal relationship with the Foster family: Mrs. Elaine Sage had been the college roommate of Mrs. Patricia Pickering, Andrew Foster's only child.

A quick look at the key board confirmed the desk clerk's recollection that 614 was not occupied at the moment.

The stunning young woman in the pageboy was obviously not Mrs. Elaine Sage. She was not even married; there was no ring on her finger. Neither was there a ring on the third finger of the left hand of the uncomfortable-looking young Marine officer standing behind her.

"Six-fourteen, Miss?"

"Please. I'm Ernestine Sage."

"Just a moment, please," the desk clerk said and walked quickly to the small office occupied by the assistant manager on duty.

"There is a young woman at the counter—a real looker, in bangs—who wants the key to 614. She says her name is Sage."

"A looker with bangs? Give it to her. That's Ernest Sage's daughter."

"She's got a Marine with her," the desk clerk said.

"Really?" the assistant manager said, and got up and walked through the door to the counter.

"Hello, Miss Sage," he said. Then, in one smooth move, he snatched the key from the key board, handed it to her, and tinkled the bell for a bellboy. "Nice to have you in the house again. And you too, Lieutenant McCoy."

"How are you," Ken McCoy responded, running the words together and flashing a brief uncomfortable smile.

"Thank you, it's nice to see you," Ernie Sage said, and turned to follow the bellboy with their luggage to the elevators.

The assistant manager picked up the telephone and asked for room service.

"Send flowers, fruit, and a bottle of champagne, Moët, to six fourteen," he ordered. After he hung up, he turned to the desk clerk. "That was indeed Miss Ernestine Sage. The gentleman with her is Lieutenant K. R. McCoy. Lieutenant Malcolm S. Pickering—who was once the bell captain here, by the way, did you know that?"

"No, I didn't."

"—Lieutenant Pickering once told me that Lieutenant McCoy was his best friend. He asked me as a personal favor to him to take very good care of Lieutenant McCoy whenever he was in the house. Is everything clear now, Tom?"

"Crystal clear."

In the elevator, oblivious to the presence of the operator, the bellboy, and a well-dressed couple in their fifties, Ernie Sage said, "Don't you *dare* look embarrassed! *I'm* not the one who doesn't want to get married."

"Jesus, Ernie!" McCoy said, flushing.

"*I* have no objection to becoming an honest woman," Ernie said, enjoying herself. "*You're* the one who insists on living in sin."

McCoy rushed off the elevator before the doors were fully open and hurried down the corridor. Ernie smiled warmly at the well-dressed middle-aged couple before following the bellboy.

Once the door was open, McCoy headed for the couch in the sitting room and picked up the telephone from the coffee table in front of it. He gave the operator a number.

"Give me the watch officer, please.

"Lieutenant McCoy, Sir. The Colonel told me to check in when I got to Washington.

"No, Sir. I'm in the Foster Lafayette Hotel. Room 614.

"Thank you, Sir."

Ernie, meanwhile, had led the bellboy into the largest bedroom, tipped him, and then watched him leave. By the time McCoy was done with the phone, she had removed all her clothing but her underwear. She was now standing in the bedroom doorway with her hip thrust out provocatively. Her arm was behind her head and a rose was in her teeth.

"Hi, Marine! Looking for a good time?"

"You're nuts, you know that?"

"I don't know about you, but I find it terribly sexy to be in a hotel room with someone I'm not married to."

"You're going to keep that up, are you?"

There was not time for her to reply. There was a knock at the door. After she closed the bedroom door, McCoy opened the corridor door to a waiter delivering a rolling cart with champagne, fruit, cut flowers, and a copy of *The Washington Post.*

The bellman refused the two dollars McCoy extended to him.

"No, Sir. Professional courtesy. Pick and I used to run bells together. Any friend of Pick's—"

"Thanks," McCoy said.

As soon as the door had closed behind the bellboy, the bedroom door opened.

"Isn't that nice?" Ernie said. "Why don't you just roll that in here?"

"I've had worse offers," McCoy said.

The telephone rang. Ernie picked up the phone on the bedside table.

"Hello?" she said, and then extended it to McCoy.

"Lieutenant McCoy.

"Yes, Sir. I'll be there.

"Sir, I have someone with me. A friend of General Pickering's. She would like to visit with him. Would that be possible?"

"Try to keep me away! I'm not in the goddamned Marines!" Ernie announced.

"Yes, Sir. I understand. Thank you, Sir.

"Whichever would be easier, Sir. I'll be here. Yes, Sir. Good night, Sir."

"You understand what?" Ernie said when he put the telephone down.

"You can see him for thirty minutes at half past seven in the morning."

"Oh, I'm so grateful!"

"Hey, I told you this was duty."

"What's it all about?"

"I don't know. I'm—which does *not* mean 'you'—about to find out. Captain Sessions is coming over here."

"Great!" Ernie said sarcastically.

"He could have made me go to the office. You're getting to be a pain in the ass, Ernie."

Her face tightened. She opened her mouth to reply, then visibly changed her mind.

"Sorry," she said.

"I'm sorry I said that," McCoy said, genuinely contrite.

She waved her hand, signifying it didn't matter.

"When's Ed Sessions coming?"

"It'll probably take him thirty minutes, maybe forty-five. He's got some stuff the Colonel wants me to read before we see General Pickering."

"I don't know about you, baby," Ernie said, "but on general principles, I have nothing against a quickie."

When Captain Edward Sessions walked into suite 614, Lieutenant K. R. McCoy and Miss Ernestine Sage, fully clothed, were sitting on the couch in the sitting room, working on an enormous platter of shrimp and oysters. It did not escape his attention, however, that despite the early hour, the bed he could see through a partially opened door seemed to have been slept in.

"Good to see you, Ernie," he said, and she stood on her tiptoes and kissed his cheek.

"Would you be crushed, Ed, if I told you I suspect something is about to happen that I'm not going to like at all?"

"No," he said.

He fumbled in his pocket for the key to the handcuff which chained his briefcase to his wrist, freed his wrist, and handed the briefcase to McCoy.

"If some kind soul were to offer me a drink and an oyster, I could occupy myself while you read that, Ken," Sessions said.

"We just had a bottle of champagne," Ernie said. "I would order another, but I don't think we have anything to celebrate. Scotch, Ed?"

"Please," he said.

McCoy settled himself in a corner of the couch and opened the briefcase. Before she made Sessions' drink, Ernie looked long enough to see TOP SECRET cover sheets on the manila folder he took from the briefcase. After a moment's thought she made one for herself.

She glanced at Ken. She recognized the look of absolute concentration on his face. She knew he would be annoyed if she offered him a drink or even handed him one.

She gave Ed Sessions his drink.

"How's Jeanne, Ed?"

"Great. If she knew you were here, she would have come. She'll be sorry to have missed you."

Five minutes later McCoy raised his eyes from the stack of folders on his lap.

"OK. I gave it a quick once-over. What's this got to do with me?"

"All I know is that General Pickering told the Colonel to send for you," Sessions said.

"Is Banning behind that?" McCoy asked.

Sessions shrugged his shoulders.

"I don't know. All I know is that the Colonel wants you 'conversant' with that stuff before we see The General in the morning."

"We who?"

"The Colonel, me, and you," Sessions said.

"I can't memorize all this by morning."

"He said 'conversant,' not 'memorize.'"

McCoy nodded and returned his attention to the folders with their TOP SECRET cover sheets. Finally he stuffed everything back into the briefcase.

"I didn't know until just now that Marines were involved in that operation."

Sessions grunted.

"I'm sorry you had to come over here," McCoy said. "I could have gone to the office."

"They don't have oysters and good whiskey in the office. Anyway, I got to see Ernie," Sessions said as he picked up the briefcase and handcuffed it to his wrist.

"Give Jeanne my love," Ernie said.

"Maybe we can get together while you're here."

"How long will we be here?"

"I guess we'll find that out in the morning," Sessions said. He shook hands with McCoy, kissed Ernie, and left.

McCoy got off the couch and made himself a drink.

"You're not going to tell me what that was all about, right?" Ernie asked.

"I don't know what it's all about," McCoy said. And then, obviously to change the subject, "Well, what should we do now?"

"I've never had any problem with 'early to bed and early to rise,' " Ernie said, and then added, "You know what I'd really like to do? Take a walk."

"A *walk*?" he asked incredulously.

"A walk. One foot after the other. It's beautiful out. Past the White House. Take a look in the windows of the department stores."

McCoy shrugged. "Why not?"

They'd stopped outside the Washington Theater to scan the posters showing Flight Lieutenant Tyrone Power of the Eagle Squadron about to climb in the cockpit of his Spitfire when the doors opened and a Marine sergeant and his girl came out.

The Marine sergeant spotted the officer's bars on McCoy's shoulders and saluted before he recognized McCoy.

"How are you, Hart?" McCoy said.

"Can't complain, Sir."

"I'm Ernie Sage, Sergeant," Ernie said, "since I doubt if the Lieutenant will introduce us."

"Ernie, this is Sergeant George Hart. He works for General Pickering," McCoy said.

"How is he?" Ernie demanded. "And a straight answer, please?"

"You can tell her," McCoy said. "She's going to see him in the morning anyway."

"He's much better. He's not nearly as strong as he thinks he is."

"Since I doubt if Sergeant Hart is going to introduce us, Miss, my name is McCoy."

"Wise guy!" Ernie said.

"Elizabeth—they call me Beth—Lathrop."

"And I'm Ernie, and I'm Ken's girlfriend, and I just decided that we should all go somewhere for a drink."

"You can't do that in public," McCoy said uncomfortably. "It's against regulations for officers to drink with enlisted Marines."

"Well, then, we'll go to the hotel," Ernie said. "Sergeant,

that's not as snobbish as it sounded. When the Lieutenant was a corporal, he was just as much a by-the-book Marine."

"I don't want to—" Hart protested.

"Nonsense," Ernie said. "I want to hear more about Uncle Fleming."

"The hotel and a drink's a good idea," McCoy said. "I've had enough walking for the night."

"I know who you are," Beth said. "You're Pick's friend."

"You know Pick?" Ernie asked delightedly.

"I know him," Beth said.

There was a strange note in her voice. Ernie concluded from it that this was one of Pick Pickering's discards. Their number was legion.

"Well, then, you have to come," Ernie said. "We can swap nasty stories about him."

McCoy, too, picked up on her uneasiness, and Hart's—his reluctance to come with them.

It's either that I'm an officer, he decided, *or more likely, that he wanted to go off with the dame and get a little and is afraid this will screw that up.*

Tough luck, if that's what Ernie wants, that's what she'll get.

XII

[One]
WALTER REED ARMY GENERAL HOSPITAL
WASHINGTON, D.C.
0725 HOURS 23 SEPTEMBER 1942

"Ernie, I hate to run you off, but we have to shuffle some paper," General Pickering said. "I'll have Sergeant Hart run you back to the hotel."

"We drove up, Uncle Fleming," Ernie said. "We have our car. You behave, you understand?"

"You call my wife and make a valiant effort to convince her that I am really in prime health, and I will behave. Deal?"

"Deal," she said, and kissed him. "You take care of Ken, too."

"I'll do my best," Pickering said. "Make sure you give your mother and dad my best."

She smiled and then turned to McCoy. "I will see you at the hotel, right?"

"I just don't know," McCoy said. "I'll call if—"

"You'll see him at the hotel," Pickering interrupted. "Now get out of here."

She blew him a kiss and left.

Pickering looked at McCoy.

"*'We* drove up'?" he quoted. "*'I* have *our* car'?" When McCoy didn't answer, Pickering went on. "You could do a hell of a lot worse than that girl, Ken. I always hoped she'd marry Pick."

"Yes, Sir. She told me. So did her father."

"Her family scare you? Their money?"

"I don't think people who earn their living the way I do should get married," McCoy said.

"I just heard about the Mongolian Operation yesterday. Is that it?"

"That's part of it, General."

"Well, since it's none of my business, I think you're wrong. Take what you can when you can get it, Ken. Life is no rehearsal."

"Yes, Sir."

"I admitted it was none of my business," Pickering said. "Maybe I'd feel the same way you do."

There was a knock at the door and Sergeant Hart came in.

"Colonel Rickabee and the others are here, Sir."

"Major Dillon, too?"

"Yes, Sir."

Pickering waved his hand, signaling Hart to bring them in.

"Thank you for coming, Jake," Pickering said. "I think it's important. Is this going to get you in hot water with General—Whatsisname?—Stewart?"

"I sent word that I was sick," Dillon replied, "and sent the film over there by messenger. It'll be all right."

"General, I can call General Stewart," Rickabee volunteered.

"Hold off on doing that a while," Pickering said.

"Jake, you don't know McCoy, do you?"

"Only by reputation. Killer McCoy, right?"

"He doesn't like that, don't call him that again," Pickering said, giving him a hard look.

"Sorry, Lieutenant," Dillon said, shaking McCoy's hand. "No offense."

"None taken, Sir," McCoy said, not entirely convincingly.

"I guess you've seen this?" Dillon said, taking a copy of the INS story about Machine Gun McCoy from his pocket and handing it to him with a smile.

"Yes, Sir, I've seen it."

"This one came by messenger this morning," Dillon said. "There's talk about making a flick about him."

"I heard they're thinking about making a movie about the Makin raid," McCoy said.

"Not thinking. They approved the treatment, a screenplay is in the works, and they signed Randolph Scott to play Colonel Carlson."

"Jesus Christ," McCoy said disgustedly. "Why not Errol Flynn?"

"Sir, does The General want Lieutenant Moore and Sergeant Hart in on this?" Colonel Rickabee asked.

"I told you to knock off that 'The General' crap," Pickering said sharply, which Rickabee correctly interpreted to mean that The General was at least slightly hung over and in a nasty mood. "And, yeah, I think so," Pickering went on. "Does that pose a security clearance problem for you?"

"No, Sir. Sergeant Hart is cleared to TOP SECRET. And no problem, of course, with Moore."

"OK, then. They stay," Pickering ordered. "I think they're going to be involved in this anyway, to one degree or another."

"Yes, Sir."

"On the security business, what is said in this room, for reasons that will become obvious, is classified TOP SECRET," Pickering said. "Everybody understand that?"

There was a chorus of "Yes, Sir."

"Let me state the problem, then," Pickering said. "Our first priority is to keep Ferdinand Six up and running. Our second priority is to get Howard and Koffler off Buka—and Reeves too, probably. Just as soon as I can get out of here, my intention is to go back to Australia and get our people to do whatever is necessary to bring Howard and Koffler back. For reasons I don't want to get into, they seem to have just written them off."

"No, Sir," Colonel Rickabee said, flatly.

"I beg your pardon?"

"You can't go back over there, General. That's out of the question," Rickabee said.

Pickering looked at him coldly. There was a long and awkward silence. When Pickering finally spoke, it was not in response to Rickabee.

"Hart has no idea what the rest of us will be talking about," he said. "And I really don't know how much McCoy knows."

"I read the file last night, Sir," McCoy said.

"Sessions has it with him, Sir," Rickabee said.

"See that Hart reads it," Pickering said. "How complete is it?"

"Enough to give him the picture, General," McCoy said.

"OK. So we'll start with you, McCoy. If you were God, more to the point, if you were a general officer, how would you go about getting those people out . . . while at the same time keeping Ferdinand Six up?"

"General," McCoy said, uncomfortably, "if Major Banning can't do that, I don't know—"

"I'll rephrase the question. If you were Major Banning, what would you do if you were *ordered* to get Howard and Koffler off Buka?"

"It wouldn't be easy," McCoy said. "Even if keeping the radio station in operation wasn't a consideration."

"You'll notice, Rickabee," Pickering said, "that he didn't say 'impossible.' "

"Maybe I should have," McCoy said.

"OK. Explain that," Pickering said. "But don't quote Banning to me. Tell me why you think it would be 'not easy' to 'impossible.' "

"Yes, Sir," McCoy said in a reflex reply. "Well, my first thought was that getting them out by air *would* be impossible. There's no airfield. So that left getting them out by water. We cannot send surface ships, even native boats, because the waters are heavily patrolled. That leaves submarines—"

Pickering interrupted him. "What's wrong with submarines?"

"Several things," McCoy said. "First of all, I doubt if we could get one."

"Let's say we can get one," Pickering said, "and take it from there."

"We probably could not get one to—" Rickabee said, and was interrupted by Pickering.

"Two things, Rickabee. One, McCoy has the floor, and, two, I told him to go ahead on the presumption that he can get a submarine."

"—make an *extraction,* Sir," Rickabee went on, ignoring him. "But, since Ferdinand Six is of great value to the Navy, they probably would give us one to insert a Coastwatcher team."

"You have a point," Pickering said, not at all graciously. "Go on, McCoy."

"A submarine could be used to land a replacement team and to take out the team that's there," McCoy said. "At least that was my first thought."

"Psychologically speaking, I think it would be a good idea," Pickering announced, "to refer to the Marines on Buka by their names. Their names are Lieutenant Joe Howard and Sergeant Steve Koffler. We're not talking about a navigation buoy we left floating around an atoll someplace."

"Yes, Sir," McCoy said.

"You were about to tell us what's wrong with a submarine," Pickering said.

"One, it would have to surface offshore someplace, obviously. That means it would have to do so at night, to lower the chances that Japanese ships, aircraft, or *Japanese* coastwatchers would see it."

" '*Japanese* coastwatchers'?" Pickering parroted.

"The Makin raid has taught the Japanese some lessons. For one, they're now afraid there'll be other raids. They are watching all their beaches."

"They don't have the manpower to watch all their coastline," Pickering argued.

"They probably have enough to watch the beaches where you could put rubber boats ashore. And rubber boats is something else."

"Explain that," Pickering ordered.

"We had trouble getting onto the beach at Makin," McCoy said. "And we damned near didn't get off. You want me to talk about putting a replacement team in by submarine?"

"Please."

"We could probably find enough people in the 2nd Raider Battalion to handle the rubber boats—"

"Why couldn't the replacement team paddle their own boats?" Rickabee asked.

"Because it's hell of lot harder than it looks, a hell of a lot harder than Colonel Carlson and Captain Roosevelt, or me, thought it would be," McCoy said simply. "It requires both skill and a lot of muscle. I just said we damned near didn't get off the beach. Seven of us didn't."

George Hart stared for a time at Lieutenant McCoy, for he found it hard to really accept it that the man now sitting across the room from him in an immaculate uniform, not even wearing any ribbons, holding a cup of coffee, the man who had entertained him and Beth the night before with stories of the trouble he'd had getting Pick Pickering through Officer Candidate School, had been one of the Marine Raiders who struck Makin Island.

"Ken," Captain Sessions asked, speaking for the first time, "you're saying you don't think we could train our people to handle rubber boats?"

"No, I don't think so. And even if we could, what about the—Lieutenant Whatsisname and the sergeant?"

"Howard and Koffler," Pickering furnished evenly.

"Yes, Sir. Howard and Koffler. They would have to be rowed back through the surf to the submarine. They sure couldn't do it themselves. The replacement team would be exhausted from rowing to shore. It's a lot harder, that sort of crap, than anyone understands until they've tried it."

"OK," Pickering said.

"Let me kill the idea, please, Sir," McCoy said. "The replacement team would be taking a radio, radios, in with them."

"*Two* radios," Rickabee said. "A replacement and a spare."

"Each weighing about a hundred pounds?"

"That's right."

"Then, Sir, based on our experience at Makin, you would have to send in *four* radios, to make sure *two* made it to the beach. And we didn't try to off-load anything that heavy from the submarines into the rubber boats. The heaviest thing we carried ashore was a Browning .50. And that was a bitch. We lost two I know about. Maybe, probably, more."

"You sound as negative about this as Banning, McCoy," Pickering said.

Although his tone was conversational, it was clear that General Pickering was both angry and disappointed.

"But just for the hell of it," McCoy went on, "let's suppose we could somehow get around the rubber boat problem. How would we get word to"—he searched his memory and came up with the names—"Koffler and Howard to meet up with the submarine?"

"We are in radio contact," Pickering said.

"I think we have to presume that the Japs are monitoring

their transmissions, and that they have broken the code," McCoy said. "They are not stupid."

Rickabee remembered again that Corporal McCoy had not applied for OCS. A report he had written about Japanese troop movements when he worked for Captain Ed Banning in the Fourth Marines in China had come to the attention of General Forrest. Forrest's reaction had been blunt and to the point. *"I think we ought to put bars on that corporal's shoulders. Right now he and I are the only two people in The Marine Corps who don't seem to devoutly believe that all Japs are five feet two, wear thick glasses, and that we can whip them with one hand tied behind our backs."*

Captain Ed Sessions had marched a very reluctant Corporal McCoy before an officer candidate selection board. Before he did that, Captain Sessions had informed the president of the board that if he found reason to reject Corporal McCoy as suitable officer material, he better be prepared to defend that to General Forrest.

"Going off at a tangent, McCoy, accepting what you just said," Rickabee asked, "why do you think the Japanese haven't located and taken out Ferdinand Six?"

"Yeah," Pickering said thoughtfully.

"They know where they are within a mile or so. So the question is really, why haven't they taken them out?"

"OK."

"That's rough terrain. Steep hills, thick jungle. Which also explains why they don't try to take them out with aircraft; it would be a waste of effort. They can't see them from the air, and even if they did, bombing or strafing them would be a waste of effort. And by the time they got within a couple of miles on the ground, the Coastwatchers would know about it. The Coastwatchers have natives who know the terrain. They can keep out of the Japs' way. And the Japs know that. They're *not* stupid."

"They must know what Ferdinand Six is costing them," Pickering said.

"Yes, Sir. But they also know that radios don't function forever in the jungle, and that white men can't live there for any length of time. They're patient; the problem will solve itself."

"You were saying that you think the Japanese have broken the code?"

"What are they using?" McCoy asked, looking at Captain Sessions.

"An old SOI," Sessions offered, meaning *Signal Operating Instruction.* "When they repeat it, they jump ahead, using Howard's serial number. I think you're right. They've broken it."

"I have no idea what you're talking about," Pickering said.

"General, they have a code book with a different code for each of thirty days," Sessions explained. "When they run past thirty days, they start over again from the beginning. But not in the same sequence this time—not one, two, three. This time, say, if Howard's serial was 56789, they use the code for the fifth day; and the day after that, they count ahead six days, the second number of his serial number. You understand how it works, General?"

"I do now."

"So what I was saying," McCoy went on, "was that even if we got a submarine, found a beach which would take rubber boats, and managed to get the replacement team and their hundred-pound radios ashore, it wouldn't do us any good, because we have no way of letting—*Howard and Koffler*—know when and where to meet the submarine. If we tried to tell them, we have to assume the Japanese would intercept the message. The Japs would then ambush them on their way to the beach. And they'd be waiting for the submarine to surface."

Colonel F. L. Rickabee was very impressed with Lieutenant K. R. McCoy. Having placed a great deal of confidence in Major Ed Banning's ability, he had not given a great deal of thought to the problems of extracting the—*Howard and Koffler*—from Buka . . . until his somewhat strained luncheon the previous afternoon with a somewhat intoxicated and very upset Brigadier General Fleming Pickering.

After giving the problem some hard thought, he had come up with very much the same conclusion that Banning had obviously reached in Australia—that getting those two guys out was impossible. It seemed pretty clear that McCoy had reached the same conclusion now that the facts were available to him.

This should shut Pickering up, Rickabee thought with a great sense of relief. *As a veteran of the Makin raid, McCoy was obviously an expert in rubber boat landings. Pickering would accept his judgment. And McCoy was a Mustang: A former enlisted Marine would not decide they couldn't go and pick up the dead and wounded unless it was really impossible.*

Better he should get this painful truth from McCoy than from me again.

"I gather that you and Major Banning are in agreement, then, McCoy, that there is absolutely nothing we can do for Joe Howard and Steve Koffler?" General Pickering asked, his voice now sounding very tired.

"No, Sir," McCoy said. "I didn't say that."

"Well then, goddamn it, let's have it!"

"I thought of two ways we might be able to carry this off," McCoy said. "One's kind of wild."

"Let's hear it, McCoy."

"I started out with the submarine idea," McCoy said. "Christ, there's so much I don't know!"

"We can get answers. Go ahead," Pickering said.

"Yes, Sir. OK. Step one. We find a beach that will take boats. Depending on what the surf and the beach are like when we get there, we put ashore the radios, the replacement Marines, and an Australian Coastwatcher. We'll also bring one, or better, two natives who know the island and can find Ferdinand Six. If the surf is bad, we just put the natives ashore. We don't try to land the radios and the replacement team. Then the natives find Ferdinand Six and tell them where the submarine will be—probably a different beach. Maybe with a little bit of luck, there would be native boats to go out to the submarine—"

"I like it," General Pickering said, looking triumphantly at Colonel Rickabee.

Oh, shit! Rickabee thought.

"Then," McCoy went on, "as I was thinking about that, I had a wild hare."

And how, Lieutenant McCoy, Rickabee wondered, *would you describe your previous "Errol Flynn Fights the Nasty Nips" idea as a tame hare?*

"Well?"

"Use an R4D, just go in, off-load the replacement team and radios, and pick up the guys that are there," McCoy said.

"I thought it was pretty well established that there was no airfield."

"There's beaches," McCoy said. "Maybe there's the right kind of sand, packed so it will take an R4D."

"I don't think so," Sessions said.

"You're talking about landing an R4D on a beach?" Rickabee asked incredulously. "It would just sink in."

"I've been nosing around for the Mongolian Operation," McCoy said. "We can make that flight only one time. If the Japs see the plane, we have to hope they think it was some guy just got lost. But if two planes got lost, they would be very suspicious. So we're going to have to take everything we'll need in with us and get it safely on the ground. And it's a one-way ride; there's no way the plane can get out again. So the question came up—they're still talking about it—of what to do with the airplane."

"I have no idea what you're talking about, McCoy," Pickering said.

"General, I'll have the Mongolia file in your hands this afternoon," Rickabee said.

"I want to hear about it now."

"General, we're getting into Need to Know," Rickabee said, gesturing toward Dillon and Hart.

"I'll decide who needs to know what," Pickering said icily. "Go on, McCoy."

"Sir, we're setting up a weather observation station in the Mongolian desert. The only way we can get in is by air. So they're going to add auxiliary fuel tanks to an R4D that will give us the necessary range from the Aleutian Islands—"

"The Japanese hold Attu in the Aleutians," Pickering interrupted.

"Yes, Sir. That's one of the problems. Anyway, we can probably get enough range to make it in. The original idea was to parachute the team in and then leave the airplane on automatic pilot and let it crash when it ran out of fuel. But they were still cutting the fuel supply so tight, they were afraid it would run out too close to the drop site. So then they thought if they didn't use parachutes and the packing necessary for the equipment, they could carry that much more fuel. So they've been wondering how they land the plane in the desert. Maybe just land it and bury it in sand. Or maybe land it, unload it, and then take off again and put it on autopilot. Anyway, they're working on how to land it on sand. I don't know whether that will work, or if it does, whether it would work on a beach in Buka, but it would sure solve a lot of problems."

"The plane that dropped Howard and Koffler on Buka was shot down on its way home," Rickabee said.

This Mongolian Operation, obviously, is just about as risky for the people involved as Ferdinand Six, Pickering thought. *And one of the reasons McCoy is so matter-of-factly willing to go on it is that he believes, as a matter of faith, that if he gets in trouble, somebody else in The Corps will do all that's humanly possible to get him out.*

I'm right about this! *Even if Rickabee, and probably Sessions, think I'm a goddamned fool.*

"We could solve that problem, too," Pickering said. "Who's 'they,' McCoy? Where are they working on this land-on-sand business?"

"At an Army Air Corps airfield in Florida, General. On the Florida panhandle, up near the Alabama border."

"That's where Jimmy Doolittle trained for his B-25 Shangri-la mission on Tokyo," Pickering thought aloud.

"Eglin Field, I think, Sir," McCoy said.

"No. It's probably an auxiliary field, between Eglin and Pensacola. I was there a while back. Is there any reason you can't go down there and find out something for sure?"

"I can go down there, yes, Sir."

"Then go."

"General, if I could have Lieutenant Moore and Sergeant Hart . . . having them with me might be helpful."

"OK. Whatever you think you need," Pickering said, and went on: "We have concluded that the extraction of Joe Howard and Steve Koffler is not impossible . . ."

You have the fantasy that it's not impossible, Rickabee thought. *Jesus Christ, landing an airliner on a beach, right under the nose of the Japanese! Fifty, sixty miles from a Japanese fighter base!*

"We will now deal with your statement, Colonel, that my going to Australia is 'out of the question.' "

"Admiral Leahy would not give you permission, General," Rickabee said. And then, anticipating Pickering's response to that, he went on. "And if you were to go without permission, he would order you home as soon as he heard about it. Among other things, that would serve to call attention to this operation, which is the last thing you want to happen."

"Jesus!" Pickering said bitterly.

It was clear to Rickabee that he had made his point. "Lieutenant McCoy," he said, "carrying a letter of instructions from you, General, to Major Banning, would, I suggest, be all that's needed."

"I don't think so," Pickering said. "McCoy is a lieutenant, Banning a major. What I have been thinking is that Jake outranks Banning."

Goddamn it, I should have known he would pick up on that, Rickabee thought. *Dillon came back into The Corps as a major while Banning was still in the Philippines as a captain.*

"Flem, for Christ's sake," Jake Dillon said uncomfortably, "I'm a press agent wearing a major's uniform. I don't know anything about this sort of thing."

"You're a Marine, Jake," Pickering said. "And all you have to do is go there and report to me that Banning is or is not doing what you tell him to do. And what you tell him to do is what McCoy tells you he wants done."

"General, that puts me in a hell of a spot," McCoy said.

"There is a limited access communications channel available to us. Moore is familiar with it . . ." Pickering said.

Jesus, he's talking about the MAGIC channel, Rickabee thought. *He shouldn't even think of using that for this harebrained scheme of his! But Jesus, except for Admiral Leahy or the President himself, there's no one to tell him he can't.*

"We will utilize that to keep in touch with day-to-day developments. As Rickabee just pointed out, the less attention paid to this operation, the better. The question, John, is whether you feel up to going back to Australia."

"Yes, Sir. I feel fine."

"General, he's walking around with a cane!" Rickabee protested.

"You're sure?" Pickering asked Moore.

"Yes, Sir, I'm sure," Lieutenant Moore said.

"OK. We're under way," Pickering said. "Now we start with the administrative details. I've got some letters to write. Can I have a typewriter sent over here, Rickabee?"

"I'll send you a secretary, Sir."

"I asked for a typewriter," Pickering said.

"Aye, aye, Sir."

"You can start on getting orders cut," Pickering said. "And

McCoy and Moore and Hart will need plane tickets right away."

"Sir," Lieutenant McCoy said, "the overnight train to Miami—'Seacoast Airline' they call it for some reason I never understood—comes through Washington at half past six. If we could get on that, we could get a good night's sleep. We could get off in Tallahassee and catch the Greyhound bus to Eglin."

"See if you can get them a compartment—compartments—on the train," Pickering ordered. "And see if you can't arrange to have somebody from Eglin pick them up at Tallahassee."

"Aye, Aye, Sir," Sessions said. "No problem, we have an officer there in connection with Operation CHINA SUN."

In the car on the way back to the Mall and Temporary Building T-2032, Captain Edward Sessions turned to Colonel F. L. Rickabee and asked, "Do you think they'll be able to pull this off, Colonel?"

"It isn't my place to think about my orders, Captain. I'm a Marine officer; when I am given an order, I do my best to carry it out. But since you asked, no, I don't think so. Do I hope they can? Yes, I do."

"Why do you suppose McCoy wanted to take Moore and Hart with him to Florida?"

"I have absolutely no idea," Rickabee said, "my mind being otherwise occupied with such mundane questions as under what authority we are going to be able to transport Major Dillon to Australia. He is assigned to Public Affairs, after all. . . . And on the subject of Major Dillon, did it occur to you that Dillon has been made privy to Operation CHINA SUN?"

"I think Dillon can be trusted to keep his mouth shut, Colonel."

"I hope so," Rickabee said. "Jesus Christ, I hope so!"

Second Lieutenant John Marston Moore waited until they were in suite 614 of the Foster Lafayette Hotel before asking the question Captain Sessions asked: "Exactly what are we going to do in Florida, McCoy?"

"I'm going to talk to an Air Corps guy I met down there. He knows all about the kind of sand you need to land airplanes on. And, more important, he invented a gimmick . . . you stick a cone, sort of, just far enough into the sand to make it stand up. Then you drop a ten-pound weight on it from exactly twenty-four inches. How far that drives the cone into the ground tells you how much weight the sand will support."

"Fascinating," Moore said.

"I want to talk to him and talk him out of a couple of the cone things—as many as he'll give me," McCoy said. "That'll probably take the better part of an hour. Two hours if he buys us lunch in their officer's club. That reminds me, Hart, you're going to have to wear civilian clothes."

"Yes, Sir," Hart said.

"And what else?"

"The beach along the Gulf Coast there is as pretty as any in Hawaii," McCoy said. "And the seafood is great. With a little bit of luck, we'll have twenty-four hours, maybe thirty-six, before Sessions gets us seats on the courier plane out of Pensacola back here."

"What do you need us along for?" Hart asked.

"Beth said she was on vacation," McCoy said. "Don't you think she'd like a day or two on the beach in Florida? And a romantic dinner on a train? I know damned well Ernie will."

"Who's Beth?" Moore asked.

"Hart's girlfriend," McCoy said. "She came to Washington to see him."

"That was the mysterious telephone call?" Moore asked.

Hart nodded.

Jesus, what the hell will happen if they find out what Beth does for a living? Hart asked himself.

It took Hart a moment to decide that McCoy was perfectly serious.

McCoy saw the look on his face, and on Moore's.

"Would you two like a few words of wisdom from an old Marine?" he asked, and went on without waiting for a reply. "In case you haven't figured this out yet, we're about to get shipped out. The way Pickering is pushing Rickabee, we're going just as soon as they can cut orders. When Pickering said he wanted me to find out about landing an R4D on sand, the first thing I thought was that I would call this Air Corps guy, tell him the problem, then send Hart down there to get the gimmicks to test the sand. *Then* I thought that if I hung around here waiting for him to come back, Rickabee and Sessions would find things for me to do. *Then* I decided that I would have to go myself, even though that's a sacrifice. *Then* I decided that it would not be fair to a wounded hero—such as yourself,

Lieutenant Moore—to leave you behind to run errands while Sergeant Hart and myself and our girlfriends are riding on a luxury train and lying on a Florida beach. Am I getting through to you two?"

Moore laughed. "It sounds like we'll be busy!" he said.

"As General Pickering said to me just this morning," McCoy said, " 'Take what you can, when you can get it.' Who am I to argue with a general?" Then he saw the look on Hart's face. "What's the matter with you? Don't you think Beth will want to go?"

"I'm sure she'll want to go," Hart said.

I'm not sure I should take her. Jesus, why did she have to be a whore?

"Then you better get your ass over to Union Station and get tickets for the girls on the Seacoast Airline Limited or whatever the hell they call it. You got any money?" he asked, as he took a sheaf of bills from his pocket.

"Pity you don't have a girl, Moore," McCoy said. "But maybe you'll get lucky in the club car."

When Major Jake Dillon walked into the Metro-Magnum Studios suite in the Willard Hotel, Veronica Wood was preparing herself for *her* day's work: Her long blond hair was pulled tightly back against her head, and she had converted the coffee table in the sitting room to a makeup table. She was wearing a really ugly brown cotton bathrobe.

"Where the hell have you been?" she asked, looking up at him. The bathrobe was hanging open.

Fantastic teats!

"I had work to do," Jake said.

"You think those cheap bastards would put a decent god-damned dressing room in here," Veronica said. "I've got an interview with that bitch from the *Post* at noon. I'm going to look like shit."

"This is Seymour's apartment," Dillon said, referring to the Chairman of the Board and Chief Executive Officer of Metro-Magnum Studios. "He doesn't like to look at himself in mirrors."

She chuckled and smiled at him.

"You had a telephone call," she said. "Couple of them. Same guy. Name of Stewart. He's pissed at something."

"Did he say he was 'General' Stewart?"

Veronica thought about that a moment, and then nodded. "Yeah. He did."

"Oh, shit."

"He said you were supposed to call him the minute you got in."

"OK, thank you, sweetheart."

"You're going to be with me at lunch, right?"

"I don't think that's possible, honey."

"Goddamn, Jake, you know I can't deal with that goddamned dyke!"

"Bobby O'Hara will be there," Jake said. "I'll call him."

"I want *you* there, *goddamn it,* Jake!"

"Bobby is very good with her," Dillon said. "They're both Irish."

He picked up the telephone and made two calls. The first was to Mr. Robert T. O'Hara, of the Washington office of Metro-Magnum Studios, Inc., to remind him he had a luncheon engagement with Miss Veronica Wood. The call lasted about sixty seconds.

The second, to Colonel F. L. Rickabee of the Office of Management Analysis, was even more brief.

"Colonel, Jake Dillon. General Stewart has been looking for me. I'm supposed to call him."

"Don't call him. Don't go near him. I'll take care of it," Rickabee said, and then the line went dead.

"*Please,* Jake!" Veronica Wood asked. "Come with me? *I* was nice to *you.*"

"That was last night. What have you done for me today?"

"You sonofabitch!" Veronica said delightedly. "That's why I love you. You're a prick but you admit it."

"If I go to lunch with you, will you promise not to say 'prick'? I don't think Whatsername from the *Post* likes that word."

The telephone rang again. Dillon picked it up. As he spoke his name, he realized that was pretty dumb. It was probably General Stewart, shitting a brick about something.

"Hey, Jake. Charley Stevens. How the hell are you?"

Charley Stevens was a screenwriter.

"How are you, Charley?"

"Got a question, Jake. I'm doing the first rewrite of the *Wake Island* script. Got a question, figured you were a Marine and could answer it. Need some love interest. Please tell me, there were nurses on Wake Island?"

"No nurses on Wake Island, Charley, sorry."

"Shit!" Charley Stevens said.

"You'll think of something, Charley," Jake said and hung up.

[Two]
OFFICE OF THE DIRECTOR
PUBLIC AFFAIRS OFFICE
HEADQUARTERS, U.S. MARINE CORPS
WASHINGTON, D.C.
1530 HOURS 22 SEPTEMBER 1942

Brigadier General J. J. Stewart summoned his deputy into his office and handed him a sheet of green paper.

"Take a look at this, will you?" he fumed.

```
                 INTEROFFICE MEMORANDUM

 DATE:       22 September 1942

 FROM:       Assistant Chief of Staff,
             Personnel

 TO:         Director
             Public Affairs Office
             Hq, USMC

 HAND CARRY

 SUBJECT:    Dillon, Major Homer J., USMCR,
             Temporary Assignment Of


   1. Effective immediately, subject officer
 is placed on temporary duty for an indefinite
 period with the Office of Management
 Analysis, Hq USMC.
   2. All records of subject officer now under
 the control of the Public Affairs Division
```

> will be hand-carried to the Office of
> Management within twenty-four (24) hours.
>   3. Discussion of this assignment or
> requests for reconsideration thereof is not
> desired.
>
>
> BY DIRECTION OF THE COMMANDANT:
>
> Alfred J. Kennedy
> Major General, USMC
> Assistant Chief of Staff, G-1

After General Stewart's deputy read the memorandum, he looked at General Stewart, but he didn't say anything.

"How the hell they expect me to do my job if they keep stealing my officers, I don't know," General Stewart said. "Who the hell am I going to get to run the war bond tour? I've got a goddamned good mind to take this to the Commandant!"

In the end, of course, he did not. He was a good Marine officer, and good Marine officers accept the orders they are given without question or complaint.

[Three]
SEA BREEZE MOTEL
MARY ESTHER, FLORIDA
24 SEPTEMBER 1942

Lieutenant K. R. McCoy, in a T-shirt and swimming trunks, opened the door to room 17 in response to an imperious knock. He found himself facing a stout woman in her late forties, wearing flowered shorts and a matching blouse under a transparent raincoat. On her head she had a World War I–style steel helmet, painted white, bearing an insignia consisting of the letters CD within a triangle. A brassard around her right arm had a similar insignia, and she was armed with a policeman's nightstick, painted white.

While McCoy was reacting to the sudden appearance of the CD lady, she pushed past him into room 17 and slammed the door behind her. Before returning to his room, he had spent three hours on the beach doing his share of the damage to a case of PX beer. After that, he attended a steak broil at the Hurlburtt Field Officer's club; each table there had come furnished with four bottles of California Cabernet Sauvignon.

"I could see light!" the lady announced in righteous indignation. "Your drapes permitted light to escape!"

"Sorry," McCoy said.

"There are German submarines out there!" the lady declared. "Don't you people know there's a war on?"

"Where do you think it went when it escaped?" Lieutenant John Marston Moore, USMCR, asked from the bed where he was resting. "The light, I mean?"

His voice was somewhat slurred, as if he had partaken of a considerable quantity of intoxicants.

"Shut up, Johnny," Miss Ernestine Sage said. She was wearing a bathing suit and a T-shirt. In three-inch-high red letters, US MARINES was stretched taut across her bosom.

The pride of the Mary Esther, Florida, Civil Defense Force stared at her; and then she looked around the room. Also in the room were Miss Elizabeth Lathrop, in a swimsuit and T-shirt reading US ARMY AIR CORPS, Sergeant George Hart, and two galvanized iron buckets filled with iced beer and several bottles of liquor.

"You girls should be ashamed of yourselves!"

" 'Let he who is without sin cast the first stone,' " Lieutenant John Marston Moore announced sonorously, "as our blessed Lord and Saviour said on the road to Samara."

Ernie Sage began to giggle.

"You keep those drapes drawn or I'll write you up!" the Civil Defense lady ordered furiously. "I mean it!"

"Yes, Ma'am," McCoy said. "We're sorry."

He turned off the lights. The Civil Defense lady left the room to return to her appointed rounds. McCoy closed the door, locked it, and then turned the lights on again.

"You're really the life of the party, aren't you?" McCoy said to Moore, misquoting *Where do you think the light went when it escaped?* "The one thing we don't need is to get hauled off to the local police station."

"Yes, Sir," Moore said, sounding not at all remorseful. "Sorry, Lieutenant, Sir."

"Are there really German submarines out there?" Ernie asked.

"Probably," McCoy replied. "They try to sink the oil tank-

ers coming out of the Texas Gulf ports and whatever sails from
New Orleans. But I don't think they're in this close to shore.
There's just too many airfields along here. There was a story
going around that they caught half a dozen Germans near the
mouth of Mobile Bay. They were supposedly landed from a
sub."

"Isn't *that* interesting?" Moore said.

McCoy flashed a cold look at him and Ernie saw it. Without
a good deal of effort, she had already concluded that whatever
Ken and the other two were doing down here had something
to do with beaches.

When they were on the beach this afternoon, Moore and
Hart had a steel cone and a square block of lead. They went up
and down the beach, pounding the cone into the sand. And
then at the Officer's Club Steak Broil—the club was right on
the beach—Ken left the party for a "walk on the beach" with
Lieutenant Mainwaring, the Marine officer who picked them
up at the train station in Tallahassee and drove them here, and
the Army Air Corps guy who gave Beth the T-shirt. They took
the cone and lead block with them. They were gone forty-five
minutes.

It does not take a wild imagination, Ernie Sage thought, *to put
that cone, whatever the hell it's for, together with Johnny's dry
crack after Ken's story about Germans caught coming ashore
from a submarine, and come up with a studied guess that what
they're about to do involves a submarine and a beach. And not a
beach in Florida, either.*

Oh, God!

"Mademoiselle," Johnny Moore interrupted her chain of
thought by handing her his empty bottle of beer, "if you would
be so kind?"

"Avec grand plaisir, mon cher," Ernie said, and went to the
beer buckets and got him one.

"What did they do to the Germans?" Beth asked. "The ones
they caught from the submarine?"

"I don't know," McCoy said. "I didn't see the file, just heard
the scuttlebutt. If they were in uniform, they were just put in a
POW cage. If they were in civilian clothing, that makes them
spies. Then they could be shot. Or maybe hung."

"What would the Japanese do if they caught Americans?"
Ernie asked.

"How did we get onto this subject?" McCoy said.

That means, Ernie decided, *that the Japanese would do nothing quite as civilized as shooting someone they caught trying to land somewhere from a submarine—these three, for example.*

There was a knock at the door. Not nearly as imperious as the previous knock. This one, in fact, was somehow furtive.

"Do you think the guardian of the beach has summoned the local vice cops?" Moore asked.

"I hope not," McCoy said as he turned the lights off, unlocked the door, and opened it.

When the lights came back on, Lieutenant Mainwaring and Captain Al Stein, the Army Air Corps officer—now that she saw him, Ernie remembered his name—and two Air Corps enlisted men were entering the small room. They had two wooden crates with them, rolling them on what Ernie thought of as a furniture man's dolly.

"Room service," Stein said.

"Why did you bring them here?" McCoy asked.

Ernie tried to read what was stenciled on the crates. Whatever had been stenciled there had been obliterated, and very recently, for the paint was still wet.

"Because I don't have the faith everybody else seems to have in this colonel of yours to fix this."

"Everything will be all right, Al," Mainwaring said.

"He said as Stein was led off in irons, destination Leavenworth U.S. Army prison."

"Help yourself to a beer," McCoy said to the Air Corps sergeants. "Or there's booze if you'd rather."

"I think maybe we'd better get the truck back," the older of the two Air Corps sergeants said.

"Have a beer," Stein ordered.

"OK, Captain, thank you."

"Have all the beer you want," McCoy said. "We really appreciate this."

"Ah, what the hell, Lieutenant," the sergeant said.

"I am sure, Captain Stein," Moore said, propping himself up against the headboard, "that an officer of your demonstrated logistical genius is aware that these crates won't fit in that Chevrolet staff car?"

Stein looked at Moore and laughed.

"I'm surprised that you're still able to talk."

"Hell, he's been quoting the Bible to us," McCoy said. "An amazing man is our Lieutenant Moore."

"We'll bring the truck back at oh six hundred, Lieutenant," the Air Corps sergeant said. "That'll give us just over an hour to make it to Pensacola. Plenty of time. We just didn't want to try to get these crates through the gate at the field in the morning."

"You have three seats on the seven A.M. courier flight and authorization for six hundred pounds of accompanied baggage," Lieutenant Mainwaring said.

"That's what these weigh?"

"Pray they don't weigh them," Stein said.

"What about the extra cone sets?"

"I've got those in the car," Mainwaring said. "All I could get you was three."

"Plus the one we have?" McCoy asked.

"Including the one you have," Stein said.

"Beggars can't be choosers," McCoy said. "Thank you."

"I won't see you in the morning, McCoy," Stein said. "So I'll say this now. In no more than seventy-two hours—probably within forty-eight—somebody's going to miss this stuff. I would deeply appreciate it if you will do whatever you can to keep Mrs. Stein's little boy from ending his Air Corps career making little rocks out of big ones at Leavenworth."

"Did you talk to the Colonel, Mainwaring?" McCoy asked. Mainwaring nodded.

"There's supposed to be TWX on the way down here."

"That ought to do it, Stein," McCoy said. "But I'll check on it myself as soon as we get to Washington."

"Good enough," Captain Stein said. He looked at his two sergeants. "Take enough of those bottles to sustain you throughout the journey, gentlemen, and then let us be on our way."

"Thanks, Stein," McCoy said. "We owe you one."

"You owe me a good deal more than one," Stein said, putting out his hand. "Good luck, McCoy. Be careful. You two, too," he said, waving at Hart and Moore.

"May the peace of God which passeth all understanding," Moore proclaimed from the bed, "go with you and yours."

"Oh, shit!" Stein said, laughing, and snapped off the lights. Just before the door slammed shut after them, Stein called out, "Mazeltov, you all!"

"Why do you think Moore got so drunk?" Ernie asked as she

made a halfhearted attempt to clean up the room when the others had gone.

"I think he was in pain," McCoy said.

"What kind of pain?"

"I think it started when he went in the water and got salt-water in his wounds," McCoy answered matter-of-factly. "And then I think he hurt his legs, either in the water, or maybe walking in the sand."

"So why didn't you do something about it?"

"Getting drunk worked as good as anything from the dispensary," McCoy said. "And if we had taken him there, they probably would have wanted to keep him."

"That's pretty damned callous!"

"He's a big boy, baby. He wanted to come down here."

"And he wants to do whatever it is you're about to do, right?"

"Right."

"And you're not going to tell me what that is, right?"

"Right."

"How about how Beth and me are supposed to get back to Washington?"

"The way Mainwaring was looking at you, I thought maybe you'd want to stay."

"Go to hell!"

"After Mainwaring drops us at Pensacola—I'm not sure we can get you on the base without a lot of hassle; you may have to wait outside the gate—he'll take you to Mobile. That's another forty miles or so. You catch a train there to Montgomery and connect with the Crescent from New Orleans to Washington."

"And by the time I get to Washington, are you still going to be there?"

"Baby, I don't know."

"In other words, I may not see you after tomorrow morning?"

He didn't reply.

"For how long?"

He shrugged.

"And if I hadn't asked, you were just going to get on that goddamned airplane tomorrow without even saying goodbye?"

"Saying goodbye to you is hard for me, baby."

"How about saying, 'I love you, Ernie'? Is that hard for you, Ken?"

"I love you, Ernie," McCoy said.

"If you love me, you sonofabitch, why won't you marry me?" she said. But she didn't expect a reply or wait for one. She walked quickly to him and waited for him to put his arms around her. When he did, she told him she loved him, too.

Two rooms down, Beth Lathrop also asked what was going to happen to her and to Ernie the next day. When she asked it, she was standing in the door to the bathroom, wrapped in a towel.

"Mainwaring is going to take both of you to Mobile to catch a train."

"Do you think she means it when she says she can get me assignments as a photographer?"

"I'm sure she does."

She doesn't know you're a whore. Maybe if she knew that, she wouldn't.

"You don't think she's just saying that?"

"You better be able to produce, Beth."

"What does that mean?"

"It better not be bullshit, you being a photographer."

"You bastard! Is that what you think?"

"All I'm saying is that if you're not a photographer, now is the time to say so. Don't make a fool of her. She's a nice girl."

"You think I've been lying all the time, don't you?"

"I don't know what the hell to think."

"That's not all. Say what you're thinking!"

"She knows Pick. He knows you. What is he going to tell her about you?"

"I didn't think about that," Beth said. "Oh, Jesus!"

"Shit," George said, and went to the dresser and opened the bottle of beer he'd brought from McCoy's and Ernie's room.

"OK," Beth said, "so what I'll do is tell her thanks but no thanks."

"No," Hart said. "No, you won't. If she says she can get you a job, you'll take it."

"What about Pick?"

"She won't be seeing him anytime soon," Hart said. "Maybe ever."

"My God, what a rotten thing to even think!"

"And anyway, what he tells her about you has nothing to do with you and me."

"Meaning what?"

"Meaning I don't give a good goddamn what anyone knows, or thinks."

That's true, goddamn it, he thought. *I don't even give a good goddamn what my father would say if he found out.*

"You say that but you don't mean it," Beth said.

"Goddamn it, I mean it."

"I mean it, George, when I say I love you," Beth said.

"Yeah, me, too," George said.

"I'll do whatever you tell me to do," Beth said.

"Whatever I tell you?"

"Whatever you tell me, honey."

"Take off the damned towel."

[Four]
WALTER REED ARMY GENERAL HOSPITAL
WASHINGTON, D.C.
1005 HOURS 25 SEPTEMBER 1942

Colonel F. L. Rickabee was in uniform when he knocked on Brigadier General Fleming Pickering's hospital room. He entered without waiting.

"Good morning, General," he said.

Christ, Pickering thought, *clothes do make the man! He is far more impressive in his uniform than in those off-the-rack Sears, Roebuck suits he usually wears.*

"Good morning, Rickabee."

"Sorry to be late, Sir. I went to the Friday Morning."

"You went to the what?"

"The Friday Morning Intelligence Summary at ONI," Rickabee explained. ONI was the *O*ffice of *N*aval *I*ntelligence.

"That's why you're in uniform?"

"Yes, Sir. That saves the usual two minutes of Naval humor when I show up in mufti."

Pickering chuckled.

"Hear anything interesting?"

"Yes, Sir. The Naval attaché in London sent an URGENT radio that he had just heard a reliable report from the English that on the twenty-third, General Rommel was flown to Germany from North Africa, ostensibly for medical treatment, and that yesterday General Halder was relieved and replaced by a man named Zeitler."

"Who's General Halder?" Pickering asked.

"He was Chief of Staff OKH—*Oberkommando* Heeres, Ground Forces Headquarters—which has *de facto* responsibility for the Russian Front. There's some thought that Hitler may send Rommel to Russia. Interesting."

"Yes," Pickering agreed.

Proving again, Brigadier General Pickering, Pickering thought, *that your total knowledge of the global war can be written inside a matchbook with a grease pencil. The only name you recognized was Rommel's.*

"And just as we were breaking up there was an OPERATIONAL IMMEDIATE in from CINCPAC that there was confirmed damage to two Japanese destroyers and a cruiser making a supply run to Guadalcanal."

"Sea or air?"

"Sea, Sir."

"I don't think you came all the way over here to report on the—what did you call it?—the Friday Morning."

"No, Sir."

"Well, let's have it."

"Sir, I have certain obligations as your deputy—"

"Cut the crap," Pickering interrupted. "Get to the point."

Rickabee's face tightened.

"I consider it my duty, General, to make it clear to you that in my professional judgment, your intended operation to relieve the men at Buka is ill-advised; it has very little chance of success; it will require the expenditure of assets, personnel, and matériel that are needed elsewhere; and it is of questionable legality."

After a moment Pickering asked, "Anything else?"

"Yes, Sir. There is a very good chance that when word of it gets out, you will be relieved as Director of the Office of Management Analysis. I would hate to see that happen, Sir, for both selfish and personal reasons."

"Selfish?"

"Yes, Sir. We need somebody who can go to Admiral Leahy directly when we need something."

Pickering poured a cup of coffee for himself. He held the pot up as an offer to Rickabee, who shook his head, no. And then he put the cup to his lip.

He lowered it without taking a sip.

"The operation goes," he said. "I appreciate your candor, Rickabee."

"Aye, aye, Sir. I thought that would be The General's reaction."

"We're back to 'The General,' are we?" Pickering asked.

Rickabee ignored the remark. He reached into the lower, bellows pocket of his blouse and took out an envelope.

"I had Sessions make this up last night, Sir," he said. "There are copies for Dillon, that's his; and for McCoy, Moore, and Sergeant Hart. They will be on the courier plane from Pensacola arriving at Anacostia about seventeen hundred."

Pickering took what Rickabee handed him and read it.

"You'll have to sign the endorsement, General. That's just to show you what it will look like when we're done. I thought about getting Major Dillon a set of ONI Special Agent credentials—McCoy, Moore, and Hart already have them, of course—but I thought that might cause people to ask questions we don't want asked."

Pickering's original orders on White House stationery, signed by Admiral Leahy, had been photographed and reduced in size by half, printed, and placed within sheets of cellophane, stapled shut.

THE WHITE HOUSE
Washington, D.C.

3 September 1942

Brigadier General Fleming W. Pickering, USMCR, Headquarters, USMC, will proceed by military and/or civilian rail, road, sea and air transportation (Priority AAAAA-1) to such points as he deems necessary in carrying out the mission assigned to him by the undersigned.

United States Armed Forces commands are directed to provide him with such support as he may request. General Pickering is to be considered the personal representative of the undersigned.

> General Pickering has unrestricted TOP SECRET
> security clearance. Any questions regarding his mission
> will be directed to the undersigned.
>
>   W. D. Leahy, Admiral, USN
>   Chief of Staff to the President

"Turn it over, General," Rickabee said. Pickering did so.

OFFICE OF THE CHIEF OF STAFF TO THE PRESIDENT
Washington, D.C. 24 September 1942
1st Endorsement

1. The following personnel of my personal staff
are engaged in carrying out the mission assigned
to the undersigned by the Chief of Staff to The
President.

Dillon, Major Homer J USMCR 17724
McCoy, 1st Lt Kenneth R USMCR 489657
Moore, 2nd Lt John M USMCR 20043
Hart, Sgt George F USMCR 2307887

2. All provisions regarding travel priori-
ties, logistical support and access to classified matériel specified in the basic order apply
to the personnel listed hereon.

3. Any questions regarding the listed personnel or their mission will be referred to the
undersigned.

Fleming Pickering
Brigadier General, USMCR

"Very impressive, Rickabee," Pickering said. "You think this will do it, so far as getting them on airplanes, et cetera?"

Rickabee handed Pickering a typewritten copy of the endorsement and a fountain pen.

"When you sign that endorsement, General," Rickabee said, "we'll photograph it, reduce it, and heat-seal the whole thing in plastic, like an ID card. With that White House stationery, it should be a very impressive document. In any event, it's my best shot at getting done what has to be done without people all over Washington asking questions."

Pickering signed it and handed it back.

"Thank you," Pickering said. "Considering your overall objections to the whole idea, I'm grateful to you."

"General, *your deputy* felt obliged to make you aware of his best judgment," Rickabee said. "This *Marine* hopes you get away with it."

XIII

[One]
SUPREME HEADQUARTERS
SOUTH WEST PACIFIC OCEAN AREA
(FORMERLY, COMMERCE HOTEL)
BRISBANE, AUSTRALIA
27 SEPTEMBER 1942

Five people in Australia were cleared for material classified
TOP SECRET—MAGIC: the code name assigned to what was
then regarded as the most important secret of the war. Navy
cryptographers at Pearl Harbor had broken some—but not
all—of the codes used by the Imperial General Staff to communicate with the Imperial Japanese Army and Navy.

In theory, of those at SWPOA, only General Douglas
MacArthur and his intelligence officer, Brigadier General
Charles A. Willoughby, were authorized access to MAGIC
messages.

Neither General MacArthur nor General Willoughby, however, had the cryptographic training or the time to decode such
messages. Consequently, two others at SWPOA administered
the MAGIC program. After Navy cryptographers at Pearl

Harbor had decoded and analyzed an intercepted Japanese message, both the message and its analysis were encrypted using an American code (which was restricted to MAGIC) and transmitted to SWPOA. There the analysis and message were decoded and placed before General MacArthur and General Willoughby.

The people who did this were First Lieutenant Hon Song Do, Signal Corps, U.S. Army Reserve, and Mrs. Ellen Feller, a civilian employee of the Navy Department who was accorded the assimilated rank of a lieutenant commander. In addition, Major Edward F. Banning, USMC, Commanding Officer of USMC Special Detachment 14, was cleared for access to MAGIC. Banning knew enough about cryptography to operate the cryptographic machine.

"Pluto" Hon, as he was known, was a very smart young man. He held a Ph.D. in mathematics from MIT and he was a trained cryptographer. That is to say, he was familiar with the esoteric theories of that craft and not just a man who knew how to work the code machine. That wasn't all that made Lieutenant Hon impressive: Hon, whose ancestry was Korean, read and spoke Japanese fluently, and understood Japanese culture better than practically anyone else you were likely to find in the United States Armed Forces. And he was as good an analyst and cryptographer as anyone you were likely to meet at Pearl Harbor. Indeed, he'd been stationed there before being sent to General MacArthur's headquarters.

Another of the best-kept secrets of Supreme Headquarters, SWPOA, was that Hon was a regular at General and Mrs. MacArthur's after-dinner bridge parties. Most often Hon and General MacArthur were partners. The General liked to win.

Of the three people who administered the MAGIC program at SWPOA—Banning, Feller, and Hon—Major Banning was senior. He was of course senior in grade to Lieutenant Hon. And as a serving officer of equivalent grade, he was senior to Mrs. Feller. All the same, Major Banning was very much aware that the one person of the three who really knew what he was doing was Lieutenant Hon. In other words—and the irony wasn't lost on Banning—the one real expert was the lowest-ranking member according to military hierarchy.

This rarely posed problems for him or for Lieutenant Hon. Or rather, this rarely posed problems *between* them. The problems were caused by the third member of the team, Mrs. Ellen Feller.

Mrs. Feller rather liked her role as a senior civilian.

Mrs. Feller came to Australia over a long and convoluted route. Her husband was the Reverend Glen T. Feller, of the Christian & Missionary Alliance. Before the war Reverend Feller had brought Jesus to the heathen of China and Japan. As a result of this experience, Mrs. Feller spoke Japanese and Chinese—though not nearly as well as she believed she did. When the Reverend Feller decided to pass the war years bringing the word of Jesus to Native American Heathen in the American Southwest, Mrs. Feller (who didn't like her husband very much) sought and found employment as an Oriental Languages Translator in the Navy Department in Washington.

When Fleming Pickering was commissioned into the Navy as a captain, he needed a secretary with the necessary clearances, and Mrs. Feller proved acceptable to him. Later, shortly after the fall of Corregidor, Pickering came to Australia. Once there, he realized that Lieutenant Pluto Hon, as brilliant and competent as he was, couldn't handle the tremendous work load on his own. As a result, he dispatched an URGENT radio to Secretary of the Navy Frank Knox requesting immediate reinforcement. Secretary Knox dispatched Pickering's former secretary.

It didn't take Major Ed Banning and Lieutenant Pluto Hon long to learn to detest Mrs. Feller, though of course each man kept his opinion private. The lady was a three-star bitch . . . no, a four-star bitch. Of that neither had any doubt.

In fact, she was worse than that; she was dangerous—and they had little doubt of that either.

For one thing, as far as Lieutenant Hon was concerned, virtually all of Mrs. Feller's analyses of MAGIC intercepts failed to catch the point of the Japanese originals. Hon credited this failure to her remarkably shallow knowledge of Japanese culture and modes of thought. Though she was shallow, that didn't mean she wasn't clever. She was as aware as Hon was that her work was weak. So she simply used his, much of the time. Often, when his own analyses disagreed in one way or another with the ones from Pearl Harbor, she "appropriated" Hon's and passed them off as her own. Thus, the analyses Mrs. Feller brought to the attention of Generals MacArthur and Willoughby were frequently not hers but his. Indeed, she had

General Willoughby convinced that she was not only a very attractive lady, indeed, but a brilliant one.

It didn't take Major Banning long to pick up on Mrs. Feller's dishonesty; his contempt for the lady had its source there. But his contempt went further than that. When Captain Fleming Pickering was in Australia, he showed an outrageous disdain for the proper security of classified documents. He left them lying all over the houses he rented.

In consequence, Banning arranged for agents of the Army's Counterintelligence Corps to sweep Captain Pickering's quarters whenever he left them. Since he didn't trust Mrs. Feller on general principles, he kept the sweep in operation after Captain Pickering's departure.

At the end of his stay in Brisbane, Pickering rented a house near the racetrack called Water Lily Cottage. After Pickering left Australia, Mrs. Feller and Sergeant John Marston Moore occupied the cottage.

Sergeant Moore, also the son of missionaries, had been sent to Special Detachment 14 as a Japanese linguist. Because of Moore's profound understanding of Japanese language and culture, Hon attempted to enlist Moore in the MAGIC analysis process without letting him know about MAGIC itself. The attempt—encouraged by Pickering, energetically opposed by Banning—was a failure . . . at least if anybody hoped to keep Moore from learning about MAGIC. It took him about two days to figure out that the documents he was analyzing had to have come from intercepted and decoded Japanese messages.

Pickering's solution to that was to add Moore to the MAGIC list—on his own highly questionable authority. Pickering's decision caused Banning not a few problems, especially after Pickering left Australia. For instance, because the First Sergeant and Company Commander of the Headquarters Company could not be told that Moore was analyzing intercepted Japanese messages for the Supreme Commander, these men often decided that Sergeant Moore's contribution to the war effort should be as Charge of Quarters or Sergeant of the Guard. To spare Moore from these tasks, and to get him as far as possible out-of-sight-out-of-mind, Banning moved Moore into Water Lily Cottage.

It took the thorough agents of the CIC only a few days to learn that Mrs. Feller was taking Sergeant Moore into her bed.

Indeed, the agents were aware that she had taught him sexual acts that were specifically proscribed by military regulation.

When CIC informed Banning of this illicit relationship, he did nothing to end it. For one thing, it didn't surprise him. For another, maybe getting a little would improve the bitch's personality. For another, calling her attention to it would make it obvious to her that she was under CIC surveillance. For another—and this was the deciding factor: Mrs. Feller arrived in Australia on the same day Captain Pickering left for Guadalcanal. According to CIC, on that day Mrs. Feller went straight from the airport into Captain Pickering's bed. After learning this, Banning realized that his hands were tied where Mrs. Ellen Feller was concerned. He could complain to only one person about her, and that person was Fleming Pickering, and that was a hornet's nest he decided not to disturb. He told this to no one, not even Pluto.

It didn't take Mrs. Feller long to prove that she was not only very skilled in protecting her ass, but dangerously ruthless in doing so.

Shortly after the Guadalcanal invasion, the First Marine Division G-2 and most of the Japanese-language interpreters of the division were killed in action. The Marine Corps liaison officer at SWPOA received orders to go to Guadalcanal as the G-2's replacement. Because he was a Japanese linguist, similar orders went to Sergeant John Marston Moore. No one in Headquarters, USMC, knew that he was privy to MAGIC and should be kept far away from any place where there was the slightest risk of his falling into enemy hands.

Mrs. Feller, meanwhile, saw in his sudden transfer the chance to end a potentially sticky situation. As nice a boy as he was, John was only a sergeant; and senior civilian employees with the assimilated rank of lieutenant commander should really not be cavorting in bed with common enlisted men. She was only too aware that eventually someone would find out.

Knowing full well that Moore should not be sent anywhere near Guadalcanal, Mrs. Ellen Feller not only kept her mouth shut about his MAGIC access, but ordered Moore to say nothing about it either. By the time Pluto Hon and Banning (who was in Townsville with Commander Feldt) learned what was going on, Moore was on a plane for Guadalcanal. And by the time Moore could be ordered off Guadalcanal, he'd been seriously wounded.

That was bad enough. But in Banning's view, this very bad situation just missed becoming a disaster. If Moore had been captured, MAGIC would have been compromised and shut down.

When it was over, Banning fully expected to be relieved or even court-martialed. He was the senior officer of the Office of Management Analysis in Australia, and the responsibility for the failure was clearly his. But Colonel Rickabee had apparently determined that since Moore's transfer was a fluke and that MAGIC was not compromised, he would leave things the way they were.

After the Moore fiasco, Pluto Hon and Ed Banning devised a system for dealing with Mrs. Feller: Her responsibility would now include only the delivery of MAGIC material to MacArthur and Willoughby. She would no longer work the decoding machine or produce analyses of MAGIC intercepts. That suited her fine. The cryptographic facilities, known as the dungeon, were in the basement of the Commerce Hotel. She didn't like it down there, anyway. And she could still present Hon's analyses as her own and thus bask in General Willoughby's appreciation of her genius.

If anything came up that Banning or Hon thought should be delivered to MacArthur personally, they did so. Usually Pluto would slip whatever it was to MacArthur before or after a bridge game.

The message from KCY to HWS came in like any other:

HWS, KCY. HWS, KCY. SB CODE.
SWPOA Radio, this is CINCPAC Radio. Stand by to copy an encoded message.

The high-speed operator, an Army staff sergeant, reached for his telegraph key and tapped out KCY, HWS, GA.

CINCPAC Radio, this is SWPOA Radio, go ahead.

He then turned from the radio equipment on the table before him to a fairly large, black device equipped with a typewriter keyboard and put his fingers on the keys.

As the message came in, in five-character blocks, he typed it out. The five-character blocks made no sense at all; and the next stage in the process was equally odd; for his typing did not form letters on a sheet of paper. Rather it made perforations, like Braille, on a narrow strip of paper. This fed out of the side of the machine into an olive drab wastebasket.

Finally the message was finished.

The SWPOA operator turned back to his key and tapped out:

KCY, HWS, UR 09 × 27 × 34 AK.
CINCPAC Radio, SWPOA Radio acknowledges receipt of your message number 34 of 27 September.

Pearl Harbor immediately replied: HWS, KCY, SB CODE.
Pearl Harbor had another coded message to transmit.
The operator tapped: KCY, HWS, H1.

CINCPAC, SWPOA, hold one moment, please.

"Charley," the high-speed operator called to another high-speed operator, "can you take KCY Code on Six?"

The other operator checked his equipment, called out, "Got it," and tapped out, KCY, HWS, GA on his key, and then turned to the tape device by his side.

The staff sergeant who had taken Message 09 × 27 × 34 left his chair, retrieved the perforated tape from the wastebasket, walked across the room to another machine, turned it on, and fed the tape into a slot in the side of the device.

This device was something like a Teletype machine. It had a roll of paper feeding onto a platen, and the keys (but not the keyboard) of a typewriter. After a moment, with a clatter, the decoded message began to appear on the paper.

FROM CINCPAC RADIO PEARL HARBOR
TO SWPOA RADIO BRISBANE
27SEP42 NUMBER 34
TOP-SECRET PKFDD DSDTS HSJS POWST
MNCOI SCHRE

"Shit!" the staff sergeant said softly, and then reached up and pushed the BREAK key. The machine stopped clattering. He pushed the EJECT TAPE button, and the strip of perforated paper began to back out of the device.

He walked to the desk of the officer on duty.

"Sir, I've got a MAGIC," he said.

The officer, a Signal Corps captain, nodded and looked around the room.

"I don't know where the hell Swift is," he thought aloud. "Can you run it down?"

"Yes, Sir," the staff sergeant said. Actually he was glad that PFC Swift, the messenger, was fucking off someplace. It gave him an excuse to get out of the radio room for a few minutes, if only down to the dungeon.

He walked to the steel door of the radio room, took from a peg a .45 in a leather holster on a web belt, strapped it on, and then left.

The radio room was on the roof of what had been the Commerce Hotel. It was necessary to walk down a flight of stairs to reach the elevators. When an elevator came, he rode it to the basement. After that, he went down a long, brick-walled corridor until he reached another steel door. This one was guarded by two soldiers armed with .45 pistols and submachine guns.

"Lieutenant Hon in there?" he asked, jerking his thumb toward the steel door.

"Yeah," the guard said and reached for a telephone. It was a direct line. When he picked it up, the other end—in the cryptographic room behind two more steel doors—rang.

"Lieutenant, there's something out here for you," the guard said, adding "Yes, Sir," and then hanging up. "He'll be right out."

Ninety seconds later, a first lieutenant of the Army Signal Corps, a tall, muscular, heavyset Oriental, came through the door. His sleeves were rolled up and his tie was pulled down.

"Hey, Sergeant," he said in a thick Boston accent, "when did they turn you into an errand boy?"

"When they couldn't find Swifty, Lieutenant," the staff sergeant said.

"Swifty is probably out spreading goodwill, or maybe pollen, among the indigenous population," Lieutenant Hon said. The staff sergeant and the guard laughed.

Lieutenant Hon took the tape, said "Thank you," and went back behind the steel door.

Lieutenant Hon passed through the second of the steel doors, closed and locked it behind him; and then, after setting it up for MAGIC, he fed the tape into his code machine. When it began to clatter, he read the message that came out:

```
FROM CINCPAC RADIO PEARL HARBOR
TO SWPOA RADIO BRISBANE
27SEP42 NUMBER 34

TOP SECRET—MAGIC
FOLLOWING NON LOG SERVICE MESSAGE FROM RICKA-
BEE WASHINGTON FOR BANNING BRISBANE

X START X THREE OFFICER ONE ENLISTED SPECIAL
DETACHMENT 14 AUGMENTATION TEAM DEPARTED SAN
DIEGO BY AIR WITH 800 POUNDS SPECIAL EQUIPMENT
0730 27SEPT42 X ADVISE ARRIVAL YOUR STATION X
REGARDS FROM BRIG GEN PICKERING X BANNING X END
```

Lieutenant Pluto Hon wondered idly why Banning was getting three more officers. What will he do with them? he asked himself. And what's the 800 pounds of special equipment? At the same time he was pleased to see the regards from Brigadier General Pickering.

General Pickering. He'd heard a rumor about that. He found it hard to understand how Pickering would get a commission in the Marines. Then he put all that from his mind.

Because it was a Service message, it didn't have to be logged in. Instead, he put a match to it, and the tape, and watched them burn. Banning would certainly call within the next twenty-four hours. When he did, Hon could tell him then that he was getting three officers and a Marine.

The four men and their equipment would probably arrive on either the twenty-ninth or thirtieth. So he called the motor pool and ordered a staff car and a three-quarter-ton truck for those days. Next he decided to put them up at Water Lily Cottage for as long as they were in Brisbane. If Ellen Feller didn't like it—in that marvelous Army phrase—she could go fuck herself.

It did not enter his mind to inform Mrs. Feller herself about the message.

Even though he was a lowly lieutenant floating around in a sea of colonels and generals, all needing wheels, the motor pool gave him no trouble about the vehicles. Three weeks before, he was late for a bridge game with General MacArthur. When he arrived, he apologized, saying that the motor pool had been unable to give him transportation.

"Dick," the Supreme Commander said to Colonel Richard Sutherland, his aide-de-camp, "make sure that doesn't happen to Pluto again."

Lieutenant Pluto Hon didn't think it would. As the man said, when you are a first-rate bridge player you fall heir to a number of social advantages.

[Two]
U.S. ARMY AIR TRANSPORT COMMAND PASSENGER TERMINAL
BRISBANE, AUSTRALIA
1615 HOURS 29 SEPTEMBER 1942

It took some time for the SWPOA telephone operator to even admit to the existence of Lieutenant Hon Song Do; and it took another minute before Hon came on the line.

"Pluto, this is John Moore," Moore said into the phone. He was standing in the passenger terminal next to a counter. The telephone was on the counter.

"John Moore?" Pluto asked incredulously. "Johnny, my God! Where are you?"

"At the ATC passenger terminal."

"We heard you were hurt and sent back to the States—"

"Can you get us some wheels? We'll need a truck, or a jeep with trailer."

It came together in Pluto's mind. Johnny Moore was the Marine in the Special Detachment Augmentation Team that the message from Rickabee mentioned.

"I just checked an hour ago," Pluto said. "There was no plane due from Pearl."

"We went into Melbourne on a Navy PB2Y," Moore replied. "The Army flew us up here on a C-46."

The PB2Y was the Consolidated Aircraft Coronado, a four-engine amphibian Navy transport, while the C-46 was the Curtiss-Wright Commando, a twin-engine, thirty-six-passenger transport taken into the Army as the C-46 and by the Navy as the R5C.

"I turned the vehicles loose," Pluto said. "Can you catch a cab to the cottage? Banning said to put you up there."

"We've got a bunch of stuff with us," Moore said, and then added, "Hold it a minute." There was a pause, and then Moore asked, "Where's Major Banning? Didn't he know we were coming?"

"He's probably at the club; we were going to have dinner there."

"Major Dillon says to tell you to ask him to meet us at the cottage."

Who the hell is Major Dillon?

"I'll get a truck started on its way over there and I'll go by the club and find Banning. Can you all get in the truck or should I come out there and get you?"

"Wait one," Moore said. And then came back on the line. "Major Dillon says he'll get wheels here to take him to the cottage, but we're going to need a truck."

"I'll have one there in twenty minutes," Pluto said. "God, boy, it's good to hear your voice. See you in a little while."

Lieutenant Hon tried to telephone Mrs. Ellen Feller to tell her there would be guests in Water Lily Cottage. But she was not in the office General Willoughby had provided for her in the SWPOA G-2 Section, and there was no answer at the cottage.

He did manage to reach Major Banning at the bar of the Officer's Club.

"Dillon? The only Dillon I know is a Hollywood press agent, and he's in the States running a war bond tour."

"I didn't speak to him, Sir. Just to Sergeant Moore."

"Well, he can't have been hurt as badly as we heard, otherwise they wouldn't have sent him back over here," Banning said. "You be waiting out front, Pluto, I'll be there in ten minutes."

At the time Lieutenant Hon was trying to reach her, Mrs. Ellen Feller was at the Officer's Class Six Store. She had charmed the sergeant in charge there to allow her to exchange the two bottles on her ration of "Spirits, Domestic" (the Army's term for gin, bourbon, or blended whiskey) to "Spirits, Foreign" (brandy, cognac, or similar). The sergeant didn't mind; there was a greater demand for bourbon than for cognac, and Mrs. Feller was one of his very few customers with a great pair of teats.

She went from the Class Six Store to the PX, where she

obtained her weekly ration of Chesterfield cigarettes (twelve packs), Hershey bars (a dozen), and Lux bath soap (three bars). Then she went back to where they were waiting for her in the Chevrolet staff car.

She'd had to beg a ride from the motor pool. Because that bastard Banning was in town, he'd claimed the Studebaker President sedan that was assigned to them.

They dropped her off at Water Lily Cottage about ninety seconds before a staff car pulled into the driveway. When the car drove up, she was on the wide stairs leading to the porch of the large, open, single-floor house. When she saw it, she stopped, turned, and went back down.

A Marine major stepped out of the car.

"May I help you?"

"You're Ellen Feller, right?"

"That's correct."

He put out his hand. "I'm Jake Dillon."

"And how may I help you, Major Dillon?"

"Well, we're going to be staying here for a while," he said. "I hope that won't be too much of an inconvenience."

"Staying here?" she parroted. "I don't think so. These are my quarters."

There was somebody else in the car, getting out of it with difficulty. It was another Marine officer, this one a second lieutenant. The driver had to pull him to his feet.

Banning is obviously behind this. I'll be damned if I will permit that man to turn my quarters into a transient BOQ for every Marine officer who passes through town.

"That's not the way I heard it," Jake Dillon said. There was neither sympathy nor kindness in his voice. He was tired from a practically nonstop flight halfway around the world, and his considerable experience with the opposite sex had permitted him to make an instant assessment of Mrs. Ellen Feller: She was a bitch.

"Oh? And how did you hear it?"

My God, that's Johnny Moore! What is he doing back here?

"Flem Pickering told me he's renting this place," Dillon said. "More to the point, he told me to use it while we're here."

She looked at him and flashed him a bitchy smile. "There must be some misunderstanding," she said. Then she walked to meet John Marston Moore. Moore was rounding the front of the staff car, supporting himself on a cane.

He smiled when he saw her. It was almost a smile of anticipation.

The last time she'd seen him was the day he'd gone off to Guadalcanal. She'd given him a farewell present in Water Lily Cottage that was as good for her as it had been for him.

She watched him closely, wondering if he blamed his going to Guadalcanal on her.

That expression on his face is not sarcastic, or angry. He remembers what we did here together. But my God, he looks awful! And he's even having trouble walking.

"You all right, Moore?" Jake asked. "Need some help?"

"I'm fine, Sir," he said. "Hello, Ellen."

"John, I'm so *glad* to see you!" She wrapped her arms around him and gave him a hug. "What are you doing here?"

"Is Major Banning around, Mrs. Feller?" Jake asked, shutting off any answer Moore might have made.

"I don't know," Ellen said. "I just came home. I don't think so. I don't see the car."

"I guess there's a phone in there?" Dillon asked.

"Yes, of course," Ellen said, smiling at him. "Come in and I'll show you."

"Can you handle the stairs, kid?" Dillon asked.

"I'm fine, Sir."

In a pig's ass you are. You look like hell.

"Is there any booze in the house?" Dillon asked. "You want a drink, Moore?"

"I wouldn't mind a little nip."

"I just happened to buy some brandy," Ellen said. "I like to have it around the house."

They watched as Moore somewhat awkwardly negotiated the steps. And then they followed him into the house.

"Be it ever so plush," Moore said, settling himself on the couch and gesturing around at the luxurious furnishings, "there's no place like home."

Ellen laughed dutifully.

"How many of you will there be, Major . . . Dillon, you said?"

"Two more."

"Things will be a little crowded, then," Ellen said. "But I'm sure we can manage."

Ellen went into the kitchen and put her packages on the sink.

She was taking a glass from the cupboard when she heard the telephone being dialed.

"Admiral Soames-Haley, please," she heard Dillon say. "My name is Dillon. I'm a major in The U.S. Marine Corps."

Rear Admiral Keith Soames-Haley, RAN, Ellen knew, had been a shipping-business friend of Fleming Pickering's before the war. Now he was high up in the hierarchy of the Australian Navy. So Dillon's words to the Admiral did not bother her—initially:

"Admiral, my name is Jake Dillon. I'm just in from the States. I have a letter for you from our mutual friend, Flem Pickering.

"Yes, that's right, Sir. It's General Pickering now. He's pretty much recovered. But knowing what he's like, they're reluctant to let him out of the hospital until he is absolutely fit.

"No, Sir. If you don't mind, General Pickering asked me to deliver the letter personally, Sir, and he hoped that you could give me thirty minutes of your time.

"I understand, Sir. Tomorrow morning would be fine. I'll be at your office at half past eight. Thank you, Admiral. Goodbye, Sir."

But then Ellen had questions: *Why does Fleming Pickering need to use this man Dillon to send a letter to Admiral Soames-Haley? If he wanted to send Soames-Haley a letter, he could have just mailed it. Or sent it via officer courier. And why did Dillon want half an hour of Soames-Haley's time? Not to discuss Pickering's physical condition. What in the world is going on here?*

She put three glasses and one of the brandy bottles onto a tray and carried it into the living room. The brandy was from Argentina, of all places, but surprisingly good.

She heard a door close, and then the unmistakable sound of Jake Dillon voiding his bladder. She put the tray on the table in front of the couch and sat down beside John Marston Moore.

"I'm so glad to see you," she said in almost a whisper. "What's going on?"

He shrugged.

She leaned toward him and kissed him, first on the cheek and then on the mouth. When she did that, she gave him just a little touch of her tongue. But when he tried to pull her closer, she pulled away, gestured toward the sound of the voiding water, and whispered, "Not now. Behave."

All the same, she let her hand run up his leg. She'd concluded that whatever was going on, having Moore on her side was a good idea.

"When did you become an officer?" she asked. Her hand was still on his leg.

"A couple of weeks ago," he said.

"I'm surprised that they sent you back—because of the cane, I mean."

He shrugged again.

Damn, he's not going to tell me anything. Not without a little encouragement, anyway.

She stood up and opened the bottle of Argentinian brandy, poured a good half inch of it into a snifter, and handed it to Moore.

He drank it hungrily, surprising her.

"That was medicinal," he said. "Now I'll have a social one if you don't mind."

"Are you in pain?"

"No," he lied. "It was a long ride in those airplanes," he said. "I'll be all right."

"Poor baby," she said, and poured more brandy into his glass.

When Jake Dillon came into the room, she was sitting with her legs modestly crossed in an armchair across from the couch.

"Help yourself, if you don't mind, Major," she said.

"Thank you," he said, and poured a healthy snort into his snifter.

"How's the leg?" he asked Moore.

"Legs, plural," Moore said. "I'm damned glad to get off them."

As he spoke they heard the sound of tires on the gravel of the driveway. After that, a car door slammed, and then they heard feet crossing the porch.

Banning saw Dillon before Dillon saw him.

"I thought you were supposed to be selling war bonds," he said, and then he saw Moore. "I will be double damned! Moore! *Lieutenant* Moore. How are you, John?"

Banning walked quickly to the couch and held out his hand.

"I'm doing just fine, Sir," Moore said. "It's good to see you, Sir. Hey, Pluto!"

Dillon waited until Hon had shaken Moore's hand, and then

he said, "He is not fine. He can barely stagger around with a cane."

"Then why is he here?" Banning asked.

"Because he told Brigadier General Pickering that he wanted to come, and Brigadier General Pickering said, 'Good boy.' "

"What the hell is this all about, Jake?"

"Why don't we wait until the other two get here, and we can get it all over at once?"

"Who's the other two?"

"Your friend Killer McCoy and a sergeant named Hart."

Ellen Feller was acquainted with Ken McCoy. And she was not happy to learn that he was on his way.

Oh, my God! I thought I'd seen the last of Ken McCoy for a while. Forever. When I woke up this morning, everything was going just fine. I've even got Willoughby just about convinced that the G-2 of SWPOA needs his own Intercept Analysis section, and that I'm obviously the person to run it. But then Moore, and now McCoy! It never rains but it pours!

During the last days that the Marines were in China, Corporal Kenneth R. McCoy was a member of the detachment of the Fourth Marines dispatched to escort the personnel and baggage of the Christian & Missionary Alliance Mission from Nanking to their evacuation ship in Tientsin.

It turned out that Corporal McCoy was a very unusual Marine enlisted man. For one thing, Mrs. Ellen Feller found that Corporal McCoy was really very sexy. For another, she was all too aware that he could be very dangerous. This was especially apparent when he discovered that the luggage of the Rev. and Mrs. Glen T. Feller contained a considerable quantity of jade artifacts and jewelry. The export from China of such artifacts was forbidden.

Mrs. Feller defused the situation by taking McCoy into her bed.

Unfortunately, the affair almost got out of hand; the damned fool fancied he was in love with her. The result was an unpleasant scene on the ship just before it sailed. Afterward, she worried for a long time that he would take revenge and turn her in over the jade. But when the Fourth Marines were transferred to the Philippines, her fear vanished—forever, she thought. There was no way they were going to get out of the Philippines, not with the Japanese there. And even if he survived the war, no one would care about jade removed illegally from China in 1941.

The trouble was that McCoy seemed to have nine lives. He got out of the Philippines somehow and showed up in Washington, as a fresh-from-OCS second lieutenant. The last she heard of him he was in the 2nd Raider Battalion. He survived the Makin Island raid, too, just as he'd survived the Philippines.

The bastard has more lives than a cat!

And what is he . . . what are all of them doing here now?

"Who's the sergeant with McCoy?" Banning asked.

"Interesting guy," Dillon said. "He used to be a detective on the vice squad in St. Louis. Rickabee plucked him out of Parris Island and made him Pickering's bodyguard."

"What's he doing here?" Banning asked.

"He's here because he told Brigadier General Pickering that he wanted to come," he said, using the line he'd used for Moore, "and Brigadier General Pickering said, 'Good boy.' "

"In other words, you're not going to tell me?"

"Not until McCoy and Hart get here, and Mrs. Feller goes shopping or something," Dillon said.

"Major Dillon," Ellen Feller said coldly, "I don't know if you're aware of this or not, but I hold the same security clearances as Major Banning."

"I didn't know that, Mrs. Feller," Jake said. "But what I do know is that General Pickering told me that the less you know about this the better."

"You won't mind, will you, Major," she said, "if I verify that with General Pickering?"

"I wish you would," Dillon said calmly. "But for the moment, I'd be grateful if you could find something else to do for an hour or two. Here comes a truck. I suspect McCoy and Hart are on it."

"How am I supposed to do my job if I am denied access to . . . whatever is going on around here?"

"Mrs. Feller, I'm just a simple Marine," Jake Dillon said. "General Pickering gave me an order and I'm going to carry it out. He said that the less you know about this, the better."

She stood up, her face white.

Whatever you do now, don't lose your temper! Just get out of here, calm down, and think this through. There is absolutely no

*reason to think you won't be able to deal with this offensive
bastard.*

"Major Banning, may I use the Studebaker?" Ellen asked.

"Are we going to need wheels, Jake?"

"Possibly," Dillon said. "Can't you call and get a staff car?"

"You can't get a staff car this time of night, and you know
it!"

Careful, Ellen! They would love it if you lost your temper!

"I think I can get you one, Mrs. Feller," Lieutenant Pluto
Hon said, and walked to the telephone.

[Three]
LADIES' BAR
MCSHAY'S SALOON & CAFE
BRISBANE, AUSTRALIA
2005 HOURS 29 SEPTEMBER 1942

"What are we doing in here?" Major Ed Banning asked Lieutenant Ken McCoy as McCoy led him into the room and to a
table.

"There aren't as many people in here as in the other bar,"
McCoy said. "I looked through the window."

A waitress came to the table. She stood about five feet tall
and measured nearly that distance around.

"And what can I get for the Yanks?"

"I want a beer, please," McCoy said. "And how about something to eat?"

"What would you like, love?"

"I would like a steak about that thick," he said, holding his
thumb and index finger an inch and a half apart. "Medium."

The waitress laughed. "But you'd settle, right, for fish and
chips?"

"How about scrambled eggs and chips?"

The waitress nodded.

"And for you, love?"

"Just the beer, please," Banning said. He waited until she
was out of earshot, then asked, "Is that why we left the house?
You were hungry?"

"I got you out of there because you were about to get into
it with Dillon and say something you would regret," McCoy
said. "And because I'm starved."

"You understand," Banning said, "that I will have to ask to be relieved?"

"Shit," McCoy said.

"What the hell is that supposed to mean?"

"That I was right in getting you out of there," McCoy said. The beer was delivered in two enormous, foamy mugs. McCoy took a swallow of his and made a face.

"It's warm," he said.

"The Aussies like it that way," Banning said.

"Jesus!"

"They get that from the English," Banning said, and then returned to his original topic. "It has been made perfectly clear that there is considerable doubt in my ability to perform my assigned duties. Under the circumstances I have no choice but to request to be relieved. Can't you see that?"

"Drink your beer," McCoy said.

"I can't understand your reaction to Pickering's idiotic idea," Banning said. "You actually seem to think it can be carried off."

"One, I'm just a simple Mustang who does what he's ordered to do. And, two, yeah, I think it can be carried off."

"Not by me!"

" 'If you're not going to play by my rules, I'm going to take my ball and go home, and fuck all of you!' Right?"

"McCoy, we've been friends for a long time, but don't push it! I'm not a child, and this is not a goddamned game!"

"It really hasn't been a long time, but it does seem like fucking forever, doesn't it?" McCoy said. "My ambition in Shanghai was maybe to make staff sergeant before I retired."

"It's hard to believe all that's happened in the last year, eighteen months."

"I wonder what's happening in Shanghai tonight?"

"Some Jap sonofabitch is driving my Pontiac down the Bund," Banning said, chuckling. "And will probably get laid in my bed later on."

"You never heard anything about Mrs. Banning?"

"No," Banning said softly, flatly.

"White Russians seem able to deal with bad situations," McCoy said.

"What do they call that, 'Whistling in the dark'?"

"She made it from Russia to Shanghai," McCoy said. "That took some doing."

"You don't think Shanghai, under the Japs, would be worse for a white woman?"

"Was that a question or what?"

"A question."

"I don't think the Japs are standing every white face they see against a wall, which is what the communists did to the White Russians. For all you know, she's just in some internment camp with other Americans."

"She's not an American."

"She's an American officer's wife. She can say she lost her passport and her other identification. I think that's what she probably tried to do, and I think she can probably get away with it."

Banning held his empty beer mug over his head.

"Right you are, love," the waitress bellowed.

"I am going to request that I be relieved," Banning said. "Can't you see that I have to?"

"We need you for this goddamned operation, don't be silly."

"That's why Pickering sent Dillon over here, right?"

"Pickering thinks you became too professional, too cold-blooded, and fell under the evil influence of the Australian swabbie."

"What the hell does that mean?"

"What's his name?"

"Feldt, Lieutenant Commander Eric Feldt, and I would appreciate it if you didn't call him an Australian swabbie."

"Pickering thinks that Feldt is too willing to write these guys off. Pickering is thinking like he's still a corporal in France, running around no-man's-land picking up the wounded. The difference, the important difference, is that Pickering has the influence. He's a general."

"What's influence got to do with it?"

"If your man Feldt gets in the way, he's going to get run over."

"That would really be the cherry on the cake," Banning said. "If it wasn't for Feldt there wouldn't be a Coastwatcher Establishment. If they relieve him, it would collapse."

"Then you better tell him not to cross Dillon, because that's the same as crossing Pickering. If he does, he's out on his ass. Your man Feldt works for the Australian Admiral with two names—"

"Soames-Haley," Banning furnished. "Vice Admiral Keith Soames-Haley."

"Right. Who is an old buddy of Pickering's. Dillon's going to see him first thing tomorrow morning, with a letter from Pickering. If it comes to Soames-Haley having to make a choice between Pickering and Feldt, who do you think it will be?"

"Sonofabitch!"

"What you better do is stop insisting this can't be done and start thinking about how it can be."

Banning looked at him for a long moment before replying.

"As you were saying, McCoy, it seems only yesterday that you were a corporal I was defending on a murder charge."

"Yeah, and you wanted me to throw myself on the mercy of the court and take my chances on getting no more than six months or a year in Portsmouth. You didn't even ask me if I was guilty."

Banning's face tightened.

"That was below the belt, don't you think?"

"It's the truth. The Colonel wanted to stay on the right side of the American Consul General and the Italians, and if that meant a corporal had to go to Portsmouth, tough luck for him. And you went along with him."

The reason I'm so goddamned mad, Banning thought, *is that it is the unvarnished truth.*

"I thought you accepted my apology for that," Banning said.

McCoy shrugged. "You brought it up. I was willing to forget it."

The waitress appeared suddenly. In one hand she held two beer mugs. In the other was a plate heaped high with french fried potatoes and scrambled eggs, topped with two slices of toast.

"In other words, you're in agreement with Pickering that I haven't done enough to try to get those two off Buka? Maybe because I don't want to make waves? Because not doing more than I have was the easiest thing to do?"

"I'm very impressed with Pickering," McCoy said.

"That doesn't answer the question."

"OK. Yeah, I am."

"That brings us back to square one. I have to ask to be relieved."

"Who are you going to ask? Rickabee?"

"He's my immediate superior."

"He works for Pickering."

"That whole thing is a sick joke. Pickering has no more right to be a brigadier general than—"

"Than what? Than Jake Dillon has to be a major? Than me to be a lieutenant? Is that what's really bothering you? You think we're all a bunch of amateur Marine officers, ex-enlisted men, who should defer to your *professional* officer-type thinking?"

"Now you've gone too far," Banning said coldly.

"Not quite," McCoy said. "Let me go all the way. Let me tell you *my* orders. From Rickabee, not Pickering. I am to advise him within forty-eight hours of my arrival here whether or not I think you're going to be in the way. If I decide you will be in the way, you'll be on the next plane out of here and you'll spend the rest of the war counting mess kits in Barstow." The Marine Corps operated a large supply depot at Barstow, California.

Banning looked at him as if he could not believe what he just heard.

"I find that hard to believe," he said finally.

"Believe it. They sent me to the 2nd Raider Battalion to see if Colonel Evans Carlson was a communist and needed to be gotten rid of. You're only a major. You're not even in the same league."

"Apparently," Banning replied sarcastically, "you decided Carlson was not a communist."

McCoy ignored him.

"Sessions has his bags packed. He's got that MAGIC clearance that I'm not supposed to know about. You wanted to know why Moore was sent here still using a cane: Moore will fill in for you doing whatever this MAGIC crap is. You want to get relieved, stay on your high horse and Sessions will be on his way here in seventy-two hours."

Banning picked up his beer mug, took a long pull at it, and then burped.

"Well, Lieutenant McCoy, I am relieved to learn that Jake Dillon's not really in charge."

"Don't underestimate Major Dillon, Major Banning," McCoy said.

"I don't want to count mess kits," Banning said.

"That's up to you," McCoy said. "I hope both you and Feldt are around to help while we do this."

"He's not going to like it," Banning said.

"The idea itself, or the challenge to his authority?"

"Either. Both."

"Then you better talk to him."

Banning nodded.

"What do you want from me, McCoy?"

"I want you to punch holes in the plan and then I want solutions to the problems you find."

Banning nodded.

"Ellen Feller's liable to pose problems," Banning said. "The way Dillon ran her off was stupid. He didn't have to tell her to butt out; he didn't have to get her ego involved. She'll be on the back channel to Pickering by morning. If she hasn't already radioed to tell him to let us in on this."

"He won't," McCoy said. "He doesn't want her to get splattered if the shit hits the fan."

"Did you know that your sainted General Pickering was fucking her?"

"No," McCoy admitted, visibly surprised. "You're sure?"

Banning nodded.

"And Lieutenant Moore has enjoyed the privilege of her bed."

"No kidding?"

"Everybody, apparently, but you and me," Banning said, and smiled.

"Everybody but you and Dillon," McCoy said. "But that was as of an hour ago."

"You, too?"

McCoy didn't respond to the question.

"Dillon's quite a swordsman," he said admiringly. "Hart told me he had Veronica Wood in the sack in Washington. He saw them."

"Veronica Wood?" Banning said. "Maybe there *is* more to Dillon than meets the eye."

Their eyes met for a moment, long enough for them both to understand that they'd resolved the problem between them.

"Speaking of women," McCoy said, "do you happen to know if our Lieutenant Howard had a girlfriend over here?"

"Yeah, as a matter of fact, he did. Does. Why?"

"Well, he's like me. No family. His home address is care of USMC, Washington, D.C. We need some really personal details about this girlfriend."

"What for?"

"Radio code, before we go in. Where is thi[...]
she?"

"She's a Navy nurse, assigned to the 4th Genera[...]
Melbourne."

"I want to talk to her," McCoy said. "Right away."

"She knows where he is, incidentally. And so does Steve
Koffler's girl. She's in the RAN. I can have both of them here
by tomorrow afternoon. I'll have to find a phone."

"It'll wait until after I eat," McCoy said. "You're sure you
don't want some of this?"

"If you *insist,* Ken," Banning said, reaching for a french fry.

"I'm glad we're back to 'Ken,' " McCoy said. "Let's keep it
that way."

Banning met his eyes and nodded.

[Four]
WATER LILY COTTAGE
MANCHESTER AVENUE
BRISBANE, AUSTRALIA
1530 HOURS 30 SEPTEMBER 1942

Lieutenant John Marston Moore was lying on the couch with
his legs elevated on two pillows.

"It says here," he said, lowering *The Brisbane Dispatch* and
reaching for a bottle of beer on the coffee table, "that they
made 488 cargo ships last year."

"Who's 'they'?" Lieutenant K. R. McCoy asked. He was
sitting at a table with Lieutenant Hon Song Do, having just
taught General MacArthur's favorite bridge partner the favorite game of Marine enlisted men, Acey-Deucy.

"Us, for Christ's sake!" Moore said.

"I wonder how many they sank?" McCoy asked innocently.
" 'They' meaning the Japs and the Germans."

"You mean despite the Air Raid Warning lady's best ef-
forts?" Moore asked.

McCoy laughed. When he saw the look of confusion on
Hon's face, he said, "Private joke, Pluto. And you go easy on
the suds, Moore."

"Aye, aye, Sir," Moore said, raising the bottle to his lips.

There was the sound of gravel crunching beneath tire wheels.

A minute later the door opened and two Navy nurses walked into the room. They were followed by Major Jake Dillon.

"Ladies, these gentlemen—using the word loosely—are Lieutenants Hon, McCoy, and Moore," Dillon said.

"Banning told me one of them was Australian," McCoy said.

"And these ladies, gentlemen," Dillon said, are Lieutenant Barbara Cotter and her friend Lieutenant Joanne Miller. They came together from Melbourne."

"Whose stupid idea was that?" McCoy said unpleasantly. "There was only supposed to be Howard's girl."

"Jesus, McCoy!" Moore said.

"It was mine, Lieutenant," Barbara said. "I thought they were bringing me here to get some bad news, and I asked her to come with me."

"I don't see any problem, McCoy," Dillon said. They locked eyes for a moment, and then Dillon said, "I was able to tell Barbara that we heard from Joe Howard at eight this morning."

"My name is Hon," Hon said, getting up from the table. "They call me Pluto."

"Barbara," Lieutenant Cotter said.

"Barbara," McCoy said, still unpleasantly, "how much does the other one—"

"Joanne," Lieutenant Miller furnished just as unpleasantly.

"—know about your boyfriend?"

"She knows he's off somewhere I can't tell her, doing something I can't tell her. I am not a fool, Lieutenant."

McCoy looked at Joanne Miller.

"Lieutenant . . . oh shit!"

"Actually, it's Miller," Joanne said.

"What the hell is your problem, McCoy?" Dillon asked.

"They call it 'military security,' Major," McCoy said. "Lieutenant, take this as an order. Everything you know about anything your friend has told you, anything you hear here, anything you might guess here, is TOP SECRET."

"It may come as a big surprise to you, Lieutenant," Joanne Miller said, "but I had actually figured that out myself."

"I didn't mean to jump on you," McCoy said.

"Really?" Joanne Miller asked.

"You come sit by me, Joanne," Moore said, "and I'll be nice to you."

She looked at him and smiled. And then she walked to the couch and sat on the edge of it.

"Jake didn't say what all this was about," Barbara said.

"We need some details," Pluto said. "Personal details, that only you and Lieutenant Howard would know, about your personal relationship."

"Why?" Barbara asked.

"We need a new code," Pluto said. "We have to assume that the code Howard's using now has been broken by the Japanese."

"I don't understand," Barbara said.

"Does he have a private name for you? Or do you have one for him?"

"You mean something like 'Baby' or 'Darling'?"

"Yes, but not those words. They're too general. How about 'Cutesy-poo'? 'Precious Doll'? Something like that?"

"Joe doesn't talk like that," Barbara said.

"I'm surprised," Moore said. "I can think of a dozen unusual terms of endearment I would use if you were my girl."

"That's the end of your beer," McCoy said. "If you can't handle the sauce, leave it alone!"

"Aye, aye, Sir," Moore said and smiled at Joanne Miller.

She surprised him by laying her hand on his forehead.

"How long have you had malaria?" she asked.

"I don't have malaria," he said.

"The hell you don't," she said. "Glassy eyes, high temperature." She looked at Major Dillon. "He has malaria and he belongs in a hospital! Doesn't anybody give a damn?"

"Shit," McCoy said.

"I'm sorry you find that inconvenient, Lieutenant," Joanne Miller said icily.

"Putting him in a hospital right now would be inconvenient."

"People die of malaria, you damned fool!"

"What would they do for him in a hospital that can't be done here?" McCoy asked.

"Well, they would put him on quinine, or a quinine substitute, for one thing. And put him in bed. And they wouldn't give him anything to drink."

"Is there any reason that couldn't be done here? Is there anything else?"

"Well, for one thing, where are you going to get the quinine? And who would take care of him?"

"Nobody's listening to me," Moore said. "I'm all right."

"Major, why don't you take the Lieutenant to the hospital and see that they give her whatever she needs? Maybe you better get a doctor over here to look at him."

Dillon considered that a moment and then nodded.

"You'd better bring a nurse, too," Joanne Miller said.

"We already have two nurses," McCoy said.

She looked at him and decided he was perfectly serious.

"I'm on a seventy-two-hour pass. I can't stay here."

"You've just been placed on temporary duty," McCoy said.

"On whose authority?"

"It can be arranged," Dillon said. "Would you mind coming with me, Lieutenant?"

"I see this," Lieutenant John Marston Moore announced, "as the beginning of a great romance."

"You're a damned fool, you know that?" Joanne said, but when she stood up and looked down at him and saw him smiling, she found herself unable not to smile back.

"Getting back to business," Pluto said, the moment the door had closed after Joanne and Dillon. "There has to be something. Maybe a place. Where did you meet? Under what circumstances? Did you ever"—he hesitated, and then went on—"go to a hotel or something?"

Barbara Cotter smiled, and Pluto thought he saw a suggestion of a blush.

"What was the name of the hotel? Did anything special happen there?"

"The first time I met Joe," Barbara said, half uncomfortably, half amused, "he was sent to me for a blood test. For syphilis. Hell of a way to start a romance, isn't it?" She looked at Pluto. "Is this the sort of thing you want?"

"I think maybe," Pluto said. "Tell me about it."

XIV

Major Jake Dillon returned from the local military hospital with everything necessary to treat a malaria patient, including a doctor. The only thing he didn't have with him was a hospital bed.

"I appreciate your coming over here, Sir," Major Banning greeted the doctor, a Lieutenant Colonel.

The doctor's bearing, haircut, and ribbon-laden tunic told Lieutenant (J.G.) Joanne Miller, NNC, that he had not been recently commissioned into military service from civilian life.

The doctor grunted at Banning and walked to the couch where Second Lieutenant John Marston Moore, USMCR, was resting.

"How do you feel, son?"

"I feel fine, Doctor," Moore said.

"Bullshit," the Colonel said. His ready use of the word con-

361

firmed Joanne's guess that this physician's patients over the years had not been in a position to complain about his bedside manner.

He examined Moore quickly but carefully.

"When did you stop taking Atabrine?"

Moore thought a moment. "About six days ago, Sir."

"Why? Did you really think they were giving it to you just so they could watch you turn yellow?"

"It was . . . inconvenient . . . for me to get more, Sir."

"Yeah, well, you see where that led us. It was inconvenient for me to come over here tonight, and it will be inconvenient to treat you here. You belong in a hospital."

"Colonel," Banning said, "did Major Dillon explain why that—"

"I've seen your orders, Major. I am suitably impressed. I said it would be inconvenient to treat him here, not that it couldn't be done."

"Yes, Sir," Banning said.

"So far as the malaria is concerned, the reason he relapsed is that he interrupted his Atabrine regimen. We put him back on Atabrine and he'll start feeling better by tomorrow morning. Now, what's wrong with your legs?"

"They're all right, Sir."

"Bullshit. You nearly jumped out of your skin when I touched them. Take your pants off."

When Moore hesitated, the Colonel said, "That wasn't a suggestion, Lieutenant. And these ladies are nurses, they've seen men with their pants off before."

Moore started to push his trousers down.

"I don't *know* that, come to think of it," the Colonel said. He looked at Joanne Miller. "You *are* an RN, right? Any specialty?"

"I'm a nurse-anesthesiologist, Doctor."

He grunted and looked at Barbara Cotter. "What about you?"

"I'm a psychiatric nurse, Doctor."

"That probably comes in handy around here," the Colonel said, and then looked at Moore's legs. "Mary, Mother of God! What moron discharged you from a hospital?"

He probed the legs knowledgeably with his fingers. Moore winced.

"Believe it or not, before I became a member of the Palace

Guard, I thought I was an orthopedic surgeon. What did that, a grenade?"

"A grenade or a mortar round."

"Well, there's no sign of infection, but you really need some physical therapy." He looked at the nurses. "Make him walk around, if nothing else. Put him on his belly and force the legs back until the threshold of pain. Fifteen, twenty movements, each leg, four times a day. Got it?"

"Yes, Doctor," they said, almost in unison.

"When I said 'walk him around,' I didn't mean he's to get out of bed or off the couch for more than thirty minutes at a time unless there's a reason. Give him all he wants to eat, aspirin for the pain, and Atabrine every two hours until tomorrow morning, when every four hours will be enough. I'll come back tomorrow. Got it?"

"Yes, Doctor," Barbara said.

"Alcohol, Doctor?" Joanne asked.

"A couple of drinks won't hurt him. Don't let him get fall-down drunk."

Why did I ask that? Joanne wondered.

"Speaking of which, if someone were to offer me some of that Famous Grouse, I wouldn't turn it down," the Colonel said.

"Certainly," Banning said. "I could use one myself. Would you be offended, Sir, if I offered you a bottle of it?"

"Offended? Jesus, how dumb do I look?"

"Just don't tell anyone where you got it, please, Doctor," Banning said.

"If you were trying to be subtle, Major, and trying to tell me to keep my mouth shut about tonight, save your breath. I don't even want to know what you and your people are up to, and I have been around the Service long enough to know what things you talk about and what things you don't."

Thirty minutes after the doctor left, the telephone rang. Banning answered it, and then a moment later announced, "The weather's clearing at Townsville. We can go."

He looked at Pluto Hon. "I just had an unpleasant thought. Will Moore be able to get into the dungeon?"

What in the world, Joanne Miller wondered, *is the dungeon?*

"With a little bit of luck, he won't have to," Hon said. "But yes, Sir. I took care of it."

"And what about the truck and the car?"

"They're supposed to be here," he looked at his wristwatch, "in ten minutes, Sir."

"Let's get Dillon's skis outside, on the porch, so they won't have to come in here," Banning said.

Dillon's skis? Joanne wondered. *Is that what he said, "Dillon's skis"?*

Two large wooden crates were manhandled through the living room and out the door.

"Pluto will come back as soon we find out if that substitution code works—or come up with something that does," Banning said to Moore. "With you sick, I hate to take him. There's no other way."

"I'm all right," Moore said.

"Yeah, sure you are," Joanne heard herself say.

"We're leaving the car for you," Banning said. "You are not, repeat not, to give it to Mrs. Feller under any circumstances."

"Aye, aye, Sir," Moore said.

Banning looked at Joanne Miller. "When Hon comes back, one of you can pick him up at the airport."

Lieutenant (J.G.) Miller decided she did not like Major Ed Banning.

"Aye, aye, Sir," she said, as sarcastically salty as she could manage. As she said it, she came to attention.

Her sarcasm went right over his head.

"Good girl," he said, and smiled and left.

Two minutes later, Lieutenants Miller and Cotter were alone in Water Lily Cottage with their patient.

[Two]
BILLETING OFFICE
OFFICE OF THE HEADQUARTERS COMMANDANT
SUPREME HEADQUARTERS
SOUTH WEST PACIFIC OCEAN AREA
BRISBANE, AUSTRALIA
1905 HOURS 30 SEPTEMBER 1942

There were only two female field-grade officers, a major and a lieutenant colonel, assigned to Supreme Headquarters, South West Pacific Ocean Area. Both of them were nurses. The Lieutenant Colonel was on the staff of the senior medical officer, and she was in charge of whatever concerned Army nurses. The Major was on the staff of the Assistant Chief of Staff, G-4 (Matériel), as the resident expert on medical supplies. Both had elected to live in the Female Bachelor Officer's Quarters provided for the nurses assigned to what was known as Mercy Forward. Mercy Forward was in fact a detachment of the Fourth U.S. Army General Hospital (code name, Mercy) sent to Brisbane from Melbourne to provide medical service for MacArthur's headquarters.

Major R. James Tourtillott, the SWPOA Deputy Headquarters Commandant, explained all this in some detail to Mrs. Ellen Feller, Department of the Navy Civilian Professional Employee (Assimilated Grade: Lieutenant Commander), to explain why there was no Female Field Grade Bachelor Officer's Quarters he could move her into.

"Where have you been living, Mrs. Feller?" Major Tourtillott asked. "Is there some reason you can't just stay there?"

Yes, there is a goddamned reason! Major Ed Banning, that bastard, has turned Water Lily Cottage into a goddamned hospital, complete with two nurses: "Sorry, Mrs. Feller, you'll have to move into a BOQ until this is over. We just have to have your room."

Obviously, there is no reason, no reason at all, why Johnny Moore could not be treated for his malaria—if he really has malaria, he looks perfectly healthy to me—in Mercy Forward. And even if there is some "security reason," as Banning said, for keeping him out of the hospital, there is no reason at all why those two Navy nurses couldn't live in the Nurse's BOQ at Mercy Forward. They're only junior-grade lieutenants, after all, and I'm an assimilated Lieutenant Commander.

"There's a project, Major Tourtillott, a classified project that I can't talk about, that seems to have evicted me."

"I could call Mercy Forward and see if they could put you up with the nurses."

"I don't want to move in with the nurses, for one thing, and for another, I have to be somewhere close to Supreme Headquarters. I'm on twenty-four-hour call."

"I'm sure something can be worked out, Mrs. Feller," Tourtillott said, thinking that the best solution for housing this lame-duck female—*I wonder what the hell she does? As an assimilated Lieutenant Commander, she's no secretary*—would probably be to move her into the Devonshire, a small, luxurious hotel requisitioned to house full colonels and one-star generals; but he couldn't do that without the OK of the Headquarters Commandant. "But not today."

"You don't seem to understand," Ellen Feller said. "I don't have a place to sleep."

Major Tourtillott handed her a printed form.

"This is a billeting voucher on Mason's Hotel," he said. "They'll put you up overnight, and if you'll come back, say at oh nine hundred, oh nine thirty, I'll have you fixed up by then."

"Where is Mason's Hotel?"

"Not far," Major Tourtillott said. "It's the best I can do right now."

The reason I am being humiliated like this is because Banning hates me, has been waiting for an opportunity to humiliate me, and now he's found it in spades. Not only is he denying me access to whatever he and that offensive Major Jake Dillon are up to, but he is rubbing that humiliation in my face by ordering me out of Water Lily Cottage.

He thinks he can just order me around like I'm one of his Marines.

And he thinks there is absolutely nothing I can do about it, because he's the senior Office of Management Analysis officer . . . even if my assimilated rank is equal to his.

Well, we'll see about that! Fleming Pickering won't let him get away with this, once he hears about it!

Room 6 of Mason's Hotel turned out to be a small, more or less square room on the upper floor of a fifty-year-old, wood-framed, tin-roofed, two-story building.

There was a bed with a visibly sagging mattress; a chest of drawers; a mirror which had lost at least half of its silver backing; a table against a wall; a straight-backed chair; a bedside table with a 25-watt lamp on it; and a bare 100-watt bulb hanging from the ceiling. There was a sink; and behind a curtain there was a tin-walled cubicle with a shower head and concrete floor. The toilet was down the corridor.

Mrs. Ellen Feller moved the 25-watt lamp from the bedside table to the table against the wall, pulled the chair up to it, and spent the next two hours composing a message to Brigadier General Fleming Pickering. It would go out that very night over the MAGIC channel, she decided, even if that meant she would have to pay for a taxi all the way out to the Supreme Headquarters, SWPOA building, spend thirty minutes in Pluto

Hon's damned damp dungeon, and then either beg a ride back here from the staff duty officer or pay for another damned taxi.

Putting her thoughts on paper, however, turned out to be much more difficult than she initially imagined. Her first draft, quickly balled up and tossed on the floor, sounded like whining. And that wouldn't do. To win her point, she had to paint herself as a member of the team who had been unjustly excluded from team activities.

Neither was Fleming Pickering going to be automatically sympathetic to her eviction from Water Lily Cottage, she realized. Banning would just tell him that John Moore's nurses needed her room.

Maybe Johnny Moore really has malaria.

And then, slowly, as her fury waned, she saw other problems. For instance, she wasn't entirely sure that Fleming Pickering would even get her carefully worded message. It would have to pass over Rickabee's desk. And Colonel Rickabee and that bastard Banning were not only brother Marine officers, but personally close. Even if she sent it EYES ONLY PICKERING, Rickabee would see it. He would be prepared to argue Banning's case by the time he handed it to Pickering.

And she couldn't send it EYES ONLY PICKERING and still look like a member of the team registering a justified complaint. Rickabee was Banning's immediate superior, not Pickering. Any complaints should be directed to him.

And finally, of course, that rude bastard Dillon just might have been telling the truth. Pickering himself just might have told him to keep Ellen Feller out of whatever it was they were doing.

Finally, she gave up. She retrieved all the crumpled-up balls of paper and put a match to them.

There were more than two ways to skin a cat.

General Willoughby was proud and sensitive about his role as MacArthur's intelligence officer. He would not be at all pleased to learn that a clandestine intelligence operation, directed from Washington, was being conducted right under his nose.

Let Willoughby send an EYES ONLY to Washington—either on his own or at MacArthur's direction.

It wouldn't be hard for Willoughby to "find out." She'd go to the dungeon in the morning, and she would personally carry to General Willoughby the first MAGIC that came through.

Willoughby almost always wanted to chat a little. He'd offer her a cup of coffee and she'd accept it, of course.

She would, she decided, wear the white cotton see-through blouse Willoughby always seemed to find so fascinating.

On that happy note, Mrs. Ellen Feller (Assimilated Grade: Lieutenant Commander) took off her clothing, climbed into the bed with the sagging mattress, and went to sleep.

[Three]

At half past nine, Lieutenant (J.G.) Joanne Miller, NNC, came back into the living room. Second Lieutenant John Marston Moore, USMCR, was regally established there in a high-backed armchair, his feet on its matching footstool. He was wearing a hospital bathrobe, pajamas, and slippers. A card table had been arranged so that Joanne could sit on one side and Lieutenant (J.G.) Barbara Cotter on the other. The three of them had been playing gin rummy.

Joanne had gone into the kitchen to make a fresh pot of tea and to get Lieutenant Moore's Atabrine. She had refused his request for another beer, and he had somewhat surprised her by not giving her an argument. Usually, when he asked for a beer and she turned him down, he gave her an argument. And that was beginning to get to her. But then he began to annoy her in a different way. Every time she glanced at him, she saw that he was looking at her.

He's just a kid, a horny kid, she thought. *If I ignore him, he'll stop.*

He swallowed the Atabrine, washing it down with a swallow of Coca-Cola.

"How old are you?" she heard herself asking.

"Twenty-two," he said.

"You don't look it."

She saw the strange look on Barbara's face.

"Did I do something wrong, or what?" Moore asked.

I'm twenty-four. What right have I got to think of him as a kid?

"That just slipped out. Sorry."

"I thought you were going to tell me it was past my bedtime or something," he said.

"It is."

He looked at his watch.

"Please, Mommy," he said. "It's only half past nine. Can't I stay up till ten?"

"I said I was sorry," she said. "I really don't give a damn if you stay up all night. I'm going to bed."

Barbara flashed her another *what's-wrong-with-you?* look.

"Just a couple more hands, John," Barbara said. "It's been a long day for me, too."

Joanne went into the bedroom recently vacated by Ellen Feller and started to prepare for bed. She had just emerged from the shower when she heard the telephone ring. A minute later Barbara called her name.

Joanne put on her bathrobe and went into the living room in time to see John Moore walking awkwardly across the room to the couch. He picked up his cane and then went into his bedroom.

"He says he has to go out," Barbara said, and gestured toward the telephone.

"Like hell he's going out!"

She pushed the door to his bedroom open. Moore was pulling his pajama top over his head.

"What do you think you're doing?"

"I've got to go to the dungeon," he said. "I'd be grateful if one of you would drive me."

"You're not going anywhere."

"Hey," he said, almost nastily, "enough of this 'me Mommy and you Little Boy' bullshit. I have to go to the dungeon. They called. I'm going."

"What the hell is the dungeon?"

He didn't answer her. He found a T-shirt and pulled it over his head. After he stuck his arms in the sleeves of a shirt, he looked at her.

"The dungeon is what they call the cryptographic room. It's in the SWPOA basement. A message there has to be decoded."

"And they don't have a cryptographic officer on duty? Why do you have to go?"

Again, he didn't reply. He turned his back to her and dropped his pajama trousers. She could see the scars on his legs. He almost fell over putting his undershorts on.

When he reached for his trousers, she went to him.

"Let me help you," she said, much more fiercely than she intended. "I don't want you breaking your leg."

He sat on the bed. She dropped to her knees, picked up his

pants, and worked them up his calves. When she looked up at him, she saw him staring down the front of her bathrobe.

She flushed and angrily put her hand to the opening, closed the robe, quickly got to her feet, and turned around.

"I hope you got an eyeful!" she snapped.

She could see him in the mirror over the chest of drawers.

He pushed himself off the bed, stood up, and pulled his trousers up. He had an erection. It stood there defiantly until he had tucked his shirt in and buttoned his waistband. As he pushed himself inside his fly and zipped himself up, he said, "If you didn't want me to look, why did you come in here dressed like that?"

A wave of anger swept through her. She spun around and slapped him as hard as she could, so hard that he fell backward onto the bed.

"You *bastard!*" she hissed.

And then, as quickly as it came, the anger passed and she realized what she had done.

"Jesus!" he said, shaking his head.

Joanne fled the bedroom, crossed the living room without looking at Barbara, went into their bedroom, and slammed the door.

She leaned against the bedroom door, breathing heavily.

A moment later she heard him ask, "Where's the keys to the Studebaker?"

"You shouldn't be going out," Barbara said.

"Give me the damned keys!" he said.

"I'll drive you," Joanne heard Barbara say. She heard the front door close. After that, the engine started, and then the headlights swept across the window curtains.

She pushed herself off the wall and went and sat on the edge of her bed.

"It's all right, I'm awake," Joanne said when Barbara came into their room without turning on the light. They had been gone two hours.

Barbara turned the lights on and started to get undressed.

"Is he all right?"

"I just gave him his eleven-thirty Atabrine," Barbara said.

"What was that all about?" Joanne asked. "Did you get to see the dungeon?"

"No. They wouldn't let me in there. Whatever it is, it's in the basement of the SWPOA headquarters building. But I did get to see General MacArthur."

"*MacArthur?* Really?"

"Yeah. In the flesh. First we went down in the basement. They made me wait outside—"

"Who made you wait?"

"A couple of sergeants with submachine guns made me wait outside a steel door. John went inside, he was in there I guess almost an hour, and then he came back out. Then we got back on the elevator, and he said, 'Now you'll get a chance to see how the other half lives,' and we rode up to the seventh floor. More sergeants with submachine guns.

"One of them said, 'The Supreme Commander is expecting you, Lieutenant.'"

"Really?"

"And the sergeant opened a door, and John said, 'I'll be right out,' and went in. MacArthur was standing right inside, walking around with a cup of coffee."

"And?"

"John said, 'Good evening, General.' And MacArthur said, 'Where's Pluto?' and John said, 'He had to go to Townsville, Sir,' and handed him a folder with a TOP SECRET cover sheet. MacArthur read it and grunted. Then he asked, 'Has General Willoughby seen this?' and John said, 'No, Sir. I just decoded it,' and MacArthur said, 'I'll see that he gets it.' And then he said, 'Have I met you before, Lieutenant?' and John said, 'I was stationed here before, Sir, as a sergeant.' And MacArthur said, 'Yes, of course, you're the fellow they sent to Guadalcanal by mistake. I'm glad to see you're recovered.'"

"Recovered, in a pig's eye!" Joanne interrupted.

"You want to hear what happened or not?" Barbara asked.

"Go on."

"So then MacArthur laid his hand on John's shoulder, sort of patted him, and said, 'I'm sorry you had to come here this late at night. When did you say Pluto will be back?' and John said, 'Probably tomorrow, Sir,' and MacArthur grunted and walked him to the door. 'Good night, son. Thank you,' he said, and then he saw me and smiled and nodded. What do you think about that?"

"I hope you're not making it all up," Joanne said.

"Well, you can go to hell!" Barbara said. She went into the bathroom.

"I'll give him his one-thirty," Joanne called after her, then rolled on her side and stretched her arm out for the alarm clock so she could set it.

Joanne pushed open the door to John Marston Moore's room and walked to the side of his bed, using her flashlight.

"Pill time," she said. "Shield your eyes, I'm going to turn the light on."

"I'm not asleep. Turn it on."

She turned the bedside table lamp on. He pushed himself up against the headboard.

"Trouble sleeping?" she asked.

She dumped two Atabrine pills from the bottle, handed them to him, and then handed him a glass of water.

"Yeah," he said after he swallowed the Atabrine.

She sat down on the bed, stuck a thermometer in his mouth, and started to take his pulse.

He smelled of soap. She remembered hearing the sound of running water half an hour after Barbara finished her shower and climbed in bed. She almost got up then to make sure he didn't fall down and hurt himself. But it occurred to her that he had been managing showers by himself with no trouble before Joanne Miller, RN, started taking a professional interest in his physical welfare. She realized he didn't need her help now.

That kept her from making a fool of herself. She did not get out of bed. She lay there, with a clear image of him in the shower. The scars on his leg. His legs. His chest. His rear end. What he had to tuck in his pants just before she slapped him for looking down her robe at her breasts. As a nurse, that word—for what he stuck inside his pants—meant nothing much to her. As a nurse, she used it easily, professionally. But now was something else . . .

"What's the matter?" she asked. "Why can't you sleep?"

"You are," he mumbled around the thermometer.

"Sssssh," she said. She wondered if her face was really flushed, or whether it just felt that way.

There was nothing wrong with his heartbeat. And when she took the thermometer from his mouth, she saw that his temperature was only slightly elevated.

"Your temperature has dropped," she said.

"That's surprising," he said.

She gave him a professional smile and then looked at his eyes to see if the pupils were dilated.

That was a mistake. I didn't assess the diameter of his pupils. I fell in.

"I'd like to apologize for . . . before. I shouldn't have slapped you."

His hand is on my cheek. Why don't I push it away? Or get up?

"Jesus, you're beautiful!"

"You shouldn't be doing that," Joanne said. "I shouldn't let you do that."

"Look at me again," he said.

"No!"

"Look at me again!"

I knew if I did that, this would happen! Joanne thought as she felt his hands on her back, pulling her to him.

She felt her heart jump when their lips touched. And she felt a weakness in her middle. And she barely had the strength to push away from him.

"This is absolutely insane!"

"Yeah, isn't it?"

His lips were now on her neck.

"We have to stop!"

"Why?"

He's pushing my robe open!

"Barbara! She'll hear us."

He touched her nipple with his tongue, and then looked up at her and smiled.

"She's probably asleep," John said.

Oh, God, I hope she is, Joanne thought as she reached down and pushed John's head back where it had been.

[Four]
FERDINAND SIX
BUKA, SOLOMON ISLANDS
1 OCTOBER 1942

It's either hotter than usual, Sergeant Steve Koffler thought, *or Ian Bruce is getting sick or something, because he's really wheezing as he pumps the pedals of the generator.*

FRD6.KCY. FRD6.KCY AK. KCY CLR.
Detachment A of Special Marine Corps Detach-
ment 14, this is the United States Pacific
Fleet Radio. Receipt of your transmission is
acknowledged. Our exchange of messages is con-
cluded.

Steve did not follow the prescribed procedure, which was to tap out FRD6 CLR before shutting down. It was a waste of goddamned time, and Ian Bruce looked worn out.

He reached for the ON/OFF switch and then stopped.

FRD6, FRD1. FRD6,FRD1. SB CODE.
Detachment A of Special Marine Corps Detach-
ment 14, this is Coastwatcher Radio. Stand by
to receive an encoded message.

What the fuck do they want?

He glanced at Ian Bruce. Ian was looking at him, waiting for the signal to stop pumping. Steve shook his head, made a keep-it-up gesture and replied to Townsville.

FRD1,FRD6. GA.
Go ahead, Townsville.

The message was not unusually long, maybe fifteen five-character blocks, but after Steve sent the usual, FRD1, FRD6. AK, Townsville came right back: FRD6, FRD1. FRD1 SB. FRD1 SB.

Townsville was standing by, waiting for an answer to their message.

Steve made a cutting motion across his throat. It would take him a couple of minutes, at least, to decode the message. Ian Bruce needed a break.

And a bath. I can smell him from here.

"Bloody hell!" Ian Bruce said.

"See if you can find Lieutenant Howard, will you?"

"Right you are."

Both Lieutenant Howard and Sub-Lieutenant Reeves came into the hut before Steve finished decoding the message.

"What the hell is this?" he asked, giving the decoded message to Howard.

USE AS SIMPLE SUBSTITUTION X JULIETS NAME X
ROMEOS NAME X WHAT SHE THOUGHT HE HAD WHEN THEY
MET X NAME OF TEST X RESULT OF TEST X

18 × 19 × 09 × 37 × 11

15 × 23 × 08 × 09 × 11

01 × 02 × 03 × 04 × 05

06 × 07 × 23 × 31 × 05

"They've gone sodding bonkers," Sub-Lieutenant Reeves said, and then added an unpleasant afterthought. "You don't think this could be from our Nipponese chums, do you?"

Steve shook his head. "No," he said. "I recognized his hand."

"I know what simple substitution is," Joe Howard said, "and so should you. But who the hell is Romeo?"

"It would have to be our lad, here," Reeves said. "Neither you nor I are romantically involved at the moment."

"Lay off him," Howard said.

"No offense, Steve, my lad."

"Go fuck yourself," Steve said. "What does that 'what she thought he had when they met' mean?"

"I think I know," Howard said.

He dropped to the dirt floor. They had two pads of message paper left. He picked up one of them. Holding it on his knees, he wrote:

```
BarbaraJosephSyphilisWassermanNegative
```

"My girl's name is Barbara," he said. "Mine is Joseph. I was taking my pre-commissioning physical in San Diego, and the doctor thought I was lying when I told him I'd never had VD. He sent me to the VD ward for a Wasserman."

"I have the oddest feeling that he actually believes he knows what he's doing," Lieutenant Reeves said.

"Barbara was the nurse on duty," Joe added.

Very carefully, he wrote numbers under the letters. When he finished, it looked like this:

```
BarbaraJosephSyphilisWassermanNegative

1234567890123456789012345678901234 5678
```

Then he recopied the numbers so there was space beneath them, and made the translation.

```
18 × 19 × 09 × 37 × 11

I    l    o    v    e

15 × 23 × 08 × 09 × 11

y    a    j    o    e

01 × 02 × 03 × 04 × 05

b    a    r    b    a

06 × 07 × 23 × 31 × 05

r    a    a    n    a
```

"Does that say anything?" Reeves asked.

"Yeah," Joe Howard whispered.

He wrote out two five-character blocks of numbers and handed them to Steve.

"You up?"

"No."

"I'll pump the goddamned bicycle. You get on the air and send that."

"What the hell does it say?" Reeves asked.

"What *they* sent says, 'I love ya, Joe Barbara,' " Steve Koffler said. "The last three letters are fillers, to fill the five-character block. What *he's* replying is none of your business."

The dials came to life. Steve's hand worked the key.

FRD1, FRD6. FRD1, FRD6.
Coastwatcher Radio, this is Ferdinand Six.

FRD6, FRD1, GA.
Ferdinand Six, go ahead.

Steve sent the reply, and then showed it to Reeves.

28 × 38 × 25 × 10 × 10

M   e   T   o   o

01 × 02 × 04 × 15 × 05

B   a   b   y   a

Townsville came right back:

FRD6,FRD1. AK

10 × 23 × 28 × 32 × 10

35 × 38 × 37 × 38 × 01

02 × 12 × 13 × 30 × 38

END

FRD1, FRD6. AK. SB.
Coastwatcher Radio, acknowledged. Standing by.

"Go pump the bike," Steve said. "Let him decode this. Maybe there's more."
There was:

30 × 02 × 35 × 13 × 07

31 × 17 × 11 × 19 × 22

17 × 19 × 19 × 10 × 22

26 × 16 × 23 × 26 × 11

38 × 31 × 14 × 11 × 24

09 × 09 × 31 × 02 × 07

END

Steven sent the reply: FRD1, FRD6. AK. MORE??

The reply came immediately: FRD1. CLR.

"That's it," Steve said as he made the cutting motion across his throat. Reeves stopped pumping.

Steve turned the radio off, stood up, and handed the last message to Howard. After that he hovered over Howard, watching him as he finished decoding the previous message.

$10 \times 23 \times 28 \times 32 \times 10$

S   A   M   E   S

$35 \times 38 \times 37 \times 38 \times 01$

T   E   V   E   B

$02 \times 12 \times 13 \times 30 \times 38$

A   P   H   N   E

"What the hell does that say?"

" 'Same Steve, signed Daphne,' " Howard said.

"Daphne is spelled with a 'D,' not a 'B,' " Steve said.

"There's no 'B' in the substitution, Steve," Howard said. "What sounds closest?"

He started working on the final block of numbers and finally handed that to Steve.

"Take a look at that, Jacob," Howard said. "What do you make of it?"

$30 \times 02 \times 35 \times 13 \times 07$

N   A   T   H   A

$31 \times 17 \times 11 \times 19 \times 22$

N   I   E   L   W

$17 \times 19 \times 19 \times 10 \times 22$

I   L   L   S   E

$26 \times 16 \times 23 \times 26 \times 11$

E   P   A   T   I

38 × 31 × 14 × 11 × 24

E   N   S   E   S

09 × 09 × 31 × 02 × 07

O   O   N   A   A

"Nathaniel Willseep At?" Reeves asked. "What the bloody hell is 'ienses'?"

"Nathaniel will see Patience soon," Howard said.

"There's no 'C' in Patience," Steve said.

"Same thing. You use what you have, in this case an 'S.' The question is, who is Nathaniel? And what the hell does it mean?"

They found Miss Patience Witherspoon washing Steve's spare utility trousers on a rock in the stream. Nathaniel Wallace turned out to be one of her friends when she was at the Mission School.

"Do you know where he is now?" Reeves asked.

"Yes, Sir. He was sent to Australia just before the war to enroll in King's College. Nathaniel is very intelligent. He did very well in school."

"And did Nathaniel know you were going into the bush with me?" Reeves asked very carefully.

"I sent him a note with the *St. James*," Patience said. "Asking him to pray for us."

"What?" Howard asked.

"The *St. James* was the last ship to leave here before the Japanese came," Reeves said. "It wasn't a ship, really, more like a powered launch."

"Bingo," Howard said. "We are about to be reinforced."

He'd caught himself just in time. He was about to say "relieved."

"Is that what you think?" Reeves asked.

"They must know our radio is on its last legs," Howard said. "And that we need supplies."

"But why take the risk of letting us know someone's coming?"

"So we'll be on the lookout for parachutes, prepared to receive them."

"You think they'd do that again?"

"There's no other way."

"And the Japs know it," Reeves said. "And they're looking
for parachutes. And when they break that child's code of
yours, they'll really be looking."

"That child's code isn't going to be as easy to break as you
think," Howard said. "It'll take them a couple of days . . . when
they start on it. And then they have to guess the meaning."

"Submarine," Steve Koffler said. "They could send people in
by submarine."

"I don't think so, Steve," Howard said. "I think we should
start looking for an airplane, and parachutes. Even if they
could talk the Navy out of a submarine, and they managed to
land somebody safely, how could he get here? Especially carrying replacement radios and equipment?"

"He's from here," Steve said. "This Nathaniel is."

"Nathaniel is very intelligent," Miss Patience Witherspoon
said. "And very strong."

[Five]
ROYAL AUSTRALIAN NAVY COASTWATCHER ESTABLISH-
MENT
TOWNSVILLE, QUEENSLAND
1 OCTOBER 1942

"We'll get into specific details later," Major Edward F. Banning said to open the first briefing session for Operation
PICKLE, "so please don't start asking questions until I'm
finished."

Just over twenty people were sitting around the tables of the
mess hall, Australians of the Coastwatcher Establishment and
Marines of Special Detachment 14. Some were drinking coffee
and eating doughnuts. The majority were drinking beer.

"The RAN is going to provide us with a submarine, HMAS
Pelican. It will take a replacement team to this beach. . . ." He
turned and pointed to a map of Buka with an eighteen-inch
ruler.

". . . According to Chief Wallace, it's approximately fifty
yards wide at low tide and has a relatively gradual slope. And
again according to Chief Wallace, it is a twenty-four- to thirty-
six-hour march from Ferdinand Six, which is about here. I

asked him to err on the side of caution. Carrying that equipment in that terrain is going to be a bitch.

"Getting it ashore in rubber boats is going to be a bitch, too. The shallow slope of the beach results in pretty heavy surf under most conditions. We won't know what those conditions are until we get there."

"We?" Sergeant George Hart thought, somewhat unkindly. *What's this we crap?* We're *not going.* These guys *are going.*

"At that time—when the *Pelican* surfaces—a decision will have to be made," Banning went on, "whether to try to land the entire team and all the equipment. If the surf or other conditions make that too risky, then we'll put just Chief Wallace and three other men ashore.

"That decision will be made by Lieutenant McCoy. Lieutenant McCoy's something of an expert on rubber-boat landings. The last one he made was on Makin Island with the Marine Raiders."

Heads turned to look at Lieutenant K. R. McCoy.

That was probably necessary, George Hart decided, *to impress these people. But McCoy sure didn't like it.*

"If it turns out we can only put four men ashore safely, two will immediately start out for Ferdinand Six. Two will remain on the beach. The two on the beach will have two missions. The first is to conduct tests of the beach, to see if the sand there will support the weight of an airplane. That information will be sent to the submarine and then relayed here. After that the submarine will immediately depart the area; it will return the following day. Their second mission will be to tell the submarine, after its return, whether or not it is safe to land the full team.

"Repeated attempts to land the replacement team and its equipment will be made until (a) they are successful or (b) the tests have indicated that the beach will take an aircraft.

"If that proves to be the case, then the aircraft will land there with the second replacement team and its equipment. That will of course solve both the insertion and extraction problems, since the aircraft will take the present team out with it, as well as the two people we insert onto the beach.

"The problem—at least in my judgment—is that the aircraft plan is not likely to work. If it doesn't, then the insertion of the replacement team and the extraction of the people now operating Ferdinand Six will be by submarine."

He looked around the room. "OK, questions?"

"Do I understand, Sir," a young Australian Sub-Lieutenant asked, "that I would be inserted regardless of surf conditions?"

"No," Lieutenant Commander Eric Feldt answered for Banning. "We will land either the entire team or none of it. Except, of course, for Chief Wallace."

"Yes, Sir."

"Question, Sir?" a buck sergeant of USMC Special Detachment 14 asked.

"Shoot."

"In case of bad surf conditions, no radios will go ashore, right?"

"Right. I just said that. The whole team goes in or none of it."

"How will the two people onshore communicate with the sub?"

"The Navy—our Navy," Lieutenant McCoy answered, "has a portable, battery-powered radio. A voice radio. Two of them are being flown in here. It has enough range to reach from the beach to the sub. And about two hours' battery life. If we can't land the whole team, I'll take one of them and a spare set of batteries with me in the rubber boat."

"Yes, Sir. But what about the airplane?"

"What about the airplane?"

"How are you going to communicate with it?"

"Shit!" Lieutenant McCoy said furiously.

"I mean, Sir, if we get it."

"I know what you mean," McCoy said. "Goddamn it, I didn't think about that!"

"Lieutenant," Chief Signalman Nathaniel Wallace, Royal Australian Navy Volunteer Reserve, asked, pronouncing it Lef-tenant, "I think we could probably modify the Navy radio so it would net with the aircraft radios. When did you say they are coming?"

"As soon as they can fly them in. Probably today," McCoy replied.

"I may be wrong, of course, but those types of short-range radios often radiate in the same general area of the frequency spectrum as aircraft radios. I rather suspect that we could make it work."

"Jesus Christ, I hope so."

Chief Signalman Wallace was the ugliest single human being

Sergeant George Hart, USMC, could ever remember seeing. He was also the only Navy man he had ever seen wearing a skirt.

But it wasn't possible to dismiss him as some quaint and ignorant savage out of the pages of *National Geographic* magazine. Hart had already long since realized that his bushy head of hair and blue-black teeth, his scars and tattoos, were not all of him. On the other side of all that was a mind at least as sharp as his own.

For one thing, Nathaniel spoke fluent English—*English* English, like the announcers on the British Broadcasting Corporation's International Service. For another, of the dozen or more radio technicians (including three Marines) who ran the Coastwatcher Establishment's radio station, he probably knew the most about radios, inside and out.

Above the waist, Chief Wallace wore the prescribed uniform for Chief Petty Officers of the RAN. Just as in the American Navy, the senior enlisted rank of the RAN wore officer-type uniforms: Instead of the traditional bell-bottom trousers and a blouse with a black kerchief and flap hanging down the back, they wore a double-breasted business suit with brass buttons, and a shirt and tie. And instead of those cute little sailor hats (as George and most other Marines thought of them), Chief Petty Officers wore brimmed caps with a special Chief Petty Officer insignia pinned on them.

The white crown of Chief Wallace's brimmed cap was not quite as wide as the mass of black, crinkly hair it rode on. It was centered with almost mathematical precision at least three inches over his skull. A neatly tied black necktie was pulled with precision into the collar of his immaculate white shirt. The brass buttons of his jacket glistened, as did his black Oxford shoes. Between the jacket and the shoes he wore a skirt, of blue denim, and knee-high immaculate white stockings. This served to expose incredibly ugly knees and skinny upper legs matted with crinkly hair.

"If we can't get the radio to communicate with the aircraft, McCoy, we could work out some sort of landing panel signals," Banning said.

"With respect, Sir," Chief Signalman Wallace said, "I don't think it will be a problem."

"Any other questions?" Major Banning asked.

"What are these beach tests, Sir?" a USMC Special Detachment 14 corporal asked.

"As I understand it," Major Banning said, "Sergeant Hart has a steel cone he pounds into the sand with a ten-pound weight. He then reads the markings on the cone. The theory is that it can be determined how much weight the sand will support."

"Yes, Sir."

"I'll say it again. Don't count on the airplane."

"Yes, Sir."

What that sonofabitch just said, Sergeant George Hart realized in shock, *was that I'm going to be in one of those rubber boats!*

[Six]
HEADQUARTERS, MAG-25
ESPIRITU SANTO
0730 HOURS 2 OCTOBER 1942

"Come on in, Jack," Lieutenant Colonel Stanley N. Holliman, USMC, Executive Officer of MAG-25, said, waving his hand at Major Jack Finch, USMC.

Major Finch entered the office. He was wearing a wash-faded Suit, Flying, Cotton, Tropical Areas, and he was armed with a .45 Colt automatic in a shoulder holster.

"Stan, I was on the threshold—" he began to complain, and then stopped. There was a stranger in Holliman's office, a non-aviator Marine in a rear-echelon uniform. "Good morning, Sir. You wished to see me?"

"This won't take long," Colonel Holliman said. "Dillon, this is Major Jack Finch. Jack, this is Major Homer Dillon."

"People call me Jake," Dillon said, putting out his hand.

"I think we'd save some time, Dillon," Holliman said, "if you would show Finch what you showed me."

Dillon took a stiff piece of plastic from the right bellows pocket of his jacket and extended it to Finch. He read it and then looked at Colonel Holliman.

"Read both sides, Jack," Holliman said.

"I'm impressed," Finch said. "I guess that's the idea, huh?"

"MAG-25, naturally, is going to do whatever it can for

Major Dillon and the Chief of Staff to the President," Holliman said.

"Yes, Sir."

"He wants a few things from you, Jack."

"Yes, Sir?"

"Starting with the best R4D you have. It will not be available for anything else until further notice."

"Yes, Sir."

"I've told him you can install auxiliary fuel tanks in a couple of hours. Is that correct?"

"Yes, Sir. The fuel lines are already installed. All that has to be done is to reload the tanks and hook them up."

"Major Dillon has also brought with him some special equipment that will have to be installed," Holliman said.

"What kind of special equipment?"

"They're something like skis," Dillon said. "They're supposed to make it possible to land an R4D on sand."

"On sand?" Finch asked incredulously.

"Certain kinds of sand," Dillon said. "We don't know yet if our sand is the right kind; but in case it is, we want to be ready."

"I don't suppose you're going to tell me where this sand is?" Finch asked.

"You understand that all this is classified?" Dillon asked.

"I thought maybe it would be," Finch said, tempering the sarcasm with a smile.

"Just for the record, I'm telling you the classification is TOP SECRET," Jake said. "The sand is on a beach on an island called Buka."

"That's way the hell up by Rabaul!"

"Right. And there is a Japanese fighter base on Buka."

"I know," Finch said. "I've seen the maps."

"There is also a Coastwatcher station on Buka. Their equipment is about shot, and we have every reason to believe that the people are in pretty bad physical shape. What we're going to do is extract them, and replace them."

"Well, I'll be goddamned!" Finch said softly. Then he added, "I guess it's that important, isn't it?" And then he had a second thought. "Just among three Marines, how did The Corps get stuck with this mission?"

"Two of the three people to be extracted are Marines," Dillon said.

"I didn't know we had Marines with the Coastwatchers," Holliman said.

"We have these people, and there are two more on the replacement team," Dillon said.

"I'll be damned," Finch said.

"Major Dillon also wants from you the name of the best R4D pilot you know who would be willing to volunteer for this mission."

"That's easy. Finch, John James, Major."

"See if you can come up with some other names, Jack," Holliman said. "I need you as squadron commander."

"Sir, I'm the best R4D pilot. I can't really think . . . of anyone with more experience."

"You hesitated," Dillon challenged.

"I'm the most experienced R4D pilot in MAG-25," Finch said flatly.

"Who were you thinking of, Major?" Dillon pursued.

"Tell him, Jack," Holliman ordered.

"Charley Galloway, Sir," Finch said with obvious reluctance. He looked at Dillon. "Galloway's a captain. He's commanding VMF-229 on Henderson Field on Guadalcanal."

"You said you needed a volunteer, volunteers," Holliman said. "I'm not sure Galloway would. Not because he doesn't have the balls, but because he would honestly figure he is more valuable to The Corps as a squadron commander than doing something . . . like this."

"Something idiotic, maybe suicidal, like this?" Dillon asked.

"Your words, Major, not mine."

"The question is, is Galloway the pilot who could most likely carry this off?"

"He was my IP," Finch said. "He's as good as there is. I don't want to sound like I'm trying to sell him for the job, but Galloway was in on the acceptance tests of the R4D before the war. He even went through the Air Corps program on dropping parachutists."

"Then in your judgment you and Captain Galloway are the two best pilots for this. Is that what you're saying?"

"Yes, that's what I'm saying."

"Colonel, would you agree with that?"

"I could lie, I suppose," Holliman said. "Maybe I should. But I won't. Yeah, they're the best."

"Well then, the next step, obviously, is to ask Captain Galloway if he'd be willing to volunteer."

"I'm going up there this morning," Finch said. "I was about to take off when I was told to come here. I'll ask him."

"If you don't mind I'll ride along with you. I'd like to see him myself. Charley's an old friend of mine."

That announcement seemed to surprise both Holliman and Finch, but they didn't say anything.

"That would mean bumping a passenger already on my plane. Or two hundred pounds of cargo," Finch said.

"You can send whoever or whatever I bump up there on the R4D you're going to install the fuel tanks and skis on," Dillon replied. "I want that ready to go from Henderson as soon as possible."

XV

[One]
WATER LILY COTTAGE
MANCHESTER AVENUE
BRISBANE, AUSTRALIA
1030 HOURS 2 OCTOBER 1942

There is a smell of pain, Lieutenant (J.G.) Joanne Miller, NNC, thought. *He's sweating because of the pain I'm causing him, and the sweat smells of pain.*

"Am I hurting you?" she asked as she bent his lower leg back until it would flex no more. She pressed harder, raising his hips off the bed.

"I'm all right," John said.

"Don't be a goddamn hero," Lieutenant Colonel M. J. Godofski, MC, USA, said. "You're not going to impress Joanne with some manly bullshit about not feeling pain. If it hurts, say so."

Godofski was leaning against the bedroom wall, puffing on a cigar.

"OK, Colonel, it hurts," John said.

"Good," Godofski said. "It should hurt a little. Not to the point where you can't stand it. We're trying to make your blood vessels down there take more blood than they're used to taking. They have to be trained to replace the ones you lost. Understand?"

"Yes, Sir."

Joanne counted *thirteen, fourteen, fifteen* and stopped.

"That's fifteen, Doctor."

"Can you take five more, son?"

"Yes, Sir."

Colonel Godofski nodded.

Sixteen, seventeen, eighteen, nineteen, twenty.

Honey, I'm sorry!

"Twenty, Doctor."

Godofski went to the bed and probed John's muscles with his fingers.

"Just give him fifteen on the other leg," he said. "It was damaged more than the other one. We don't want to overdo it."

"Yes, Doctor."

"I'll see you tomorrow, son," Godofski said. He looked at Joanne. "I think he's out of the woods with the malaria. No sweats. No diarrhea. His temperatures seem constant. We'll leave him on the Atabrine regimen for a couple more days and see what happens."

"Yes, Doctor."

"They called up from Melbourne about you yesterday. Wanted to know when they can have you back. You must be a pretty good gas passer."

Joanne nodded.

"They're getting in a bunch of wounded from New Guinea," Godofski said.

"I didn't ask for this assignment," Joanne said.

"I didn't ask for mine, either," he said and walked out of the room.

"But are you sorry you came?" John asked as he picked up his ankle. "That's what it sounded like."

"Shut up," Joanne said.

One, she began to count, *two.*

She saw the sweat suddenly pop out on his forehead.

Thirteen, fourteen, fifteen.

"Jesus!" John said.

Oh, honey, I'm sorry.

She sat on the bed beside him and wiped the sweat from his face and neck.

"I like that," he said, then caught her hand and kissed it.

She slapped him on the buttocks and stood up.

"Go take a bath, you stink."

"I like *that,* too," he said.

"Will you stop? Barbara will hear you."

"You don't think she doesn't know?" John asked.

The doorbell went off; it was an old-fashioned turn-to-ring device.

"That's probably the Colonel," John said. "He's had second thoughts. He wants you to give me twenty."

He rolled onto his back. She put her hand on his cheek.

He caught it and used it for support as he pulled himself to a sitting position. Next he swung his legs out of bed; the movement made him wince.

"You're all right? You're not going to fall down in there?"

"No," he said as he made his way into the bathroom.

She was pulling the sweaty sheets from his bed when Barbara put her head in the door.

"Taking a shower," Joanne said. "If that's what you were about to ask."

Barbara, who looked upset, walked to the bathroom and opened the door.

"John, Daphne Farnsworth is here. Would you come out, please?"

"Be right there. Offer her a cup of coffee. *Tea,"* John replied.

"I've wanted to meet her," Joanne said.

Barbara didn't reply.

There were two women in the living room. One of them was obviously Daphne Farnsworth, Royal Australian Navy Women's Volunteer Reserve, and Barbara's friend. *She's not in uniform; I wonder why not,* Joanne asked herself. Though Daphne looked damned unhappy at the moment, that didn't detract from her looks; she was a pretty young woman, with light-brown hair, hazel eyes, and that soft peaches-and-cream skin English women seem to have.

Or Australian women, Joanne thought. *Same blood. I wonder why she's so unhappy? Or is that shame I see in her eyes? What's going on here?*

The other woman was wearing what looked like a man's suit with a skirt, and she was old enough to be Daphne Farnsworth's mother. But Joanne was sure that wasn't the case.

"Daphne, this is Joanne Miller," Barbara said. "I've talked about her to you."

Daphne Farnsworth, with effort, managed a smile.

"This lady is a policeman," Barbara said. "I'm sorry, I've forgotten your name."

"*Constable* Rogers," the woman said, unsmiling. "How do you do?"

"Won't you please sit down?" Barbara said. "Can we offer you something? Tea? Something to drink?"

"No, thank you," Constable Rogers said, but she sat down on the edge of the couch, her knees together, and rested her black purse on them.

That looks, Joanne thought, *like a midwife's bag.*

"Daphne, can't I get you something?" Barbara asked.

Daphne offered another weak smile and shook her head, no.

There was an awkward silence while they waited for John Moore to come in. It lasted no more than two minutes but seemed much longer. Still drying his hair with a towel, John Moore finally walked into the living room.

"Hel*lo*, Daphne!" he called cheerfully, and then he saw Constable Rogers and bit off whatever else he had intended to say.

"I'd heard you were hurt," Daphne said. "I'm glad to see you're all right."

"May I ask who you are?" Constable Rogers asked, rising to her feet.

"My name is Moore. Who are you?"

"I'm Constable Rogers—"

"*Constable?*"

"—and I am instructed to place Mrs. Farnsworth into the custody of Major Edward Banning, of the United States Marine Corps."

"Into the custody? What the hell are you talking about?"

"Can you tell me where I might find Major Banning? This is the address I was given."

"Major Banning is not here. I work for him. Will that do?"

"If you would, I'd like to see some identification, please," Constable Rogers said.

"Daphne, what the hell is going on here?" John asked, and then saw tears in Daphne's eyes.

He went into the bedroom and came back out holding his credentials in his hand. Constable Rogers examined them carefully.

"That will be sufficient, thank you," she said. Then she fished in her purse and came out with a form, in triplicate, with carbons, the whole thing neatly stapled together. "If you would be good enough to sign that, Sir?"

Moore took the form, glanced at it, took the fountain pen Constable Rogers extended to him, and signed his name in the block provided for SIGNATURE OF INDIVIDUAL ASSUMING CUSTODY OF DETAINEE.

Constable Rogers tore off one of the carbons and handed it to Moore.

"Thank you very much," she said as she neatly folded the rest of the form and stuffed it in her purse.

She turned to Daphne. "When you are finished here, Mrs. Farnsworth, if you will come to the Main Police Station, room 306, they will arrange for your transportation back to Melbourne."

Daphne nodded but didn't say anything. With a curl of her lips she probably thought was a smile, Constable Rogers gave a nod to Moore and then to Barbara and Joanne and walked out of the living room.

"Daphne, what the hell is this all about?" John Moore asked.

"She called you *Mrs.* Farnsworth?" Barbara said.

"Yeoman Farnsworth," Daphne said softly, looking at Barbara and then averting her eyes, "has been discharged for the good of the Service."

"What?"

"I'm pregnant," Daphne said. "About four months, they tell me."

"Oh, my God!" Barbara said. "Steve?" she asked; and then a moment later, with horror in her voice, she blurted, "I'm so sorry I asked that."

Daphne shrugged. "Steve," she said.

"What's this . . . ? Who was that terrible woman?"

"Banning said Feldt would arrange for Daphne to come here," Moore explained.

"They came to where I was working," Daphne said. "Two policemen brought Constable Rogers. Then they took me to my room and let me pack a bag. And then they took us to the railroad station and put us on the train."

Goddamn Major Banning! Joanne thought.

"That's outrageous!" Moore said.

And what if you're in the family way, too, Joanne Miller? You didn't think about that, did you, carried away on the wings of love? Oh, God!

"They can't do that!" Barbara said furiously. "You didn't do anything wrong!"

"Oh, yes they can," Daphne said. "They read me the appropriate passages from the Emergency War Powers Act. Any citizen may be detained for ninety-six hours when it is considered necessary in the prosecution of the war."

"Damn them!" Barbara said.

"What does Major Banning want with me?" Daphne asked. "I'm afraid to ask, but does it have something to do with Steve?"

"Yes, but he's all right, Daphne," Moore said.

"Then what?"

"We needed a new code to communicate with them," Moore explained. "Pluto Hon came up with a simple substitution code based on personal things that only Barbara and Lieutenant Howard would know. He wanted to do the same thing with you and Koffler."

"He's all right?" she asked.

"Yes, he's all right."

"Daphne," Barbara said, "I wish I was pregnant."

What the hell is the matter with you, Barbara? That's absolute idiocy! Joanne thought. *God, don't let me be pregnant!*

"It's not quite the same for you, Barbara," Daphne said.

"I believe Joe's coming back," Barbara said. "Steve will, too."

"You're in love with Joe," Daphne said.

"You're not in love with Steve?"

"How could I be in love with him? I hardly know him."

How could I be in love with Johnny? I hardly know him, either.

"You're upset," Barbara said. "Understandably."

"Actually, I think I'm thinking pretty clearly," Daphne said. "What happened—and I was with him only that one night—happened because he came to Wagga Wagga—"

"Where?" Moore blurted and was immediately sorry.

"My family has a station, Two Creeks Station, in Wagga Wagga, New South Wales," Daphne explained. "You'd call it a farm, or a ranch."

He should not be hearing this, Joanne decided. *This is between women, and none of his business.*

"Why don't you go get dressed?" Joanne snapped.

"Hey, I'm trying to help," John replied. "And I do have to get the stuff for a code from her."

"You know all about codes, too?"

"I know what Pluto told me to get from her when she showed up," Moore said. "What about . . . *Wagga Wagga*?"

Daphne smiled.

"Steve thought it was funny, too," she said. "I thought you knew all this, John?"

"I wasn't here," Moore said. "I came after Koff— Steve and Lieutenant Howard jumped into Buka."

"That's right, isn't it?" Daphne said. "I'd forgotten."

"You don't have to talk to him about this," Joanne said.

"It would be helpful if she would," Moore said coldly.

"It's all right. If it will help Steve," Daphne said.

"I'm not trying to pry," Moore said, looking at Joanne. "I just need words we can use for a code. Wagga Wagga sounds fine." He looked at Daphne. "Steve would remember that?"

"Oh, I'm sure he would. He got lost twice trying to find it," Daphne said.

"What was he doing there?"

"After I learned that my husband was killed in North Africa," Daphne said, "there was a memorial service for him. When Steve heard, he wanted to do something for me. So he drove out. In that Studebaker, I think," she said, gesturing outside. "With a box of candy and flowers and a bottle of whiskey, he didn't know what was appropriate, so he brought one of each."

"Steve's a nice kid, John," Barbara said gently.

"Yes, a nice kid," Daphne said. "And I rode back from New South Wales to Victoria with him. He had to stop at Captain Pickering's place. What was it called?"

"The Elms, in Dandenong," Barbara furnished.

"And everybody was there, and they ran you and me off, and we eavesdropped—"

"I was sent from the hospital to give them their shots," Barbara said, looking at Joanne. "I didn't even know Joe was in Australia until I walked in there. We had only the one night, too."

"—and we heard what was going to happen to them the next day," Daphne went on, "and I decided—helped along by several gins—that the two loneliest people in the world were Yeoman Farnsworth and Sergeant Koffler, and . . . I'd always heard that all it takes is once; but even that didn't seem to matter."

"Steve's in love with you," Barbara said.

"You said it, Barbara," Daphne said. "Steve is a nice kid."

So is John Moore a nice kid. You should have realized, Joanne Miller, that your maternal instincts and/or hormones were getting out of control. You should have reminded yourself that all he is is a nice kid.

"He's more than a nice kid," Moore said. "He's one hell of a man. I don't think I like that 'nice kid' crap."

Go to hell, you bastard!

"You're right," Barbara said. "I didn't mean that the way it sounded."

"He's a kid," Daphne insisted. "Even if he were here, even if he wanted to marry me, even if I wanted to marry him, I couldn't. He's a minor, and your regulations don't permit your sergeants to marry; they have to be staff sergeants or above."

"You're sure about that?" Barbara asked.

"Yes," Daphne said.

"They'd probably waive that, considering . . . the child," Moore said.

"Australian law considers the child to be my husband's," Daphne said.

"But he was in Africa," Barbara protested. "He couldn't possibly—"

"I'm telling you what the law says," Daphne interrupted.

"And you're determined to have it?" Joanne asked.

God, I hate to talk about abortion with John sitting there with a shocked look on his face! But somebody, obviously, has to start thinking practically about this.

"Oh, I thought about that," Daphne said. "How am I going to support the child?"

"But it is getting a little late for an abortion, isn't it?" Barbara said.

"Yes, it is," Daphne admitted.

"What about your family?"

"My family can count. They will want nothing to do with me or the baby when they find out. God, it was conceived the night of my husband's memorial service."

"Your family doesn't know?" Joanne asked incredulously.

"Don't worry about support," John Moore said. "That's not one of the problems. This can be worked out with The Corps."

"And if it can't?" Joanne snapped.

"There's money available," he said.

"Whose?" she demanded.

"Mine, all right?"

He actually believes that. More evidence that he's no less a child than the child who made this pathetic young woman pregnant.

"In the end I decided that God had a hand in what's happening to me," Daphne said.

"God?" Joanne asked. "What's God got to do with it?"

"I thought that maybe I was being punished for being an adulteress . . ."

"That's nonsense!" Barbara protested.

"Or that God wanted Steve to leave something behind, a new life. Anyway, I'm going to have his baby. I'll work it out."

"Not alone," Barbara said.

"Right," Moore said. "And for one thing, you're not going back to Melbourne. You're going to stay here with us."

"I've got to have a job," Daphne said.

"I told you, you don't have to worry about money."

Goddamn you! The one thing she doesn't need is false hope!

"Can we get her a job here?" Barbara asked.

"Yeah, sure," John Moore said. "Detachment 14 has authority to hire Australians. But that's not what I was talking about."

He turned to Daphne.

"I'm going to put my clothes on. Then we're going to have to take care of the *Wagga Wagga* business."

Daphne nodded.

"Won't that wait, for God's sake?" Joanne snapped.

"I don't know what the hell is the matter with you," Moore

responded furiously, "but everybody else around here is breaking their ass trying to get the boyfriends off Buka."

"Is that what you're really doing, John?" Barbara asked very quietly.

Moore didn't respond. He simply turned and went into his bedroom. As he left, Daphne's eyes followed him. *God! That's admiration in those eyes of hers—awe!* Joanne thought. *As far as she's concerned Johnny Moore might as well be the Angel Gabriel, come to set all the evils of the world right.*

Barbara, meanwhile, with tears in her eyes, went to Daphne and put her arms around her.

And Joanne pursued John Marston Moore.

She found him naked, awkwardly trying to put his leg into his underpants.

He modestly turned his back to her.

"You sonofabitch!" she hissed. "You make me sick to my stomach."

"Are you going to tell me why?" he asked over his shoulder.

"You had absolutely no right to tell that poor girl you'd take care of her. That was incredibly cruel. She needs to hear the truth; she doesn't need you giving her false hope."

"You're talking about the money?"

"Of course I'm talking about the money!"

"I hadn't planned to tell you this . . ." Moore said. Instead of finishing that thought, he squatted, wincing, to pull his shorts up; and then he turned to face her, ". . . until our wedding night. But among all the worldly goods I'm going to endow you with is a lot of money. Pushing three million, to be specific."

My God, he means it!

"More than enough for you and me, and our kids, and Koffler's kid," Moore said. "OK?"

"I never said I was going to marry you," Joanne said softly.

"Well, what do you say?"

"You may have to," she said. "I'm probably pregnant."

"That would be nice," he said, and held his arms open for her.

[Two]
154° 30″ EAST LONGITUDE 8° 27″ SOUTH LATITUDE
THE SOLOMON SEA
1229 HOURS 4 OCTOBER 1942

When Sergeant George Hart, USMC, looked out of the port
waist blister of the Royal Australian Navy Consolidated
PBY-5 Catalina, he saw beneath him the expanse of blue
ocean—absolutely nothing but blue ocean. He'd been riding in
the Catalina for four hours; for the last twenty minutes it had
been flying slow, wide circles . . .

It just might happen that blue ocean was all he was going to
see. He found it hard to believe that the pilot up front really
had any precise idea where he was.

There was no land in sight, and there hadn't been for a long
time. He remembered from high school enough about the modern miracle of flight and airplanes to recall that there were such
things as head winds and tail winds—and presumably side
winds, too. These sped up or retarded an aircraft's passage over
the Earth, and/or they pushed the aircraft away from the path
the pilot wished to fly.

It was possible, he recalled, to navigate by using the known
location of radio stations. This pilot was obviously not doing
that, because there were obviously no useful radio stations
operating anywhere near here.

What the pilot was doing was making a guess where he was
by dead reckoning: He'd have worked that out by plotting how
long he'd been flying at a particular compass heading at a
particular speed.

That would work only if there were no head winds, tail
winds, or winds blowing the airplane to one side or another.

How they expected to find a boat as small as a submarine this
far from land was an operation he simply didn't understand.

Curiosity finally overcame his reluctance to reveal his ignorance.

A RAN sailor was standing beside him looking out the
blister. "I don't see how you're going to find the submarine,"
George confessed to him with as much savoir faire as he could
muster.

"For the last hour," the sailor answered, "she's been surfac-
ing every fifteen minutes, long enough to send a signal . . . They
just hold the key down for ten or fifteen seconds. You saw that

round thing on top?" He gestured toward the wing above them.

George nodded.

"Radio direction finding antenna. Sparks just turns that until the signal from the sub is strongest and gives the pilot the heading."

"Yeah," George said. "That always works, huh?"

The sailor pointed down at the sea. There was now a submarine just sitting there. It looked even smaller, even farther down, than he expected.

The submarine was the HMAS *Pelican*. George knew a good deal about HMAS *Pelican*. On his desk in Townsville, Commander Feldt had a book with photographs and descriptions of every class of ship in the major navies of the world, as well as descriptions of many individual ships, too.

Since the *Pelican* was in the book, he looked it up; after all, he was going riding—correction, *diving*—in it.

It—correction, *she*—began life as HMS *Snakefish* in 1936, at the Cammell Laird Shipyard in Scotland. In 1939 she was transferred to the Australian Navy and renamed *Pelican*.

Does the Royal Navy treat the Royal Australian Navy the way the U.S. Navy treats The U.S. Marine Corps? George wondered. *As a poor relation, only giving it equipment that's no good, or worn out? Probably,* he decided.

According to Commander Feldt's book, HMAS *Pelican* had a speed on the surface of 13.5 knots and a submerged speed of 10. Elsewhere in the book George read that Japanese destroyers could make more than 30 knots. That meant that the Japanese would have a hell of an advantage if they spotted the *Pelican* and wanted a fight. Particularly since destroyers had a bunch of cannons, of all sizes, and depth charges. And the *Pelican* had only a single four-inch cannon and a couple of machine guns.

Of course the *Pelican* had torpedoes, but this did not give George much reassurance. He didn't think it would be very easy to hit a destroyer while it was twisting and turning at 30 knots and simultaneously shooting its cannons and throwing depth charges at you.

The Catalina suddenly began to make a steep descent toward the surface of the ocean. George grabbed one of the aluminum fuselage members. A moment later he saw blood dripping down onto his utilities.

The Catalina straightened out for a time, but then it made a really steep turn, after which it dropped its nose again.

A moment later there was an enormous splash, and then another, and then another. They were on the surface of the ocean. He looked around for the *Pelican* but couldn't see it.

The crew of the Catalina opened a hatch in the side of the fuselage and tossed out two packages. In a moment these began to inflate and assume the shape of rafts.

Lieutenant McCoy, wearing utilities, scrambled through the hatch and into one of the boats. A moment later Chief Signalman Wallace, wearing his skirt and his Chief Petty Officer's cap and nothing else, dropped into the other. Then two of the other three Marine members of the replacement team, a staff sergeant named Kelly and a corporal named Godfrey, got in the rafts. That left Sergeants Doud and Hart in the Catalina. Because of their strong backs, they'd been chosen to transfer the equipment from the Catalina to the rafts.

Before they took off, Hart told McCoy that he suspected this would be a bitch of a job. And McCoy told him he thought it would be worse than a bitch of a job. He was right. One of the radios almost went in the water. And when a swell suddenly raised one end of McCoy's raft, one of the tar-paper–wrapped weapons packages did go in.

No problem, there was a spare.

Finally everything was loaded onto the rafts, and Sergeants Doud and Hart half fell, half jumped into them.

The Catalina's hatch closed and there was a cloud of black smoke as the pilot restarted his port engine. The plane swung away from them, gunned its engines, and started its takeoff.

George felt a heavy sense that he was far removed from anything friendly. And he didn't get any relief from that when he finally spotted the submarine.

The Pelican's *crew are not waving a friendly hello,* he realized after a moment, *but gesturing angrily for us to get our asses in gear and paddle over.*

One of those thirty-knot Japanese destroyers with all those cannons and depth charges is charging this way.

Why am I not afraid?

Because this whole fucking thing is so unreal that I'm unable to believe it. What the hell am I doing paddling a little rubber boat around in the middle of the Solomon Sea?

The *Pelican* was a lot farther away than it seemed. By the time the raft bumped up against her hull, he was breathing so hard it hurt. And the saltwater stung like hell on the slash in his hand he'd got in the Catalina.

The *Pelican*'s crew threw lines down to them. These were fastened to the equipment they were taking aboard, and then the crew dragged that up to the submarine's deck. Finally, the raft paddlers crawled aboard—with considerable help from the crew.

Just before passing through a hatch into the conning tower, George took one last look around him. He was surprised to see that one of the rafts was drifting away from the *Pelican.*

Why're they loose? They were securely tied.

But then he saw that the other raft was loose, too.

And then there was a burst of machine-gun fire from above him.

Jesus Christ! They're shooting holes in the rafts! What the hell for? What are we going to use to get ashore?

They're shooting holes in the rafts because they expect one of those thirty-knot Japanese destroyers, that's why they're shooting holes in them. It would take too much time to deflate them and bring them aboard.

He went inside the conning tower and down a ladder. He was almost on the main deck, thinking, *Jesus, it stinks in here,* when a Klaxon horn went off right by his ear.

Faintly, through the squawk of the Klaxon, he heard a loudspeaker bellow, "Dive! Dive! Dive!"

[*Three*]
OFFICER'S MESS, MAG-21
HENDERSON FIELD
GUADALCANAL, SOLOMON ISLANDS
0730 HOURS 5 OCTOBER 1942

The officer's mess of Marine Air Group 21 was pretty much the same as the enlisted mess. They differed mainly in location and in size. The officer's mess (a sandbag enclosure topped by an open-walled tent) was on the north side of the communal kitchen (a sandbag enclosure topped by an open-walled tent). The enlisted mess (an open-walled enclosure topped by an open-walled tent) was about twice as large as the officer's mess, and it was on the south side of the communal kitchen.

Lieutenant Colonel Clyde W. Dawkins, USMC, in a fresh but already sweat-soaked cotton flight suit, sat on the plank seat of what looked like a six-man picnic table. Both hands were on a mug of coffee. The remnants of his breakfast tray (a steel tray holding mostly uneaten powdered eggs, bacon, toast and marmalade) were pushed to the side.

Before he spoke, Colonel Dawkins carefully considered what he intended to say.

"It's bullshit, Charley, is what I think," he finally said to Captain Charles M. Galloway, USMCR, commanding officer of VMF-229. Galloway was sitting on the other side of the picnic table.

Charley Galloway shrugged.

"And I'll tell you something else, I think your Major Dillon's orders are bullshit, too," Dawkins said.

"You don't mean phony?" Galloway asked, surprised.

"Not *forged*," Dawkins said. "I think that there is a General Pickering, even if I never heard of him, and that he works for Admiral Leahy."

"I've got a kid named Pickering in my squadron," Galloway said. "He got two Bettys his first time out, a Zero the second."

Dawkins ignored that aside. "It's the endorsement that I think is bullshit."

"I think you mean that," Galloway said, surprised.

"Think about it," Dawkins said. "Think about two things. First ask yourself if it's reasonable that the President's Chief of Staff—Jesus, he used to be Chief of Naval Operations, and now he got promoted higher than that!—I find it hard to accept that *Admiral Leahy* is personally concerned with two guys on a tiny island he probably couldn't find on a map. He's got better things to do."

Galloway looked at him and shrugged again.

"For the second thing," Dawkins went on, "it wouldn't be the first time in the recorded annals of military history that an officer with a set of vague orders giving him lots of authority went ape shit."

Galloway did not reply.

"Did you know, for example, that just before the Spanish-American War, the American Ambassador to Spain went to the Spaniards and *ordered* them to get out of Cuba? He had absolutely no orders from Washington. Nada."

"Really?" Galloway found that fascinating.

"Really. He didn't have two cents' worth of authority; he just decided that's what he wanted to do, and did it."

"I don't think Dillon's that kind of guy. He used to be a sergeant with the Fourth Marines in China."

"And now he's a major running around with orders on White House stationery. You're making my point for me, Charley. I can easily see where that would go to an ex-sergeant's head, having orders to do just about anything he wants to do." He hesitated. "Present company excepted, of course."

"Yeah, sure," Galloway said. "I think it's just as reasonable to assume that this General Pickering . . . I agree, I doubt if Admiral Leahy knows where Buka is, or didn't—"

"I don't follow you," Dawkins interrupted.

"OK. This General Pickering. He knows (a) that we have our ass in a crack here; (b) that about the only reason the Japanese don't bomb this place into oblivion, and bomb the hell out of the supply ships coming here, is that the Coastwatchers on the islands let us know when they've launched their aircraft from Rabaul; and (c) that the Coastwatcher station on Buka is pretty fucking close to going out of business. I just thought of another one: and (d) that nobody here seems to give a damn. Maybe because the Navy thinks it's MacArthur's responsibility, since the Coastwatchers are under the Australians, and he's sort of in charge of the Australians. But MacArthur figures it's the Navy's business, since Guadalcanal and Buka are CINC-PAC's concern; they're not in his SWPOA. So Pickering goes to Admiral Leahy and gives him a quick rundown, and Leahy says, 'OK, General, take care of it.' "

"That's possible, I suppose," Dawkins said reluctantly.

"I think that's more likely than what you're suggesting," Charley said.

"How about an URGENT radio from Leahy to both CINC-PAC and SWPOA: 'Settle it between yourselves, but make sure Buka stays in operation. Love and Kisses, Admiral Leahy'?"

Galloway chuckled.

"All Dillon asked me to do, Colonel, is make a quick trip up there and back. And only if they can't reinforce Buka by submarine."

"In an unarmed transport, landing right under the nose of

the Japanese on a beach that may or may not take the weight."

"They'll know if the beach will take the weight before I go,"
Galloway said.

"You and Finch, from our vast pool of qualified squadron
commanders who are otherwise unoccupied," Dawkins said
sarcastically.

"We have more time in the R4D than most people," Galloway said.

"Speaking of the R4D. Why the R4D?"

"You saw the skis. I think they'll work. The problem with
the regular landing gear, I think, is not that the airplane might
stick in the sand while it's landing or taking off. But when it's
stopped. If it's not moving, it might sink. The skis will fix that,
I think."

"You think," he said, and gave him a look. "But I meant,
why the R4D in the first place? Specifically, why not a Catalina? It could land in the water, for one thing. For another, it
has .50 calibers in the blisters and a .30 in the nose. The R4D
has zero armament."

"Dillon said they considered the Catalina—"

"Who's 'they'?"

"I guess Dillon and this General Pickering."

"And?"

"Decided against it. Dillon said that getting rubber boats
through the surf on the Makin Island raid wasn't as easy as it
came out in the newspapers. And the Japanese don't have an
airplane that looks like the Catalina. But they do have a bunch
of R4Ds . . . actually, they're not R4Ds but DC-2s; Douglas
licensed the Japs to make DC-2s before the war. But they look
like R4Ds from a distance."

"And your General Pickering thinks the Japanese will think
your R4D is one of their DC-2s and leave it alone?"

"The Japanese would *not* think a Catalina was one of
theirs," Galloway said.

Colonel Dawkins decided not to argue the point. Charley
Galloway had volunteered for this idiotic mission because he
was gallant. There was no other word for it. That also applied
to Major Jack Finch. Major Finch and Captain Galloway were
both gallant. They fit the classic definition of gallant: warriors
who knew goddamned well they were likely to be killed, and
were willing to take that risk, (a) because the mission was

important, and (b) because they might possibly save the lives of other warriors.

But as a responsible commander, Lieutenant Colonel Dawkins decided, the cold reality was that he could not indulge their gallantry. If they remained in command of their squadrons, they would ultimately be of greater value to the overall mission, and would ultimately be responsible for saving more lives, than if they soared nobly off into the wild blue yonder on an idiotic mission dreamed up by an ex–China Marine sergeant and a paper-shuffling rear-echelon brigadier general back in Washington.

He also decided it would do no good to take the matter up with either Lieutenant Colonel Stanley N. Holliman, USMC, Executive Officer of MAG-25, or Brigadier General D. G. McInerney, the senior Marine Aviator on Guadalcanal. While he had a great—in the case of General McInerney, nearly profound—professional admiration for these officers, both men were also awash in the seas of gallantry. They would not understand why Dawkins did not wish this idiotic mission to take place.

They will understand the gallantry. They will be touched by the gallantry.

If they can find the time, they will be standing at attention, saluting and humming the Marine Hymn as Galloway and Finch and their goddamned R4D on goddamned skis roar down the runway.

There is only one man who can bring this idiocy to a screeching halt, Colonel Dawkins decided, *and therefore it is my duty to go see him.*

"When are you going, Charley?" he asked Galloway.

"Whenever they send word. Here to Port Moresby, then to Buka, then back here."

"Why Moresby? It's just as close, direct from here."

"Moresby has landing lights," Galloway explained. "We want to make the leg up there in the dark."

"I see," Dawkins said. He stood up. "I've got to go see G-3 Air at the Division CP. You need a ride anywhere?"

"No, Sir. Thank you."

"Well, hello, Dawkins," Major General Alexander Archer Vandergrift, Commanding General of the First Marine Division, said when he came out of his office and saw Dawkins sitting on a folding chair. "We don't see much of you."

Colonel Dawkins rose to his feet.

"Sir, I'd hoped the General could spare me a few minutes of his time."

Vandergrift's eyebrows rose in surprise. He glanced at his watch.

"I can give you a couple of minutes right now," he said, then held open the piece of canvas tenting that served as the door to his office.

Vandergrift went to his desk (a folding wooden table holding a U.S. Field Desk, a cabinetlike affair with a number of drawers and shelves), sat down on a folding chair, crossed his legs, and looked at Dawkins.

Dawkins assumed the at-ease position. He put his feet twelve inches apart and folded his hands together in the small of his back.

The formality was not lost on Vandergrift.

"OK, Colonel, let's have it," he said.

"Sir, there's an officer visiting, Major Dillon—"

"Jake came by to make his manners," Vandergrift interrupted. "What about him?"

"Did the General happen to see Major Dillon's orders?"

"The General did," Vandergrift said dryly. "Interesting, aren't they?"

"He has laid a mission on one of my squadron commanders, and on Major Finch of MAG-25—"

"I'm familiar with it," Vandergrift said. "You obviously don't like it. So make your point, Colonel."

"That's it, Sir, I don't like it."

"Because of the risk?"

"Yes, Sir."

"I don't think you've been to see General McInerney about this, have you, Colonel?"

"No, Sir. I'm out of the chain of command."

"I won't give you the standard speech about the chain of command. You're a good Marine and you know all about it. And, in a way, since you do know the consequences of violating it, I admire your conviction in coming to see me directly."

"Sir, they have one chance in five of carrying this off."

"When he came to see me, it was General McInerney's judgment that they have one chance in ten," Vandergrift said.

"Yes, Sir. General McInerney is probably right. It borders on the suicidal, and it will deprive us of two good squadron commanders."

Raising his eyes to meet Dawkins', Vandergrift started to say something, stopped, and then went on: "After we'd accepted the obvious fact that we've gotten an order and we have no choice but to obey it, General McInerney and I also concluded that General Pickering was certainly aware of the risk and that he considers it acceptable."

"I don't know General Pickering, General. I've been searching my mind, and—"

"He and General McInerney were together in France. With Jack (NMI) Stecker, by the way. At about the same time Jack got his Medal of Honor, Pickering got the Distinguished Service Cross. I met him here. When Colonel Goettge was killed, he filled in as G-2 until they could send us a replacement. I was impressed with his brains, and his character."

"Yes, Sir."

Well, I tried and I lost.

"He was then a Navy captain," Vandergrift went on, "on the staff of the Secretary of the Navy. He showed up here the day after the invasion and told me he just couldn't sail off into the sunset with the Navy when they left us on the beach. I tell you this because . . ." He paused a moment, then began again. "While I don't know how he got to be Brigadier General of Marines, General McInerney and I both think it was a wise decision on somebody's part."

"Yes, Sir."

"Have you any other questions, Colonel?"

"No, Sir."

"I'm going to give you the benefit of the doubt, Colonel, and conclude that before you went over General McInerney's head, you gave it a lot of thought. So far as I'm concerned, this discussion never took place."

"Yes, Sir. Thank you."

"One more thing, Dawkins. One of the Wildcat pilots in VMF-229 is General Pickering's only son. I think we may presume that the lives of Marine Aviators on Guadalcanal are never out of General Pickering's mind for very long."

"General, I knew none of this."

"There's no way you could have. That's why I have decided to forget this conversation. That's all, Dawkins."

[Four]
THE OFFICE OF THE SUPREME COMMANDER
SOUTH WEST PACIFIC OCEAN AREA
BRISBANE, AUSTRALIA
1625 HOURS 5 OCTOBER 1942

Double doors led into the Supreme Commander's office. Master Sergeant Manuel Donat, of the Philippine Scouts, pushed open the left-hand one of these, waited until the Supreme Commander looked up, and then announced:

"Lieutenant Hon is here to see you, General."

"Ask the Lieutenant to come in, Manuel," General Douglas MacArthur said. He was slouched down in his chair, reading a typewritten document.

"Good afternoon, Sir," Pluto Hon said, saluting. He had a large manila envelope tucked under his arm.

MacArthur touched his forehead with his hand, returning the salute.

"That looks formidable," he said, pointing at the envelope Hon now extended to him.

"It's rather long, Sir."

"Manuel, get the Lieutenant a cup of coffee. Get us both one, as a matter of fact. Have a seat, Pluto. I'll be with you in just a moment."

"Thank you, Sir," Pluto said, sitting down on the edge of a nice, possibly genuine, Louis XIV chair. He was convinced the chair had been placed where it was because it was delicate and tiny by comparison to MacArthur's massive desk and high-backed leather swivel chair. Anyone sitting in it could not help but feel inadequate.

Holding a stub that was once a large black Philippine cigar between his thumb and index finger, MacArthur rested his elbow on the leather-bound desk pad and carefully read a document before him.

Finally, as Master Sergeant Donat appeared with a silver coffee service on a tray, he pulled himself out of his slouch, closed the TOP SECRET cover sheet on the document, and tossed it in his out basket. Then he looked at the cigar butt between his fingers.

"It offends Mrs. MacArthur that I smoke them so short," he said. "But of course, for a while, there will be no more of these. I have to smoke them all the way down."

"Yes, Sir," Pluto said.

"Captain . . . *General* Pickering found these for me, as a matter of fact, in Melbourne. Did you know that?"

"Yes, Sir. I actually went and picked them up, Sir."

"Well, when they're gone, that's it. There will be no more." He looked at Hon and smiled. "How are you, Pluto? I understand you were out of town."

"Yes, Sir. I'm fine, thank you, Sir."

"Townsville, was it?"

"Yes, Sir."

MacArthur pulled the MAGIC material from the manila envelope. It had two parts. One was an analysis of intercepted Japanese messages; the other was the messages themselves, and their translations. He pushed the messages and translations to one side and began to read the analyses.

He read carefully. There was a good deal to read and consider.

Finally he looked at Hon.

"Very interesting," he said. "I see again—how shall I phrase this? *that there are subtle differences of shading,* how's that?—between your analyses and those of the people in Hawaii?"

" 'Subtle differences of shading' does very well, Sir. We are in general agreement with Pearl Harbor."

"We? Does that mean this is not your analysis? Mrs. Feller's perhaps?"

"Actually, Sir, *those* analyses were done by Lieutenant Moore. I'm in complete agreement with them, Sir."

"Fascinating, don't you think, that I picked up on that?" MacArthur said. "That I could tell it wasn't you?"

"You're used to my style, I suppose, Sir."

"Yes, *literary* style, one could say, right? I seem to be able to recognize yours, don't I?"

"Yes, Sir."

"Actually, a day or two ago, I paid Mrs. Feller something of a left-handed compliment," MacArthur said. "Willoughby was in here, impressed with an analysis Mrs. Feller had prepared; and I said, yes, it's quite good, it sounds like Pluto."

He knows! Why am I surprised? He's a goddamned genius!

"Yes, Sir."

"If we are to accept this analysis," MacArthur said, "plural, *these analyses,* we are forced to the conclusion that a reason—a major reason, perhaps even *the* major reason—why the Japanese have not thrown the Marines back into the sea at Guadalcanal is that there's a breakdown in communication between the Japanese Army and Navy. I find it difficult to accept that."

"Sir, why the analyses, Pearl Harbor's and ours—"

"Yours and the other lieutenant's, what's his name?"

"Moore, Sir."

"What's the condition of his health? When he was in here, he looked terrible."

"There has been a recurrence of his malaria, Sir. They have it back under control."

"He was walking with obvious discomfort, using a cane," MacArthur said. "I wonder if Pickering did the right thing sending him back over here in that condition."

"He's getting physical therapy, General."

"Good. We were talking about a breakdown in communication between the Japanese Army and Navy."

"Yes, Sir. I was saying that Pearl Harbor, Moore, and I all agree that Japanese pride got in the way of efficient operation. Neither the Navy nor the Army was willing to ask each other— or the Imperial General Staff, for that matter—for help. If they did, that would admit to some kind of inability to deal with the situation. The honor of the Army and Navy and of the individual commanders would then be open to question."

"That's what I said," MacArthur said somewhat coldly. "A breakdown in communication."

"An *absence* of communication, Sir, rather than a *breakdown.*"

MacArthur gave him a frosty look.

"I suppose that semantics are your profession, Pluto, aren't they?"

"Actually, Sir, I'm a mathematician," Pluto said.

MacArthur looked at him for a moment and then laughed. "You're also a skilled semanticist, Pluto," he said with an airy wave of his hand.

"So it is your analysis that that situation no longer prevails," he went on, "and we may now expect from the Japanese more coordinated activity, more interservice cooperation, and less prideful, selfish rivalry?"

"Yes, Sir."

"And why would you come to that conclusion? What made them, so to speak, see the light?"

"They had to go to the Emperor and confess failure, Sir. And their worlds didn't come to an end."

"'They' being the senior officers of the Army and Navy?"

"And of the Imperial General Staff, Sir."

"They did do rather well in the opening days of this war, didn't they? Everything they set out to do, they did."

"Yes, Sir, they did."

"No confessions of failure were needed, were there?"

"No, Sir."

"And you think they led the Emperor to believe then that our Guadalcanal operation was something they could easily deal with? . . . almost certainly because they believed it themselves."

"We have the intercepts to prove that, Sir. I could get them for you if you'd like to see them."

MacArthur waved his hand grandly.

"I've seen them," he said.

The implication, Pluto thought, *is that once he's read something, he is incapable of forgetting it.*

"What I'm saying, Sir, is that the Guadalcanal landing was on 7 August. That was almost two months ago, and the Marines were not thrown back into the sea. Not only are they still there, but Henderson Field is operational. So the Japanese commanders had to confess that the American presence could not be easily dealt with. For all intents and purposes, the battle of Bloody Ridge simply wiped out *Kawaguchi Butai.* Prisoners have reported that its commander, Major General Kiotake Kawaguchi, actually committed hara-kiri—"

"Has there been confirmation of that?" MacArthur interrupted.

"No, Sir. Not as far as I know."

I wish to hell there was. MacArthur is fully aware that Kawaguchi Butai wiped out the last American resistance on Mindanao. He'd be pleased to know that their general has disemboweled himself after a defeat by Americans who are only slightly better fed and equipped than the Americans he had such an easy time with in the Philippines.

"It was a humiliating defeat for them, wasn't it?" MacArthur asked rhetorically.

"Yes, Sir. I think the senior people expected to be relieved,

Sir. They weren't. But now they're dealing with the changed situation."

"And this assessment of their change in attitude is based on what, Pluto?"

"On the language, Sir. In our judgment, there is less intentional obfuscation. That's based on word choice, Sir. I don't know if I'm making myself clear."

"You're doing fine," MacArthur said. "Go on."

"It's as if they've decided that their mission now is to regain Guadalcanal . . . as a *national* mission, not as a task the Army or Navy can handle by itself."

"And are they going to be more difficult to deal with? Is there a chance we will be thrown off Guadalcanal? That there will be more efficient resistance to our operations on New Guinea?"

"Yes, Sir. To a degree; we'll have to wait and see to *what* degree. But, yes, I think we can expect greater naval activity against Guadalcanal. I don't think they'll be able to throw us off, though."

MacArthur nodded, spun around in his chair, and for a moment stared thoughtfully at the huge map on the wall behind his desk. Then he turned around again.

"All right, Pluto, I would now like to hear how General Pickering's clandestine operation is going."

Christ, talk about getting taken by surprise!

What do I do now, lie? You can't lie to the Supreme Commander, South West Pacific Ocean Area!

"What would you like to know, Sir?"

"General Willoughby came to me a day or so ago, agitated. He said that an impeccable source had informed him that a clandestine intelligence operation is being conducted here by people acting on Pickering's orders."

"Sir, I wouldn't define it as a clandestine intelligence operation," Pluto said. MacArthur waited for him to go on. "It's more on the order of support for the Coastwatchers."

"The Coastwatcher Establishment is an intelligence operation. General Willoughby feels that anything connected with intelligence is his responsibility."

"General Pickering is attempting to relieve the Coastwatcher detachment on Buka, to replace it with fresh men and equipment."

"And he decided that this was none of General Willoughby's business?"

"I wouldn't know how to answer that, Sir."

MacArthur tilted his head toward Pluto and examined him carefully.

"I asked how the operation is going," he said.

"An attempt to land the replacement team and equipment from a submarine will be made as soon as possible. If that fails, an attempt will be made to make the insertion and extraction by airplane."

"Show me," MacArthur ordered, pointing at the map.

Pluto outlined the operation.

"Presumably thought has been given to a diversionary attack on Japanese air bases on Buka and New Ireland?"

"It was decided, Sir, that was not feasible."

"Nonsense," MacArthur said. "An unarmed airplane will have no chance without a diversionary attack to draw their fighters off."

"Yes, Sir."

"Not feasible! Whose decision was that?" MacArthur asked. But he did not expect a reply; he was already picking up the telephone: "Get me General McKinney," he ordered. A moment later, imperiously, he said, "Then send the senior officer present in here right away."

An Army Air Corps colonel appeared a minute or so later, marched to MacArthur's desk, and saluted.

"Colonel," MacArthur said, "this officer is Lieutenant Hon. He will brief you on the details of a clandestine operation which is about to take place. In my judgment, a diversionary attack on Japanese fighter bases in the Rabaul/Buka area is essential to the success of this operation. If there is some reason General McKinney feels this is not *feasible,* please ask him to be good enough to explain this to me personally."

"Yes, Sir," the Air Corps Colonel said.

"That will be all," MacArthur said. "Lieutenant Hon will be with you in a minute."

"Yes, Sir," the Air Force Colonel said, saluted again, did an about-face, and marched out of the room.

"Would you be free, Pluto, for a little bridge tonight? Say, half past seven?"

"Yes, Sir. Of course, Sir."

"Sometime between now and then, get this off, will you?"

He handed Hon a folded sheet of paper.

"Yes, Sir," Hon said, saluted, and marched out of the office.

The Air Corps Colonel was waiting for him.

"If you're free, Lieutenant, I think it would be best to discuss this in my office."

Pluto looked at the sheet of paper MacArthur had handed him.

"Colonel, if you'll give me the room number, I'll be there in fifteen minutes. I have to go to the dungeon and get off a Personal for the Supreme Commander."

"Of course. I'm in 515."

"Thank you, Sir," Hon said.

XVI

From the very moment Sergeant George Hart stepped off the train in the middle of the night at Port Royal, S.C., and boarded the truck for transportation to The U.S. Marine Corps Recruit Depot at Parris Island; from the moment, in other words, that he realized he was *really* in The Marine Corps and would almost certainly go into battle, he had given a good deal of thought to his first time in harm's way.

In the image of himself he conjured up most often, he was pictured in utilities, with USMC and the Marine emblem stenciled on his chest. Neatly buckled under his chin, he wore a steel helmet covered with netting that bore a camouflage of twigs and leaves. He was laden down with field gear and armed with a rifle—possibly even the new one, the semiautomatic Garand—and bandoliers of ammunition and hand grenades.

415

He heard the roar of artillery and the rattle of machine guns. And he was led by a captain who looked like Tyrone Power and by a sergeant who looked like Ward Bond (both men had made a lot of money playing Marines in the movies). One or the other of them shouted, "Let's go, Marines! Let's go kill the dirty Japs! Semper Fidelis!" And then he blew a whistle as he jumped up and charged toward the enemy, firing a Thompson submachine gun from the hip.

In the event, that wasn't exactly what Sergeant George Hart got.

What he got was a very young-looking lieutenant who didn't look anything like Tyrone Power or Ward Bond. He was wearing swimming trunks, had black grease smeared all over him, and his call to battle was, "With just a little bit of luck, we can make it onto shore without the Japanese seeing us. I will personally castrate anybody who loads, much less shoots, his weapon unless we're fired on."

Sergeant Hart took some reassurance from his conviction that Lieutenant K. R. McCoy knew what he was doing. After all, he'd been on the Marine Raider raid on Makin Island. They hadn't been ashore on Makin more than two minutes, he'd told everybody on this expedition more than once, when some asshole accidentally fired his rifle, telling the Japanese they had visitors.

As far as Hart was concerned, Lieutenant McCoy's castration threat was not total hyperbole, either. McCoy was skilled with knives. He'd earned the "Killer McCoy" nickname, for instance, by killing people with one—several people. And at this moment Lieutenant McCoy had a non-issue, nasty-looking dagger affair adhesive-taped to his upper leg. There was no way of knowing it for sure, but Hart had a strong suspicion that it was *the* knife he'd used on the Chinese and Italians he'd killed when he was a corporal in China.

Sergeant Hart himself had a non-issue knifelike device adhesive-taped to his upper right leg. This had started life as a dull-edged bayonet for the U.S. Carbine, Caliber .30 M1, and had been converted to a kind of dagger by putting a sharp edge on both sides of the blade and then blueing the blade so it wouldn't reflect light.

Sergeant Hart was not only armed with a modified bayonet from a U.S. Carbine, but he carried the Carbine itself, as well.

Compared to the .30-06 cartridge used by the Springfield and Garand rifles and the light Browning machine gun, the .30 caliber Carbine cartridge looked puny—more like a long pistol cartridge than a real rifle cartridge.

During a briefing to the members of the landing team on board the submarine, McCoy did not challenge this notion: "Think of the carbine as a pistol with a stock, not a rifle," Lieutenant McCoy had advised them. "If you make sure of your target before you fire, it will put him down."

During the briefing, all the members of the landing team showed an intense interest in the Carbine. For everybody was to be armed with one—with the exception of Chief Signalman Wallace and Lieutenant McCoy, who were armed with Australian Sten 9mm submachine guns.

"There are two reasons we're not taking anything heavier," McCoy had explained. "For one thing, a Garand would be harder to handle in the rubber boats. For another, we are not *invading* Buka, we're sneaking ashore. And with a little bit of luck, we won't even see a Japanese soldier."

There had been some grumbling about this at Townsville and on the *Pelican,* particularly from Staff Sergeant Tom Kelly, who was an expert with the Thompson submachine gun, and from Sergeant Al Doud, who wanted to bring a light Browning machine gun. But the grumbling had quickly dissipated. Not only was McCoy *a veteran of the Makin Island raid,* but he was just not the sort of officer you fucked with.

They were taking very little field equipment with them, just packs stuffed with field rations, clothing, and some first-aid equipment. And they would paddle in, McCoy had informed them, because outboard motors were unreliable and made too much noise.

In the boats, they would wear swimming trunks; paddling the rafts was easier that way; and it was hard to swim in water-soaked utilities.

The plan was now a little different from the one McCoy and Banning had first put together. Now Lieutenant McCoy, Staff Sergeant Kelly, and Corporal Harry Godfrey would go in on one raft, while Chief Signalman Wallace and Sergeants Al Doud and George Hart would be in the other.

"Yes, the boats will be unbalanced," McCoy said, in answer to a question from Staff Sergeant Kelly, "but they will also be

150 or 180 pounds lighter than if we had four people in each one. We need that weight for the radios."

When his briefing was over, McCoy required each member of the team to recite not only his own role in the landing operation, but that of each of the others. If anyone didn't know exactly what he was supposed to do, Hart thought, he really had to be stupid:

On landing, McCoy would immediately radio the *Pelican* that they had made it through the surf. After that, he and Wallace would remove the weapons from their waterproof packs, and then select from their equipment those items to be carried inland. Meanwhile, Sergeant Doud and Corporal Godfrey would deflate the rafts, and Sergeant Hart would begin to test the sand. Staff Sergeant Kelly would accompany him to provide what assistance was required.

Without changing out of their bathing suits, Sergeant Hart and Staff Sergeant Kelly would run a test every ten yards or so along the beach. While they were doing this, the others would dress; then the boats would be deflated, the weapons distributed, and the rafts, the radios, and the supplies they weren't taking to Ferdinand Six would be moved to some spot off the beach where they could be concealed.

After departure of the party going to Ferdinand Six, the party that was staying behind—that is to say, Sergeant Hart and Corporal Godfrey—would complete the concealment of the radios and supplies, put on their uniforms, and wait for the others to return. Presuming they didn't encounter Japanese en route and that Chief Signalman Wallace could really find Ferdinand Six (it was some ten or twenty or thirty miles away in the mountainous jungle), the journey would take from thirty-six to seventy-two hours.

Assuming it did not encounter a 30-knot Japanese destroyer and/or a Japanese patrol aircraft, HMAS *Pelican* would surface each morning at the same time to see how things were going on the beach. If the people from Ferdinand Six had not returned within seventy hours, it would be presumed they were not coming and Sergeant Hart and Corporal Godfrey would be free to make an attempt to paddle back through the surf to the *Pelican* for evacuation.

Even if the tests suggested the sand on the beach could take the weight, Sergeant Hart privately concluded, there would be no point in sending in the airplane if the people from Ferdinand Six weren't there to meet it. And they certainly wouldn't take the risk just to pick up a sergeant and a corporal. The Marine Corps had more important uses for an airplane like that. *Semper Fi!*

Sergeant Hart heard electrical pumps. Then he thought he sensed movement, but he wasn't sure. A moment later he decided he was wrong. There was no movement, he was just nervous—read scared shitless.

And then there were more mysterious submarine-type noises, and now he was sure he sensed movement.

An Aussie officer appeared, climbing halfway down a ladder. "We're ready for you, Mr. McCoy," he announced courteously.

Hart followed McCoy up the ladder. When he reached the level of the next deck, there was the absolutely delicious smell of fresh air.

We're on the surface, and the hatches are open, otherwise there would be no fresh air.

While he waited his turn to follow McCoy and some Aussie sailors through a hatch, the *Pelican's* hull trembled. It was her diesel engines starting.

He stepped through a hatch onto the deck. It was light enough to see that the surface of the sea was smooth, so smooth it looked oily.

Thank God for that!

McCoy started aft. When Hart started to follow him, McCoy stopped him and gestured toward the bow of the submarine, where Aussie sailors were manhandling the radios and supplies through hatches.

Two minutes later, as he watched Staff Sergeant Kelly kneel beside one of the two rafts to inflate it, McCoy spoke in his ear.

"Just one, Kelly," McCoy said.

"Sir?"

"There's no way we can get loaded rafts through that surf," McCoy said. "The waves are ten, twelve feet, close together."

Hart felt light-headed; this was instantly followed by a sudden chill. He knew why McCoy only wanted one raft. It was because he'd decided they had to shift to Plan B. He had confided this plan only to Chief Wallace and Sergeant Hart, since they were the only ones who'd be involved in it.

If the surf was so rough that passing through it in heavily laden rafts was impossible, Plan B would be placed into effect.

They had not rehearsed Plan B as carefully as Plan A, but Plan B was a little simpler. It required only one raft to attempt making it to shore. This would contain Lieutenant McCoy, Chief Signalman Wallace, and Sergeant Hart. They would carry with them only their personal weapons, three days' supply of rations, and two of the radios Chief Signalman Wallace had modified so they could communicate with both HMAS *Pelican* and aircraft (on air-to-ground frequencies).

When they reached the beach, McCoy and Wallace would wait to see if Hart's tests of the beach sand suggested that an R4D aircraft could land successfully. The results, one way or the other, would be radioed to the *Pelican,* for relay to Townsville.

If the test results were favorable, Lieutenant McCoy and Chief Signalman Wallace would head for Ferdinand Six, while Sergeant Hart would remain on the beach, there being no good reason to subject him to the hazards of the trip through the jungle. Presuming McCoy and Wallace found Ferdinand Six, they would radio Townsville the estimated time of their return to the beach. Then they'd return there with sufficient manpower to handle the supplies which would come in with the R4D.

If the tests indicated that a safe landing could not be made, Sergeant Hart would go with Lieutenant McCoy and Chief Signalman Wallace to Ferdinand Six. And they'd all wait there until some other, better, *workable* plan to reinforce Ferdinand Six and extract its garrison could be devised.

It had to be presumed, finally, that if they couldn't land on Buka through the surf, then that was it. There was no other way in. Swimming was out of the question. Sharks.

"You're going to try it with just one rubber raft?" Staff Sergeant Kelly asked, a little confused.

"Chief Wallace, Sergeant Hart, and me," McCoy replied. "None of the equipment."

"Lieutenant, I'd like to try," Staff Sergeant Kelly said.

"You would only be another mouth to feed," McCoy said. "But thanks, Sergeant Kelly."

"I really want to go, Lieutenant," Kelly said.

"When you get that raft over the side, Sergeant, you better start getting everything else below."

"Shit!" Sergeant Kelly said.

Lieutenant McCoy did not seem to hear him.

About a hundred yards from the beach, the surf turned the rubber raft end over end, and George Hart found himself suddenly underwater, instinctively swimming toward the surface.

I am going to drown on this fucking beach!

He broke through the surface much sooner than he expected to. When he glanced around, another wave was about to fall on him; he took a quick breath and ducked under the water.

When he came up again and started treading water, he became aware that the bag containing the sand-density measuring equipment was banging against his back. He had looped the rope handle around his neck. It was a good thing he had his life preserver on, he realized. That stuff was heavy.

Then he saw McCoy. The Lieutenant was in the act of wrapping the weapons package in a life preserver, with the idea it might float in to shore. The next person he saw was a stranger. But in a moment he became recognizable; it was Chief Signalman Wallace. When Hart was previously with Wallace, his hair was a six-inch-high support for his Chief Petty Officer's brimmed cap. Now that it was soaking wet, Wallace's hair was hanging down over his face, almost to his chin. He looked like a really ugly woman.

Hart pointed at him. McCoy followed the pointing hand and laughed. Wallace at first looked surprised, and then his face clouded.

"Sod you both!" he called. Pushing the hair out of his face, he turned and started swimming toward the beach. He was towing two other packages, also hastily wrapped in life preservers.

That's all of them, then. The weapons, the radios, and our clothes.

Another wave came in and crashed over Hart. It took him so much by surprise that he breathed some water in.

He coughed and gagged a moment or two, and then he started swimming after McCoy and Wallace.

Ahead of him, he saw the rubber raft. It was now right side up, and a wave was gently depositing it on the beach.

Forty yards from the sand, treading water again, his feet touched sand. So he started walking the rest of the way ashore.

He almost made it, walking in water not even waist high, when another wave took him by surprise, knocked him down, and scraped him along the bottom.

The beach turned out to be much wider than they expected, even wider and flatter than it appeared from the raft. Even so, the first thing he started to do was what they'd told him to do: He began taking measurements right down the middle.

But then he decided that they'd given him those instructions because they'd been thinking of beaches like the ones in Florida. This one was twice, three times, that wide. With a beach that wide, there was no telling where the tide would go—how far the water would come up the beach at high tide.

Instead, because the beach stopped dead in a mass of roots and trees, he stepped off from its inland side a distance that was twice the length of the wing of the Air Corps C-47 (he'd measured one in Florida). Then he looked around again, saw where he was, and stepped off that distance again. And then, after another look around, he stepped off one more wing length.

Even taking into account the foliage, there was room for at least two R4Ds to sit wingtip to wingtip between the trees and the place where he decided to pound the cone into the sand. And to seaward, there was even more sand.

Then he put the cone down and pounded it in. Next he was on his knees, bent over to read the cone's markings.

I don't believe this, George thought, *it's too good to be true!*

He picked the cone up and moved five feet closer to the water; then he stood the cone up and dropped the weight on it.

The cone went into the sand no farther than it did on the first try.

Jesus! Maybe there's clay or rocks or something here! This can't be right!

He scraped at the sand with his fingers, but could move only an inch or so away without difficulty.

He jumped to his feet and ran fifty yards down the beach and repeated the test. And then he ran a hundred yards down the beach and did it again.

He went back to where he started.

McCoy intercepted him, holding out for him a set of utilities. "Put these on."

Amazingly cheerful, Hart replied, "Afraid I'll get sunburned?"

"For the bugs," McCoy said.

Hart was so excited he'd forgotten he'd been waving his hand in front of his face and swatting at various parts of his body. When he looked now, he was spotted all over with insect bites.

"The antibug grease is in the first-aid stuff," McCoy said, gesturing toward the *Pelican*.

Hart nodded.

"How does it look?"

"Too good to be true," Hart said. He pulled the utilities over his swimming trunks and ran farther down the beach.

Five minutes later he ran back to McCoy, who was holding the battery-powered shortwave radio.

"What do I tell them?" McCoy asked.

"Two, repeat Two, this is no mistake, Two," Hart said.

"You're sure?" McCoy said.

"I'm sure," Hart said, beaming.

McCoy put the microphone to his lips.

"Bird, this is Bird One, Over."

"Go ahead, Bird One."

"Message is Two. Repeat Two. This is not a mistake. Two. Over."

"Understand Two No Mistake Two, Over."

"The message is Two. Over."

"Good luck, you chaps. See you soon. Bird out."

McCoy and Hart smiled at each other.

"Wallace is snooping around the boondocks looking for some water for you," McCoy said.

"Good," Hart said.

What the fuck am I so cheerful about? As soon as he finds the water, he and McCoy are going to take off and leave me alone on this fucking beach.

Wallace appeared five minutes later, wearing only a loincloth. There was a compass on a thong around his neck. In one hand he held his Sten gun, and in the other was one of the funny-looking machetes Hart had seen in Townsville. His hair was now dry, and it seemed to have snapped back into place, but not to the carefully configured coiffure Hart had grown used to. Wallace did not now look like a Chief Signalman of the Royal Australian Navy Volunteer Reserve.

He looks like a fucking cannibal.

McCoy told him what Hart's tests of the beach had turned up.

"I thought it might turn out that way," Wallace said thoughtfully. "Once I saw the beach, it occurred to me that the wave action is ideal to pack the sand. And the odd large wave tends to provide the right amount of moisture to keep it from drying out."

Hart had no idea whatever what Wallace was talking about.

"I found a place where you might be comfortable," Wallace went on. "And I've been thinking, Lieutenant McCoy, that it would be a rather better idea if you stayed here with Sergeant Hart."

"Why?" McCoy asked.

"No offense, Lieutenant McCoy, but I can move faster alone."

Please God, let him agree with Wallace.

"If you think so, OK," McCoy said.

Wallace nodded.

"Well, let me help you two get settled, and then I'll be on my way."

[Two]
ROYAL AUSTRALIAN NAVY COASTWATCHER ESTABLISHMENT
TOWNSVILLE, QUEENSLAND
0555 HOURS 6 OCTOBER 1942

FRD1, KCY. FRD1,KCY. SB CODE OI.
Royal Australian Navy Coastwatcher Radio, This is Commander in Chief Pacific Radio. Please stand by to receive an encrypted Operational Immediate message.

Signalman Third Class Paul W. Cahn, RANVR, threw the switch to TRANSMIT and tapped his key quickly KCY, FRD1. GA. As the message came in, in the familiar five-character blocks of gibberish, he turned to the device that made cryptographic tape and began to type.

Without stopping his typing, Signalman Cahn called out to Sergeant Vincent J. Esposito, USMC, "Vince, you better go get the brass. I think they're in the mess. Whatever this is, it's Operational Immediate."

Operational Immediate was the second-highest priority for message transmission.

Sergeant Esposito put down his coffee cup and walked quickly out of the radio room.

Less than two minutes later, Signalman Cahn reached for his key, tapped out,

KCY, FRD1, AKN UR OI. CLR.
CINCPAC Radio, Coastwatcher Radio acknowl-edges receipt of your Operational Immediate transmission and is clearing the net at this time.

He waited for the reply, FRD1, KCY. CLR, and then took the strip of paper which had been fed out of his tape machine and fed it into the cryptographic machine. In a moment, the keys began to clatter:

```
FRD1, KCY.
KCY 6OCT34
OPERATIONAL IMMEDIATE
FOLLOWING RECEIVED 0545 FROM BIRD FOR RELAY
START
PART ONE
PLAN BAKER RPT BAKER EXECUTED AS OF 0530 RPT
0530
PART TWO
EGGS AND CHICKS IN NEST RPT IN NEST
PART THREE
CONDITION TWO RPT TWO THIS IS NO RPT NO MISTAKE
END
```

By the time Cahn removed the decrypted message from the machine, Lieutenant Commander Eric Feldt, RAN, and Major Edward Banning, USMC, had come into the radio room. Banning had a large manila envelope in his hand.

Signalman Cahn handed the message to Commander Feldt. He read it and handed it to Major Banning, who read it and handed it to Sergeant Esposito, who had been desperately trying to read it over Banning's shoulder.

"Christ, they couldn't get through the sodding surf! Or

something else went wrong! Bloody hell!" Commander Feldt said.

"McCoy and Wallace are ashore," Banning said. "And Condition Two!"

McCoy's orders were to assess the condition of the sand on the beach on a scale of One to Five: One meant it was Perfect and Five meant it was Extremely Hazardous.

Banning took a sheet of paper from the manila envelope. He had prepared a number of messages beforehand to cover all the contingencies he could think of. The message he was looking for had three spaces that he'd left blank. He wrote BAKER in one of them and 0530 06OCT42 and TWO in the others. Then he handed the sheet to Cahn.

"The sooner the better, Cahn," he said.

"Aye, aye, Sir."

Cahn set the switch on the tape machine to CLEAR, then typed the message.

FOR CINCPAC RADIO
OPERATIONAL IMMEDIATE
FROM OFFICER COMMANDING RAN COASTWATCHER
ESTABLISHMENT

FOR RELAY TO COMMGENERAL 1ST MAR DIVISION

FOLLOWING FOR MAJOR HOMER DILLON USMC X PLAN BAKER SUCCESSFULLY EXECUTED AS OF 0530 06OCT42 X CONDITION TWO REPEAT TWO X EXECUTE PLAN VICTOR X ADVISE ONLY DELAYS AND REASONS THEREFORE X FELDT

He then moved switches on the encryption device to ENCRYPT, fed the tape to it, and waited for the message to appear.

Two minutes later, CINCPAC Radio acknowledged receipt of Coastwatcher Radio's encrypted Operational Immediate message. Four minutes after that, CINCPAC sent another message.

FRD1, KCY. FYI 1STMARDIV AKN UR OI.
Coastwatcher Radio, this is CINCPAC Radio. For Your Information, First Marine Division Radio has acknowledged receipt of your Operational

Immediate.
KCY, FRD1. THANKS. FRD1 CLR.

"They've got it, Sir," Cahn reported.
"When do we net with Ferdinand Six?" Banning asked.
"Six-fifty, Sir," Cahn said after consulting his Signal Operating Instructions for 0001-2400 6 October 1942. "About ten minutes, Sir."
"Try them now," Commander Feldt ordered.
Cahn did so. There was no reply from Ferdinand Six. Neither was there a reply at the appointed hour.
"Keep trying," Feldt ordered.
At 120-second intervals, Cahn tapped out FRD6, FRD1. FRD6, FRD1.
At 0710, twenty minutes late, FRD6 came on the air:

FRD1, FRD6. FRD1, FRD6.

"He's calling us, Commander," Cahn said. "Not responding to us. Maybe his reception is bad."
"Try him again."

FRD6, FRD1. FRD6, FRD1.

FRD1, FRD6. UR 2 × 5.

FRD6, FRD1, SB CODE.

FRD1, FRD6. GA.

FRD6, FRD1.
USE AS SIMPLE SUBSTITUTION
FIRST NAME BELLE OF WAGGA WAGGA
SECOND NAME DITTO
MODEL RPT MODEL BANNINGS CAR

05 × 08 × 15 × 16 × 02

05 × 21 × 12 × 02 × 04

15 × 04 × 21 × 11 × 10

13 × 14 × 24 × 25 × 13

11 × 23 × 06 × 17 × 02

15 × 21 × 23 × 24 × 02

ACKNOWLEDGE UNDERSTANDING
FRD1, SB

Signalman Cahn listened carefully, making minute adjust-
ments to his receiver for half a minute.

"I lost his carrier, Sir. He probably shut down to decode
that."

"We hope," Banning said. He turned to Sergeant Esposito.
"Esposito, get on the Teletype and send what we have to Brisbane. Eyes only, Lieutenant Hon."

"Aye, Aye, Sir."

"Tell him I suggest—use that word, suggest—that he relay to
General Pickering on the special channel."

"Aye, aye, Sir."

"Are you sure you want to do that?" Feldt asked. "Falsely
raised hopes are worse than no news at all."

"O ye of little faith," Banning said. "Send it, Esposito."

Sergeant Esposito picked up the various messages and sat
down at the Teletype machine and started typing.

[Three]
FERDINAND SIX
BUKA, SOLOMON ISLANDS
0715 HOURS 6 OCTOBER 1942

"I hope you know what the hell Wagga Wagga is," Lieutenant
Joe Howard, USMCR, said to Sub-Lieutenant Jakob Reeves,
RANVR. "Because I don't."

"It's a backwater town in New South Wales," Reeves said.
"A town?"

Reeves nodded. "Using the term generously. And as far as I
know I don't know a living soul there, much less the belle
thereof."

"My girl's from Wagga Wagga," Sergeant Steve Koffler
said.

"That must be it," Howard said.

"I thought your girl was down at the creek, washing your linen," Reeves said.

"I told you, goddamn it, you sonofabitch, to knock that shit off!"

"That's enough, Koffler."

"Fuck him, I told him to stop!"

"That's enough, Sergeant Koffler," Howard said firmly.

"Shit!"

"He *has* been diddling—"

"That's enough out of you, too, Reeves," Howard said.

"*You* don't give *me* orders, Lieutenant!"

With a great effort, Howard controlled his temper, although he did not flinch under Reeves' angry glare.

Eventually Reeves shrugged.

"Sergeant, I apologize," he said. "I was making a joke. Or thought I was."

"Forget it," Koffler said, sounding not at all sincere.

"For reasons I can't imagine, I think all of our tempers are on a short fuse," Howard said. "None of us can afford to let things get out of hand."

"Just for the fucking record," Koffler said, the picture of righteous indignation, "that happened just *once,* and I was drunk."

Howard had a terrible urge to laugh.

"On that beer shit that Reeves makes," Koffler said.

"Well, fuck you, Sergeant," Reeves said. "If you feel that way, you can't have any more of my beer shit."

Howard laughed out loud. Reeves looked pleased with himself.

"You just dug your own grave, Koffler," he said. "No more of Lieutenant Reeves' splendid, tasty beer for you."

"That shit sneaks up on you," Koffler said.

The flare-up seemed to have passed, Howard decided with relief.

"What do you think they mean by 'model of Banning's car'?" Reeves asked.

"Studebaker," Howard said. "Right? Or are they talking about that English car, the Jaguar, that Captain Pickering was driving?"

"It says 'model repeat model,' " Koffler said. "I think they mean 'President,' a Studebaker President. If they meant the Jaguar they would have said 'Pickering.' "

"I'm sure Steve's right," Reeves said.

"Let's try it," Howard said. It did not go unnoticed by him that Reeves had used Koffler's first name.

"Well, it's English," Howard said five minutes later, "but what the hell does it mean?"

Reeves and Koffler looked down at the sheet of paper. On it Howard had written the message in code blocks, then his interpretation of that:

N A T H A

N S W A N

T H I S N

O R N T O

S E E P A

T I E N S

Nathan Swan This Norn to See Patiens

" 'Norn' is maybe 'North'?" Koffler guessed.

"There's no 'M' in 'Daphne Farnsworth Patiens,' " Reeves said. "Make it 'swam' and 'morn.' "

"Nathan *swam* this *morn* to see Patience," Howard said. "That makes more sense, but what does it mean?"

"Nathan is obviously the Nathaniel of the first message," Reeves said. "What it could mean is that he came ashore, swam ashore, from a submarine or something."

"This morn? This *morning*?"

"Yes. If that's what it means. This morning."

"Could he do that?" Koffler said.

"He could try to do it. That's not quite the same thing. The reason there are so few ports on Buka is that the surf is so rough in most places—this time of the year especially. Presumably they know that. That means he would either have to try to make it ashore near a port, which would place him very far away, or through the surf somewhere near here. Which would be quite difficult."

"They know what shape we're in supplywise," Howard said. "Maybe they figured it was worth the risk."

"You think there's a chance he's not alone?" Steve asked.

"This could very well be wishful thinking, Steve," Reeves said. "Certainly, it is. But if I were the man in charge and were going to all the trouble of sending someone up here, I would go the extra mile and try to send in more than one person—and supplies, of course."

"Get on the air, Steve," Howard ordered. "Send, 'Message acknowledged and understood.' "

"That's all?"

"That's all. If they wanted to tell us more than they did, they would have."

"Aye, aye, Sir."

[Four]
COMMAND POST, 2ND BATTALION, FIFTH MARINES
GUADALCANAL, SOLOMON ISLANDS
0830 HOURS 6 OCTOBER 1942

Using his arm as a pillow, Major Jack (NMI) Stecker, USMCR, was curled up asleep on his side on the deck of the S-3 section. His Garand rifle, with two eight-round clips pinned to the strap, was hanging from a nail in the wooden frame of the situation map.

When the flyboy from Henderson Field walked into the command post asking to see the Old Man, Stecker's S-3 sergeant was reluctant to disturb him.

"He was up all goddamned night, Captain," he said. "Can this wait a couple of hours?"

Captain Charles M. Galloway, USMCR, shook his head, no, and then said it aloud: "No, it won't, Gunny."

"Aye, aye, Sir," the gunny said, and went to Stecker and knelt beside him and gently shook his shoulder.

"Sir? Sir?"

Stecker woke reluctantly, shrugging off the hand on his shoulder. But then he was suddenly wide awake, forcing himself to sit up.

"What's up, Gunny?" Stecker asked as he looked at his watch.

"An officer to see you, Sir."

Stecker searched the dark area and found Galloway.

"This better be important, Captain," Stecker said, matter-of-factly.

"Sir, my name is Galloway. I have VMF-229."

Stecker saw the look on Galloway's face.

"Give us some privacy, will you, Gunny?" he said softly.

He waited until the gunny was out of earshot and then said, "OK, let's have it."

"Your son crashed on landing about twenty-five minutes ago, Sir," Galloway said.

"You're here, that means bad news," Stecker said.

"He's pretty badly banged up, Sir, but he's alive."

"Define 'pretty badly,' would you, please?"

"Both of his legs are broken; he has a compound fracture of the right arm; his collarbone has probably been cracked. He almost certainly has broken ribs, and there are probably some internal injuries."

"Jesus Christ!" Stecker exhaled. "Is he going to live?"

"Commander Persons—I just left him—said that barring complications—"

"Persons?" Stecker interrupted. "Mean little guy?" He held his hand up to nearly his shoulder level, to indicate a runt.

"Yes, Sir."

"Barring complications, what?"

"He will recover and will probably even be able to return to flight status."

I'm telling you that because that's what Persons told me, and because I want to believe it, not because I do believe it. When they pulled him from the wreck, I was surprised that he was alive.

"I don't like to think what Mrs. Stecker will do when she gets the telegram," Stecker said. "I suppose you've already set that in motion?"

"No, Sir. I haven't. MAG-21 handles that, Sir. You could probably talk to Colonel Dawkins—"

"What happened? 'Crashed on landing'? Is that a polite way of saying it was his fault?"

"It looked to me as if his right tire was flat, Sir."

"You saw the accident?"

"Yes, Sir. I was right behind him in the pattern."

"And?"

And a second after he touched down, he started to ground loop to the right, and then he was rolling end over end down the strip; the only way it could have been worse was if there had been more gas in his tanks and it exploded.

"He was attempting to make a dead-stick landing, Sir. He was out of fuel."

"How did that happen?"

"They hit us pretty badly this morning, Major—"

"I was up earlier, I saw it."

"—and he stayed up as long as he thought he could, as long as he thought he had fuel to stay."

"You encourage that sort of thing, Captain, do you? Staying up there until you have just enough fuel to *maybe* make it back to the field?" Stecker asked nastily, and then immediately apologized. "Forgive me. That was uncalled for. And you were up there, too, weren't you, presumably doing the same thing?"

"We lost three Wildcats this morning, Sir. And the Air Corps lost two of their P400s."

"Counting my son?"

"No, Sir. Not counting him."

But including a Wildcat piloted by Major Jack Finch. Finch wouldn't have been up there if I hadn't told him he could, for auld lang syne.

"All lost? Or just shot down?"

"One of the P400 pilots made it back to the field, Sir. Just him."

"Tell me about this flat tire," Stecker said after a moment.

"He told me that he'd taken some hits. . . . Major, I didn't mention this, but he shot down two Bettys and a Zero this morning. He's an ace. That makes it six total for him."

"All I knew he had was one," Stecker said. "The flat tire?"

"He called and said he'd taken some hits, so I pulled up beside him and took a look, and there were holes in the area of his landing gear."

"And you told him this?"

"I signaled him, Sir. His radio was not working. But he understands my signal."

"Then why didn't he try to make a wheels-up landing?"

"I can only presume he thought he could make it, Sir."

"And that he wanted to save the airplane?"

"Yes, Sir. I think that probably had a lot to do with the decision he made."

"What about the Pickering boy?" Stecker asked. "Was he one of the other three you lost?"

Galloway was surprised at the question.

"No, Sir. He made it back all right. He was flying on your son's wing, Major."

And he landed three minutes before your boy—time enough for him to be walking away from his revetment when your boy came in, to see the crash, and to run to the plane and listen to your boy scream for the five minutes or so it took to pry him from the wreckage. He made it back all right, but I'm going to have trouble with him. I know the look he had in his eyes.

"I know his father," Stecker said.

"Yes, Sir. Major, I have a jeep—"

Stecker met his eyes.

"I've been trying to decide if I have the courage to go see him. Jesus Christ, they ought to skip a generation between wars so that fathers don't have to see their children torn up."

"They're going to fly him out, to Espiritu Santo, Sir."

"If I ride down there with you, can I get a ride back up here?"

"Yes, Sir. No problem."

"Squadron commanders at Henderson have their own jeeps?" Stecker asked.

"I borrowed Colonel Dawkins' jeep, Sir. I didn't think he'd mind."

Stecker pushed open the canvas flap.

"Gunny, I've got to go down the hill for a while," he said.

"Major, I'm goddamned sorry," the gunny said and glowered at Galloway as if it were obviously his fault.

"Thank you, Gunny," Stecker said. "It is not for dissemination."

"Aye, aye, Sir."

"Hello, Pick," Major Jack (NMI) Stecker said to Second Lieutenant Malcolm S. Pickering. "How are you?"

Pickering was on a hospital cot next to the one where Second Lieutenant Richard J. Stecker lay. Tubing ran from Pickering's arm into Stecker's; a transfusion was taking place.

"Jesus Christ, I'm sorry!" Pick said and sat up. There were tears in his eyes.

Stecker quickly pushed him back on the cot.

"Watch out for the tubes," he said. Then he dropped to his knees and put a firm hand on Pick's shoulders.

"There was just too fucking many of them!" Pick said. "I just couldn't cover him!"

"I'm sure you did the best you could, Pick," Stecker said, and then he turned and looked at the adjacent cot.

The suit, Flying, Cotton, Tropical Climates, had been cut from Second Lieutenant Richard J. Stecker's body. He was clothed now in undershorts and vast quantities of bandage and adhesive tape. There were splints on both legs. He was unconscious.

Major Jack Stecker laid a very gentle hand on his son's face and held it there for a long time.

Captain Charles M. Galloway felt like crying.

"Major, I'll go find Commander Persons," he said.

Stecker nodded.

Major Jake Dillon found Captain Galloway before Galloway found the medical officer.

"I thought you'd be here," Dillon said.

"What the hell do you want?"

Dillon handed him a message form:

FOLLOWING FOR MAJOR HOMER DILLON USMC X PLAN BAKER SUCCESSFULLY EXECUTED AS OF 0530 06OCT42 X CONDITION TWO REPEAT TWO X EXECUTE PLAN VICTOR X ADVISE ONLY DELAYS AND REASONS THEREFORE X FELDT

"Victor means go to Moresby, right?" Galloway asked.

Dillon nodded.

"What are you going to do for a copilot?" Dillon said. "Sorry to hear about Major Finch."

"The way you were supposed to say that, Jake," Galloway said nastily, "was, 'Sorry about Jack Finch,' and *then* ask what I'm going to do about a copilot."

"OK, I'm sorry. But what are you going to do about a copilot?"

"I'm going to take the other kid in there, the one giving blood to Stecker."

"What kid?"

"Pickering."

"He's not a qualified R4D pilot. What the hell are you talking about?"

"He's a pilot. And he's not a bad one. And besides, all he'll have to do is put the wheels and flaps up and down and talk on the radio. I'll be flying."

"I don't understand, Charley. There must be another guy qualified in R4Ds somewhere on Henderson."

"If Pickering stays here, he's going to fly. And in the mental condition he's in, if he flies, he's *going* to get killed. If he comes with me, he only *might* get killed."

"That doesn't make any sense. It has nothing to do with his father?"

"Don't try to tell me about flying or pilots, Jake, OK?" Galloway replied.

"Forget it Charley. How long will it take to get going?"

"I don't know, Jake. It will have to wait until he's finished giving his buddy blood, OK? This idiot idea of yours will have to wait that long."

[Five]
CRYPTOGRAPHIC CENTER
SUPREME HEADQUARTERS, SOUTH WEST PACIFIC OCEAN
AREA
BRISBANE, AUSTRALIA
0935 HOURS 6 OCTOBER 1942

Lieutenant Hon Song Do, Signal Corps, USA, had just about finished decryption of the Overnight MAGICs when one of the two telephones in his cubicle rang. Of these, one was a Class A switchboard line, and the other a secure Class X line that connected with only a few telephones in SHSWPOA. Brass hats too important to use the ordinary system had Class X phones—the Supreme Commander, the Chief of Staff, the four Gs (Personnel, Intelligence, Plans & Training, and Supply), and a few of the Special Staff officers, including the Provost Marshal.

"Lieutenant Hon, Sir," he said, hoping that it wasn't the Supreme Commander and that his annoyance at being disturbed did not show in his voice.

"Major Banning, please," a voice Pluto did not recognize said.

"I'm sorry, Sir, Major Banning is not available."

"When will he be available?"

"I'm not sure, Sir."

"Where can I reach him?"

"May I ask who this is?"

"Colonel Gregory."

The name did not ring a bell.

"I'm sorry, Sir, I'm not permitted to divulge Major Banning's location. May I take a message?"

"My name is not familiar to you, Lieutenant?"

"No, Sir. I'm sorry, but it's not."

The phone went dead in his ear.

"Well, fuck you, too, Colonel Whatsyourname," Pluto said and hung the telephone back on the wall.

Fifteen minutes later, a .45 automatic jammed in the small of his back, a locked leather briefcase handcuffed to his wrist, Pluto made sure that everything was turned off. And then, feeling like Bulldog Drummond, Master Detective, he rigged a thread between a pin stuck in the brick wall and one of the chairs. If anyone entered the room, he would disturb the thread.

Banning's orders.

A little melodramatic, Pluto thought, *but if Banning thought it was necessary . . .*

He locked the door and went down the corridor to the guard post.

"Make sure you feed the dragon, Sergeant," he said to the senior guard as he signed himself out. "I thought I heard his tummy rumbling."

The little joke fell flat. The sergeant gave a small, just perceptible jerk of his head down the corridor. There was an officer down the way in the gloom.

One of the MP officers, Pluto decided, *checking to see that the enlisted men are not cavorting with loose women.*

"Lieutenant Hon, I'm Colonel Gregory," the officer said. He was a small, natty man in pinks and greens. A *Lieutenant*

Colonel, not a full bird, wearing the insignia of the General Staff on his lapels.

"Yes, Sir?"

"Have you got a minute, Lieutenant?"

"Actually, Sir, no," Pluto said, holding up the briefcase.

Colonel Gregory held out a leather folder to Pluto. It held a badge and a photo identification card. It was something like the ones Banning and Moore carried, identifying them as Special Agents of the Office of Naval Intelligence. The credentials Gregory held out identified him as an Agent of the U.S. Army Counterintelligence Corps.

"Yes, Sir," Pluto said.

"Ed Banning and I are sort of friends, Lieutenant. I really would like to talk to him."

"I'm sorry, Colonel, I can't help."

Gregory's eyes appraised him carefully.

"You going upstairs with that briefcase, Lieutenant? Or out to Water Lily Cottage?"

How the hell does this guy know about Water Lily Cottage? More important, what the hell does he want?

When Gregory realized that Hon was not going to answer him, he said, "No offense, Pluto, but you look more like a Japanese spy than I do, don't you think?"

How the hell does he know that people call me Pluto?

"I don't know who you are, Colonel," Pluto said.

"I really hoped to avoid using the word until we were alone, but I'm here to talk about your Buka operation," Gregory said.

Shit! We're compromised. Who the hell told him?

The first possibility that came to his mind was Mrs. Ellen Feller, but that couldn't be. Banning had gotten her out of Water Lily Cottage before anyone mentioned the word Buka.

Then who? In a moment the answer came: *That fucking Air Corps Colonel that MacArthur summoned to his office.*

"You're not compromised," Colonel Gregory said, reading his mind. "Nobody knows a thing who is not supposed to. Are you going to Water Lily Cottage?"

Pluto nodded.

"Let me ride out there with you then. We might have to get Moore involved in this anyway."

This sonofabitch knows a hell of a lot about Water Lily Cottage.

"I don't know how long I'll be out there, Colonel. How would you get back?"

"We keep the cottage under surveillance. There'll be a car there to bring me back. Shall we go?"

"I'm not going to tell you where Major Banning is, Colonel."

"You've made that perfectly clear, Pluto," Gregory said.

Gregory volunteered to drive the Studebaker. After a moment's hesitation, Pluto agreed: *He is a CIC type; he is not going to commandeer the car and take me someplace where they will stick lighted matches under my fingernails to make me tell them where Banning is. And besides, driving a car with a briefcase chained to your wrist is difficult, even dangerous.*

It soon became apparent that Gregory not only knew where Water Lily Cottage was, but the shortest route.

"I've got a question," Gregory said.

"Sir?"

"Just idle curiosity. When you gave me the hard time on the phone and I realized that I was going to have to deal with you personally, I went to look at your personnel file. You don't have one. What do they do, keep it in Pearl Harbor or Washington?"

I honestly don't know.

"What I was wondering is, how do you get paid?"

"They send me a check," Pluto said. "I take it to Finance and they cash it."

Gregory grunted. Then he changed the subject.

"I got a copy of that Transfer of Detainee form that Moore signed for Mrs. Farnsworth. The Kangaroo FBI sent it to the Provost Marshal, and he didn't know what to do with it, so he sent it to me. What the hell was that all about?"

"The Kangaroo FBI?"

"His Majesty's Royal Australian Constabulary," Gregory said. "What are you going to do with her?"

Pluto again elected not to reply.

"I know she's staying in the cottage, for Christ's sake," Gregory said. "I told you we keep it under surveillance. At Ed Banning's request."

"She's a fine young woman," Pluto said. "Her heinous crime was to get herself impregnated by one of our Marines. Banning didn't know that when he sent word we wanted to talk to her.

The Kangaroo FBI, as you so aptly describe them, went overboard."

"They tend to do that," Gregory replied. He didn't speak for a moment or two. "And so she'll become one of yours, I presume?" he asked when he was ready to talk again. "As in Special Detachment 14, rather than The U.S. Marine Corps generally?"

"Right. I think we'll hire Mrs. Farnsworth."

"As soon as Banning gets back from wherever he is?"

Pluto declined to reply.

Gregory chuckled, and then remained silent until they pulled up the drive to Water Lily Cottage and stopped. As Pluto reached for the car door handle, he touched his arm.

"Do you think we could send the ladies shopping or something? I'd really rather have our little chat in private."

"Well, Lieutenant," Colonel Gregory said to Moore as soon as the Studebaker with Barbara Cotter, Joanne Miller, and Daphne Farnsworth in it had nosed out of the driveway, "you seem to have recovered from your recurrence of malaria. And congratulations on your promotion."

"You seem to know a hell of a lot about me, Colonel," Moore said.

"You provided my people with a lot of laughs when you were here the first time . . . humping Mrs. Feller," Gregory said.

"Son of a bitch!" Moore blurted.

"From the look on your face, Pluto, I don't think you knew that, did you? I guess Banning decided you didn't have the Need to Know," Gregory said.

He chuckled at Moore's flushing face.

"Your secret is—*secrets are*—safe with me. Believe it or not, I was reluctant to bring that up, but I wanted to make the point quickly that I know a good deal about you—and about what goes on here—because Ed Banning wanted me to know."

"What the hell is this all about?" Pluto asked.

"This is a very delicate situation, gentlemen," Gregory said. "One of those aberrations where people of our lowly ranks and positions have to make decisions involving our superiors."

"I have no idea what you're talking about," Pluto said.

"At his first opportunity, Colonel Armstrong went to General McKinney and told him he had been ordered by the Supreme Commander to stage diversionary air attacks in connection with a clandestine operation being conducted in or around Buka—"

"That must be the Air Corps officer who was in General MacArthur's office?" Pluto interrupted.

"Right," Gregory said, "—under the auspices of Lieutenant Hon. Or Banning, who is Hon's boss. I don't mean to sound cynical, but that sounds like bullshit to me; Ed Banning is a nice guy, but he's only a major. I'd like to know what authority, if any, there is for this operation."

Moore looked at Hon for instruction.

Without those orders for authority, Hon thought, *what we are is two pissant Lieutenants surrounded by very senior brass who are likely to fuck this whole thing up on general principles. Jesus, I wish Banning or Dillon was here!*

"Show him your orders, John," Pluto said.

Moore went into his bedroom, returned with his plastic sealed orders, and handed them to Colonel Gregory.

"Well," Gregory said after reading them and handing them back, "I suppose that operating under the auspices of the Chief of Staff to the President gives you all the authority you could ask for."

"Is that what you came to find out?" Pluto asked.

"Not exactly," Gregory said. "So General McKinney, who is not exactly on General MacArthur's fair-haired-boy list, went to General Willoughby. He did that on the reasonable presumption that as the G-2, Willoughby would know all about this clandestine operation and could tell him what was going on. But it turns out that all Willoughby knows he got from Mrs. Feller. I.e., that there's a clandestine operation he knows nothing about. He was pissed off about that—understandably, I think. But what really upset him was that MacArthur was in on the secret. Obviously, since MacArthur laid this air-raid diversion mission on McKinney."

"We didn't ask for that," Pluto said. "That was MacArthur's idea."

"That's the problem," Gregory said. "By definition, any tactical or strategic mission invented by MacArthur is brilliant. And not subject to cancellation."

"I don't know what you're talking about," Pluto said.

"Buka is not within the boundaries of South West Pacific Ocean Area," Gregory said. "It belongs to CINCPAC. MacArthur cannot order an operation in CINCPAC's area. If he does, the shit will hit the fan all the way back to Washington. The Navy is just as sensitive about its territory—about infringements thereon—as MacArthur himself."

"So there will be no diversionary air attack?" Pluto asked. "No problem. We didn't think it was feasible in the first place."

"You miss the point, Pluto," Gregory said. "There *will* be diversionary air activity; MacArthur has ordered it. It's entirely possible, I think, that he hopes it will cause the shit to hit the fan. He knows damned well where his boundaries are."

"I'm confused again," Pluto said.

"General Willoughby has a number of other virtues, I'm sure, but the one I admire most is his determination to keep his boss out of trouble. While simultaneously keeping his own ass out of trouble with MacArthur, of course. He and McKinney have come up with a possible solution. Willoughby sent me to present it to you."

"Why didn't Willoughby just call me in?" Pluto thought aloud.

"Since MacArthur never told Willoughby about his order to McKinney, he doesn't officially know about it."

"What do they want from us?" Moore asked.

"They want Hon to go back to Colonel Armstrong and request aerial reconnaissance of your operations area—in other words, of Buka. Because the only aircraft with the range to do that are bombers, B-17s, it can be described to General MacArthur as a diversionary raid. At the same time it can be described as reconnaissance activity to CINCPAC. They don't object to that. Actually, they're glad to have it. McKinney can offer daylight reconnaissance for four days."

"Why don't we just tell MacArthur that we'd rather not have any aircraft involved in this, period?" Moore asked.

"I tried that," Pluto said. "General MacArthur has decided we need a diversionary attack."

"When is this thing going to happen?" Gregory said. "And don't tell me I don't have the Need to Know."

Hon pointed to the briefcase.

"By now the R4D should be on its way to Port Moresby.

Townsville sent me a copy of the message just before you called me."

"I happen to know that Colonel Armstrong is in his office right now," Gregory said, "if you have anything to say to him."

"We don't have any wheels to get back to SWPOA," Hon said.

"I told you that wouldn't be a problem," Gregory said.

He walked out on the wide porch of Water Lily Cottage and waved his arm. Thirty seconds later, a black Humber four-door sedan with a man in civilian clothing behind the wheel pulled into the driveway.

XVII

[One]
FERDINAND SIX
BUKA, SOLOMON ISLANDS
1005 HOURS 7 OCTOBER 1942

Sergeant Steve Koffler, USMC, sat on the dirt floor of his hut, carefully scraping at the rib cage of a wild pig Ian Bruce had beheaded with his MACHETE, SUBSTITUTE STANDARD. They'd roasted the pig whole over an open fire like in the movies about the South Pacific, at a luau or some such bullshit.

The difference was that the pigs they cooked in the movies were great big porkers, and this one had been about the size of a medium-sized dog. It had lasted just one meal, not counting the stew they'd made with the leftovers.

He wasn't scraping the rib cage to get food from it. There wasn't anything edible left, just some stringy shit. He was scraping the rib because there wasn't a goddamned thing else to do.

Steve had sort of hoped there would be another message for them when he'd gone on the air with a Here-They-Come report, but there hadn't been. And there hadn't been when he'd made the regular net check-in either.

So that left the bullshit message of the day before, about that guy Nathan swimming to see Patience.

And that bullshit simple substitution code with Daphne's name . . . which made him think of Daphne, practically all fucking night. That was a bitch, because there was absolutely no fucking way he was ever going to see Daphne again in his entire life, no matter how the fuck long that lasted. It didn't look like it was going to be long at all, frankly.

He was going to die on this fucking island, and the goddamned ants would pick his bones as clean as they'd picked the rib cage of Ian's fucking pig.

Better sooner than later, this shit is really getting me down.

He put his knife aside. But then he picked it up and worked the edge under one of the scabs on his legs, just prying it loose enough so he could force the pus out.

Jesus, if Daphne walked into this fucking hut right now, and saw me, she'd run away screaming. I look like I got fucking leprosy or terminal syphilis or something.

Patience Witherspoon stuck her head in the opening.

You had to show up right now, right? When I was thinking of Daphne?

"Oh, Steven, come quickly!" Patience said excitedly, holding her arm across her bosom.

"What's up?"

Jesus, maybe Ian got another pig! He hasn't been around since yesterday. Reeves had to pump the fucking bicycle.

"Oh, come quickly!" Patience said, and disappeared.

Maybe I should fuck her again. That once wasn't bad, and if I'm going to die, what the fuck difference does it make if she looks like something out of National Geographic *magazine?*

Fuck that. Don't even think that. You may be holding the shitty end of the stick in the absolute asshole of the world, but you're a white man, and a Marine, and you know better than fucking cannibals.

He rose to his feet and picked up the Thompson and left the hut.

Well, there's Ian. He doesn't have a pig. Who the fuck is that with him? I never saw that cannibal before. What is this, Cannibal Homecoming?

Patience came running back and caught his hand and pulled him to the new cannibal, slowing as they got close.

"Steven," she said shyly, "I want you to meet my old friend Nathaniel Wallace. Nathaniel, this is Steven."

"Chief Signalman Wallace, Sergeant," the cannibal said, putting out his hand. "I've been looking forward to meeting you."

"You have?"

"You have a fine hand," Wallace said. "I tried to copy your style."

"I'll be goddamned."

[Two]
HENDERSON FIELD
GUADALCANAL, SOLOMON ISLANDS
1105 HOURS 7 OCTOBER 1942

Captain Charles M. Galloway ran the engines up, saw that all the needles were in the green, and looked back over his shoulder toward Major Jake Dillon. Dillon was standing behind the pilots' seats, wearing a headset. Galloway took the microphone from its holder and moved the switch to INTERCOM.

"Strap yourself in, Jake," Galloway ordered, jerking his thumb to show Dillon a fold-down seat behind him. "I don't want you in my lap if I have to try to stop this thing."

He looked at Second Lieutenant Malcolm S. Pickering, in the copilot's seat.

"We have twenty degrees of flaps," he said, pointing. "There's the gear control. The way we're going to do this is move onto the runway, run the engines up, remove the brakes, and see if we can get it to fly. You follow me through on the throttles. When I give you the word, you will raise the gear and then the flaps. Got it?"

Pickering took his microphone and pressed the switch.

"Got it, Skipper."

"Call the tower," Galloway said.

Pickering moved the switch to TRANSMIT.

"Cactus, this is"—he stopped, searching the control panel in vain for the aircraft's call sign—"Eastern Airlines City of San Francisco on the threshold for takeoff."

"Eastern *Airliner,* you are cleared for takeoff as number

one," the Cactus tower replied. The amusement in his voice came through even over the frequency-clipping radio.

Pickering dropped his microphone in his lap and watched as Galloway moved onto the runway, lined up with its center, stopped, locked the brakes, and put his hand on the throttle quadrant. Then he put his hand over Galloway's as Galloway ran the throttles forward to TAKEOFF POWER.

The engines roared and the airplane strained against the brakes.

Galloway released them, and the R4D started to roll. He pulled his hand from under Pickering's and put it on the wheel.

Pickering picked the microphone from his lap.

"Cactus, Eastern Airlines rolling."

The aircraft slowly began to gain speed. It was over the Recommended Maximum Gross Weight for the temperature and available runway length. And the runway was not smooth concrete but wet dirt, patched here and there with pierced steel planking.

Galloway was more than a little worried about blowing a tire, but he kept that to himself. As soon as he could, he eased forward on the wheel to get the tail wheel off the ground.

Then he kept his eye on the end of the runway, dropping his eyes every second or so to the airspeed indicator, which had come to life at 40 knots.

The speed climbed very slowly. But then Galloway sensed life in the controls. He eased back on the wheel, felt the airplane want to try to fly, and then eased the wheel back just a hair more.

The heavy rumbling of the undercarriage suddenly quit.

"Gear up!" he called.

Pickering took his hand from the throttle quadrant and dropped it to the wheel-shaped landing gear control ten inches down and to the rear. He put it in RETRACT.

The wheels took a long time coming up. On Jack Finch's orders, the pilot who had flown the airplane to Guadalcanal from Espiritu Santo had also tested and timed how long it took to get the gear up with the added weight and wind resistance of the skis. It hadn't taken appreciably longer than normal, a tribute to the strength of the hydraulic system.

A moment before he expected the GEAR UP light to go on, Galloway ordered, "Flaps Up!"

The GEAR UP light went on as Pickering moved the flap-control lever.

"Gear up," Pickering's voice came over the earphones, and then a moment later, "Flaps retarded."

The airspeed indicator needle pointed at 110. Galloway put the airplane into a shallow climb to the left and kept it there until the surf on the Guadalcanal beach passed under his wing. Then he straightened it out, retarded the throttles, and set up a shallow climb.

It was just about 900 miles in a straight line from Henderson to Port Moresby on New Guinea, but Galloway was planning for at least a thousand-mile flight, in case he ran into weather, and because he knew that flying dead reckoning, the airfield was probably not going to be where he expected it to be.

To conserve fuel, he would cruise somewhere around 8,000 to 10,000 feet and at an indicated 180 knots. A thousand miles at 180 knots translated to right at six hours. That would give them an Estimated Time of Arrival at Port Moresby of 1700, 1710. The worst possible case—if they failed to find the field for another hour or so—would still see them on the ground at 1800. Before nightfall.

There was plenty of fuel. An R4D in this configuration could officially carry twenty-eight fully loaded paratroops, or 5,600 pounds. Galloway's experience during the C47/R4D acceptance tests had taught him that was a very conservative estimate of Maximum Gross Load.

Dillon had told him five people would be going into Buka. That would be less than 1,000 pounds, because they would not be fully equipped paratroopers. But call it a thousand anyway. And they would have with them an already weighed 950 pounds of supplies. So call that a thousand pounds, too. That left 3,600 pounds of cargo lift weight available.

More than that, really. Galloway had concluded that the Maximum Gross Weight erred on the side of caution by about 20 percent (a thousand pounds). So that left him 4,600 pounds.

AvGas weighed about seven pounds a gallon. And he had auxiliary fuel tanks mounted inside the cabin over the wing root. He'd ordered these filled with 600 gallons of gasoline.

One of the Rules for Over Water Flight that Captain Galloway devoutly believed in was that as long as you could get the airplane to stagger into the air with it, there was no such thing as too much fuel aboard. If necessary, they could fly to Australia.

Galloway turned to Pickering.

"Can you hear me?"

Pickering nodded.

"You've never been in one of these before?"

"Not sitting up front," Pickering said.

"They're a very forgiving airplane," Galloway said.

"That's nice," Pickering said. "May I ask a question?"

"Shoot."

"From the movies I've seen, people are supposed to be asked to volunteer for a mission they can't be told about."

Galloway smiled.

"You volunteered the day you joined The Corps," he said. "And again when you went through P'Cola. You had two chances to say no."

"Where are we going?"

Galloway threw the map into his lap. "First stop, Port Moresby. It'll take us about six hours—"

"We have that much fuel aboard?" Pickering asked, and then realized the stupidity of his question. "I guess we do, don't we?"

"—and then—turn the chart over—Moresby to Buka and return."

"The Japanese hold Buka, right? Where are we going to land? Or *are* we going to land?"

"We're going to pick up some people and equipment at Moresby and fly to Buka. We'll land on the beach, off-load the people and their equipment, and pick up three passengers."

Pickering looked at him. "Christ, you're serious!"

Galloway nodded.

"There's something I think I should tell you, Captain," Pickering said. Charley picked up on the "Captain"; Pickering usually called him "Skipper."

"You're not Alan Ladd or Errol Flynn, right?"

"No," Pickering said. "I used to think I was a pretty good pilot."

"You are. With the Zeke you shot down this morning, that made five, you're officially an ace."

"That's not what I meant," Pickering said. "I mean, when I

got my first ride in a Yellow Peril at P'Cola, the IP thought I
was a wiseass—"

I can certainly understand that, Mr. Pickering.

"—and tried to make me airsick, and couldn't. So he turned
it over to me and told me to take it back to the field and land
it and I did; and then he was really pissed because he thought
I already knew how to fly and hadn't told anybody."

"No kidding?"

"No kidding," Pickering said. "I had no trouble learning to
fly the Wildcat, either, and . . . shit, just before I came over here,
I took my grandfather's Stagger Wing Beech up, the first time
I'd ever sat behind the wheel, buzzed Marin County, and then
flew under the bridge."

"You flew under the Golden Gate Bridge?" Galloway asked
incredulously.

Pickering nodded.

"Both ways, I flew in from the ocean, went under the bridge,
did a one-eighty over Alcatraz, and flew back out under the
bridge."

"That's a little hard to believe."

"I did it. And I wasn't scared. And I wasn't scared here until
this morning."

*I'll be a sonofabitch if I don't believe him about flying under the
Golden Gate.*

"Maybe you grew up this morning," Galloway said.

"Could be. After I saw what happened to Dick Stecker, I was
about to hand you my wings and take my chances with a rifle.
I don't want to end up like that."

He means that, too.

"So why didn't you?"

"Because wherever you were going was away from Henderson, from Guadalcanal," Pickering said. "I figured I could
hand you my wings wherever we landed."

"You're out of luck, Pickering. At least until this mission's
over," Galloway said. "You want to turn in your wings, that's
your business. But not until we get back."

"You can't make me get back in this airplane once we land."

"Yes, I can. You're a goddamned Marine officer, and you'll
do what you're ordered to do."

"Or what?"

"There is no 'or what,'" Galloway said. "The subject is
closed, Mr. Pickering."

Pickering shrugged and folded his arms across his chest.

Galloway put his hand on the wheel and reached up and turned the automatic pilot off.

"Put your hands and feet on the controls," he ordered. Pickering looked at him. After a moment he unfolded his arms and put his left hand on the wheel.

"You have the aircraft, Mr. Pickering," Galloway said. "Maintain the present course and rate of climb until reaching nine thousand feet."

Pickering nodded.

They rode in silence for a minute or so. Galloway had enough time to judge that Pickering was telling the truth about that—the rate-of-climb and airspeed-indicator needles didn't even flicker, nor did the attitude of the aircraft change a half degree. He was one of those rare people you heard about but never actually saw: He was born with the ability to fly.

A glint of light at his left startled him. He snapped his head and looked out.

First Lieutenant William Charles Dunn, USMCR, Executive Officer—and at the moment, acting Commander—of VMF-229 waved cheerfully at him from his F4F.

Galloway furiously signaled him to return to base.

When Dunn brought the subject up before they left, Galloway expressly told him not to escort the R4D.

It would have been nice if a whole squadron of Wildcats could escort the R4D away from Guadalcanal, to protect it from Japanese bombers. They'd be delighted to shoot an R4D down if they saw it. But a whole squadron of Wildcats could not be diverted from their primary mission for that—they couldn't even divert two or three of them.

And a single Wildcat wouldn't do any good. Not only that, it would place itself in unnecessary jeopardy.

Bill Dunn continued to wave cheerfully, apparently choosing to interpret Galloway's furious signals as a friendly return of his own greeting. Galloway remembered that back at Henderson, Bill seemed to cave in to the logic of his arguments far easier than Galloway expected.

"We're at nine thousand feet, Sir," Pickering reported.

"See if you can trim it up for straight and level flight at an indicated 180 knots, Mr. Pickering, without running into Mr. Dunn."

Pickering looked at him in confusion, and then saw Dunn in

the Wildcat. He took his left hand from the wheel and, smiling, waved at him.

Meanwhile, the R4D leveled off. The altimeter indicated 9,000 feet, and the rate-of-climb indicator needle stopped moving. It was right in the center of the dial.

In direct violation of a specific order to the contrary, Lieutenant Dunn remained on the wingtip of the R4D until he had only enough fuel, plus ten minutes, to return to Henderson Field.

Then he waved one more time and entered a slow 180-degree turn to the left.

When he was out of sight, Galloway unfastened his shoulder and seat belts and got up out of his seat. Pickering looked at him.

"Piss call," Galloway said. Pickering nodded.

He'll be all right, Galloway thought. *He had every reason in the world to go a little crazy. Bringing him along was the right thing to do.*

[Three]
ROYAL AUSTRALIAN AIR FORCE STATION
PORT MORESBY, NEW GUINEA
1340 HOURS 7 OCTOBER 1942

RAAF Moresby was located too far forward to have the most advanced cryptographic equipment. It was necessary, therefore, to decrypt both incoming and outgoing classified messages by hand.

A loose-leaf notebook kept locked up in the safe of the cryptographic officer held a number of codes printed on chemically treated paper. It would readily burn—almost explode—if a match were applied.

Each day there was a new code. But the change did not follow the calendar. Rather, it occurred upon notification from RAAF Radio, Melbourne. In other words, a code might be valid for eighteen hours, or twenty-six, or two, depending on when RAAF Radio, Melbourne, decided to change it.

The cryptographic officer's notebook also contained a number of codes for special use. A new set of these codes was sent in every two weeks by officer courier.

The RAAF Moresby Cryptographic Section consisted of a

Flight Lieutenant and two Leading Aircraftsmen, RAAF. When the message came in from RAAF Radio Melbourne for Lieutenant Commander Eric Feldt, RANVR, these men were frankly annoyed. Now that action against the Japanese on New Guinea was finally getting in gear, they had enough work as it was without having to handle the classified traffic for a goddamned sailor and his motley command—four American Marines and a Bushman wearing a RAN Petty Officer's uniform.

So they decrypted the Commander's message as far as his name and address, and stopped there. It was their intention to let the rest of it wait until they'd taken care of the regular traffic. But that idea didn't work out. Air Commodore Sir Howard Teeghe, Commanding RAAF Moresby (his rank was equivalent to Brigadier, Commonwealth Ground Forces and Brigadier General, U.S. Army and Marine Corps), made the first visit anyone could remember to RAAF Moresby Cryptographic Section and informed the Lieutenant that Commander Feldt was expecting some rather important material. Whenever that came, Air Commodore Teeghe said, he'd be grateful if they got right on it.

While the Air Commodore waited, the Lieutenant himself decrypted the rest of the message and handed it to him:

MOST URGENT
MELBOURNE 1250 7TH OCTOBER NUMBER 212
FROM ADMIRALTY MELBOURNE
VIA RAAF MELBOURNE
FOR OFFICER COMMANDING RAAF MORESBY

MOST SECRET

START
PART ONE
INFORMATION TO LT COMMANDER E. FELDT RANVR
PART TWO
START FOLLOWING FROM BANNING:
SUB A
SWIMMER WITH PATIENCE AS OF 1010 7OCT
SUB B
GREYHOUND DEPARTED STATION ABLE 1110M ETA STATION BAKER 1700M RPT 1700M
SUB C STATION C COORDINATES 06 13 21 XXXX 14 16 07

RPT 06 13 21 XXXX 14 16 07
SUB D RENDEZVOUS STATION C 0550M 9 OCT RPT 0550M
9 OCT
END FROM BANNING
PART THREE
ADVISE ADMIRALTY MOST URGENT SIGNAL
SUB A ON ARRIVAL GREYHOUND
SUB B READINESS TO EFFECT SCHEDULED RENDEZVOUS
SUB C CAUSE OF AND EXPECTED TIME OF REMEDY ANY
DELAY
SUB D ON DEPARTURE GREYHOUND FOR STATION C
SUB E RETURN OF GREYHOUND TO STATION B
BY AUTHORITY: SOAMES-HALEY, VICE ADM RAN
END

When the R4D with MARINES lettered along the side of its
fuselage made a low approach from the sea and touched down
smoothly, Lieutenant Commander Eric Feldt, RANVR, was
standing outside RAAF Moresby Base Operations. It was 1655
hours (Melbourne Time).

A BSA motorcycle with a sidecar onto which a FOLLOW ME
sign had been bolted led the R4D to a sandbag revetment. The
driver signaled the aircraft where to shut down, then a ground
crew appeared and manhandled the airplane into the revetment.

The rear door opened and a ladder was lowered. Once that
was done, Major Jake Dillon climbed down.

"Hello, Jake," Feldt said. "How are you, old man?"

It was not the profane and/or obscene greeting Dillon expected.

"Can't complain, Eric. Yourself?"

Captain Charley Galloway appeared and climbed down the
ladder.

"Captain Galloway, Commander Feldt," Dillon said.

Galloway saluted.

"You're the Coastwatcher commander, Commander?" Galloway asked.

Feldt nodded.

"A lot of people where I come from have a lot of respect for
your people, Commander," Charley said.

Feldt looked uncomfortable.

"I hope you had a good flight," he said after a moment. Then

he put out his hand to Second Lieutenant Malcolm S. Pickering
as he turned from climbing down the ladder. "My name is
Feldt, Lieutenant. Welcome to Port Moresby."

"Thank you, Sir."

"Is the aircraft all right, Captain?"

"It ran like a Swiss watch, Sir. I'd like to go over it before we
leave, of course."

"There's plenty of time for that. You're not due at Buka
until six the day after tomorrow. Major Banning sent some
steaks and whiskey. The rest of the lads are guarding it from
the RAAF boys. I've got a car whenever you're ready."

MOST URGENT
RAAF MORESBY 1705 7TH OCTOBER NUMBER 107
FROM OFFICER COMMANDING RAAF MORESBY
FOR ADMIRALTY MELBOURNE FOR VICE ADMIRAL
SOAMES-HALEY
VIA RAAF MELBOURNE

MOST SECRET

START
PART ONE
REFERENCE YOUR 212 7 OCT PART THREE SUB A: 1655M
RPT 1655M
PART TWO
REFERENCE YOUR 212 7 OCT PART THREE SUB B: NO RPT
NO PROBLEM ANTICIPATED
END
FELDT LT COMM RANVR

[Four]
FLIGHT OPERATIONS BRIEFING ROOM
ROYAL AUSTRALIAN AIR FORCE STATION
PORT MORESBY, NEW GUINEA
1800 HOURS 8 OCTOBER 1942

The four Marines and the RANVR Signalman First who were
to land on Buka, along with Major Jake Dillon, Captain
Charles M. Galloway, and Lieutenant M. S. Pickering, were

sprawled in chairs in the small, airless, steaming hot room. Most of them clutched beer bottles.

"I rather doubt if any of you people are sober enough to understand any of this, but permit me to go through the motions," Lieutenant Commander Feldt said.

Their laughter sounded just a bit forced.

"The last word we had from Ferdinand Six was at 9:55 this morning. Chief Wallace reports that the party that will carry the supplies up to Ferdinand Six from the beach, and the people who are being extracted, all departed at noon yesterday, that is, 7 October. Using as a guide the time it took Wallace to get from the beach to Ferdinand Six, it should take them about thirty hours to reach the beach. That means, barring any trouble, they should be getting there right about now.

"Of course they may not have been able to move as quickly as Wallace did alone. We don't know what shape Reeves, Howard, and Koffler are in. That may delay them. On the other hand, since they know where they were going, and Wallace had to look for Ferdinand Six, they may have got to the beach hours ago. Either way, we have just about twelve hours in the schedule to take care of the unexpected; the pickup is scheduled for ten minutes to six tomorrow morning.

"There are several potential problems. One is that they will run into our Nipponese friends; that could delay them beyond the twelve-hour cushion—"

"Or forever," one of the Marines said.

There was more forced laughter.

"Thank you ever so much, Sergeant, for that encouraging observation," Feldt said.

The sergeant held up his beer bottle.

"My pleasure, Commander."

"If I may continue?"

"Certainly, Sir."

"Or, as you have so cleverly deduced, Sergeant, it could well keep them from reaching the beach at all," Feldt said. "Second, since we were unable to land a Hallicrafters through the surf, the only radio now on the beach is the hand-held, battery-powered voice radio. That has a limited range and a limited battery life.

"In other words, Captain Galloway can't use that radio as a radio direction-finder; it's not powerful enough. Thus he'll have to find the beach on his own. If—and when—he finds it, he'll attempt to contact the beach, code name Greyhound Base, by radio.

"Now, if the radio is working, the officer in charge there, Lieutenant McCoy, will radio—"

"Sir, what if he's not on the beach?" another Marine sergeant asked; he sounded both very concerned and completely sober. "I thought he was supposed to go to Ferdinand Six. And you just said that they may not make it back to the beach."

"Sorry, I should have got into that. When they landed from the sub, they decided that Wallace could make better time to Ferdinand Six traveling alone. So Lieutenant McCoy stayed with Sergeant Hart."

"Did you say McCoy?" Pick Pickering asked.

"Yes, I did."

"Is he one of your people?" Pick asked.

"As a matter of fact, Lieutenant, no, he is not. He's sort of a rubber-boat expert they sent from Washington."

"Is that Killer McCoy?"

"Yes, but when you meet him, Lieutenant, I strongly suggest that you do not so address him."

"Aye, aye, Sir," Pick said.

"You know this guy?" Charley Galloway asked; they were sitting together.

"We went through OCS Quantico," Pick said.

Galloway shrugged.

"If I may continue?" Felt asked sarcastically. "As I was saying, if the battery-powered radio is working, the beach will communicate with the aircraft. If it is not working, McCoy has two signal panels, one red, meaning Do Not Attempt Landing, and one blue, meaning the beach is Safe to Land. If they display the red panel, the Hallicrafters aboard will be kicked out of the airplane into the water. If we're lucky, their packaging will float them and they will be washed ashore. The aircraft will then return here."

"I'm willing to jump in, Commander," the sober-sounding sergeant said.

"We all are," the other sergeant said, the one who obviously had had one or two more bottles of beer than his metabolism could handle.

"We considered that and decided against it," Feldt said. "You will return here so we can try this again. Clear? I don't want any heroics out there."

There was no reply.

"What I am waiting for, gentlemen, is an acknowledgment of that order."

"Aye, aye, Sir," the two sergeants said. Feldt looked at the other three members of the team and waited for them to say, "Aye, aye, Sir."

"If the green panel is displayed, the aircraft will land," Feldt said. "The radios and other supplies will be off-loaded, Reeves, Howard, and Koffler will be taken aboard, and the aircraft will depart."

"What happens to the two guys on the beach?" one of the Marines asked, "if the airplane can't land?"

"They're fucked," the drinking sergeant said.

"They will remain in position for seventy-two hours if they wish," Feldt said matter-of-factly. "In case we can restage the landing. At the end of seventy-two hours they will make their way to Ferdinand Six."

"Like I said, they're fucked," the drinking sergeant said.

"That will be quite enough, thank you, Sergeant," Feldt said. "If the people from Ferdinand Six are on the beach, they will of course lead everybody back there. If they are not there, the landing team, plus Lieutenant McCoy and Sergeant Hart, will carry one of the Hallicrafters and the equipment in bags marked with red tags and make for Ferdinand Six. The other equipment will be concealed somewhere near the beach for pickup at a later time. We've been over all this, of course, in great detail before.

"Are there any questions?"

There were none.

"There is one case of beer left, plus a few other bottles. When that's gone, that's it. My advice is try to get some sleep. We'll wake you at 0100. There will be breakfast, the rest of the steak and eggs, and then you will board the aircraft. I remind you there is only a bucket aboard the aircraft for bowel movements, and that can get messy. So try to take care of that before you get on the airplane.

"I thank you for your kind attention, and please be generous when the hat is passed."

There was more laughter. This time some of it seemed genuine.

[Five]
NORTH PHILADELPHIA STATION
PENNSYLVANIA RAILROAD
PHILADELPHIA, PENNSYLVANIA
0915 HOURS 9 OCTOBER 1942

"That must be him, Lieutenant," Sergeant Howard J. Doone, USMC, said to First Lieutenant J. Bailey Chambers, USMC, discreetly pointing down the platform to a Brigadier General of The U.S. Marine Corps who had just stepped from the train.

Lieutenant Chambers moved quickly down the platform, saluted, and inquired, "General Pickering, Sir?"

Fleming Pickering returned the salute.

"Admiral Ashworth's compliments, Sir," Lieutenant Chambers said.

"My compliments to the Admiral," Pickering said. "We have a car?"

"Yes, Sir."

"Do you know where to find Tatamy, Sergeant?" General Pickering asked.

"Yes, Sir. It's a small town just north of Easton. About sixty-five, seventy miles, Sir."

"Let's go, then," Pickering said. "Where's the car?"

"The General's traveling alone?"

"My aide is otherwise occupied, Lieutenant. Let's go."

"Aye, aye, Sir."

Mrs. Ellie Stecker heard the car door slam. She pushed aside the lace curtain and watched a Marine brigadier general get out of the backseat before the driver could run around the front and open it for him.

Oh, dear God, please no!

She heard footsteps on the narrow wooden porch of the row house, and then the twisting of the doorbell.

If I don't answer it, it won't be happening.

The Brigadier General had his cover tucked under his arm when she pulled the door open.

"Mrs. Ellie Stecker, please. My name is Pickering."

"I am Mrs. Stecker."

"Mrs. Stecker, I'm afraid I—"

"Dick? Or my husband?"

"Dick. He's been in a crash."

"Is he alive?"

"Yes, Ma'am," Pickering said.

Thank you, God!

"How bad?" she asked.

"He's rather badly hurt, I'm afraid," Pickering said.

"What, exactly, General, does that mean?"

Pickering reached in his pocket and handed her a sheet of paper.

URGENT
FROM HQ FIRST MARDIV 1130 6OCT42
TO COMMANDANT USMC
  WASHINGTON DC
  FOLLOWING PERSONAL FOR BRIG GEN FLEMING PICK-
ERING USMC
REGRET TO ADVISE THAT 2ND LT RICHARD J STECKER
USMC SERIOUSLY INJURED PLANE CRASH TODAY X OF-
FICIAL NOTIFICATION WILL FOLLOW X IF POSSIBLE
WOULD APPRECIATE YOUR RELAYING ELLIE MY DEEP
REGRET AND OFFER ANY HELP NEEDED X JACK SAW HIM
BEFORE AIR EVACUATION ESPIRITU SANTO THENCE
NAVY HOSPITAL PEARL HARBOR X PROGNOSIS FULL RE-
COVERY X YOUNG STECKER AND YOUR BOY BOTH ACES
AND FINE MARINES X REGARDS X VANDERGRIFT
  END PERSONAL GENERAL VANDERGRIFT TO GENERAL
PICKERING

"That was very kind of General Vandergrift," Ellie Stecker said, "and of you, General, to come here with this."

"Jack and I are old friends," Pickering said. "And I'm fond of Dick, too."

"Oh, my God, I didn't put that together. You're Pick's father, of course. But I thought you were a captain in the Navy?"

"That was a mistake that was straightened out," Pickering said. "By the time you get to California, we should have more specific word for you on exactly what happened."

"I don't understand."

"Arrangements have been made to fly you to Pearl Harbor," Pickering said.

"How can that be done?" she asked.

"It's done," Pickering said. "One of my officers will have the details worked out by the time we get back to Philadelphia."

"It wouldn't be fair to the other wives and mothers—"

"The Commandant seems to feel, Ellie, that someone who has put as many years into The Corps as you have is entitled to a little special treatment."

When he telephoned Walter Reed with Vandergrift's message, the Commandant's precise words were, "You seem to have a lot of influence, Pickering. Why don't you use some of it to get Jack's wife out to Hawaii to be with her boy?"

"Oh, I don't know how I could—"

"Nonsense," Pickering said. "This won't be the first time you've picked up and gone somewhere on no notice at all."

She looked at him.

"No," she said finally, "it won't. I'll throw some things in a bag."

[Six]

```
MOST URGENT
RAAF MORESBY 0410 9TH OCTOBER NUMBER 21
FROM OFFICER COMMANDING RAAF MORESBY
FOR ADMIRALTY MELBOURNE FOR VICE ADMIRAL
SOAMES-HALEY
VIA RAAF MELBOURNE

MOST SECRET

START
PART ONE
REFERENCE YOUR 212 7 OCT PART THREE SUB D: 0315M
RPT 0315M
END
FELDT LT COMM RANVR
```

It began to grow light a little after five. Captain Charles M. Galloway, who was flying, reached over and touched the sleeve of his copilot, who was dozing. His arms were folded on his chest; his head was tilted to one side.

He woke startled.

"Go back and find somebody to come up here," Galloway ordered.

Pickering nodded, unstrapped his seat and shoulder belts,

and went back into the cabin. He returned with the Marine sergeant who had given the Aussie Naval officer all the trouble during the briefing. He looked—and was—more than a little hung over.

Galloway waited until Pickering had strapped himself back in.

"You have the aircraft, Mr. Pickering," he said, and then unstrapped himself and got up.

Pickering looked over his shoulder to see what Galloway was up to.

Galloway unfolded the step that let you stand and take navigational observations through the Plexiglas dome on top of the fuselage. Then he installed the hung over sergeant on it, facing to the rear.

He returned to his seat and strapped himself back in.

"What was that all about?"

"I don't know what I'll do if it happens," Galloway said. "But if we are spotted by a curious Japanese, I think it would be nice to know it before he starts shooting."

"I'm sorry I asked," Pickering said.

[Seven]
APPROXIMATELY 40 MILES SOUTH OF CAPE HANPAN
BUKA, SOLOMON ISLANDS
0550 HOURS 9 OCTOBER 1942

The call came in loud and clear over Pickering's earphone; he even recognized the voice:

"Greyhound, Greyhound, this is Greyhound Base. Over."

"I'll be damned," Captain Charley Galloway said.

Pickering picked up his microphone.

"This is Greyhound. Read you five by five. Over."

"Greyhound, I have you in sight. You are approximately two miles south. Over."

"Shit!" Charley Galloway said and pushed the nose of the R4D down.

"Understand two miles. Winds, please? Over."

"The wind is from the north. About ten knots. Over."

"Understand north, ten knots. Over."

"I suppose if there was something wrong with the beach, he

would have said so," Galloway said as he began to retard the throttles.

"Yeah, I think he would have," Pickering said. "But let's check."

"How's the sand down there, Killer? Over."

"Condition Two. Repeat Condition Two. Over."

"Thank you, Killer. Please make a piss call before boarding."

Galloway glanced at him and smiled before ordering, "Twenty degrees flaps. Put the wheels down."

A moment later Pickering said, "Twenty degrees flaps. Gear extended."

"OK, here goes," Galloway said.

Just before he eased back on the stick to put the tail wheel on the ground, two men with arms waving jumped out of the foliage onto the beach. By the time Charley Galloway very carefully stopped the R4D, turned it around, and taxied back to them, they had been joined by what looked like twenty others; most of them wore loincloths and had bushy hair.

Less than five minutes later, Lieutenant K. R. McCoy came into the cockpit.

"Everybody is aboard, Sir," he said to Galloway, "and the door is secure."

"How goes it, Killer?" Lieutenant Pickering asked.

"Fuck you, Pickering, you know how I feel about that Killer shit!"

"I guess you two know each other," Charley Galloway said, as he put his hand to the throttle quadrant and shoved them forward to TAKEOFF POWER.

[Eight]
U.S. ARMY AIR CORPS B-17E TAIL NUMBER 11354
17,500 FEET
OFF WEST COAST, BOUGAINVILLE, SOLOMON ISLANDS
0805 HOURS 9 OCTOBER 1942

"What the hell is that down there?" Second Lieutenant Harry Aaronson, the bombardier, inquired over the intercom.

"Down where, for Christ's sake, Aaronson?" First Lieutenant Joseph Wall, the Aircraft Commander, replied.

"At maybe eight, nine thousand, two o'clock."

"I can't see it," Wall replied.

"It looks like a C-47," First Lieutenant Thomas Killian, the copilot, said.

"What the fuck would a C-47 be doing up here? That must be a Jap bomber or something."

Wall banked the airplane to the right and put the nose down so that he could see.

"That's a C-47," he pronounced with finality and straightened the airplane up.

"Then it would have to be a Japanese C-47," Killian argued. "Nobody on our side could be *that* lost. And the Japs don't *have* any C-47s."

"The Japanese have L2Ds," Lieutenant Wall announced. "They stole the C-47 blueprints and they build them in Japan."

"Bullshit," Lieutenant Harry Aaronson said. "You couldn't get all the blueprints for an airplane in a boxcar."

"Well," Lieutenant Wall said slowly, having never considered that before, "the Japs had L2Ds that are C-47s, and that's one of them."

"Let's go shoot the sonofabitch down," Lieutenant Aaronson said.

Lieutenant Wall's orders—for the flight the day before yesterday, for the flight today, and probably for the flight the day after tomorrow—were to conduct an aerial observation of the west coast of Bougainville Island. During these observations they would take aerial photographs of a list of topographic features and of any naval activity in the waters adjacent thereto. They were not carrying any bombs—which frankly struck Lieutenant Wall as a pretty goddamned silly way to make war.

On the other hand, shooting down an unarmed Japanese airplane didn't seem right.

Fuck it, Remember Pearl Harbor!

"I don't want one shot fired until I say so, you got that?"

He put his hand to the throttle quadrant to take power off and pushed the nose of the airplane down.

"The sonofabitch *is* lost," Lieutenant Aaronson said. "That's one of ours. Shit! It says 'Marines' on the fuselage."

"I didn't know the Marines had C-47s," Lieutenant Killian said.

"They don't, that's a mirage, you asshole."

"Tom, see if you can raise them on the radio," Lieutenant Wall said to Lieutenant Killian.

"Captain," Sergeant George Hart reported, "there's a B-17 behind us."

"A *B-17?*"

"Yeah. I think. I never heard of a Japanese plane with four engines."

"*I* have," Galloway said and unstrapped himself to have a look.

"Oh, shit!" Lieutenant Pickering said.

It was not possible to establish radio communication between the two aircraft, but the navigator of the B-17 made a sign with a question mark and an arrow on it and gave it to Lieutenant Killian. He held it in the window so the pilot of the transport could read it.

He nodded, and in a moment a sign appeared in the pilot's window of the transport plane: MORESBY.

Another sign was prepared in the B-17.

ON OUR WAY. WANT COMPANY?

Whereupon the pilot of the Marine transport enthusiastically smiled and shook his head up and down in the affirmative.

[Nine]
MERCY FORWARD
BRISBANE, AUSTRALIA
1130 HOURS 11 OCTOBER 1942

"Hello, Steve," Daphne Farnsworth said. "How are you feeling?"

My God, he looks awful!

"I'm all right. How you doing?"

"I'm fine, thank you," Daphne said. She thrust a box of candy at him.

He's one ulcerous sore from his shoulders to his fingers!

"Thank you."

"I would have brought you some whiskey, but Barbara said they meant it; with the medicine they're giving you, it would make you sick."

"You mean the worm medicine," he furnished helpfully.

"I suppose."

"Doctor Whatsisname said—"

"Colonel Godofski?"

"Yeah. He said it was poison. That was the only way to get rid of them."

"He said you'll be well soon," Daphne said.

"So how come you're wearing a dress?"

"I'm out of the Navy," Daphne said.

"No fooling? How come?"

"It's not important," Daphne said, wanting to tell him.

"Just curious, that's all. I thought you had to join up for the Duration Plus Six Months, like you do in The Corps."

"I'm going to have a baby," Daphne said. *Well, there, it's out.*

"Oh," Steve said.

"That's why I'm out of the Navy."

"Yeah, sure. Who's the father? You married some Australian guy, right?"

"I'm not married, Steve."

"Why the hell not?"

Daphne shrugged.

"The sonofabitch won't marry you? What the hell is the matter with him? You give me a couple of days to get out of this goddamned hospital, and I'll fix his ass all right."

"He didn't know about the baby," Daphne said. "He was away."

"When did he get back?"

"Yesterday," Daphne said.

He looked at her for a long moment until she could bring herself to meet his eyes, and he saw the answer in them.

"No shit, just that once?"

"It wasn't just once," Daphne said.

"You know what I mean," Steve said. "Well, what do you know about that?"

Daphne averted her eyes.

"I don't want you to feel that you have any obligation, any responsibility," Daphne said.

There was no reply and she forced herself to look at him. He had his lower lip under his teeth, and his body was shaking, and tears ran down his cheeks.

"Steve, what's the matter?"

"I thought I was never going to get off that fucking island, and now I'm going to have a baby!"

And then the sobbing came, and she went to him and put her arms around him, and he put his arms around her, and it didn't matter that they were ulcerous from his shoulders to his wrists.

Coming soon in hardcover

W.E.B. Griffin

In Danger's Path

A Corps Novel

Putnam

THE *NEW YORK TIMES*
BESTSELLING SERIES!
THE CORPS
W.E.B. Griffin

Author of the bestselling
BROTHERHOOD OF WAR series.

THE CORPS chronicles the most determined branch of the United States armed forces—the Marines. In the same gripping style that has made the BROTHERHOOD OF WAR series so powerful, THE CORPS digs deep into the hearts and souls of the tough-as-nails men who are America's greatest fighting force.

___I: SEMPER FI	0-515-08749-1/$7.50	
___II: CALL TO ARMS	0-515-09349-1/$7.50	
___III: COUNTERATTACK	0-515-10417-5/$7.50	
___IV: BATTLEGROUND	0-515-10640-2/$7.50	
___V: LINE OF FIRE	0-515-11013-2/$7.50	
___VI: CLOSE COMBAT	0-515-11269-0/$7.50	
___VII: BEHIND THE LINES	0-515-11938-5/$6.99	

Prices slightly higher in Canada

Payable in U.S. funds only. No cash/COD accepted. Postage & handling: U.S./CAN. $2.75 for one book, $1.00 for each additional, not to exceed $6.75; Int'l $5.00 for one book, $1.00 each additional. We accept Visa, Amex, MC ($10.00 min.), checks ($15.00 fee for returned checks) and money orders. Call 800-788-6262 or 201-933-9292, fax 201-896-8569; refer to ad # 269

Penguin Putnam Inc. **P.O. Box 12289, Dept. B** **Newark, NJ 07101-5289** Please allow 4-6 weeks for delivery. Foreign and Canadian delivery 6-8 weeks.	**Bill my:** ☐Visa ☐MasterCard ☐Amex _____ (expires) Card#_____ Signature_____

Bill to:

Name_____

Address_____ City_____

State/ZIP_____

Daytime Phone #_____

Ship to:

Name_____	Book Total	$_____
Address_____	Applicable Sales Tax	$_____
City_____	Postage & Handling	$_____
State/ZIP_____	Total Amount Due	$_____

This offer subject to change without notice.

W.E.B. GRIFFIN

The electrifying *New York Times* bestselling saga by the author of *The Corps*.

BADGE OF HONOR

From the cop on patrol, to the detectives, to the chief of police—their story—the saga of those behind the badge, their hopes and fears, their courage and heroism.

__ **I: MEN IN BLUE**   0-515-09750-0/$7.50
When a cop is killed in the line of duty the men in blue are set on solving the murder...no matter where it leads.

__ **II: SPECIAL OPERATIONS**   0-515-10148-6/$7.50
A spree of kidnapping and rape challenges Inspector Peter Wohl, commander of a new task force, to stop the reign of violence.

__ **III: THE VICTIM**   0-515-10397-7/$7.50
After a Mafia slaying, Officer Matt Payne takes on the ultimate battle between organized crime—and his own police force.

__ **IV: THE WITNESS**   0-515-10747-6/$6.99
The robbery ended in murder, and the only cooperative witness feared for his life. But Officer Matt Payne never thought that he himself would be the one who needed protection . . . .

__ **V: THE ASSASSIN**   0-515-11113-9/$7.50
A mad assassin's ready to make his move, and the department's only clue is a single, perfectly typed bomb threat.

__ **VI: THE MURDERERS**   0-515-11742-0/$7.50
Four deaths that originally seemed unconnected, trigger a massive convergence of corruption, cops, and the mob that could tear the Philadelphia police department apart...

Prices slightly higher in Canada

Payable in U.S. funds only. No cash/COD accepted. Postage & handling: U.S./CAN. $2.75 for one book, $1.00 for each additional, not to exceed $6.75; Int'l $5.00 for one book, $1.00 each additional. We accept Visa, Amex, MC ($10.00 min.), checks ($15.00 fee for returned checks) and money orders. Call 800-788-6262 or 201-933-9292, fax 201-896-8569; refer to ad # 329

Penguin Putnam Inc. **P.O. Box 12289, Dept. B** **Newark, NJ 07101-5289** Please allow 4-6 weeks for delivery. Foreign and Canadian delivery 6-8 weeks.	Bill my: ☐Visa ☐MasterCard ☐Amex _____(expires) Card#_____ Signature_____

Bill to:

Name_____

Address_____ City_____

State/ZIP_____

Daytime Phone #_____

Ship to:

Name_____	Book Total $_____
Address_____	Applicable Sales Tax $_____
City_____	Postage & Handling $_____
State/ZIP_____	Total Amount Due $_____

This offer subject to change without notice.